Further Encounters of
Sherlock Holmes

Also Available from George Mann and Titan Books:

Encounters of Sherlock Holmes

Sherlock Holmes: The Will of the Dead
Sherlock Holmes: The Spirit Box (June 2014)

The Casebook of Newbury & Hobbes
The Executioner's Heart: A Newbury & Hobbes Investigation
The Revenant Express: A Newbury & Hobbes Investigation (July 2014)

FURTHER ENCOUNTERS OF SHERLOCK HOLMES

BRAND-NEW TALES OF
THE GREAT DETECTIVE

Edited by George Mann

TITAN BOOKS

Further Encounters of Sherlock Holmes
Print edition ISBN: 9781781160046
E-book edition ISBN: 9781781160114

Published by Titan Books
A division of Titan Publishing Group Ltd
144 Southwark Street, London SE1 0UP

First edition: February 2014
10 9 8 7 6 5 4 3 2 1

What did you think of this book? We love to hear from our readers.
Please email us at: readerfeedback@titanemail.com,
or write to us at the above address.

To receive advance information, news, competitions, and exclusive offers online,
please sign up for the Titan newsletter on our website: www.titanbooks.com

CONTENTS

Introduction by George Mann

INTRODUCTION

S herlock Holmes. A name that strikes fear into the heart of criminals and lackadaisical policemen alike. A name that rings out across the centuries, across language barriers and cultural divides. But who is Holmes? What is it that gives him such longevity? Why have terms such as 'elementary' and 'the game's afoot' entered our lexicon?

Clearly, Holmes has become something greater than Sir Arthur Conan Doyle, his creator, could ever have imagined. Tales of his exploits have passed into legend. His name has become a by-word for a great detective, shorthand for 'genius'.

Sherlock Holmes has become an archetype. It's probably fair to say that Holmes is one of the most successful and popular fictional characters of all time. Indeed, he's no longer *just* a fictional character from the latter days of the nineteenth century, and nor does he remain the creation of one man alone.

Holmes is now a part of our literary heritage. More than that, he's been woven into the rich texture of our mythology. Everyone knows who Sherlock Holmes was, as surely as they recognise any of the great historical figures: Winston Churchill, Alexander the Great, Cleopatra, Abraham Lincoln, Marie Curie, to name but a few. I've heard it said that there are more people who believe Holmes to be a real historical figure than people who know him to be a fictional character, although surely that must be apocryphal? Perhaps not.

Certainly, I'm convinced that more people paraphrase Doyle's famous sleuth than will ever read the original stories in which he appears. More still know him from feature films, television shows, computer games, comic books, radio plays – the list is almost endless. He's appeared in almost every storytelling medium, in enough stories to give a completist like me terrible, terrible nightmares.

Holmes is a character who won't – who *can't* – die. He's been resurrected innumerable times; not only by his creator, who relented and breathed fresh life into Holmes after his murderous attempt to send his creation to his doom, but by writers, actors and artists all across the globe. He's been reinvented and reinterpreted, turned into a vampire and a zombie, reconstructed as a hologram in the far future, transposed into a talking animal. Always, however, he remains recognisably Holmes. Always, his true character shines through. The archetype is so strong, so powerful, that all it takes is a pipe and a deerstalker, or perhaps only a single word – 'elementary' – to invoke him.

For that reason, Holmes will never die. No matter what a succession of writers might choose to do with him. There'll always be an untidy sitting-room in Baker Street, London, in which a man wearing a tatty old dressing-gown sullenly smokes a pipe, ekes sounds out of a violin and contemplates the nature of the criminal mind.

Like all good heroes, you can't keep Holmes down for long.

My point is simply that Holmes has grown beyond the page, beyond the screen. He's become a part of the fabric of our society, a name that's recognised in every single country in the world. A name that carries meaning wherever you go. Like Robin Hood or Hamlet, Santa Claus or Sleeping Beauty, Sherlock Holmes belongs to us all.

In this anthology, the great detective is restored to us once again for twelve brand-new cases, leading us from mysterious London embassies to the distant sands of Mars, from the dizzy heights of the Victorian era to the waning years of Holmes's life. Here we meet the siblings of Moriarty and the child of Watson, sinister wax dummies, time travellers and drug-fuelled alter egos. Here is adventure and mystery. And most importantly, here is Sherlock Holmes.

Once more, the game's afoot, and Watson is ready to relate his tale.

George Mann
October 2013

The Adventure of the Professor's Bequest

BY PHILIP PURSER-HALLARD

I

"This is a quite surprising telegram, Watson," Sherlock Holmes remarked without preamble, as he tossed me the slip of paper which Mrs Hudson had brought him some minutes before. I perused it, considering.

HELP URGENTLY REQUIRED BROTHER JAMES PAPERS STOLEN YESTER-NIGHT CONSEQUENCES INCALCULABLE MRS BANISTER MOST DISTRAUGHT MONEY NO OBJECT PLEASE COME SOONEST BANISTER

"I see nothing remarkable about it, unless perhaps it is written in code," I replied at last. "Despite this Mr Banister's evident urgency, it seems indistinguishable from a dozen similar requests since your return."

"And yet it is quite unique," he insisted. "Not in its substance, which is precisely as it appears, but because of its sender. Professor Redmond Banister, with whom I have had certain dealings, is not only a leading authority on the morphologies and life-cycles of annelid worms, but also one of the last people I had ever expected to approach me for help."

"And why's that?"

"Because he is also one of the few living relatives of the late Professor Moriarty, albeit by marriage. Mrs Abigail Banister, whom he describes as being so very distraught, is Moriarty's younger sister, making our erstwhile nemesis Redmond Banister's lamented brother-in-law."

It was at this time some six months since Holmes's return from the continent following his presumed death at Moriarty's hand, and the sequence of events which it had set in train, including the arrest of the professor's lieutenant, Sebastian Moran, for the murder of the Honourable Ronald Adair. As the true scope of Moriarty's criminal enterprises – continued after his death by Moran and his fellows – had emerged, the talk of the town had turned to a knighthood for my friend, and clients had begun arriving in their droves at our old rooms in Baker Street. Holmes had received the latter courteously, while doing his utmost to discourage the former.

"So brother James is none other than Moriarty himself," I surmised.

"That seems the likeliest conclusion, although there is an outside possibility that the papers in question belong to the colonel."

I knew already that the two brothers unusually shared one forename. The appearance in the national newspapers of letters from Colonel James Moriarty, pressing for Holmes's arrest on charges of the homicide of his brother Professor James Moriarty, had been the sole, if somewhat confusing, stain on the otherwise unblemished pleasure of my friend's homecoming.

"What papers did he leave with them?" I wondered. "And who profits from stealing them now?"

"The first is a question I endeavoured to resolve some small while ago. When I learned that Moriarty had bequeathed a packet of papers to his sister and brother-in-law, I approached them for permission to read the contents. I was curious to know what matters our notoriously secretive criminal Edison had seen fit to commit to paper, but given the view of me taken by the colonel, the family was set against helping me in any way."

Holmes stood, galvanised suddenly, and knocked out his pipe against the hearth. "This new development has changed their minds, at least. Come, Watson, if we are at King's Cross by eleven we can make a good start in learning more of the professor's bequest and its whereabouts."

The Banisters resided in the northern city where Moriarty had held his academic chair, before beginning his second career as the outstanding criminal mind of the century. Indeed, it was through the university that Moriarty had made the acquaintance of Dr Redmond Banister, an association which had led in time to Banister's marriage to Abigail Moriarty.

Their house formed part of a hillside terrace in the outskirts of the town, a row of generously proportioned slate and tile homes built to house members of the faculty. Steps led up to the door and down to an area beneath, divided from the sloping street by sturdy railings. A servant admitted us at Holmes's knock, and conveyed us to a drawing-room at the rear of the house where a modest but pretty garden boasted two small plane trees. It sloped up towards a mews which had been converted into servants' quarters when the new houses were built.

We were greeted by Banister himself, an elderly white-haired man with watery grey eyes, quivering with nervous tension, and his wife, some twenty years younger than he and still handsome.

"Thank you for coming, Mr Holmes," the eminent biologist gasped when he saw us. "I understood the instant I made this morning's shocking discovery that you and only you could aid us in this terrible plight. I am strongly conscious, however, that not every man of your stature, nor even for that matter of a more modest one, would have been so forgiving as to extend us that necessary aid, given the unconvivial history of our intercourse prior to today. I can only thank you, sir, for your indulgence, from the bottom of my heart and, if you will allow me, from my pocket as well."

I almost think he would have brought out his pocket-book on the spot, had not his wife placed an admonitory hand on his shoulder. Mrs Abigail Banister had the unusual height, the slenderness and the prominent, intelligent forehead which my friend had remarked on in his descriptions of her late brother. The cold, reptilian quality he had found in the master criminal, had in her case been transmuted into a calmness in the face of crisis which contrasted strongly with the agitation of her husband. The telegram had certainly misled us: of the two, it was Professor Banister who was the more distraught.

Mrs Banister was a forbidding woman nonetheless. "My husband talks with too great a freedom when he is excited," she informed us, frowning. "I beg that you will pardon him."

"Perhaps it will help to focus your discourse, professor, if you confine yourself to the facts," Holmes suggested.

"Very well," our host said, composing himself with some effort. "As you know, I have been the keeper of my brother-in-law's papers for some three years, since he was declared dead – along with yourself, of course – on the basis of Dr Watson's testimony and the evidence left behind at the Reichenbach Falls. He left few material possessions, and of those he did, some have since been proven deplorably to have been come by illegally. The Gutenberg Bible, for example –"

"The facts," Holmes reminded him languidly, "would be specifically those pertaining to the current case, professor."

"Yes, quite. Well, the family received little enough, but Jimmy and Tom – Abigail's other brothers, you understand – between them inherited everything of value. Our legacy was the packet of papers that you came asking after some months back, Mr Holmes, and nothing else. From the weight of it, it is perhaps as much material as might make a monograph or dissertation, assuming of course that all the pages are covered."

Holmes frowned. "You have not read it?"

"No, sir." The professor looked pained. "The packet was double-wrapped, with a letter inside the outer package. It was the unopened inner envelope which was stolen; I have the letter here."

At this point the vermeologist did indeed produce his pocket-book, and withdrew a single sheet of notepaper, written upon on both sides. He handed it to Holmes, who sniffed it, rolled the corner gently between thumb and forefinger and held it up to the light from the window before reading it.

"My dear sister," Holmes read, "and you, Banister,

I would send you cordial greetings, but they would mean little. I fear that when you receive this I will be dead, and quite without capacity or will to feel cordially disposed to any person, no matter what degree of consanguinity or professional brotherhood may in the past have put us in one another's way.

I merely charge you, then, with the care of these papers after I am deceased. I will not tell you, nor do I recommend that you attempt to ascertain before time, what is contained within them. While neither of you has the capacity to understand their contents, you will both – unlike my imbecile brothers or my lumbering business associates – be dimly capable of grasping their import, which is the only reason I entrust them to you.

I insist that they are to be preserved at all costs for posterity's sake, but I absolutely forbid their being published until the new century has dawned. That time, if any, will be fitting for the revelations contained herein. You know that I am not given to overstatement, nor do I exaggerate now when I say that these papers have the capacity to bring down the whole of Christendom.

An ambition to be hastened, you may think; yet I find the persistence of civilisation, however despicable in its own right, agreeable to my ends, and so I would wish it to be quite certain that I am dead before such matters are set in motion – if, indeed, the world persists in its existence after my death, a matter which I confess remains of interest to me, although I will *a priori* never see it resolved.

I will conclude by observing that, of the disagreeably inferior intellects in this wholly unsatisfactory sphere, it is yours, sister, with which I shall most deplore having no further contact after my death – though I naturally expect that my personal regrets on the occasion will more than eclipse such sentiment.

Your fond brother,
James Monroe Moriarty

"Dear me, how very agreeable of the man," Holmes opined, with a smirk that under the circumstances did him very little credit.

"He was raving, surely?" I said. "Bringing down Christendom? The world ending with his death? It can be nothing but rampant megalomania."

"If that is a medical term, Dr Watson, it is not one that I recognise," said Mrs Banister with considerable asperity.

"You will concede, however, that the claim is a rather grandiose one," Holmes declared over my stammered apologies. "Although the professor's letter purports to rule it out, we must allow ourselves to assume some degree of embellishment. Still, Moriarty's intelligence network was extensive, and his methods remorseless. I could well believe that what is to be found within that package might cause serious embarrassment to some of the royal families of Europe, for instance; perhaps even to the Church. In either case, we might say that Christendom had been dealt a blow."

"It sounds as if the contents of this package are a danger to the social order, at least," I said. "Unless it's a hoax."

"It would be reassuring to imagine so, Watson, but I think not. A hoax would not be in the late professor's style. I see there is a postscript in the margin: 'P.S. If publisher is so pusillanimous as to insist on an editor, V.K.C. is the man.' Who, pray, is V.K.C.?"

Banister frowned. "Some fifteen years ago, he was one of James' students. Now he is a researcher in his own right. He has published extensively on the mathematics of telegraphy, of all things. James considered him quite the most promising mind he had taught, I believe."

There was a note of reservation in our host's voice, which Holmes observed. "But you do not?"

"He's... a rather excitable little fellow. I worry that he is less than reliable. I opposed his election to the faculty myself, but others outvoted me."

"We will need to speak to him," said Holmes decisively. "Had you informed him that he was named in your brother-in-law's letter?"

Our host shook his head firmly. "Not I, sir. I cannot see how he could have learned of it, unless from James before his death."

Banister took us to see the scene of the robbery: a large laboratory-cum-study, located in the basement of the house because, as he told us, his colonies of live worms distressed the servants, who lived in constant fear of their escape. Open books of taxonomy stood in piles, earth-filled glass tanks seethed with vermiform activity, and formaldehyde jars displayed some distinctly unprepossessing specimens. The room was very dusty.

"We're trying to find a girl who'll clean it," Banister explained. "The last one who tried left in hysterics after breaking a vivarium of *Didymogaster sylvaticus*."

The only broken glass in the room now came from the window, which looked out at ground level across the rear garden. Holmes insisted that everyone but himself stop at the door, and spent some minutes on the floor with his magnifying glass, examining footprints in the dust.

Eventually he rose. "Tell me, professor, do any of your servants wear size thirteen boots? Rather muddy ones, I fear."

Banister looked in confusion at his wife. "I suppose Burrows the gardener might," she supplied. "The man has extraordinarily large feet."

"What on earth would *he* want with James' papers?" Banister asked in astonishment.

"Very little, I suspect," Holmes replied. "Mrs Banister, would you enquire whether Mr Burrows has had a pair of boots go missing last night, or whether he noticed anything unusual about them this morning?"

The lady hurried off, and her husband showed us the locked drawer where Moriarty's package had been kept, along with various of his own notes and papers.

"The drawer was not forced," Holmes observed. "Either the man was a proficient lock-picker, or he had the key. That is, if we assume that the drawer was locked at the time. Professor?"

Banister flushed. "I cannot swear to it, Mr Holmes. I use that drawer to file all my confidential documents: records of my research, departmental finances and the like; I am often referring to them. I also keep my bond certificates in there. It is my practice to keep it unlocked during the day and to lock it at night, but I admit that I am sometimes preoccupied. It would not be the first time that I have forgotten, I am sorry to say."

"Then we have too few data to theorise," my friend said. "Especially since it will turn out that Mr Burrows' boots have been borrowed. There is, I presume, a Mrs Burrows? The housekeeper, perhaps? And they live in the mews behind the house? As I thought. A woman of the meticulous habits befitting a housekeeper would not tolerate muddy boots in her own quarters. She would insist on them being left outside, where the burglar might readily have come upon them."

"But surely the criminal would have worn his own footwear?" our host expostulated. "How else could he have come here?"

"I can see that you are more familiar with the anatomy of worms than that of mankind, professor. The prints of, say, a pair of size eight men's shoes would tell us that the intruder's feet were at most a cramped and uncomfortable size nine. That alone would eliminate perhaps half the adult population of this city. Almost anyone, however, may wear size thirteen boots. Several thick pairs of woollen socks may transform a criminal of readily identifiable stature into one of entirely unknown dimensions."

"The thief seems to have gone to some lengths to disguise himself," I observed. "Almost as if he knew you were coming, Holmes."

Holmes nodded as if the thing were settled. "Given the papers' connection with the late Professor Moriarty, he would be a fool not to assume it. Tell me, Professor Banister, do your brothers-in-law visit often? The living ones, I mean."

"Why, yes," said Banister. "That is – we see little of Tom. He is a station master, you know, and his work and his young family keep him at his station."

"Of course – the cadet branch of the Moriarty family," Holmes murmured gravely. "How charming."

"Jimmy passes through town often, though. Indeed, we were to expect him today."

"Really?" Holmes looked pained. "I could wish that you had mentioned the fact. He is not a man I have any great desire to meet. And has the colonel ever –" he began to ask, but was interrupted by a cry from upstairs.

"He's here? The blackguard!" It was a man's voice, though

accompanied by agitated feminine murmurs. "I'll teach him to meddle in the affairs of this family! Why, that insolent vulture murdered poor James, and now I find him sloping around my sister!"

"Oh, dear me," whimpered Banister.

The door was thrown wide with a crash, and Colonel Moriarty stood before us.

Like his brother and sister, he was tall, with a face that, though shrewd, showed little of the remarkable intellect they displayed. Unlike his siblings, he was wiry and muscular, a man physically powerful in proportion with his height. Despite his broad military moustache, his expression reminded me of one of the more vicious snakes: a cobra, perhaps, caught in mid-strike.

"Colonel James Madison Moriarty, I believe," Holmes purred. "How delightful to make your acquaintance at last."

"Oh, delightful, is it? As delightful as pitching my brother off a cliff-top, eh? Did that delight you?" The colonel was almost incoherent with rage. "Why are you here, Mr Sherlock Holmes, you liar and slanderer and murderer, at my sister's house? Do you plan to seek out and destroy my family one by one, hmm? I shall horsewhip you, sir – no, better still I should kill you!"

"Jimmy, please calm yourself." Abigail Banister stood behind her brother now. "Mr Holmes is here at our invitation. He is investigating a theft."

"A theft, is it?" the colonel raged. "Then he should look no further than this room! When misfortune befalls our family – when crimes are committed against us – who else should be there but the invidious Holmes? Investigating his own perfidies, by God! A pretty trade for those with the gall to practise it!"

"I think we'd better leave, Holmes," I suggested.

Holmes smiled tightly. "Indeed, I think we can accomplish little here under the present circumstances. Mrs Banister, Professor Banister, I thank you for your hospitality. You may find us at the Crown Inn."

The colonel moved to bar our way, but Abigail Banister placed a warning hand on his arm and he stepped aside without halting his tirade. His abuse followed us up the stairs and down the street.

II

"What made you of the colonel, Watson?" Sherlock Holmes asked later, as he smoked a postprandial pipe in our rooms at the Crown. Despite our hasty retreat from the Banisters' house, neither of us had given a moment's thought to resigning the case. Whatever Colonel Moriarty's wishes in the matter, we had been engaged by the Banisters; besides, the alleged import of the stolen bequest was too much to let go on any account.

"He scarcely seemed sane," I replied truthfully.

"No; I fear mental stability is not in plentiful supply among the Moriarty family line. The level-headed Mrs Banister may have monopolised her generation's supply. Yet I wonder whether any relative of the late professor could truly be so blustering a fool as he appeared. You noticed that the colonel wore civilian clothes?"

I had indeed noticed this. "I assumed he has retired."

"He has, but only recently, and not by free choice. His staunch defence of his disgraced brother's reputation made his position in his regiment intolerable."

"I see. So he blames you for the loss of his career as well as that of his brother?"

Holmes looked startled for the moment. "Well, perhaps. I had in mind a more material consideration, however: his loss of income. The legacy left by his late brother was not large. Most of the capital earned from Moriarty's illicit profession seems to have made its way into the hands of such co-conspirators as Moran."

"You think Colonel Moriarty stole the papers to make money out of them? If the contents are as scandalous as you suppose, they could enable him to blackmail some influential people."

"So I fear, Watson, so I fear."

We smoked in silence for a minute, before I asked, "Should we perhaps tell your brother about this?" Mycroft Holmes was a figure of considerable, if rarely acknowledged, significance in the civil service, and had the ear of the highest in the land. "He might forewarn –"

"Forewarn whom, pray? At present we have no idea of the persons to whom these papers may pertain – if indeed they do contain personal information, and not some other matter altogether.

Our best chance of such a hint must lie with the mysterious Mr V.K.C. No, we will leave Mycroft unburdened by our misgivings for the moment."

I agreed, though privately I wondered whether this was altogether wise. "There is a third brother, however. If Colonel Moriarty is to be suspected, then we should consider him so as well."

"Indeed. It would be opportune, I think, for me to undertake a rail journey. I understand the connections are excellent."

"And yet," I said, "the papers were stolen here. Surely our search should take place in this city?"

"Whoever has taken them has shown a great deal of intelligence in disguising their steps. They will not be readily found by an ordinary search. No Watson, this is a theft of information, and it is only with *more* information that we shall solve it. Data, my dear fellow, data! Only on a foundation of solid data can our theories be built. Besides, I intend that you should stay here, for the moment at least. While I approach Mr Thomas Jefferson Moriarty, you will speak to Mr V.K.C."

"That should be easy enough. Professor Banister gave us no surname, but he will surely be in the university directory."

"I have no doubt of it. We will regroup in London tomorrow morning. Ask Professor Banister to call on us… oh, let us say Friday of this week. If I have no answer for him by then, I fear that one may never be forthcoming."

"Just as you say, Holmes."

He continued, "There is, too, another point of concern. The hierarchy of criminality that Moriarty left behind him, controlled from London but with its tendrils pervading the country and the continent, was run until recently by his lieutenants. Moran's arrest has put paid to that. A decapitated organisation will soon collapse, yet what has once been ruined may perhaps be rebuilt more easily than if one were to start from nothing. Conceivably one of the brothers feels that the late professor's position might become available to him too, if he were to press the information in those papers to his advantage."

"Not the colonel, surely. He hardly seems like a criminal genius."

"No indeed, but many men fail to understand their own limitations.

Two brothers, in fraternal rivalry since childhood, the older and cleverer becoming so much more powerful in later life… one can understand how the younger might develop the urge to prove himself within his brother's sphere, can one not?"

I glanced at him, but his eyes were hooded by those heavy lids.

I will say at once, regarding Professor Banister's assessment of him, that Mr V.K. Chakraborty was not especially little for a man of his race and caste; nor did I find him unusually excitable, though he was an ardent enthusiast for his specialism.

"Information itself – all information – is applied mathematics, you see," he explained to me as he called for a pot of tea. He had received me in the senior common room of his college, and I had made the mistake of opening the conversation by politely asking about his work on telegraphy. Dark-skinned and delicate of feature, Chakraborty wore a herringbone suit and his hair was neatly parted.

"There are of course the mundane calculations of speed and volume of transmission in a system, the limitations of human and mechanical operation and so forth," he went on, "but there is also the question of encoding human knowledge in mathematical form. To be sure, at present we send words along the wires, rendered into a signal which the medium may pass, but in future, who knows? Pictures, sounds, objects, perhaps even states of mind, might be just as easily transmitted and received, for assuredly all of those things may be equally analysed as information."

"Imagine that," I said rather weakly, for his voice was soothing and musical, and I had eaten a heavy luncheon.

"But I am tiring you, Doctor," Chakraborty added at once. "I understand. My work is overly theoretical for the layman, and your business with me lies elsewhere, I suppose."

I nodded. "I have come to ask you about Professor Moriarty."

The Brahmin's face turned grave. "Ah yes, the poor fellow. I still find it difficult to credit everything they say about him."

"It's quite true, I can assure you," I said, perhaps a little too coldly, for the mathematician looked up at me in alarm.

"Don't misunderstand me, Dr Watson. I have seen the evidence summarised in the newspapers, and I have no doubt that he committed the crimes associated with his name. My concern is that he may not have been fully aware of what he was doing, as he was so much changed after his breakdown. Previously he could be arrogant of course, sometimes jealous or vindictive: such, I am afraid, are the sins of academia. But he was a considerate, patient tutor, and very kind to me when I first came to this country."

I had heard rumours of a scandal accompanying Moriarty's dismissal from the university, but this was the first I had known of a breakdown. I enquired after its cause.

"I cannot tell you," Chakraborty replied. "It came at a time when his research was entirely successful, so far as anyone else can determine. He was, you must understand, at the very vanguard of our profession. I am considered no mean intellect myself, I am flattered to say, but compared with Professor Moriarty I was playing blind-man's-buff in a treasure house. When he assured us that his researches progressed well, we could do little but take him at his word. There are, perhaps, three men in the world who might have gainsaid him on the matter: an American, a Russian and a Swede, all of whom unfortunately refuse to speak to one another. Of his colleagues here, I came the closest: indeed, some of his findings have served to inform my work on the theory of telegraphic communication.

"Even as his work flourished, however, the professor's moods became grimmer and more unpredictable. He would at times fly into a temper over the most trivial of provocations, though at others he would still show the patience and forbearance I had known of old. I once asked him the meaning of one particular formula, entirely obscure to me, only to have him round on me in a fury, seize me by the arms and pin me against a wall. He was not a physically strong man, but I found myself utterly unable to escape his grip. He cried, 'It means that you, Chakraborty, are *nothing*! Nothing, do you hear me? Why should I interrupt my work for you, you evanescence?'"

"What a peculiar thing to say," I exclaimed.

"Dr Watson, the whole incident was peculiar. And yet the next day he was as polite and conciliatory to me as if the whole event had never happened. At the same time he became interested in politics, of the most detestable kind."

"Really?" I had heard nothing to suggest that Moriarty's depravities had had a political dimension.

"It was a most surprising reversal. He had always followed the life of the mind, and topics relating to the material world were of little interest to him. The first sign of it came a few days after what I suppose I must call his assault on me, when he started an argument which nearly came to blows with the university chaplain, a perfectly harmless man named Smithson. Without any provocation I could see, Professor Moriarty began berating him in this room, in the most vulgar terms, calling his church a cult, his god a sham and his Bible random words upon a page, devoid of meaning. Smithson was terribly upset, and resigned shortly afterwards. Not wishing to lose a scholar of Moriarty's brilliance, the faculty kept the matter quiet.

"Some weeks later, however, a graduate student was caught distributing socialist pamphlets of the most scandalous nature, calling for an end to the monarchy and the hereditary peerage, and even hinting at the assassination of the Queen herself. The young fellow told the police that he owed his views to the influence of his tutor, Professor Moriarty. It was assumed that he spoke out of malice, and that part of the evidence never reached court, but it was shared with the senior faculty members.

"Matters really reached their head when in a lecture – a mathematics lecture, mind you – he began railing against the monarchy, the law and Parliament, declaring that all such structures were false and must be done away with. That was the scandal which the university was finally unable to ignore, and which ended with his dismissal."

"And you believe that these outbreaks were symptoms of some kind of nervous breakdown?" I asked. Despite my previous, rather airy diagnosis of megalomania, I knew little of psychoanalysis. "Brought on by overwork, perhaps?"

Chakraborty spread his hands. "What else could it have been? In any case, he left the university immediately, and took a position as an army tutor which his brother arranged for him. That was evidently when his criminal career began in earnest."

"What contact had you with him after that?"

"None at all, I am afraid. He severed all his ties with the university, save with Dr Banister as he then was, to whom he was bound by family connections."

"He gave no indication that he still held you in esteem?"

"Rather not. I passed him on the street once, on an occasion when he was visiting the Banisters, and he ignored me. I am not an easy man to miss in this city, Dr Watson: I do not exactly blend in with the crowd. No, I am convinced that after he abandoned his mathematical work my friendship held no further interest for him."

From the Brahmin mathematician's friendly manner and the ease with which he had confided in me, I believed that I could trust the man. Enjoining him to secrecy, therefore, I apprised him of the unexpected mention of his name in Moriarty's final communication to his sister and brother-in-law.

At first he professed himself baffled, but as I was about to leave he remarked, "I have just one thought. This letter of the professor's – was it amicable in tone?"

"Rather the reverse," I said. "The Moriarty Holmes and I had dealings with was not a warm man. He expressed a perfunctory fondness for his sister, but that is all."

"Then I have one suggestion," Chakraborty told me, "though perhaps not a very useful one. Professor Banister has never liked me. He is one of those on the faculty who are ungracious enough to object to my complexion, though it is no fault of mine and affects my academic capabilities not a jot. If Professor Moriarty was in a vexatious mood, he might have mentioned my name merely to annoy his relative."

The speculation certainly seemed in keeping with the letter's tone. I bade the mathematician farewell, and made arrangements to return to London, not forgetting to send a message to Redmond Banister, appointing our meeting for the Friday. I asked the messenger particularly to ensure that Colonel Moriarty was absent before delivering it.

* * *

Sherlock Holmes and I reconvened for breakfast the next morning at 221B Baker Street. Over coffee and Mrs Hudson's finest kedgeree he informed me, "Either Tom Moriarty is innocent, or he is the most consummate actor I have ever encountered."

"Really?" I said.

"Oh yes. The man appears absolutely guileless; as far as I can judge he is not even a good station master. His children, on the other hand, have certainly inherited the tendencies of the Moriarty line. They are devious, amoral and utterly without remorse. As the eldest is but six years old, however, I fear we must rule them out of our inquiries."

I told him of the words I had exchanged with Chakraborty. He brushed aside the talk of mental breakdown ("It hardly matters to us how Moriarty came to be a criminal, since he is beyond hope of reform now"), but seized on the story of the young anarchist and his pamphlet.

"This may be the key to deciphering the affair, Watson," he said. "I knew that Moriarty had contacts among the political radicals – communists, nihilists, Fenians and their ilk – but I had assumed that theirs was a mere consulting relationship, like his many others. Perhaps I was wrong. Perhaps his convictions were actually engaged in this part of his work. After all, who but an anarchist would take delight in the prospect of demolishing Christendom?"

"I thought your theory was that the thief intends to use the papers for blackmail?"

"Well, they may yet – but how complicated and cumbersome to arrange meetings with representatives of everyone involved, to wheedle out the money discreetly and to avoid the ever-present threat of corporal reprisal that dogs the blackmailer. How much simpler, safer and more elegant to sell the information to a solitary third party, who wishes nothing more than to make the information public and to revel in its effects."

"That's monstrous!" I protested. After a moment's thought I added, "And not nearly as lucrative. I don't know many nihilists, but I don't believe they have the same funds at their disposal as the typical royal family."

He beamed at me. "Excellent, Watson! We'll make a criminal mastermind of you yet. Still, we know nothing as yet of the burglar's motives. He may be a communist himself, and have no interest in money. We must at least investigate this new avenue, for in our other lines of investigation I confess myself at a loss."

Over the next few days I saw little of Holmes, and that in the late hours of the morning, when he would arrive grimy with the soot of the capital, eat a hearty breakfast and then retire to bed until mid-afternoon. His attire during this time was characterised by soiled shirts, ragged trousers and flat caps, and he ceased shaving. Our coffee table grew a great crop of ill-printed pamphlets calling for everything from the overthrow of the capitalist system to the reform of the licensing laws, and of posters for public meetings to be addressed by men (and the occasional woman) whose names were as often as not prefaced with "Comrade".

"We seem to be assembling a catalogue of the most infamous individuals in the capital," I ventured once, to which Holmes replied with uncharacteristic acerbity.

"On the contrary, Watson, many of them are merely hungry, desperate or overworked, and feel themselves without the power to direct their fates in a world run by men like you and me. They do not mean ill, for the most part – unlike the late professor, the greater number of them maintain a strong moral sense. The conclusions to which it leads them diverge from your own largely because of the differences in your circumstances."

My dismay at hearing my friend talk in this way may be imagined, but I put it down to the need to maintain his character for his nocturnal excursions.

Thursday evening came, and I was anticipating our meeting with the Banisters with a heavy heart. Professor Banister had written to say that he and his wife were travelling down on Thursday afternoon, and staying at the Metropole. Holmes had invited them to call on us at nine the next morning.

"What will you tell them?" I asked. As far as I knew, his investigations among the radicals and socialists had come to nothing, and we were no nearer to knowing the location of the stolen package. For all I knew, it could have found its way to Barcelona or Gdansk, and be waiting there to erupt like a pustulent boil.

"I have hopes that there will be some news," Holmes replied.

"Have you found the papers, then?" I asked eagerly.

"No, but I have spoken to the man who once acted as go-between for Moriarty and the London Nihilist League. He changed his precise allegiance some time ago – you would not believe the ferment of divergent factions that is the radical fringe, Watson – but he retains friends in that brotherhood. He has heard rumours that their presses are being readied to print a document of explosive potency, unprecedented in the annals of revolution. There is a name attached to these rumours."

"Moriarty!" I surmised.

He nodded. "I have been observing the League with interest. I believe the exchange will be made at midnight tonight, in the shadow of Blackfriars Bridge. I have invited Inspector Lestrade and a half-dozen sturdy constables to join us there."

"Do you expect the colonel to appear?"

"Consider, Watson: it is apparent that the burglar knew the house. No other window was broken, nothing else in the laboratory was touched – not even the other papers, some of them valuable, in Banister's confidential drawer. Burrows' boots were taken from outside the mews. The burglar was careful to leave no clues of identity, knowing that given the gravity of the theft I might be involved. Thus far our only leads have come from Moriarty himself, through the letter he left, and from Mr Chakraborty, to whom it directed us. Yet a new Moriarty is emerging, with all the criminal predilections of that name, and we must assume that this new Caesar is older than six. If we have a man to catch, the colonel is he."

Lestrade arrived at ten p.m., gleeful at the prospect of arresting a real nihilist cell. "I don't mind telling you, Mr Holmes," he said, "these fellows have had it coming for a long time. We've seen their pamphlets, calling for Parliament to be blown up and Her Majesty assassinated and heaven knows what else. If you can lead us to them there'll be a medal in it for us all, I shouldn't wonder."

"Arrest them if you must, Lestrade," my friend said, "and if you can. I am concerned only with retrieving the package and bringing it safely back here. Anything beyond that is your remit, not mine."

"You have my sympathies, Mr Holmes," Lestrade said with a wink. "Must be difficult in your line of work, not always being your own boss. The lads and I are happy enough to back you up, though, if it gets us nearer to these anarchist swine."

By eleven we were in wait in the shadows of the great bridge. Lestrade, Holmes and I carried pistols; the constables had their truncheons. The night was cold and foggy, and the footfalls of pedestrians on their way home from the public houses, and even the clattering of hooves from the hansom cabs, were distant and muffled. We had been standing quite still for half an hour when a group of five men arrived and began to loiter at the corners of the square of road roofed by the bridge. All of them were dressed much as Holmes had been during the past few days, with no sign of the black cloaks or masks I had been rather wildly imagining.

Lestrade had chosen his men well. None of the anarchists saw us, although the challenge of staying perfectly still and silent for the half-hour that remained was excruciating.

As the chimes of midnight sounded, a hansom approached, proceeded briskly to the middle of the area under the bridge, then drew to a halt. The fifth man, who had been loitering on the nearby pavement, stepped up to the door. Low voices, dulled by the fog, exchanged a few words, and then objects changed hands: the man produced a purse from his satchel, which he replaced shortly afterwards with a heavy roll of paper.

The cabman raised his whip, and at once Lestrade's whistle sounded.

Policemen poured forth from the shadows, grappling with the men. "Watson, the cab!" Holmes cried as the cabman's whip cracked, and the two of us ran in front of the vehicle, brandishing our pistols. I fired a shot into the girders of the bridge above, and the horse reared and whinnied. The cabman leapt down, crying "Nothing to do with me, gents, just making an honest fare!", and took the horse's reins, trying to calm it while he cringed from the sight of my weapon. Holmes seized the ringleader's satchel and busied himself with it.

At the same time, a tall shape in a heavy overcoat and muffler leapt from the cab and hared away towards the other exit from the bridge. Lestrade was waiting, though, and even as the final nihilist was being cuffed by the constables, he tackled the figure, wrestling it to the ground.

"Sit tight now, you, you're under arrest!" Lestrade cried, then a moment later: "Coo! It's a woman!"

Holmes produced the roll of papers with a triumphant cry. I ran across to Lestrade, who was hauling his captive upright, unwilling to let his temporary discomposure rob him of his prize.

He pulled away the scarf to reveal the face of the would-be-fugitive. It was Abigail Banister, née Moriarty.

Lestrade's whistle had brought more officers to the scene, and the nihilists were quickly bundled up and taken to Scotland Yard in a four-wheeler. Holmes commandeered the cab, and he, Lestrade and I followed with Mrs Banister.

"You were the obvious suspect, of course," Holmes told her as we rode. "You will recall, Watson, I said that *if* we had a man to catch, the colonel was he? I thought it unlikely enough then, though I knew you would appreciate the joke."

Mrs Banister appeared as outwardly composed as before. I wondered whether in her case the family instability had expressed itself as its opposite: whether her insanity showed itself in an incapacity for feelings of any kind.

She said, "You must have guessed the burglar was familiar with the house. I thought of breaking another window and blundering around smashing things up, but that would have been too great a risk. Far better to commit the burglary the day before my fool of a brother was due to visit, and throw your suspicions on him instead."

"I say, this one's a piece of work," Lestrade commented cheerfully.

"My dear lady," Holmes said, "neither of your living brothers is capable of such cunning as the burglar displayed. It is all too plain that, with the passing of your late brother, the brains in the family have fallen entirely to you."

"And what brought you to that conclusion, Mr Holmes?" she sneered. "Instinct? The same jumping to judgement which allowed you to execute my brother James and boast of a clear conscience afterward?"

"Not at all," Holmes replied gravely. "In fact it was my respect for your brother's professional judgement. His letter to you made it clear enough that he considered your intellect superior to your brothers'. Furthermore, whatever his family feeling, the man made ruthless use of such resources as he had available. If he felt that Tom or Jimmy had the talent to join him in his criminal enterprises, he would have involved them, but I have found no trace of any such association. If there was indeed a Moriarty capable of such an ingenious burglary, why was he not already part of your brother's felonious empire? Unless, of course, she was barred by her sex from such a role. Despite his radical notions, your brother evidently retained some traditional sensibilities.

"The fact that your husband called me in – that, I confess, gave me pause. It was perfectly evident that you had sufficient influence to direct him in this matter, so why would you allow him to invite me to solve a crime of which you yourself were guilty? The packet was unopened, after all. You could have taken it at any time, replacing it with a similar one so that your husband would not remark the difference. Why should the crime have even been discovered, let alone myself involved?

"It was the realisation that the criminal end was nothing so petty as blackmail, but an assault on civilised values themselves, that caused me to reassess your motivations.

"I killed your brother: that is common knowledge; and you would not be alone in wanting to avenge him. What better way to humiliate a man of my reputation, than to bring the Empire crashing down about my ears, and let it be known that I had been unable to prevent it? Such a plan would have justified the risk of discovery. It is, if you will permit me to say so, worthy of your late brother's memory."

Mrs Banister nodded. "I thank you, Mr Holmes. That is a question you are the only person alive competent to judge."

"I will inform your husband of your arrest," Holmes told her. "I am sure that he will stand by you, since he seems so little capable of standing on his own. In the meantime, perhaps you will permit me to take custody of your late brother's papers."

"Keep them," she said. "I wish you all the benefit of them. They drove my brother mad: perhaps they will do the same for you."

The hansom clattered on through the foggy night.

III

I awoke the next morning to find Sherlock Holmes wild-eyed, pacing the carpet in the sitting-room, flicking feverishly through the bundle of pages.

"Absurd, Watson!" he barked at me, before I had had time to say a thing. "The entire matter is quite ridiculous. And yet…" He whirled and resumed pacing. "And yet, and yet…"

"Why, whatever is the matter, Holmes?" I urged him, alarmed. "Are you ill?"

"No, nothing of the kind. Kindly do not burden me with trivialities."

"It's freezing in here." I poked at the embers of the fire, then rang the bell for Mrs Hudson.

He paced impatiently as the good woman stoked the fire, then bustled off to get breakfast. As she left he seized me by the shoulders, and sat me down bodily in an armchair. "Your telegraphy expert, Mr Chakraborty. He told you, did he not, that all human experience could be rendered in mathematical code? Even states of mind, he said?"

"I believe that was the gist, yes."

"Dear me, Watson, these are deep waters indeed – too deep for you and me, I fear. Small wonder that the man lost his connection with reality."

"Chakraborty? He seemed sane enough to me. A little full of himself, perhaps, but –"

"Not Chakraborty, Watson, Moriarty!" He brandished the papers at me. "It seems that he anticipated much of Chakraborty's work – anticipated, surpassed and transcended it. Oh, I am no mathematician, but I can follow an argument, and dear God, if what this purports to say is true…"

"What is it? Do you mean to say this whole affair was about a mathematical paper? That's absurd! Holmes, sit down, you're frightening me."

"I am frightening myself," he whispered. He sat, his knee jiggling with impatience. "Where Chakraborty's work is in the theory of communication, Moriarty worked along more abstract principles. What he has created here is something we might call *theory of information*. Great masses of data, existing in dynamic conditions, undergoing processes whose results are used to inform the next round of processes. Whole systems of information, in rigorously regulated communication with one another. Have you heard of Babbage's calculating engine, Watson?"

I had not.

"As the name suggests, it is a mechanism sometimes used to facilitate the working of repetitive mathematical processes. Moriarty's paper envisages something like a Babbage engine, but many times faster and more powerful, and capable of being linked with other such engines to make them more powerful still. Imagine all the types of information that might be worked by such a machine. What was it Chakraborty told you? Images, sounds, physical objects – or their simulacra, at least – even the human mind. Even the human mind, Watson!"

Mrs Hudson brought in the breakfast then. I frowned. "You mean to say that such a machine might think like a man? But then it would be…"

"Conscious, yes! Self-aware – but not aware of its true nature. For if the simulacrum of a human mind is fed with simulacra of sights, sounds, smells, feelings – if it sits at a simulated table, and warms itself by a simulated fire, and drinks a cup of simulated coffee – thank you, Mrs Hudson – then how is it to know that it is a simulacrum at all?"

"It would believe itself a living man," I said slowly.

"And now imagine millions of such machines! A huge array of Moriarty engines, each maintaining the illusion of a human mind. Imagine them feeding information to one another. They might speak together, argue, fight, fall in love, engender simulated children

– and all without knowing for a moment that they were anything other than real!"

I stared at him. His eyes were fervent, fanatical even. It was plain that he was half convinced by this nonsense.

"It's fantastic, Holmes. An astonishing conceit, I grant you. Moriarty must have had a remarkable mind to imagine such a thing. But surely those papers don't argue that what he has imagined is actually possible?"

"More than that, Watson." Holmes gazed at me, for such a long time that I wondered whether he had finally fallen asleep with his eyes open. "Moriarty's argument purports to prove that all of this has already happened; that we live in just such a world. That all of us – you and I, Mrs Hudson, Lestrade, Abigail Banister, Mr Chakraborty, Moriarty himself – are mere facsimiles of reality."

I tried to laugh. "Come now, Holmes. It's a fantasy, surely? Even if Moriarty believed it, he was a madman."

"Oh, yes. Moriarty was mad, but in a very particular way. It may even have been this discovery that first convinced him that conventional moral rules were useless – for after all, if our entire world is an illusion, what should we care for the consequences of our actions? If all the world is false, then what of others? Even believing in their capacity to suffer becomes an act of faith – and whatever else he may have been, Moriarty was not a man of faith. He came to believe himself the only conscious thing in the world."

"You see? How can we possibly trust such a man's conclusions? As you said yourself, you're no mathematician. You may be able to see what Moriarty was getting at, but you surely can't verify it. Even Chakraborty couldn't fully follow his theories."

"Oh, it will need to be verified," Holmes whispered. "The Russian will need to see it, and the Swede, and the American. But if they pronounce it true –"

"That's a big 'if', Holmes."

"Then it is truly no exaggeration to say that Christendom will fall. Who would believe in God, when *we ourselves* may not exist? Darwin's theory of evolution was bad enough for the Church, but when Moriarty's theory of simulation becomes accepted…"

"We mustn't allow that," I told him sternly. "It is precisely what Moriarty wanted. Mrs Banister, too, and the Nihilist League. He knew the effect this would have on the world; he said as much in his letter. This is his final legacy, a legacy of anarchy. We mustn't let it come out."

"And yet," he said again. "If it is the truth, Watson... the truth must not be suppressed. The truth will always out. What use is it to live in a world one knows to be a lie?"

I spoke gruffly. "It will turn out to be so much nonsense, old man, depend on it. Show it to the mathematicians and they'll say so. Ponder it for weeks first, probably, but in the end they'll say he was as mad as everyone thought he was."

"Perhaps you're right, Watson," he said. "Perhaps, indeed, you are right. We must lay our plans carefully."

"Of course," I told him soothingly. "But there's no hurry. Moriarty's theories aren't going anywhere. Go and get some sleep. Come back to it later, when your mind is rested. We can work out the right thing to do together."

"I cannot sleep," he murmured. "But perhaps... there is the violin. Even if the sound it makes is false, music itself is mathematics, and still beautiful."

"That's right, old fellow. Beautiful numbers. Go and play for a while. I'm sure it will help."

I took him by the shoulders and steered him, still murmuring, to his room. A few minutes later, the violin's sound pervaded the house, and I stood still for a moment, shocked by what I had just witnessed.

I picked up the papers and flicked through them. They were completely impenetrable: page after page of mathematical symbols and equations, annotated with scarcely less abstruse commentary. The word "simulation" appeared a great deal, however.

I wondered anew about Mrs Banister's motivations: firstly for staging the burglary, and then for involving Sherlock Holmes in its investigation. If her aim was truly to advance the nihilists, to enrich herself and set herself up as the new Napoleon of crime, why risk the attention of the one man with the knowledge and skill to destroy her?

Had she really been setting him up to fail? Or did she intend him to succeed? Was it her hope that the knowledge which had doomed her brother would end up in Holmes's hands? Could that even have been what Moriarty himself intended?

Was this, after all, the professor's truest bequest – to his archenemy, an insoluble dilemma? Had he hoped in the end, not to ruin the world, but to drive one man insane?

Holmes was right. These waters were too deep for me.

I gathered up the papers and flung them on the fire.

ABOUT THE AUTHOR

Philip Purser-Hallard edits official documents by day, looks after his family by night, and writes in the folds of conceptual time between the two. He has written stories of diverse lengths for shared-universe series including *Faction Paradox*, *Time Hunter* and *Doctor Who*, and edits anthologies set in the City of the Saved, where the historic human population of the cosmos is resurrected after the Big Crunch. (The next one, *Tales of the Great Detectives*, features multiple iterations of Sherlock Holmes.) His urban fantasy thriller *The Pendragon Protocol*, the first book of the Devices Trilogy, will be published in May 2014.

THE CURIOUS CASE OF THE COMPROMISED CARD-INDEX

~✦~

BY ANDREW LANE

During the many years I spent assisting my friend Sherlock Holmes in his various investigative cases, I often heard him described – usually by disgruntled members of Scotland Yard – as an unemotional calculating machine. This was far from the truth. Holmes was as emotional as the next man, and I frequently saw him in the grip of strong feelings: angry at the police when they had missed an obvious clue or arrested the wrong man; morose due to lack of intellectual stimulation; ecstatic at a well-performed piece of violin music; or curious about almost everything that crossed his path. I can, however, only remember once seeing him uneasy, and that occasion coincided with an appalling violation of his lodgings at 221B Baker Street.

I recall that this was in the year 1890, just following a visit that we made to the United States of America. The trip, which took us most of a month to accomplish and which led to the discovery of a plot to invade Mexico by a group of Confederate supporters and claim it as a new state, is vivid in my memory not just because of the various sights that we saw in that great country but because Holmes uncharacteristically told me stories about his early life, and the huge influence that an American tutor named Amyus Crowe had on his development when he was of school age.

When we arrived back in England we went immediately to Baker

Street. I was living elsewhere at the time, having recently remarried, and my wife had taken the opportunity to visit friends. Rather than let me stay in an empty house Holmes offered me the use of my old bedroom until she returned. "It is a little untidy," he admitted, "as I have been using it to store some of my files, but I am sure Mrs Hudson can clear a space for you in no time."

For Holmes to refer to anything as "untidy" made me worry. He could normally work surrounded by piles of newspapers, plates of half-eaten food and scattered pipe tobacco without either noticing or caring.

There was a curious smell in the house when Holmes opened the door to the street. As a friend of his I was, of course, used to all manner of chemical odours, but as a medical man I knew the smell of death. So did Holmes, and we shared a concerned glance before he bounded up the stairs and threw open the door to our sitting-room.

I was close behind him, and over his shoulder I saw one of the most grotesque sights I have ever witnessed. There, in Holmes's own armchair, was what appeared at first glance to be the body of a child. The blue sailor suit in which it was dressed suggested that it was a boy, but it was difficult to tell because the face was wizened like that of an old man, and the jaw protruded in a most unusual manner.

Holmes made a "tch" sound, and immediately began to search the shelves and the desk, ignoring the body altogether. I crossed the room and stared down at the lined face, feeling a shudder run through me. The eyes were mercifully closed, while the hair on the body's head was thick and black, and stuck out in all directions. I also noticed a curious scattering of small cuts on the crepe-like skin of the neck and cheeks.

"Holmes…" I started.

"Not now," he snapped. "I am checking for clues as to what has happened."

"There is a dead body in your armchair," I said, my voice wavering with shock. "Is that not the most obvious of clues?"

"The body will tell us little," he said, still searching, "and what it does tell us is wrong."

I was about to remonstrate with him when I heard Mrs Hudson's footsteps on the stairs. I quickly crossed to the doorway and intercepted her, blocking her view of the sitting-room. I wanted to save her from the sudden shock.

"Dr Watson!" she cried. "It has been such a time since I have seen you!" She eyed me critically. "You have lost weight," she said. "Your wife has not been feeding you properly."

"It was the Atlantic crossing," I said, painfully aware of the dead body just a few feet away. "It was so rough I could hardly eat."

"I will prepare luncheon straight away," she said. "You will be staying for a while?"

"For a few days," I replied. "Has anyone been up in Mr Holmes's rooms, by the way?"

"There *was* a man, a few days ago," she said, frowning. "He delivered a package. He said it was some chemical experiment, and he had to set it all up ready for Mr Holmes's return. He had a letter signed by Mr Holmes. I know the strange kinds of thing that get delivered here sometimes, so I left him to it." She wrinkled her nose. "I know I usually do not mention anything, but this experiment smells a lot stronger and a lot worse than the others."

"How long was he here?" I asked.

She shrugged. "I was preparing the pastry for steak and kidney pie, and I lost track of time. When I went back up to check on him, he was gone and the door was shut."

"Thank you," I said. "I will pop down later and tell you about our trip."

"That would be lovely." She left, and I turned back to the room. Holmes was on his hands and knees, checking the carpet.

"Holmes," I said firmly, "we need to alert the police."

He glanced up, frowning. "For what reason?"

"A child has been murdered, and in the most appalling way!"

"Really? Where?"

I sighed, and indicated the wizened body in the armchair.

"Nonsense," he cried. "That is merely the corpse of an ape that has been shaved to make it look passably human. Just look at that jaw!"

"An *ape*?"

"Yes. It almost certainly belonged to a zoological garden. And far from being murdered, it died of natural causes."

"How can you tell that?"

He sighed. "Is it not obvious? There are no marks of violence, and none of the contortions or foaming at the mouth that would have been expected of poison. Strangulation is a possibility, but the ape would have fought back and there would have been traces of its attacker's flesh and blood beneath its nails. No, the most likely explanation is that it died of old age, or perhaps pneumonia. The climate in England is hardly conducive to the health of an ape, after all."

My head was reeling. "But why an *ape*? Why *shave* it? Why leave it *here* for us to find?"

"Well, it is a shaved ape because it looks like a child and will attract our sympathy, of course, and it is here to distract my attention."

"From what?"

"From the real reason someone entered these rooms." He stood. "I overheard Mrs Hudson's remarks. Someone has been in here, and for some time as well, having faked a letter from me to gain entrance. They have taken something, or left something, and the ape's body is a transparent attempt to get me onto the wrong track, investigating this supposed child murder rather than finding out what has been done."

"What could they possibly have wanted?"

"That is what worries me."

I glanced around wildly. "Could they have left a bomb? An infernal device that might explode at any moment?"

"Unlikely," he said scornfully, shaking his head. "Consider: our intruder would not know for sure when we might return, and would thus have difficulty in setting an appropriate timing mechanism. And besides, why take the trouble of distracting our attention with this badly shaved primate, thus alerting us to the fact that we have played unwitting host to an intruder? Why not just hide the bomb under a table and wait for it to go off?"

"Then what?" I was stumped. "Perhaps a current case…?"

Holmes smiled thinly. "I never make notes on current cases. I keep all relevant information in my head."

"An experiment, then? Some ongoing chemical examination of a clue that might tell a guilty party that you are on the right track?"

"I cleared everything away before we left for America."

"Then I confess I am at a loss. What could they have wanted?"

"There is one obvious possibility."

I looked at him, raising an eyebrow to invite him to continue. Instead, he crossed to the shelves that had been fixed from the chimney breast to the wall. The shelves were lined with the thick ledgers in which he kept notes of anything that attracted his attention: reports in newspapers, extracts from journals, gossip and tittle-tattle that he had picked up while lurking, disguised, in taverns and on trains. How many times could I remember us sitting beside the fire and Holmes saying something like: "Pass me the ledger for the letter 'B', would you, old chap?" and then sitting there, leafing through it, murmuring: "Ah, yes, 'Borthwick' – the Southwark cannibal... 'Bears, Russian' – the underground fighting arena where destitute men would pit themselves against those vicious and unpredictable creatures... 'Balham' – the area of London containing more poisoners per square mile than any other in the world..." and so on.

"My data," he said quietly. "The raw material which my brain uses as fuel for its deductions. I may keep the information on current cases in my memory, but once a case is over, or when I read or hear about something that may become a case one day, I write it down here, archiving it for when I might need it." He sighed. "You, of all people, Watson, know how important this data is to me. If I hear that a man has vanished into thin air in Theydon Bois then I can immediately look up 'V' for vanishing, and cross-reference it with 'T' for Theydon Bois, and thus see whether any other similar events have happened in the area, or if anything *else* strange has happened in the immediate vicinity. If I am engaged to save a duke from blackmail then I can instantly look up a list of all the blackmailers currently working in London, and rank them by the importance of the victims they choose."

"I am aware of the importance of these ledgers," I replied carefully. "But I am lost as to their relevance now."

"What if," he murmured, "the information in these journals has been interfered with? What, for instance, if three or four blackmailers have been erased from the list? What if a strange event in Theydon

Bois has been excised, so that it will never come to my attention?" His voice dropped lower, and I could detect anger in it, and worse: a desperation, a vulnerability. "If someone was planning a crime, and knew that I would be called in to investigate, and that I would most likely solve the crime because I had information on a previous similar event, then why not sneak in here and *change* that information so that I would ignore it, thinking it of no relevance?"

"Surely you would notice?" I ventured. "An entry could not be cut out or erased without you noticing. Even a page carefully sliced out would leave traces, and any additions would be obviously in a different handwriting and a different ink, no matter how carefully the forger tried to emulate your style."

He shook his head silently, then walked across to the door leading to my old bedroom. I followed.

"It might be necessary to take a ledger away and make a careful forgery of the whole thing," he said over his shoulder, "with a few things changed. It might also be possible for a skilled forger to *add* new information: fictitious entries that might take my investigations in the wrong direction altogether. However, I have been engaged on an activity which might, inadvertently, have left me more vulnerable to compromised data."

He threw open the door to my old room, and I gasped. Every available surface, including the bed, the floor and the dressing table, was covered with piles of file cards, some five inches across by three inches high. Most of the ones I could see were covered with Holmes's fine, spidery writing, but they were also pierced by holes in different locations.

"It occurred to me, some time ago," he said, "that my data was not organised as efficiently as it could be. If I wanted to know the name of every bald criminal in London, for instance, I would have to look up 'London Criminals', then check each of their names in a different ledger to find out whether or not they were bald. Spurred on by the work of Mister Charles Babbage, I have been transferring my files to these cards. If I have a card for each known criminal in London – and that would run to hundreds of thousands of cards – I could punch a hole in one place if they were bald, or in another place if they were blond haired, or black haired, or wore a wig. Then, if I want to sort out all the bald criminals, I merely have to shuffle them in a clockwork machine of some kind and have the machine touch each card with a thin rod to see whether there is a hole in the right place. The machine could then spit out every relevant card and ignore the irrelevant ones."

"I see the potential," I said, "and I admire your cleverness and your industry, but –"

"It should be obvious," he snapped. "Rather than cut out or erase an entry in a ledger, leaving traces, all the intruder has to do is remove all the cards that implicate them – or the person they are working for."

"Ah." My heart fell as I realised the implications of what Holmes was saying. In the ledgers his data was difficult to access, but difficult to change or delete. On the file cards he could access it much more easily, but that also made it easier for any intruders. "What can you do?"

"What can I do?" he repeated. "I must recheck every card against the original ledgers and against the original source material, looking for discrepancies. I must also persuade Mrs Hudson to invest in some proper window locks, and not to let strangers into my rooms, even if they have letters purportedly from me. He glanced at me. "And you must dispose of the body of that poor ape. I understand that some sailors have developed a bizarre taste for monkey flesh. See if you can peddle it down at the docks."

Ignoring his last remark, which I took to be facetious, I said, "But checking every card against the entries in your ledgers – that would surely take weeks, if not months, and the opportunity for errors due to lack of concentration is immense."

He sighed. "You are right, of course. Even if I called for assistance from people I could trust – and I am thinking of Wiggins and his band of street urchins, or at least those of them who can read – the task would still be vast. It also occurs to me that it would still not provide me with reassurance."

"How so?"

"Even if I spent all that time rechecking every single card and found that no changes had been made and no cards removed, I would have had to turn down a large number of cases in order to complete the work. Is it not conceivable that this entire affair is a double bluff? The perpetrator expects me to see through the badly designed corpse and realise that my files had been interfered with. The perpetrator *wants* me to spend time checking all my information in order to distract me, to keep me from investigating a particular crime – not one that *has* happened, but one that is *going* to happen in the near future!"

"I suppose." I tried to put a brave face on the situation. "But at least you will know that all your data is accurate."

"Yes," he said, but he did not sound convinced. Flinging himself into my old armchair, he slouched with his head thrown back, staring at the ceiling.

I was naturally concerned for Holmes, but I could think of little I could do that would be of help. He was so dependent on his data that, bereft of it, he was like a steam engine deprived of coal. Sooner or later he would run down and stop – which was, perhaps, the aim of this whole macabre exercise.

I did the only thing I could under the circumstances – I bundled up the corpse of the ape in an old rug, carried it downstairs (fortunately without Mrs Hudson spotting me and inquiring what I was doing with her furnishings) and took it outside. Rather than follow Holmes's suggestion that I should hawk it down at the docks as some kind of bizarre culinary delicacy, I paid two passing scallywags a halfpenny each to take the rolled up rug away and burn it. I impressed upon them that they must not, under any circumstances, unroll it before setting it on fire. Even as I was speaking I suspected that they would not follow my instructions, in which case they would receive a salutary shock, but they were of a class and an age that made it unlikely they would notify the police, and the natural affinity between children and matches made it likely that the rug and its contents would be eventually burned, rolled or unrolled.

Returning to Baker Street in a better mood than I had left it, I found Holmes also in a lighter frame of mind. He was standing by the fire in our drawing-room examining a handful of the cards through his magnifying glass.

"Have you found something?" I asked.

"Indeed I have. This is most indicative. Come – look more closely."

He handed me the cards. I examined them, reading the text and looking at the holes that had been punched through them, but I could not identify whatever it was that had lifted Holmes's mood. I said as much.

"As I have said before, Watson, you see but you do not observe. Look closely at the edges of the cards."

I did so, not without a slight flare of anger at Holmes's casual dismissal of my abilities, and suddenly I realised what he was talking about. "There are pinch-marks on the cards!" I exclaimed. I held one of them up to the light. "It seems almost as if the cards have been pulled through some kind of roller."

"That is exactly what has happened. Each card that I have examined bears very slight marks of having been fed into a device equipped with rollers made of some material with elasticity but also some resilience – gutta-percha, or something similar."

"*Every* card?" I walked across to the door to my old bedroom and looked at the mass of information in there.

"Indeed, and that tells me exactly what it was that our intruder wanted."

"And what is that?"

"It tells me that they have already constructed or procured a computational machine similar to the one that I have envisaged, and wish to obtain data for it, rather than building it up for themselves."

"Surely," I said carefully, "that would imply that they were setting up as a consulting detective as well, and wanted to take advantage of your exceptional collation of historical information. What are the odds that there might be room for more than one consulting detective in London? Are there enough cases to go round?"

"It takes more than information to be a consulting detective," Holmes responded airily. "There is a more likely hypothesis, however, and that is that someone wants to set themselves up as a master *blackmailer*."

"A blackmailer?" I repeated, stupidly. I could not see where Holmes was going.

"Consider," he said. "I have collected significant amounts of information on the illegal or immoral habits of numerous citizens of this, and other, countries. A large proportion of these people appear to be respectable members of society. I know otherwise, but only through hearsay or rumour, or from evidence that is enough to convince me but which would be too abstruse for a judge or a jury to follow. Suppose, for instance, I were to have a card on Lord X, who I suspect of having killed his first wife with a toxin derived from the Japanese coral *limu make o hana*. Suppose then that this information fell into the hands of an unscrupulous man. That man might seek to extort money from Lord X by threatening to spread this incriminating rumour."

The grandiose nature of the scheme left me nearly breathless. "Good Lord, Holmes – how many potential victims are there in your files?"

He shrugged indifferently. "Including suspected murderers, arsonists, burglars and blackmailers, along with those people whose various unsavoury romantic arrangements I have noted in passing – perhaps ten thousand."

"But this is terrible!"

"Not so terrible," he replied, "for these people have, by and large, brought their fate on themselves." He frowned. "However, I am loath to allow my own information to be used for criminal purposes. If anyone is to bring justice to these people it will be myself or the police, and at the right time and through channels approved by the law or by God. I am not in the business of providing fodder for further criminal activities. This must be stopped."

"But how?" I asked. "Surely we still have no idea who stole your information? The only other blackmailer of that scope I am aware of was Charles Augustus Milverton, and he died fully two years ago."

"That is true, but as with Mr Charles Darwin's theory of natural selection, if there is a niche vacant in the criminal world then someone will move into it. We merely have to determine whom." He thought for a moment, hand to chin. "The arrangement of the cards in your bedroom is exactly as it was when I left. I have seen no difference, and I have looked most carefully. The cards would, however, have had to have been taken away to be run through this mechanical calculating device. In order for them to be returned and replaced intact, the thief would have had to employ a man of singular ability – an eidetic mind that could remember exactly where everything came from and where it should go back."

"A photographic memory?" I frowned. "I thought such people were few and far between – if they are real at all. I have never met one."

"Indeed, and I am aware of only one such in London at the moment – billed as the Miraculous Master of Mental Muscularity, he is appearing at the King's Theatre on Shaftesbury Avenue. His real name is Solomon Shavetsky. I suggest that we pay him a visit."

We took a hansom directly to the King's Theatre. It was late afternoon, and the sun was low in a sky layered with clouds. Mr Shavetsky was in his dressing-room when we arrived. Holmes gained access through the stage door by dint of having once boxed with the stage manager, and burst into the room unannounced.

"Solomon Shavetsky!" he cried, pointing his finger dramatically at the tall, thin man with pale blond hair who cowered at this display of Jovian wrath, "you have infiltrated my rooms without permission and been party to a theft!"

"Mr Sherlock Holmes," the man said in a tremulous voice, gazing up at my friend from where his contorted form was twisting nervously in his chair. "Three thousand five hundred and twenty-eight successful cases. Twenty-nine unsuccessful cases. Two hundred and fifty-eight examples where events were allowed to unfold to the detriment of the criminal but without the involvement of the police. Contacts with ten separate Scotland Yard inspectors. Eighty-nine –"

"Yes, yes," Holmes interrupted. "I am not here for a demonstration of your skills. I wish to know who exactly hired you."

"I did nothing wrong!" Shavetsky cried, raising his hands to shield his face. "I touched nothing!"

"Your guilt or innocence are debatable, but irrelevant. I just want a name."

"And you will leave me be?"

Holmes nodded. "You are small fry, Mr Shavetsky. It is the shark I want, not the sprat."

"Aloysius Morgan," the pale man whispered. "Twenty-seven Byron Avenue, Hampstead Garden Suburb. Green door. Five steps up. Flowers in the front garden are: hyacinth, hydrangea, lavender…"

We left as the poor man was still reciting names of flowers. His mind was obviously deficient in some important social regard, presumably to make up for his prodigious memory skills.

Holmes instructed the cabbie – who had waited for us, buoyed up by a half-shilling advance – to drive to the address we had been given. As we clattered through the noisome streets of London, heading north and then up Hampstead Hill, I suggested to my friend that a direct assault was not necessarily the best option.

"Nonsense," he said, jaw set grimly. "This man has dared to infiltrate and exploit my very thought processes. He needs to be set right, and quickly, before he can profit from his unsavoury acts."

I let it be. Once Holmes had an idea in his head there was no shifting it.

Aloysius Morgan's house was an impressive edifice overlooking the park. I could not help but wonder, as I looked up at it, how many lives and reputations had been ruined in order to pay for it. Holmes rang the doorbell and pushed past the boxer-like butler when he opened the door. The butler tried to grab at me as I passed too, but I floored him with a jab to the solar plexus. Being a medical man *and* a military man I am well versed in ways to bring an opponent down in a fight.

Aloysius Morgan was not in his drawing-room. Holmes rapidly searched the ground floor for the man, but in vain.

"Perhaps he is not here," I pointed out. "It is not as if we had an appointment."

"Hark!" Holmes said, cocking his head to one side. "Do you hear that?"

I listened, and detected a whirring, clicking sound, like the noise made by some gigantic clock that was preparing to strike. It seemed to come from beneath our feet.

"His mechanical calculating machine is in the cellar," Holmes said. "And if it is operating then I suspect that he will be there as well, monitoring it."

He rushed for the door that led to the cellar, and I followed, wishing that I had placed my revolver in my coat pocket before leaving Baker Street.

By the time I got to the bottom of the stone steps my friend was already standing in front of the house's owner, but I confess that it was the machine he stood in front of that took my immediate attention. It filled the cellar, and seemed to have aspects of a printing press and an adding machine, but scaled up immensely. There were cogs and axles, springs and chains, levers and struts, all in service to a pile of index cards, like the ones in my old bedroom back in Baker Street, which were being taken, one by one, and fed through to a plate where they were held while an array of narrow rods, like knitting needles, were pressed against them. Some of the rods were stopped by the unyielding cardboard, but others went through the holes in the cards and hit something on the other side, making a series of ringing musical tones. Depending on some configuration of the levers, the cards were sent in one of several directions, forming piles in hoppers. It was a mechanical monstrosity whose purpose was now obvious to me, thanks to Holmes's explanation.

"This cannot be allowed to go on," Holmes said to Aloysius Morgan. He was a small man, in a red velvet smoking jacket. His hair was thin, and brushed back over his scalp, and his cheeks were pocked with the scars of some childhood disease.

"Mr Holmes," he said, "I thought you would be visiting soon."

"You must stop," Holmes said darkly.

"Stop what?" He indicated the massive machine behind him. "Which law have I broken? I had this machine built for me, and I paid for it in coin of the realm. Each of these cards you see feeding through was purchased by me. I see nothing illegal going on here."

"You have mechanised the foul process of blackmail!"

Morgan raised his hands. "Where in there is blackmail taking place?"

"And you have stolen my data… *my* data… to do it with!"

"Can you point to a particular card and tell me that it is yours? Does it have your writing on? Have you impressed it with a special seal of your own?" Morgan smiled. "Please contradict me if I am wrong, but all of your data is exactly where you left it – in your lodgings."

"To which you gained entry using a subterfuge!"

"An accusation for which you have no proof."

"And left a shaved monkey behind!"

"A mere practical joke – if it occurred at all, given that I doubt you can produce this shaved monkey that you speak of or connect it to me in any way."

"Those cards contain information which is potentially slanderous or libellous," Holmes said, and I could tell from his tone that he was clutching at straws now. After all, he had a similar set himself. "They should be destroyed."

Now Morgan actually laughed. "They are merely cardboard slips with holes in! Can you show them to a judge and jury and point to where this scandalous information is? I think not!"

"What do I have to do to *make* you stop?" Holmes asked bleakly.

Morgan nodded slowly. "So, now we come down to it. Well, if you truly believe, in your own inflamed mind, that I am preparing some massive campaign of blackmail, then you could always make an estimate of how much money I would get from my victims and offer me… oh, let us say *double*." He stared at Holmes, and Holmes stared back. "No response? No bargaining? No counter offer?" He sighed. "So be it. Now, if all you wish to do is to throw accusations around then I will have to ask you to leave. You grow wearisome."

Holmes stood there, glancing from Morgan to the clockwork mechanism and back again. Abruptly he spun around and stalked away, towards the stairs.

I looked at Morgan, who was now looking at me with a questioning expression on his face.

"Nice meeting you," I said, rather fatuously, and followed Holmes out.

The cab ride back to Baker Street was conducted in silence, apart from Holmes's mutter of "The man is apparently fireproof!" as we passed Paddington Station. When we arrived back at our lodgings Holmes locked himself in his room. I ate alone. Later, when I was talking to Mrs Hudson downstairs, I heard the outer door open and close. I presumed he had gone out, possibly in one of his disguises. I hoped that he was not going to do something drastic.

I returned to my own digs, on the basis that my old bedroom was still filled with Holmes's infernal cards, and returned the next morning. Holmes was either still in his room or had not returned from his peregrinations, but Mrs Hudson kindly offered me breakfast. I was reading the newspaper and sipping a cup of tea when I noticed a small article on page four:

Man Eaten by Machine!

In Hampstead Garden Suburb last night a man, by name one Aloysius Morgan, was crushed and mangled most horribly when he fell into the bowels of a machine in his own cellar. Scotland Yard state they have no idea what the machine was designed for, but add that there is no reason to suppose that Mr Morgan's death was anything but an accident. Sources close to the investigation have said that the machine may have been a printing press, and that Mr Morgan may have been involved with some form of currency forgery...

"Ah," Holmes said from behind me, "you have seen the report on the death of Mr Morgan." He was wearing his mouse-coloured dressing-gown, and standing in the doorway of his bedroom.

"Holmes –" I started, but he raised a hand to stop me.

"I did not push Mr Morgan into his calculating machine," he said, "nor did he fall in while we were arguing. I did not return there after we left."

"Then it is a strange coincidence that he has died," I pointed out.

"Indeed," he said in a non-committal tone.

"If I may ask – where did you go last night? I know that you left here late, and did not come back until after I had returned home."

"I went to send a message," he replied.

"To whom?"

He sat at the table and busied himself loading bacon and kedgeree onto a plate. "There is a man in London," he said, apparently apropos of nothing, "who is to crime what I am to detection. He is an academic, of sorts. I have never mentioned his name to you on the basis that I did not want to put your life at risk – he is that dangerous. One day he and I will cross paths, and the results will be dramatic for one or both of us, but for the moment we are content to circle each other like wary jackals." He paused, and inspected his plate. "I sent an anonymous message to him alerting him to the fact that information mentioning his name had been stolen from me. I thought he ought to know."

"And did you bother sending a similar message to anyone else whose information was on your cards?" I asked, in a very quiet, very controlled voice.

"I was saving that for today," he replied, smiling slightly, "but I see there is no need now."

I felt a cold chill in my soul, not so much because of what Holmes had done but because of the calm way he spoke of it, as if his actions were the most obvious thing in the world. I opened my mouth to chide him, to point out that his actions had led directly to the death of Aloysius Morgan, but I knew already what his answer would be. He would look me in the eye, smile slightly, and say, "Which law have I broken?" – the very same words that Aloysius Morgan had used against him. I closed my mouth and said nothing.

It was a very awkward breakfast.

Soon afterwards, Holmes burned the file cards and abandoned his attempts to systemise his data. And in the weeks, months and years that passed, I would occasionally see him glancing up at his ledgers with a grim and worried expression on his face, still wondering just how much he could trust the information they contained.

ABOUT THE AUTHOR

Although he originally qualified as a physicist and subsequently worked for twenty-seven years in the Civil Service, Andrew Lane has also written twenty-seven books, split more or less evenly between fiction and non-fiction. At the moment he is in the midst of writing a series of Young Adult novels about the early life of Sherlock Holmes. The first of these books – *Death Cloud* – was published by Macmillan Children's Books in 2010 and the sixth – *Knife Edge* – in 2013. *Death Cloud* has subsequently been republished in thirty-seven other countries. Andrew lives in Dorset with his wife, his son and four cats, two of which just wandered in from somewhere else and decided to stay.

SHERLOCK HOLMES AND THE POPISH RELIC

BY MARK A. LATHAM

I start this tale in an unconventional manner, for it is an account of an adventure with my friend, Mr Sherlock Holmes, which led me to ask many questions about my own investigative powers, the nature of the world around me, and, perhaps, my own credibility. The fact that I have waited well over a decade before committing the tale to paper is not to protect our client in the matter – for the names of those involved have, as always, been changed – but perhaps to protect my own reputation. This adventure, then, does not begin in those Baker Street rooms so familiar to you, Dear Reader, but in a little flat on Thread-needle Street, within the long shadow of the Bank of England, where I was in company less renowned than that of the famous detective.

My business at the house was a séance. Goodness knows what Holmes would have said. My friend has always been most dismissive of the supernatural, for which reason I was accompanied that night by other associates, all of sound professional credentials and no less estimable standing. They were members all of a particular London society that has an interest in matters esoteric, with which I – for reasons most personal – have an association kept entirely separate from my adventures with Sherlock Holmes.

On the night in question, four of us went to bear witness to the celebrated spiritualist talents of a certain Ms B—. This lady had built something of a reputation for her mastery of the spiritualist arts, and the greatest debunkers of the age had visited her both openly and covertly, coming away with no evidence of charlatanry or histrionics. So, then, had she come to the attention of my society, and I – as a colleague of the great detective and being well known for my rational mind and no small deductive powers – had been invited along to bear witness.

I shall not dwell long on the events of the séance, save that they were undoubtedly eerie. We were seated in a room, dark but for the light of three candles in the centre of a large circular table. As well as the four of us, gentlemen all, there was a pregnant young lady and her brother, an ageing widow, and a sad-looking young man of perhaps five and twenty. Ms B— sat between myself and the pregnant lady, with a thin old woman standing behind us; her *amanuensis*, I thought, and whom I scrutinised at every opportunity throughout the séance to ensure no trickery was performed on her part. When proceedings began, Ms B— asked several questions of supposed spirits, and "received" answers that seemed to have a profound effect on some of the guests. The pregnant lady, for example, was told that her late husband had set sail to some faraway land, whereupon he had met his end. The young woman confirmed that he was indeed a soldier, and had been killed in action on the final day of fighting in Majuba. What followed were various soothing words about the father of the child being in a "better place" and "at peace"; the usual sort of thing.

The séance continued much in this manner, punctuated occasionally by a rather violent rapping and tipping of the table that, although I was at a loss to explain how it was achieved, was nothing more than mediums had produced for decades. It seemed that, as the event drew to a close, there was not a single prediction or reading from the clairvoyant that could not be put down to mere parlour tricks – things that my friend Sherlock Holmes would have called deduction rather than spiritual intervention. That was, until the very end of the evening.

After half of the attendees had received some vague, platitudinous message "from beyond", and the rest of us were sorely disappointed and beginning to fidget somewhat in our seats, a most peculiar thing happened. Ms B— suddenly froze, as if gripped by some unseen force, and tightened her grasp upon my hand accordingly. Her head lurched backwards, her eyes opened wide, and a strange croaking sound emerged from her throat. "A-ha!" I thought at first, "This is where the theatrics begin!" But immediately after I had thought so uncharitably, doubts began to creep into my mind. The little old woman lurched towards her mistress, with a look of grave concern etched upon her face, but checked herself, stopping shy of interfering. The temperature of the room dropped considerably, I am sure; although there was no breeze in the slightest, the three candle flames guttered dramatically, and one was extinguished. I had been momentarily distracted by the smouldering candle, and when I turned back towards Ms B— I almost jumped with fright, for she had leaned in closer and was staring right at me; only, she was not staring, for her eyes had rolled back into her head, revealing the whites. I almost tore my hand from her grasp and shook the woman, for I was certain that she was having some kind of seizure, but before I could act she began to speak in a voice most unlike her own.

"You are not a believer," she croaked. "But a day will come when you will be. You have a friend, a great man, who believes in nothing beyond his own formidable five senses. One day soon, the two of you will be lost in an endless catacomb, and you will have a choice. Follow your friend as you have always done, or follow that which you know to be folly. If you depend upon reason, you will be lost forever in darkness and nightmare. Hearken to these words, or your end will find you!"

As she spoke this ghastly prophecy, many of the assembled party began to murmur most discontentedly. Finally, the old woman turned up the gas jets, and the room was brightly lit once again. Ms B— seemed to come around almost immediately, though she was not herself, and we were informed that the séance was over, and thanked for our understanding.

Once we were all ushered outside, my companions and I made light of the events, and I must confess that, after a glass of Tokay and a cigar, I felt rather foolish for being so affected by an obvious trick. I gave the matter no more thought. That is, until six months later, when Sherlock Holmes and I were visited by a certain Sir Daniel Hotchkiss.

* * *

When Mrs Hudson had first shown Sir Daniel into the sitting-room of 221B Baker Street, I noticed immediately that this gentleman was on edge. Though a young and healthy man, his handshake was not firm, his manner distracted, and it did not take a detective of Holmes's character to see that the baronet was as agitated as any visitor to our door had ever been. We greeted him with all courtesy, but I could tell from Holmes's look that the baronet was not going to have an easy time of the interview. My friend had just concluded a case involving the capture of a disgraced officer of the Pretorian army, and was flushed with success. As ever in such times, Holmes was apt to select his next engagement most choosily, and with scant regard for the querent's feelings.

After Mrs Hudson had provided our guest with tea, Holmes bade him tell his story.

"Mr Holmes; Dr Watson," began the baronet, "I have come to you in the hope that you will lend me aid where the regular authorities have failed me. You see, I have recently been notified that I have come into a substantial inheritance, the estate of my uncle, Lord Septimus Bairstowe."

Upon hearing the name, Holmes waved a hand at me, indicating that I should look into his files for information on the Bairstowe family, which I did at once. "Congratulations," he said to our guest. "I take it Lord Bairstowe was a wealthy man?"

"Yes, he was, by all accounts. But it is not congratulations I seek, Mr Holmes. You see, my uncle is something of an eccentric. Though he is believed to be dead, no body has yet been found. I have been told that I will inherit his estate, Tattlesby Abbey, when such time has passed that there can be no doubt as to the old man's demise."

"Hah!" cried Holmes, most inappropriately. "Watson, forget the search – instead bring me the file for Tattlesby Abbey, Buckinghamshire!" Sir Daniel cast Holmes a queer look, but he had no need to be worried; I knew from Holmes's sudden burst of enthusiasm that there was something about the case that excited him. I found the file, and handed it to my friend.

"Here it is," said Holmes. "A clipping from the *Chronicle*, almost two weeks old. Lord Bairstowe missing, feared dead. Tattlesby Abbey left deserted. It struck me as odd at the time. Do carry on with your story, Sir Daniel."

"Quite simply, Mr Holmes, I refuse to take on the estate if there is any hope at all that Lord Bairstowe is alive and well, and in the absence of a body… I have to hope that he does indeed live still. The Buckinghamshire police are certain that he has met some unfortunate fate, and have called off the search. I have heard, of course, of your prodigious talents, and wish to engage you in finding my uncle… or his body."

"But there is something you are not telling me," said Holmes, matter-of-factly. "Why are the police so quick to dismiss the disappearance of such a wealthy man? There are many private agents who would take on a missing persons case such as this, so tell me, what is it that troubles you so? What is it that makes this case fit for Sherlock Holmes? Tell me the whole story, every detail – for the greatest clues often lie in the most mundane trivia. Tell me plainly, sir, and I will decide whether I can help you find your uncle."

Sir Daniel looked taken aback at first, but Holmes was right, of course. The man was clearly on edge, frightened even.

"Very well," said Sir Daniel. "But I must have your word that none of what I am about to say will leave this room. And yours, too, Doctor." We acquiesced at once. He bowed his head and told his story, as my friend Sherlock Holmes sat and listened attentively, his fingers pressed together, and his brow furrowed in concentration.

"My uncle Septimus is seventy years old, and not well disposed towards company or even familial ties. He is an eccentric and solitary soul, and I am ashamed to confess he is not well liked amongst the family. I believe I got along with him better than anyone, and even I saw him infrequently. The estate is large and rambling, and as my uncle grew older, it became a lot for him to manage. My mother, Lady Hotchkiss, née Bairstowe, being Uncle Septimus's closest living relative, attempted to have him committed to an asylum for the old and mentally feeble, and to do so quietly, avoiding any possible scandal. I objected strongly, for although my uncle is indeed…

peculiar in his habits, he is not mad!" I observed Sir Daniel's earnestness, and I believed that his fondness for his uncle – and faith in the old man's mental state – was genuine indeed. "Eventually my mother relented," he continued, "and let it be. However, when Uncle Septimus disappeared, my mother felt obliged to disclose these circumstances to the chief inspector at Bucks constabulary…"

"At which point, the officious policeman carried out the most perfunctory search for your uncle, before giving up all hope of finding him, yes?" Holmes interjected, with a derisive snort at the mention of lax policing.

"Indeed, Mr Holmes. I attempted to rally the police using my good name and standing, but by then the damage was done. They believe that my uncle wandered off during some kind of turn, and has come to mischief along the way. None of his outdoor clothes were missing from the house, so they believe he went walking in his nightshirt, in winter, and has perhaps caught his death in the woods nearby."

"And yet no body was found?"

"No. They made a search of the estate grounds, and half a mile in every direction. That's two miles from the house. They also passed word around the local villages; every gamekeeper and, I daresay, poacher, has been on the lookout for him in the hopes of securing a reward."

"Why do you say 'poacher', specifically?" asked Holmes, sitting upright. "There is something else, is there not?"

"Yes… I was coming to it, Mr Holmes, but it is most unusual, and I am still not sure how to express it. I mentioned poachers because I received a visit from one three days ago. He did not confess to his occupation, of course, but it was plain enough to me. I have been staying occasionally at an inn at Chalgrave, the nearest village, so that the locals could report their news to me directly, rather than go to the inspector."

"Most prudent," said Holmes, approvingly.

"This poacher told me that he had been on my uncle's land some two nights hence, and had experienced something that had alarmed him greatly. He claimed that he had been taking a shortcut home through the woods near the house at around ten o'clock, when he had heard a strange sound, like that of tin pots banging together and ringing out like a bell. This noise, he said, was quite faint, and he couldn't at first place it. Remembering the promise of a reward for information about my uncle, he walked close to the house, where he thought the noise was coming from; but as he approached, a different noise started up – a low, grumbling noise that caused the very earth to tremble. Startled, he looked around, and realised that a light blazed in a window of the empty house where none had been apparent before, and began flickering on and off, growing dimmer and brighter each second, until he felt sure that the place must be haunted. The poacher made off through the woods, but as he chanced to look back over his shoulder, he swore he saw a hooded figure, like a monk, following him, dashing furtively from tree to tree. The reason the man came to me, cap in hand, was to offer his condolences, for he was sure that my uncle must be dead, and that his ghost is haunting the estate."

"The man must surely have had one too many nips from his flask," I ventured.

"I cannot testify to his character, Doctor," replied Hotchkiss, "though he seemed sober enough at the tale's telling. I gave him half a crown and promised that if his story could be confirmed, I would ask after him for further reward. This seemed to satisfy the man. After he left, however, I was most troubled, for it was not the first report of strange occurrences on the estate."

Holmes raised an eyebrow. "Indeed?" he prompted.

"Twice a week, a local woman – a Mrs Drebbins – calls in at the house to ensure all is well; she's a housekeeper, though not on the permanent staff. It was she who first reported my uncle missing, for he does not have a full staff and instead rather fends for himself."

"Forgive the interruption," said Holmes, "but on what days does the good Mrs Drebbins attend your uncle's house?"

"Sundays and Wednesdays."

"The newspaper article reported Lord Bairstowe missing on Monday, the 25th of last month – so Mrs Drebbins found the house empty on Sunday 24th?"

"Yes, Mr Holmes, with the back door unlocked, too, she said."

"But it is possible that he could have left the house for the last time any time between that Sunday and the previous Wednesday?"

"I'm afraid so. That is another reason the police were so keen to put an end to the matter – if he had been missing so long, then they felt there was no hope of finding him at all."

"Fascinating," Holmes said, ruminating on something. "Please, continue the story of our good housekeeper."

"It is a similar story, Mr Holmes. Mrs Drebbins had decided to continue the upkeep of my uncle's house, lest he should return, and thus continued her usual routine. On Wednesday 27th the lady was too frantic with worry to visit the house, and so she sent two maids, whom she regularly appoints to do the cleaning, without her. The women complained that the house had taken on a ghostly aspect; that there were chill draughts, strange noises and objects disappearing. They refused to go back to the 'haunted house', and Mrs Drebbins cursed them for empty-headed children. On the Sunday – a full week after she had reported Lord Bairstowe missing – Mrs Drebbins had stayed at the house later than usual, but had asked her husband to meet her on his way back from his shift at the local chalk mine, to walk her home. The hour grew late, and she said strange draughts started to blow through the house, bringing with them the smell of stale air 'like the stench of an old crypt'. She could find no source of the draughts, for the house was closed up tight." Sir Daniel paused to take a sip of water, and I saw that he was trembling slightly; was it from worry for his uncle, or fear of the phantoms? Composed again, he continued.

"When it was time for her husband to arrive, she set about to leave the house, when she claims to have heard a terrible banging noise, echoing all around her. She rushed outside to find her husband walking along the drive, and he had also heard the noise. Before they could enter the house, they were both suddenly frightened by the appearance of a hooded figure walking towards them from the treeline of the old forest. Despite being practical folk, they both hurried away from the house as fast as possible. I am rather afraid that this story reached the public houses before it reached me, and now the locals are full of ghost stories and tales about an ancient curse put on the house by the Catholic monks centuries ago. There is no way, it seems, to untangle the facts from the fiction; that, Mr Holmes, is why I called upon you."

A thin smile passed Holmes's lips, and I knew that my friend was already considering countless possibilities.

"You were wise to come here," said Holmes. "And I believe I can help you. I urge you to return to the inn at Chalgrave as soon as possible, and listen for any further news. Watson and I will travel down on the first train tomorrow. Please have a key to your uncle's house ready for us, and we will soon get to the bottom of this strange matter."

Sir Daniel seemed greatly encouraged, and thanked us effusively for our time. When he had departed, Holmes – as was his usual custom – refused to be drawn on his theories, for half-thought deductions were no deductions at all. All he would do was advise me to pack appropriately for outdoor pursuits, for we would be staying in an empty house with few creature comforts. Thus, we ensured that our affairs were in order, and prepared for our morning journey to Buckinghamshire.

We arrived at Chalfont Road Station shortly before nine o'clock the following day. The weather bode ill, for winter was in full swing and a freezing wind whipped about us as soon as we disembarked our train. A greyer, lonelier little place I could not have imagined, but thankfully Sir Daniel had sent a local man with a small gig to collect us. Half an hour later we were warming ourselves by a hearty fire at the Traveller's Rest in the small village of Chalgrave. We exchanged pleasantries with our employer, but Holmes was determined to set straight to business, beginning by interviewing the landlord as soon as coffee was served.

"Aye sir," Mr Turnham, the landlord, confirmed when asked about the old legends of Tattlesby Abbey, "it's well known around these parts. They say that the conspirators behind the Popish Plot hid their relics around Britain, so as not to have their Catholic idols seized by the king. And Tattlesby, being a Catholic stronghold back then, had no shortage of sympathisers. They say a relic of a saint, in a priceless golden chest, was given to the owner of Tattlesby Abbey, who was hisself related to the last abbot, from back in the day. He buried the relic somewhere on the land, and every so often some local lad will go off in search of this buried treasure. No one's ever found nothin', leastways, not as far as I know. The lads always get chased off by a gamekeeper, or else come home crying about ghosts of faceless monks wandering the woods at night. I don't hold with tales of the relic myself, but mark my words: there's something queer about that place, sure enough."

As Turnham related his tale, in a most conspiratorial manner, the first regulars had started to drift into the bar, and those who caught the tail end of the conversation eyed Holmes and I suspiciously. We thanked the man and returned to Sir Daniel.

"Well?" said the baronet. "What did you make of the legend? Quite the story, isn't it?"

"Oh yes," I replied. "Especially seeing as the 'Popish Plot' was a fiction – an elaborate hoax devised to discredit important Catholics."

"Don't be so sure, Watson. There may be more truth to the tale than you give credence for."

"Really?" I asked, wide-eyed. Holmes was not one for fanciful stories.

"The plot was a fiction, of that you are correct. But that does not mean the story cannot be true. After all, those men accused of conspiracy to murder Charles II feared for their lives before the truth was revealed. They may well have disposed of their relics in the manner described. After all, many old Catholic families were known to be in possession of such items after the dissolution." Holmes's knowledge of obscure trivia frequently astounded me, though this time I suspected he had been examining his remarkable files into the small hours to learn what he could of the local lore of Tattlesby. "Sir Daniel," Holmes resumed, quietly, "before Watson and I go up to the house, I would ask for an introduction to Mrs Drebbins, and for one other favour."

"Anything, Mr Holmes."

"When we leave the village, I would like you to make it known that we intend to stay the night in the 'haunted abbey', in order to disprove the talk of ghosts and goblins. Say it just so, do you understand?"

"Why, yes, of course. But…"

"Ah, no questions yet, Sir Daniel. I have my methods, and must be given time to practise them. Watson," he turned to me with a twinkle in his eye, "from now on, every time someone talks of the hauntings at the abbey, or the myth of this 'Popish Plot', I want you to act as a believer in such things. Behave as though you are interested, or nervous, at all times. Agreed?"

Of course, I agreed at once, although I did not see at that stage what use it would serve. And had Holmes known already the extent of my own dabblings in such matters, he would have known that it would be no hardship to me to behave interestedly in the affair. We finished our coffee, and procured a day's provisions from the inn, and with that we left to see the housekeeper.

Mrs Jemima Drebbins was a stout, respectable-looking woman of middle age. When we happened upon her she was doing the laundry, and her husband had long left for his morning shift. We questioned the woman gently, for she seemed to display some affection for her missing employer. She confirmed her story exactly as Sir Daniel had related it to us. When she had finished, Holmes asked: "May I ask what time this terrible event occurred?"

"About half-past nine, sir; maybe a bit after."

"And neither you nor your husband ventured into the house to find the source of the disturbance; either before or since?"

"Oh, Lord no, sir!" the woman remarked. "We didn't dare, not after we saw the figure. All in dark robes it was, with a hood pulled down low. It near scared the living daylights out of us both. If Mr Drebbins hadn't been there to shepherd me home, I would have gone out of my mind. And I ain't been back!"

"I'm not sure we should be going there tonight," I said, playing my part, "but duty calls!"

"And what do you suppose the robed figure was?" Holmes asked, ignoring my remark.

"It's well known around here, sir. They say there's a priceless Catholic treasure, buried somewhere on the land. They say that the last abbot told the secret to his kin before he died, and that it's been guarded by the lords of Tattlesby Abbey ever since. But there's a curse on that old place, and anyone who goes looking for the treasure will get set upon by the ghosts of them monks, who guard it for all eternity. Whatever is happening up at the abbey, you mark my words sirs: there's something not right about that place."

With no further questions, we bade good day to Mrs Drebbins, and set off along the road to the abbey. At the foot of the mile-long lane to the estate, we said goodbye to Sir Daniel, who promised to send the gig for us the following morning. "I won't be able to find anyone willing to come over after dark, I'm afraid," he'd said, "but I'll be sure the lad comes to get you first thing." We thanked our client, and made our way to the "haunted abbey".

It was a cold, blustery day, and it looked like rain, although thankfully the heavens did not open upon us on our dreary walk. When we reached the abbey, we were greeted by a pair of tall black iron gates, rusting on their hinges and unlocked, which opened onto a gravel drive. To our right, a dense forest of skeletal trees stretched off as far as we could see, whilst to the left lay several acres of overgrown gardens and lawns, dying off in the wintry weather. As we made our way along the path, we observed here and there ancient stones jutting out of the earth like stalagmites until, rounding a small hillock, we saw part of the ancient abbey ruins towering above us. Its broken Gothic arches looked both handsome and foreboding against the pale grey sky. Beyond the largest section of ruins, the path wound round to the house itself, which in parts seemed to grow from the abbey ruins almost organically, and low protuberances of ancient buttresses jutted out from the stone foundations. Holmes explained (reciting verbatim from his notes on the place) that the house was originally late Tudor in design, but had been added to significantly over the centuries. What stood now was a grey, frowning sort of place – tall, square and sturdy, with pointed roofs and small arched windows. It was almost castle-like in appearance, and the dense ivy smothering the north and west walls would have lent Tattlesby Abbey a romantic air, had it not been so stout and formidable a building. Rarely have I seen a house so suited to ghostly habitation, and the thought forced me to suppress a shudder.

The house was as cold and stern inside as out, but I knew that we would not set about making it homely, for Holmes at once began scrutinising the place. In the tiled entrance hall, he pointed to several deposits of mud, undoubtedly from dirty boots, which looked at home in the rather dusty, unkempt environs. I examined the mud closely.

"Is that chalk?" I asked.

"Excellent, Watson!" Holmes remarked. "Your powers of observation grow daily."

"But what is the significance?"

"Everything has significance – see what you can deduce from it."

He continued his investigations whilst I pondered, searching every room, store cupboard, bookshelf and drawer, sometimes with his magnifying glass. He stopped several times, making excited noises – a "Hmm…" when he searched the hall closet, a "Haha!" when he looked over the windows in the master bedroom, and a muttered "Interesting," when he examined the larder. As was his custom, he did not reveal to me what he found so fascinating, but instead invited me to deduce it for myself, which I attempted to do, but never to his satisfaction. We continued in this manner for several hours, searching every room, attic and cellar. The house was in remarkably poor condition, given that it had been vacated for only a couple of weeks. The kitchen stores, basement pantry and wine cellar were virtually bare, and I was very glad of our provisions from the inn. There was barely enough firewood to last the night, and no coal in the scuttle, so we made only the most meagre fire in the small study, and confined ourselves to that room where possible, saving wood for the stove.

"I must say, Holmes," I said, when we finally sat down, "whatever the old man paid those girls from the village to clean this place was too much. And I don't think much of Mrs Drebbins' stocktaking either."

"You have hit on an interesting fact, my dear Watson. However, let's not be too hard on the staff – it is clear that the principal rooms were cleaned more recently. This study, for example, and the master bedroom. But did you observe the unusual deposits of dirt in the bedroom?"

"Actually, yes, Holmes. More of that mud, although someone had at least tried to clean it up."

"And the curtains?"

"No, I confess I saw you looking around the windows, but I could not see what you were looking for."

"I was not looking for anything, Watson. I was merely observing with a keen eye, and letting the facts speak for themselves. The curtains had faint smudges of chalk upon them."

"Well, Holmes, you have a better eye than me, that's for certain. But I still don't see the significance…"

"And did you observe, in various rooms, the absence of certain items rather than merely the placement of some foreign substance?"

"Nothing of note, other than the lack of food and a good cellar," I said, ruefully. "A drop of claret would help make the day go a little better."

"Nothing of note, you say! You look, but you do not see. Come Watson, help me with the books from the library – we should learn all we can of the history of the manor, and then prepare ourselves for a hair-raising night in a haunted house!"

Holmes was adamant that the secret to the whole affair lay in the house, and stubbornly refused to make a search of the grounds beyond the most cursory inspection of the perimeter, whereupon he periodically stopped and smiled to himself as was his way. Inside, we read and made notes, and discussed and hypothesised until darkness fell. By night, the place took on a dreamlike quality, worsened by the fact that there was very little lamp oil to be found, and only one packet of candles! It was hard to make do, as there were no gas jets, and only the lower floor had electric lights (and even then not in every room). Holmes took one of the candles and went from room to room, checking that there were no draughts of any sort, and satisfying himself that the doors and windows were uncommonly sound. I managed to rustle up a small pot of stew as I had learned to do in my army days, and we made the best of things until it was time for bed. We had chosen the two rooms closest to the stairs so we would be alerted easily by any commotion; not that I was able to get much sleep, given the ascetic surroundings and freezing temperature, but eventually I managed to nod off.

I had a most peculiar dream that night (perhaps brought on by my culinary efforts). I dreamt that some noise had awakened me, and that I was tiptoeing about the corridors of Tattlesby Abbey in the dark; only, there were no doors or exits of any kind, just a maze of carpeted halls, with ancient paintings of stern old men looking down at me from the walls in silent mockery. I became hopelessly lost, and my panic began to grow, before suddenly I found myself at a dead end, looking into a stone well that was inexplicably placed at the end of a corridor. From its bottomless blackness came a faint glow, which slowly grew into a small orb of soft, golden light, until that light was floating before me. It drifted past, illuminating the corridors for the first time, and wherever its light fell, the familiar doorways appeared once more, so that I was no longer lost. A soft voice spoke to me. "Watson... follow me; come, Watson..."

And then I awoke, at first in great confusion, for before me, in the darkened room, was a small golden light that at first dazzled me. Then I realised it was a candle flame, and Holmes was holding it, shaking me awake and hissing: "Wake up Watson. Come on, follow me." I came to my senses in an instant, and leapt out of bed. As advised by Holmes earlier, I had slept in my spare clothes, and I followed Holmes to the door as he crept out into the corridor, snatching my dressing-gown from a peg for warmth.

Once in the corridor, I heard faintly a ringing sound, like the distant chiming of a bell or the striking of steel in a blacksmith's forge. It was definitely coming from downstairs somewhere, and Holmes beckoned me towards the landing. No sooner had we stolen halfway down the stairs than I detected a most curious, gusting draught, carrying with it a smell of mildew and the damp of ages. It chilled me to the bone and caused Holmes's candle to gutter. Had our ghost proven to be real after all? Holmes did not seem to think so, as he continued down the stairs fearlessly. If he was creeping so carefully, it must mean that he aimed to disturb a human intruder, and so, when we reached the hall, I slid my cane from the umbrella stand to use as an improvised weapon – or, at least, to make me feel better about creeping round a supposed haunted house in the dark!

The ringing noise continued, though more sporadically, and did not seem to get any louder no matter where we went – it seemed to emanate from all around us. Holmes checked the direction that his candle flame was blowing, and determined that the horrid draught was coming from the kitchen, and so we set forth. However, no sooner had we inched open the kitchen door than the flame sputtered its last and blew out altogether! Our senses were assailed by a stale odour, and then the draught stopped quite suddenly. There was silence and stillness for a few moments, during which Holmes rushed to the window, for he had evidently observed something by the wan moonlight outside. I was about to join him, when a tremendous noise rang out that startled me greatly: a grinding, thrumming sound that set the pots and pans hanging in the kitchen to rattling, and seemed to vibrate the whole house to its foundations.

"There's someone outside, Watson!" cried Holmes over the din. Sure enough, as I stared out into the night, into the black forest before us, I could see a light dancing about amidst the trees, smudged into a blur by the rising October mist. "Ghosts need no lanterns. After him – the game is afoot!"

I was given pause about chasing after strange lights by the troubling dream I'd had, but there was no time to lose, and my senses quickly got the better of my jarred nerves. I ran from the house into the cold night air, and raced into the woods after the swinging lantern as fast as my legs would carry me. I heard Holmes's steps behind me, crunching through the crisp leaf litter, and knowing my old friend was near to hand girded me to tackle whatever might lie ahead. Anything, that is, except the thing that confronted me! Just in the instant that I thought I was gaining upon the bearer of the light, a figure stepped out in front of me from behind a dense cluster of jagged trees, and I skidded to a halt in alarm as I recognised the ghastly figure of a robed monk, his face shrouded in utter blackness. I staggered backwards (I was, I am ashamed to say, momentarily unmanned by the experience), and instantly became aware of another presence at my back. I turned, and saw not Holmes but a second ghostly monk! I had no time to gather my wits before I felt a sharp pain at the base of my skull, which knocked me to the ground almost senseless.

The next thing I knew, I was being half-carried along the gravel drive, my legs working automatically as Holmes struggled to drag me towards the house. I was always surprised at how such a rakish fellow could be so possessed of such wiry strength, but I was very glad of it that night! The last thing I remember before passing out was seeing the yawning door of that dreadful dark house, threatening to swallow us whole as the downstairs lights flickered on and off like the blinking eyes of a waking demon.

The lad had come for us first thing, as promised, and I was glad to get away from Tattlesby Abbey. I rubbed the lump on the back of my head, and glowered at the famous detective as he fidgeted excitedly in his seat, smiling to himself in a display of extreme self-satisfaction.

"I do wish you'd tell me what amuses you so," I snapped. Holmes put a finger to his lips and glanced askance at the driver, before leaning forward and whispering.

"My dear Watson, I am sorry – I do not wish to make light of your ordeal. But I believe the pieces of the puzzle are falling into place. And yet, we must have complete privacy before I can speak of it. We shall meet Sir Daniel and discuss our plans."

"But Holmes, if you cannot even trust this simple lad, whatever makes you think you can trust the man who stands to profit most by Lord Bairstowe's disappearance?"

"All in good time, Watson; all in good time." And he would say no more.

Holmes was no more forthcoming back at the Traveller's Rest, where we fortified ourselves with an excellent breakfast, and deflected the probing questions of Mr Turnham, who was eager for gossip. After breakfast, we went for a stroll around the village, and Holmes asked to be taken directly to the home of one of the two maids who had earlier fled the abbey – he asked for the most sensible one, whichever that might be. Sir Daniel took us to a small worker's cottage on the edge of the village, where we gained permission from the girl's mother to speak with her daughter, Connie. Once the girl had been reassured that she was not in any trouble, she answered Holmes's questions earnestly. He was most intrigued about the objects that she said had gone missing during her last time at the house. She claimed that things were not in their usual place, and items that she had seen that very day vanished before she could use them. Holmes's grey eyes seemed to glitter when the girl named, amongst other everyday items, paraffin oil, matches, the parlour coal scuttle, a bread knife, bed linen, some polishing rags, and thick twine. Holmes was even more interested when the girl said that some of the curtain ties had gone missing in the bedrooms, so she had been unable to "set the room right".

When we left the girl, Holmes could contain himself no longer.

"Gentlemen," he said, "we are not dealing with a ghost of any sort, but rather with a flesh and blood villain; and more than one, if I am not mistaken. Sir Daniel, I believe there is a chance that your uncle is still alive, although I do not wish to raise your hopes falsely. We have much to do if we are to catch the villains in the act, and we can only do that with careful preparation. I am afraid I must keep you both in the dark for now, but I must have your word that you will carry out my instructions exactly."

We consented at once, for Holmes's confidence was infectious. With our compliance, he continued: "Sir Daniel, I wrote a letter to the chief inspector last night, and I am pleased to say that, now my suspicions have been confirmed, it was not a wasted effort. Would you be so good as to travel to High Wycombe this afternoon and deliver it by hand? Watson," he turned to me without waiting for Sir Daniel's reply, "I am about to engage our worthy driver one more time and ride back to the abbey. When I have departed, I would have you return to the inn and pay in advance for a room for yourself. Tell Turnham and whoever else is listening that I, Sherlock Holmes, have failed to solve the case. Tell them that I have returned to the abbey in a fit of despair, but that you refuse to go back. Tell them of your firm belief in the ghosts of the abbey, and how Sir Daniel has left the village to make arrangements for his uncle's funeral. He will, of course, be burying an empty coffin, thanks to my failure." I looked at Sir Daniel upon this comment, in case his feelings were hurt; but I wondered whether Holmes was trying to get the baronet out of the way. Was he a suspect?

"Before dark," Holmes went on, "you will decide to take an

evening stroll, but you will actually come back to the abbey via the back roads. I apologise, dear fellow, as it is quite the walk, but no one must see you approach. I will leave the back door open for you – let yourself in, and be very quiet. Go to the study directly. Do you both understand?" We nodded, dumbly. "Then let us waste no more time, because I fear these villains will not tarry!"

I followed Holmes's instructions to the letter, but the superstitious locals had kept me talking about the "defeat" of my friend for far longer than I had wanted. It was already dark by the time I reached the abbey, and I was shivering. I let myself in and crept to the study. I found the curtains drawn, and risked lighting a candle, whereupon I discovered that Holmes had left me a flask of brandy and a scribbled note:

Watson,
Wait until nine o'clock and then go to my room. Make as much noise as you like. If you hear the strange noises again, go to the cellar and check the dumbwaiter. Be careful!

SH

I had not been involved in quite such a cloak-and-dagger investigation since the notorious business on Dartmoor, and I fancied spending time alone in that house about as much as I fancied a reunion with the Hound. And yet I took a nip of brandy and followed Holmes's instructions to the letter.

At a little after nine o'clock I clomped around Holmes's bedroom, before settling in a chair to read a book for the remainder of my vigil. Sure enough, at about a quarter-to-ten I heard the ringing noise again. Eager to discover the fiend that had assaulted me the previous night, I flung open the door and hurried down the stairs carrying a shielded lamp rather than a candle. This time, I made it to the cellar stairs before the dreadful thumping and grinding noise began, but I was set on my course. I checked the dumbwaiter as Holmes had said, and to my surprise when I raised it I found an open panel in the ancient stone wall behind, which was broken through into some passage that ran parallel to the cellar. The raising of the dumbwaiter sent a sudden rush of foul air towards me. I took up my cane and lamp, and set forth into the passageway.

It was cramped at first, filthy and criss-crossed by cobwebs, but ahead I saw a flight of worn old steps and a low, vaulted ceiling, and I realised at once that I was in a crypt beneath the ruined abbey! The noise came again, vibrating the walls and causing crumbling mortar to fall on me. At the bottom of the stairs I saw a soft light, and so I turned down my lamp to avoid detection. As I neared the foot of the stairs, I heard a terrifyingly loud crash; the grinding noise stopped, and I could hear two people laughing giddily. I popped my head around the corner and saw that I was in a tiny corridor, at the end of which was a brightly lit chamber. I could make out some sort of machinery in the chamber, and moving shadows of people cast on the walls by the light. There was nothing else for it – I had to trust to Holmes, and so I crept along the tunnel to confront the party.

When I reached the chamber, I was able to see the cause of the commotion. In the room was an electrical generator, which thrummed and sputtered, and powered several lanterns that were suspended from the ceiling. To my right, I saw a frail old man, tied and gagged and very still, lying in a funerary niche. Lord Bairstowe, I presumed! To my left the old stone wall had been caved in to reveal an antechamber, and there was a man within standing next to a large mining machine. This machine had, it appeared, just broken through a thick wall into yet another chamber, and the man was using some kind of ratchet-jack to support the new opening. He was not alone – I recognised at once the figure of Mrs Drebbins helping him! I stepped into the room, brandishing my cane, but my courage almost failed me immediately. At the far end of the room, a long, flagged corridor ran off into darkness, but before the entrance to that tunnel stood the robed monk! It was perhaps less frightening in the lighted chamber than it had been the previous night, but I was still unnerved by the prospect of battling a phantom. It stood quite motionless, and I heard a cry of alarm from the antechamber, and knew that the others had seen me.

"Get 'im! Stop 'im!" shouted the miner, and at his call the "monk" stepped threateningly towards me. Mrs Drebbins came to the entrance of the chamber, wielding an iron bar.

"You're for it now! Come on, Harry, don't just stand there!"

But "Harry" took only one step towards me, before changing direction, quick as a flash. He grabbed Mrs Drebbins by the wrist, and jerked her into the chamber, forcing her to drop her weapon. As she screamed, the monk yanked back his hood, revealing the austere features of Sherlock Holmes!

"That's enough struggling, my good lady. I'm afraid the game is up. And Mr Drebbins; you might as well give yourself up right now!"

The miner, who I now knew to be Mr Drebbins, approached the opening with a pickaxe in his hands.

"You leave go of my missus," he growled, "or there'll be the devil to pay."

"The devil indeed!" came another voice from the corridor behind Holmes. Several figures barged into the chamber; a policeman – who was wrestling another hooded monk into the room – and a stern-looking man with a bristling moustache. "I am Inspector Denby," said the man, "and I suggest you come quietly, before I add more charges to the list."

Drebbins looked at me, then at Holmes, and then at the inspector, his eyes wild. Finally, he submitted to his less rational urges, and raced off into the antechamber and down the newly opened tunnel.

"After him, Watson!" cried Holmes, handing Mrs Drebbins to the inspector. "Inspector, take this woman into custody, and see to Lord Bairstowe." The woman continued to struggle, and I was away before the inspector had time to respond to Holmes's haughty instructions. I was aware of Holmes hot on my heels as I plunged past the mining machine and into the dark passageway beyond.

The tunnel was blacker and longer than I could have expected, and I was very glad of my lantern as I hurtled along it after Drebbins. Holmes stayed close behind, and I pitied my tall friend in the vaulted tunnel, for even I had to duck every few feet to avoid hitting my head. As my lantern swung to and fro, its light was cast upon more of those burial niches and the frontages of plain tombs and, here and there, skulls set into tiny nooks in the brickwork. It was a frightful environ for a pursuit, and I looked away from the remains of the long-dead and concentrated on my footing, lest I slip on the mossy flagstones.

The passageway took a definite downward slope, and twisted and turned most irregularly – why the builders of the old abbey would construct such a labyrinthine catacomb was beyond me – but it seemed to stretch for some distance. At last we reached an intersection of passages, where Holmes and I had to stop to catch our breath and listen carefully for the sounds of Drebbins' footsteps echoing off the stone floor. Eventually we picked up the trail again, but found ourselves at a T-junction, then a crossroads, then a fork; again and again we were forced to slow, and even Holmes seemed to be losing his sense of direction. We had no means of knowing whether we were going around in circles, or getting hopelessly lost in the dark – nor even if Drebbins was lying in wait around the next corner to stove in our heads!

Finally, after what seemed an age, we stopped at another junction and distinctly heard a man's voice, giddy with joy and laughter. A moment later Drebbins ran across the passage ahead of us, freezing briefly in the light of my lantern like a rabbit caught in a poacher's lamp. In his arms he clutched an oblong box of shining gold.

"I've found it!" he cried. "And I will not give it up!" With that, he ran once more, and we gave chase again. But before we could reach the end of the passage, we heard a terrible scream. Holmes and I rounded the corner, and saw that Drebbins had run into a dead end – closed that is, except for an ancient well set into the floor of the small apse. He clung to the crumbling bricks of the well's lip with one hand, and my light showed his eyes, wild with fear.

Holmes rushed to the man immediately and tried to pull him up, and I set down my lantern and tried to help. The well seemed impossibly deep; even when the light shone down it, no bottom could be seen, and I knew that if Drebbins fell, he would be forever lost. And yet, no matter what we said, or how much we struggled, he would not let go of the heavy golden casket – the relic of the Popish Plot that he had worked so illicitly to secure had now driven him to the madness of gold-fever.

Holmes tried one last time, using all of his wiry strength to heave at the man's arm, but Drebbins, in his lunatic state, attempted to fight the detective, and in doing so spelled his own doom. First, the relic fell from his grasp, striking the sides of the well several times before vanishing from sight forever. Then, incensed by this loss, Drebbins attempted to strike out at Holmes, who lost his grip on the man as he tried to defend himself. The exertion forced Drebbins to loosen his own grip on the bricks, and in the terrible moment when he knew he was lost, his eyes seemed to regain their lucidity, and pleaded with me for salvation; but it was too late. He fell, with a blood-curdling scream that lingered long after he had disappeared from sight, into that Stygian gloom. The man, and the relic, were gone.

I wish I could say that was the end of the tale, but it is not. What followed was one of the most daunting and strangest episodes of all my adventures with the great detective, for when we attempted to find our way out of those tunnels, we seemed unable to retrace our steps. Every passage and chamber seemed unfamiliar, and Holmes cursed himself for a fool, for being so hasty in his efforts to catch the criminal that he had gotten us terribly lost. We struggled to keep our composure, but after an hour or more had passed, the lantern started to gutter and smoke as the last of the oil was expended. We groped our way around those terrible catacombs like blind men, recoiling when our hands alighted on an ancient skull, or when we walked into a massive, dusty cobweb; feeling the scurrying of crawling insects and spiders running across our trembling hands, hitting our heads on the arched supports, and almost falling on the slimy stones many times. Who can say how many hours elapsed? We began to give up hope that Inspector Denby would come looking for us at all, for we heard not a sound except for our own footsteps and breathing.

It was at our darkest moment, when it had dawned on us that we might be as lost as poor Drebbins, a most peculiar thing occurred. We had just felt our way to a crossroads, and at the end of one passageway I saw a soft, golden light, which I first took to be a policeman's lantern. But the light seemed to hover and dance, casting very little illumination on the surrounding stones. I took a tentative step towards it, and asked Holmes if he could see the light.

"What light?" he asked. "No Watson, but fear not. I believe I have found our salvation. The passage to our right has a marked incline, and I think we have been here before. If I am not mistaken, there is a faint draught coming from it, too. Come, Watson, this has to be the way out."

Holmes took a step down the right-hand tunnel, but I reached out and grabbed his arm. For the first time in months I remembered what the medium on Thread-needle Street had told me, and I knew that what I was seeing was no figment of my imagination. I *knew* it was a sign!

"No Holmes," I hissed, "the way out lies directly ahead. I am certain."

"I'm sorry, Watson, but the stress of the events has addled your mind. And perhaps the blow to the head you received yesterday, courtesy of Drebbins as I'm sure you now understand, has taken its toll. The passage ahead will take us deeper into these catacombs."

He turned to leave once more, but this time I seized him with all the strength I had, and stated as forcefully as I could: "Holmes, for once in your life trust me! I have never been more certain of anything. Your deduction will get us even more lost; follow me."

Holmes was so surprised by my forcefulness and earnestness that he eventually submitted, albeit grudgingly. He was most unused to taking orders, or being in any way undermined. I was careful not to mention the hovering orb of light, which I could still see up ahead at the end of the passageway, but which Holmes evidently could not. And yet I followed it, praying that I had not taken leave of my senses, as Holmes had surmised. The light hovered tantalisingly out of reach, but led us past every junction and round every turn; Holmes was amazed by my surety, and asked repeatedly how I knew where I was going, but I told him merely that "I was certain".

After the longest time, we rounded a corner, and saw a real light up ahead – the light of the little mineshaft that Drebbins had constructed. As we staggered towards it, we became aware of the inspector's voice calling out to us.

"Come on quick! The jack won't hold – you'll be stuck!"

We saw that the large metal jack was buckling most severely, and that rubble had already begun to fall from the cavern ceiling. Indeed, the mouth of the tunnel was half the size it had been earlier, and a police constable was desperately trying to brace the supports with the tools to hand.

We needed no second warning, and stumbled forward as fast as our weary legs would carry us, almost falling into the antechamber as the ratchet-jack strained and bucked under the weight of the earth above it. The inspector herded us to the safety of the next room as the metal support finally gave way, and a pile of bricks and rocks collapsed into the newly excavated catacombs with a tremendous crash.

Seeing that her husband was not with us, Mrs Drebbins let out a woeful cry. She was sitting on the cavern floor next to her accomplice, "Harry" – none other than Mr Turnham, the landlord of the Traveller's Rest. But even that was not the biggest surprise of the evening.

"He didn't make it out then?" said the inspector. "You fellows took your time – I was about to send my lads in after you."

"About to…" I started, incredulously. "We've been lost in those catacombs for goodness knows how long!"

The inspector gave me a queer look. "About twenty minutes or so, I should think. We got the old man to wake up, thankfully, and he told us that the old crypt doesn't extend a great distance underground, so you can't have wandered far."

"Well, I… I…" was about all I could say. Holmes, looking even paler than usual, simply put a hand on my shoulder to steady me, before going over to where Lord Bairstowe sat. The old man was in a severe state, filthy and scrawny, and swaddled in dirty linen sheets.

"I think we should get this man to the village," said Holmes, calmly. "I will make a full statement to you, Inspector Denby, especially concerning the fate of Mr Drebbins." At the mention of Drebbins' name, his wife let out a huge heartfelt sob.

"Indeed, Mr Holmes. I should like to know just how you came to solve this case. You have certainly lived up to your reputation."

* * *

The night had been a long one, and Holmes and I were not able to return to our rooms at the now-managerless inn until the small hours. Sir Daniel had returned with the police, and was extremely thankful to us for the discovery of his uncle, and to his credit was not in the least bit concerned that he had missed out on a large inheritance. I spoke not a word to Holmes, nor he to me, and we went to our rooms and slept until late morning the next day. We departed Chalgrave in silence, and it was only when we were safely in our quiet train compartment on the journey back to London that I asked Holmes how he'd done it.

"It was really quite simple, Watson," he said, a sardonic smile on his thin lips indicating that he was returning to his old self. "I suspected from the start that Septimus Bairstowe had not left his home at all. If he had done so, someone would surely have seen him – the estate is bordered by three large villages, and a working chalk mine, not to mention the poachers who patrol the local woods. I was first alerted to Mrs Drebbins as a suspect when Sir Daniel told us of her testimony. Her husband, a miner, had come to walk her home from the abbey 'on his way back from work'. But of course, miners start early (as we saw when we visited the Drebbinses on that first morning) and cannot legally work more than twelve hours. It would have been a stretch for him to collect his wife so late at night, unless some other business had kept them at the house. And he did enter the house, despite what his wife said, for we saw for ourselves the chalk dust throughout the old place. The reports of the various hauntings were curious, but sadly obvious. The ringing noise was the sound of hammer and pick on stone walls, the grinding was the generator and the mining machine – which also, I must point out, caused the electric lights in the house to flicker. When we first went to the house, we failed to find any secret passages, but I knew one must be there, as it was the only thing that would explain the draughts. The Drebbinses and Turnham entered the tunnels through an old hidden grate in the woods – which, incidentally, is where I apprehended Turnham and took his costume. From there, the crooks stole into the house to avail themselves of supplies whenever they needed to: fuel for the generator, food and fresh linen for the old man, and curtain cords for their ridiculous monk costumes. I believe the maids gave Mrs Drebbins the idea of using a ghost story to frighten away the locals, and the young girl, Connie, confirmed all the items that went missing from the house, which were just as I suspected. The story of the Popish relic and the haunted abbey were told to us by both Mrs Drebbins and Harry Turnham, so similarly in their style that I knew they must have been rehearsed. Their activities had succeeded in frightening away every visitor to the house, and they could not resist adding me to that list when you told them of my 'failure'. That overconfidence allowed me to discover their hiding place, and set my trap." He leaned back in his seat, closed his eyes and smiled thinly.

"And all of that – including harming a frail old man – for a piece of treasure that may or may not have been real!" I exclaimed.

"Oh it was real enough, Watson," said Holmes, not opening his eyes. "We saw it for ourselves. Mr Drebbins found his prize before falling to his death. His avarice was, quite literally, his downfall."

"I'm not sure I understand why they didn't kill Lord Bairstowe. Surely they risked everything by keeping him alive?"

"I believe it was Mrs Drebbins' compassion that stayed their hands, Watson. You saw for yourself how fond she seemed of the old man, and added to that none of the conspirators were hardened criminals. They turned to crime purely for monetary gain, and doubtless planned to leave the village as soon as the relic was found. Besides, Lord Bairstowe was kept blindfolded at all times, and of course he was in a fragile state of mind. He may never quite be himself again."

"But there are things you cannot explain," I said, tentatively. "About our time in the tunnels… of the catacombs that weren't there, and of…"

Holmes opened his steely eyes, and fixed me with a gaze so singular it stopped me dead. "The tunnels were not as deep as we thought, Watson, but surely deeper than the old man knew. He was muddled, and perhaps always will be after his ordeal. As for our perception of the passage of time, and our confusion, I put it down to the foul air – perhaps some ancient gas which, when combined with the pitch darkness and the eerie events of the past few days addled even my acute senses. Your lantern burned down because you forgot to fill it.

This was likely due to a mild concussion, thanks to the blow to the head you sustained the previous night. I trust you will let the issue rest; I am not proud of my lapse in mental fortitude last night."

I stared at Holmes, but his eyes told me he would brook no reply. I knew what I had seen, and, as I have previously related, I had been warned at the séance of the events that came to pass. I said no more to Holmes – I simply opened my newspaper and tried to read, though the words would not sink in.

"Oh, and Watson," Holmes said.

"Hmm?"

"I think that from now on we ought to concentrate on more worldly matters. Let us leave the flights of fancy to your friends at the Golden Dawn."

I did not know how he had deduced my involvement with that secret society, or exactly how much he knew about my attendance at various séances around London; and I did not ask. I was merely silently thankful that he did not press the matter. He knew that the loss of my dear Mary had shaken me, though we had rarely spoken of it. I have often said that Sherlock Holmes lacked the warmth and compassion that defines most men; but by keeping his own counsel in this affair, Sherlock Holmes proved to me that he was my most dear and steadfast friend.

ABOUT THE AUTHOR

Mark A. Latham is an author, editor and games designer from Staffordshire, UK. Formerly the editor of *White Dwarf* magazine, Mark is now a writer of short stories, novels and tabletop games. Mark has been ensconced in the worlds of science fiction and fantasy for many years, but his real passion is for history. Mark has a deep obsession with the past, especially the nineteenth century; an affliction that can only be salved by writing on the subject for far longer than can be considered healthy. Visit Mark at www.facebook.com/thelostvictorian, or follow him on Twitter @ alostvictorian.

THE ADVENTURE OF THE
DECADENT HEADMASTER

BY NICK CAMPBELL

August 2013

*T*he London heat is intolerable, but in the apartment the blinds have been lowered all day. I turn off my phone and leave it in the box room with my cardigan and shoes. I am escorted to an inner room, where a figure waits at a desk. I feel as if one word from my lips would demolish her perfect stillness.

Thankfully my escort is going to do the talking.

"An unusual task for you this afternoon, Madame. Mr Campbell is a writer, he says, of sorts. He has been invited to write a short story about the Great Detective, Mr Sherlock Holmes. He has been having some difficulty with his task."

As he speaks, I think again of that humiliating episode in Cox and Co., the pleasure that girl in pinstripe took in turning me away. The days of frustrated searching in the British Library; the temptation to simply invent something…

"Mr Campbell would like you to contact a man for him. A man called John Watson. To ask him for an untold story of Mr Holmes. He is aware that such a request is rather – mercenary. But the Society is in favour."

The figure remains perfectly poised in the shadows. Her hand moves to attention. A point of lead glints.

The secretary of the Chelsea Psychical Society is holding his breath. I draw strength from his belief. I never believed in the ineffable before, but needs must… Now I hear him give a high, dry chuckle.

No – what I hear is the pencil scribbling in the woman's hand, whispering in silver across the page:

Concerning my literary output, Sherlock Holmes was never shy in offering his reviews: "I flatter myself I have run to greater feats of ingenuity than this – what a pity none of them involved the arrival of an exotic animal by moonlight"; "Once again, Watson, you over-sweeten your medicine, deliver a heady rush and little of real sustenance"; "Scarce meat for the intellectual member of society in this month's number, I see." My friend would have preferred to see his methods dispassionately described – and, incidentally, I am certain, limned in gold leaf – and he absolutely deplored any tendency toward obscurity, however germane to a case. The adventure of Meadowbank College contained one intrinsic element which, inevitably, fell under just this category my friend always insisted I downplay, or preferably skirt altogether. Thus I never even considered setting it down in print.

For another reason, though, it was never (in life) even alluded to. The princes of central Europe are one thing, but to describe a scandal in so venerable an institution as Meadowbank, where certain of Britain's greatest figures were forged, might have ruined me.

I recognised the crest on the letter as soon as I laid eyes on it, that dark November evening at the end of the century. It was in that period after one sad loss and another strange return which found me living once more in Baker Street, and typical of Holmes's model of domesticity, the reverse of this venerable missive had been used to total up the last fortnight's spending on shag, laundry bills and theatrical greasepaint.

"Holmes," I said hotly.

"Watson." He was stretched upon the divan in what he insisted on describing as an Ayurvedic pose.

"Are you in the habit of reading my post?"

"Certainly not," he replied. "I regard it more as a chore than a habit, and if you will forgive a tortured quotation, I read only the mad, bad and dangerous to know."

"How can you possibly tell without opening the envelope?!" I ejaculated.

He sighed and shifted position, lazily. "The signs are always there, Watson, believe you me."

I gathered the scattered leaves. "I doubt a schoolmaster can be a danger to anyone – so long as he has done his Latin prep."

"A spurious comment," Holmes replied. "But give it voice, Watson and we shall learn all we can."

My Dear Dr Watson,

I write as a long-standing admirer of your chronicles of the career of Sherlock Holmes. Long have I marvelled at his genius for deduction and his firmly British moral character. Sadly, whilst a letter of appreciation is certainly overdue, this is not it. It is instead a call for your assistance – and that of your friend, particularly.

I am a master at Meadowbank College for Boys. You will know that our reputation in education is unique, and the hundred boarders lodged within these walls has been a happy garrison since before our present monarch's reign. Alas, it has become evident to me that the present Headmaster is not what he should be – that is, of sound mind.

Given the particular prestige associated with the school, I must ask that such a delicate statement is not repeated beyond yours and Mr Holmes's sitting-room. Tolerance for eccentricity has long been an English virtue, but I am confident I can distinguish it from more dangerous modes of mind. Indeed, I would be entirely willing to turn the blindest of eyes on Mr Marcus Crawthew, were it not for certain circumstantial events.

I could not fail to notice the absence midway through term of one of our most promising students, named Bragg. An exceptional scholar in history, and moreover a minor favourite amongst the boys, it transpired that Bragg had been quietly removed from Meadowbank due to a change of circumstances regarding his father, and there I thought best the matter should lie. Since I am no housemaster, nor in any way close with the boys, I felt no responsibility for the absent student.

However, it chanced that I was asked by Bragg's pals to pass correspondence to their departed comrade, along with a quantity of personal effects he had left behind: books, smoking materials, playing cards *etc*. The quantity of these personal objects surprised me somewhat. However, I made my colleagues aware, in case any of them wished to include a note or sustaining epigram.

Soon afterward, I was informed that the parcel was against the traditions of the school, and that it had been destroyed. My amateur investigations suggest that Bragg Snr's estate is secure. The disappearance of Bragg Jnr presents itself therefore as a mystery.

I made no great publicity of my suspicions. However, as a result of my role in the saga of the destroyed parcel, I was inducted into certain alternative views of our Headmaster. It is said that his personal rooms are decorated in the most exquisite Chinoiserie, and that when disturbed at night he has been witnessed sporting a silken robe of the deepest crimson. He is unmarried and known to be a reader of certain yellow-backed literature. The most perturbing detail, I offer as evidence, though I cannot explain it myself.

It took place in July of this year, when the majority of boarders were holidaying, and only a few boys and schoolmasters remained. I am told the atmosphere of this old pile becomes rather ghostly in the sunshine and deep silence, when students and staff are engaged elsewhere and one is alone.

It seems that one afternoon, the diminished population of the school was employed on the playing fields, a modest expanse at the rear of the school, adjacent to the railway, when a master had occasion to pass the Meadowbank entrance, and observed the Headmaster greeting a brougham waiting in the drive. He was disturbed to see the door of the carriage open, and a woman's body lowered to the ground, where she lay at the gentleman's feet. According to his testimony, Crawthew then lifted her into his arms and carried her back towards the school, at which point my confidant returned to his fellows, keen not to be recognised by his employer.

You will, I hope, forgive certain oddities of procedure due to the sensitive nature of my enquiry. My obligations at school forbid me to leave the grounds; in the meanwhile, I am unable to speak with colleagues on the matter. If we are to meet, it must be done clandestinely. There is a cricket pavilion on the school playing fields which at this time of year is rarely frequented. If you would meet me there on the last day of the month, at about ten in the evening, I would be much obliged; I feel powerless to intervene in a drama which may have more unpleasant acts in store.

Yours,
A Concerned Individual

"I appreciate the letter's aim is to secure your services," I said mildly, "but I fail to see why you have not mentioned it. You planned to attend in my absence?"

"I did not," Holmes replied. "In point of fact, I have no intention of visiting the aforementioned cricket pavilion whatsoever."

I was bemused, to say the least. "But the fellow describes the most disturbing series of events! What reason could you have for not answering him?"

Holmes turned a weary expression on me. "Why, Watson, surely it is obvious to the most casual reader?" He rose from his louche attitude and joined me at the fireside. "To begin with, the penmanship is remarkably fine. It suggests a man whose habits routinely require great volumes of impeccable composition. Then the odd stipulation in meeting us on school grounds. Is any schoolmaster so put upon in term time that he cannot spare an evening in town, in extremes such as these?

"It is unmistakably the work of a schoolboy at Meadowbank who hopes to gain our interest. Observe his exaggerated formality in contacting you instead of me, and his juvenile reiterations of patriotic feeling: the unmistakable English public schoolboy. Most glaring of all, the *grand guignol* of the demonic headmaster who, we are led to believe, operates a trade in schoolboys and murdered females on school premises. Even the most gullible man would raise an eyebrow at that, I hope."

"You suspect it to be a fraud?"

"Either to embarrass ourselves or his Headmaster," Holmes replied, sneering at the paper as I held it to the lamp. "After all, Christmastime is almost upon us, and boys must have their entertainments."

As was customary, after this interpretation the truth seemed simple and self-evident. I felt slighted at having been baited by some arrogant youth, and mildly censured by my friend, though he gentlemanly refrained from re-emphasising my error. If I had not received such a double wound to my pride that evening, it may be that I would have made no connection at all when, precisely one week after we missed our appointment on the playing fields, I learned in the *Standard* of a master found dead in his room at Meadowbank.

I was suffused with a chill sensation; passing the newspaper across the breakfast table, I could only muster a few words to direct Holmes to the item. Inspection of the scene had conclusively showed Mr Tournier to have made a violent end to his own life, drinking a dose of arsenic in a glass of fortified wine. Colleagues, forcing the locked door, found a note beneath the empty glass, explaining that heroic death was preferable to the *ennui* of life. The *Standard* took care to stress the unromantic circumstances of Mr Tournier's death throes. I watched Holmes consider and remember. Then he lowered the paper and, unexpectedly, smiled.

"So, another light shines on the matter," he said.

We lost no time in departing for Primrose Hill. It was the first week in December, and the morning sky was the mottled hue of an antique cheese. As our carriage passed under the brow of the hill, the massed black skeletons of bare trees did nothing to alter my sombre mood. Holmes, a similarly stark silhouette in such meagre light, gazed into the bowl of his pipe, deep in rumination. We stopped at a tobacconist on the corner, which I took as a sign we were embarking on an investigation, not merely restitution with the author of the letter.

Indeed, we spent almost ten minutes (Holmes demolishing a bowlful of malodorous leaf) before even gaining the front door of the school, as he perused the wide gravel drive detailed in our correspondent's story. I reminded him that he had himself dismissed the apocryphal event as fantastic. "The delivery of a woman's body in broad daylight –"

"Is patently absurd," he said, measuring the length of the drive in the steady strides of a patient heron. "Possibly the incident was invented solely to excite our appetites for the grotesque. Alternatively, in August of this year, when solitude was thought to be assured, Meadowlands College received what appeared to be a body – but was not."

"But what could arouse more interest than dressing such an object in female clothing?" I asked, keeping pace beside him as best I could, without arousing suspicion. He was, after all, nearing the front door.

"What indeed?" he murmured. "Did you ever hear of the Marvel of Montmartre?"

"Isn't that a public house in Soho?"

"And you do not recall the vanishment of several government ministers this summer?"

I admitted a certain haziness on the matter. "Did you put that one down to the mirrored Underground carriage in the end?"

"In point of fact," he replied, "I did not. No trace of the men was ever found."

"I presume you believe young Arnold Bragg to have gone the same way," I deduced, looking back at the empty, overcast drive. I tried to imagine the thing in woman's clothing lying prostrate on the gravel, the mysterious carriage departing in a haze of summer heat, perhaps with a sedated schoolboy slumped inside. It was difficult to make sense of – but if I had expected immediate clarification, I should have been frustrated: Holmes had disappeared through the front door.

The interior was hushed and gloomy, and would have done credit to Henry VIII: a cavern of varnished wood in which a massive Christmas tree charged the air with an odour of resin. Above our heads, antlers gleamed bone-white, and craning to examine them I caught sight of a figure on the staircase. This was Mr Crawthew, the much-maligned Headmaster, beaming munificently and extending his hand. An unprepossessing figure, he resembled a mother hen shortly after death. "I watched you from the window," he said. "You make an interesting pair."

"I was calculating if it would take one man or two to carry a body in from the gates," Holmes explained, which Mr Crawthew received with a charitable laugh. He apologised for the cool reception, explaining that no serving staff were retained over the Christmas holiday.

"Merely a handful of schoolmasters and barely that of boys. I'm afraid you've picked a poor time to make your visit."

"It is villainy that has brought us here, Mr Crawthew," replied my companion. "I suspect we have not arrived one moment too soon."

It fell to me to make our introductions, but the Headmaster remained unstirred by this fresh information. "I know you by reputation, of course," he said, "but I am past the age for detective stories. In this moment of history, one must show more interest in the condition of the soul, Dr Watson."

I expressed the opinion that the chronicles of our adventures took human morality as their prime concern. Crawthew, smiling, voiced his disagreement.

"Mr Holmes is in the business of maintaining the assurance of authority," he said, "and the authority he defends is that of logic and positivism. There are more difficult problems to be faced, I believe, and stranger answers."

"The ineffable has never struck me as being much use, practically," said the detective.

"And yet a great deal may escape such confined vision."

Holmes received the criticism coolly. "I don't deny that the mystic spends his days in raptures of mystery," he said, "but it is my curse to never suffer a mystery for long. The good doctor is far more inclined toward mystification."

"Recent experience has taught me to keep an open mind," I said modestly, having no wish to go deeper into my personal interests.

The Headmaster looked approvingly at me. "I have no doubt the new century shall see more men of Dr Watson's type than yours, Mr Holmes. But forgive me, what wicked behaviour brings you to our little encampment?"

My friend surprised me by making no reference, either to the schoolboy's letter or the schoolmaster's suicide. "We are on the trail of the Marvel of Montmartre," he said. "A Parisian construction, lately exhibited in the foyer of the Langham Hotel. Do you object to our searching the premises?"

"I would not dream of obstructing you," Mr Crawthew answered, addressing me particularly. "Though why such a thing should be brought here, I cannot imagine. I hope you do not view any of my boys with suspicion!"

"The criminal schoolboy is far from an impossibility," Holmes replied, "and it would make a refreshingly original addition to Watson's casebook."

"There was the case of the charred sphinx," I noted.

"Ah, but Watson, you forget," Holmes replied, "in that instance the culprit was merely a very, very small person in disguise."

His benevolence having been tried, I thought, almost to its limits, Crawthew granted us the freedom of the school, asking only that I repair to his study after our searches for a festive brandy and debrief. The invitation was quite pointedly not extended to my companion.

"You have not had a good report from the Headmaster," I observed, as we made our watchful way through the halls of Meadowbank.

"His literary taste seems not to have been misrepresented in our client's letter," Holmes said. "Perhaps we ought to have asked to see him in his dressing-gown."

I hesitated a moment when we passed a wall of tributes emblazoned in oak, to names distinguished on turf or foreign battlefield. The deathly silence of the place gave me the strange sensation of visiting an abandoned, haunted ruin. The memory of Arnold Bragg and the dead schoolmaster only deepened my sense of trespass.

Holmes was now awaiting me at the door that led out to the playing field, like a looming bundle of firewood brought into the dry. Through a glass pane I saw that the fields had been softly painted out by a new fall of snow. "Watson, I trust you are not unduly disturbed by the chance that the Headmaster is a student of the occult."

"I must admit," I told him, "the very idea of corruption in a place for the young has had me unsettled from the outset."

He cast a look around the building. "This also has been one of the dark places of the Earth, Watson," he said. "But as an aside, Mr Crawthew is a quite obvious dilettante. The ideas he expressed are absorbed from elsewhere and merely parroted."

"So you do not, after all, consider him a threat?"

"He is credulous and easily manipulated – otherwise he should not have allowed us, particularly me, the run of the place." He opened the door to the bare winter fields. "We must now uncover what malign element he has permitted to enter his school." And at that, he was off across the fields and bound for the cricket pavilion.

I should never have suspected there to be anyone waiting within, but as Holmes later remarked, such a rendezvous is not chosen lightly. Moreover, the schoolboy's haunts are few, and he guards them, quite literally, for all he is worth.

There were twelve boys lounging in their den, of all ages, most of them squat and wild looking. They had built a small fire and were taking turns to singe slices of bread on an antique toasting fork; through the resultant fog of sweet-smelling smoke, the scene was disquietingly prehistoric. The first one to notice our arrival gave a cry of, "What ho!" and soon half of them were on their feet. The toasting fork was levelled directly at us.

"Hold, gentlemen," Holmes intoned. "We are here to confer with you, not disrupt your meeting."

The lad with the toasting fork stuck it under his arm and peeled the piece of toast from its tines, but remained wary. "State the terms of your business," he said, through the mouthful. "I cannot say I recognise your faces."

"I bally well do," said a voice from amongst the dark clouds. They parted, and a boy of twelve stood before us. In the dim light, the violet blazer of Meadowbank's uniform looked bloody. "Not wishing to be unwelcoming, chaps, but this is a damnable late showing for your appointment."

"We must beg your forgiveness," Holmes replied, seriously. "I have honed my powers of observation to such a degree that the slightest deviation from honest testimony reeks like a rotten egg. I failed to realise, of course, that in such a place as this, deception is a necessity."

"It was the devil's own task, perfectin' that letter," said the small creature I had mistaken (on paper) for one of his masters. "But I knew you'd write me off straightway if I told you I wasn't yet sixteen. Then, naturally, I had to keep you off Dorian."

"Dorian?" Holmes frowned in concentration.

"I suspect he means Mr Crawthew, the decadent Headmaster," I murmured. "Places like these run on pet names, as I recall, and Dorian Gray would suit him." I was conscious that Holmes's own experience of school had been somewhat unorthodox.

"Ah," he said, gratefully. "So, a herring in a red dressing-gown?"

"Not entirely. Come into the circle, Mr Holmes, Dr Watson."

"I don't believe your brethren share your confidence in us," I said, hunkering down beside the blaze as best I could, propriety and my leg permitting. Holmes assumed the position with an acrobat's grace, delved in his overcoat and produced three tins of Balkan Sobranie, which in hindsight I saw were the object of our trip to the tobacconist. This mollified the boys, who soon settled down in an even thicker billow of smoke to listen to Holmes's interview with Tiger (*vis.* Kit, *vis.* his family name of Marlowe).

"Tell me of Arnold Bragg."

"A stout fellow," quoth the Tiger, in the manner of someone four decades older. "Able mind, fine batsman, and not voluble. Never a gloat from that quarter."

"I assume this quiet soul's disappearance went unremarked," said Holmes, "until after the fact?"

"You see aright," said the boy, looking sideways at his peers. "We failed the young fellow, it's true. Questions were asked in the House, of course, but as I say, we were jolly well fobbed off. Froggy told me it was unmanly to enquire too deeply."

"Dash it, Tiger, don't blame the masters," said an older boy. "When a blighter's pater finds himself stoney, you're an utter beast to make an inquisition about it."

This produced a round rebuke from Tiger. "Do I have to make myself hoarse sayin' it, Beetle? Bragg Senior isn't a bit of him stoney. Father says he's as much in clover as a heifer in the west of Ireland."

"So you have approached your father for help," I interjected.

"Not as baldly as the proverbial," he answered. "Father doesn't approve of me hectorin' him – he says, what's the point of puttin' a hundred and twenty miles between us, otherwise? I wrote to him for facts, and that's that. It's odds against him swallowing such a story in any case."

"What were the circumstances of his disappearance?"

"Impossible to say," said Tiger. "It must have taken place at night. Durin' term time, a fellow couldn't have any time alone in Coll' for ready money. But then he shared a dormitory with nine other boys, and nothing was heard, not even by the chap who shares his bunk."

"And you have discounted the most obvious explanation," Holmes said, questioningly. "That he has simply run away?"

"And told no one? He had his friends, Mr Holmes," said Tiger, "and what is more, his team-mates. I've interrogated 'em all, and gone over his tuckbox with a glass, as per your stories. I can show you later, if you like?"

"I will accept your findings," the detective replied solemnly, as he rarely if ever was wont to do with professional men. "And whilst Dr Watson talks symbolism with the charming Mr Crawthew, I will be looking over the effects of your late master, Mr Tournier. Did any of you consult him about the disappearances?" The boys solemnly shook their heads. "Prior to his fatal glass of Madeira wine, of course."

"I remember saying to him what a loss to the Coll' Bragg was," an upright, athletic-looking boy remarked. "He was games master, you know, and I'm Captain of the First XI. Bragg really was an asset to the squad. Couldn't catch a blind thing, but he had a drive like a Greek hero."

"And Tournier had something to say on the matter?"

"Nothing extraordinary. Our loss was some other place's gain, that sort of a thing," said the Captain. "The masters sincerely believe he's been taken out by his father. And I don't see why Tiger's old man should be an expert on such things."

Tiger made some aside about the Captain seeing little that happened outside the frame of a cricket pitch, a remark that was soon being frenziedly debated by all other individuals seated around the fire.

Sherlock Holmes closed his eyes and considered. He then produced a perfectly composed set of smoke rings. This silenced the crowd. "He interests me, this games master of yours. Can you tell me anything of his history?"

Nobody was quick to volunteer this information. I could imagine just such an uncanny task, attempting to sum up the character of someone who had been so recently lost – and in such a strange fashion.

"He didn't confess to any of you," I added, "any reasons for unhappiness…?"

Again there was silence. "The most important thing is," said Tiger, "he wasn't to blame for – whatever is taking place here at Meadowbank."

"Boney was a jolly decent old boy," said the Captain.

"He may have been a frog," said another boy, "but he was nothing like Froggy. Boney was a true sportsman."

"He wasn't liked by the other masters," said Tiger. "I'd bet you all the money there is, he was bullyragged by one of them, pushed too far. Someone who knows what's really going on."

"But why should he feel such responsibility," I asked, "that he took so dramatic a course of action?" Once again, silence had fallen like the afternoon snow.

Holmes tapped the ash from his pipe, once again drawing attention. "I fear we are in an impossible situation, Watson. We have, in the past, been accustomed to the solidarity of thieves, men whose code of honour may be somewhat selective but is generally resistant to the probing arm of the law. Yet here we find an even tighter ring of steel." He looked about the room. "However, I wonder about

Bragg's personal effects – books, tobacco and playing cards. The late Mr Tournier was a noble sportsman. Did he play cards with Arnold Bragg?"

There was still no sound in the pavilion beside the soft pad of snow on the roof and the hiss of the fire. At last, however, the silence itself became too full of significance to be endured. It was Tiger who broke it. "Most of us played cards with Boney at one time or another, Mr Holmes. He ran the games club, after all."

Holmes's eyes were suddenly as bright as spirit lamps. "Aha! And Bragg was a frequent visitor, I assume?"

"By the end of the term, it was only Bragg and a handful of others who kept it going," the Captain replied. "Most of us found it rather dry."

"Yes, but look here," Tiger responded, "such information can only look incriminatin', when nothing links the poor chap to this foul business at all."

"Are any of those other members here now?" asked Holmes, to no response. "None of them? Fascinating! I suppose one or two of them may have gone home for the holiday, but even so… who else attended? Any other masters?"

"Only –" It was the Captain. "Well, I did talk with Bragg about it once, and he said there was, sometimes – a woman."

The silence that followed this was only a brief hush, before hilarity broke upon the room. The very idea of a woman being invited into the school, and to do anything but press these young firebrands' clothes and cook their dinner, struck them as the most outrageous joke. He might as well have said there had been fairies present.

The fire had begun to burn low, and the laughter had broken the dramatic atmosphere of the gathering. Holmes looked at me. "If we are not to make the Headmaster suspicious of us, Watson, I think we had better not spend much longer here. Tiger, it is better if we are not seen together."

"Oh," he said, looking away, "I unn'erstand."

"I do not doubt we shall meet again before this matter is resolved," Holmes said, "and I must thank you for your openness in these matters. One final question: which man was seen, carrying the dead woman's body? The Headmaster? Or Mr Tournier?"

"My hat," said Tiger, "you *are* misled. It wasn't either of them. It was Froggy, the French master."

As we walked back across the playing fields, I found myself wondering at all of these queer mysteries, and remarked to Holmes that it was extraordinary none of them had spoken to any but us about it.

"The child occupies a world even I can never fathom," he agreed. "One wonders what other fearful events go on daily within their hermetic communities…"

Knocking and entering, alone, the Headmaster's domain, I was at once unnerved. The study was filled with schoolmasters. I had wondered at the silence of the school, and here was the explanation: a room of variously severe and ascetic gentlemen, gowned in black. There were seven of them in all, already engaged in the promised consumption of brandy: the air was heady with its aroma, and rumbling with their conversation. Mr Crawthew made brief introductions, and I made note of the French master, a handsome, bearded young man called Lemaitre, who greeted me with a smile.

"You must return next term Dr Watson, and speak to my boys of your many great successes with Mr Holmes," he said, "not least your facility with the pen."

Struggling to reconcile this charming fellow with the so-called "Froggy" of macabre reputation, I accepted a crystal tumbler from Mr Crawthew and an armchair by the fireplace, and prepared to say bland things about the weather for a good hour or so. The masters were more interested in Mr Holmes's investigation, and the item we were engaged in exploring the school in search of – a conversational topic I found something of a strain, given that this particular piece of information had not yet been divulged to me.

I asked as many inoffensive questions as I could muster about the College, learning that Mr Crawthew and his staff – draped variously, like great black cats, over chairs and occasional tables throughout the room – were bidding *au revoir* for the season to the mathematics master, a Mr Grimes, I believe. The remaining men, with no friends or family to spend Christmas among, would be staying on. They had all manner of extra-curricular activities in mind for the holiday period, from a visit to Drury Lane's pantomime to their own staging of *Dick Whittington*, an evening of carols on the longest night and a plunge in the Serpentine on Christmas morning.

Mr Grimes, who was merry with the prospect of freedom as well as the Headmaster's drink, made a friendly conversational partner while the other masters laid their plans. Inevitably, the matter of Tournier's death came to the fore, Grimes having been one of the unfortunate men to discover the body. "I hope you will exercise some caution, not to say decency, in drawing any conclusions from his sad demise. Mr Tournier's private agonies need not become a public one for his more innocent fellows of Meadowbank."

I asked him if he had known the man, and had any clue to his actions. He pulled a very particular face, not so different from the schoolboys' silence in the face of the same question.

"I did not know him well," he said. "Such an event makes a man question what he knows of any of his brethren. There was a note of some sort – in French, of course – but nothing in that, save a request for forgiveness."

"For taking the arsenic?"

"What else?" He frowned deeply. "As a medical man, you will know that such a death is no easy solution to a problem. I was struck, as we carried the man from the room, rigid and cold, that in his agonies he had smashed his Hunter pocket-watch so badly it had stopped, and the face cracked right across."

"A peculiar detail!" Holmes said later, when I recounted the conversation to him over a pot of tea in Baker Street. "There may be something in that, don't you agree?"

"Signs of a struggle, you mean?" I suggested.

"As suspicious deaths go, it certainly distinguishes itself," he replied, musingly. "A schoolmaster is admitted to one of England's great schools by a headmaster with a susceptibility to a certain type of man. He is noble, vital, well liked. And yet when he invites them to play cards and chess on a Sunday night, he has some uncommon attendees. One of them, probably more, vanishes. The other –"

"Belongs to the French master?"

At this, Holmes's eyebrows became two steep, dark arches. "No longer, Watson!" With a flourish, he drew back a bed-sheet from a curious shape in the corner of the room.

The firelight lit up the dark orbs of her eyes, and ran in strange pools across her almost beautiful face. It could not quite make her flush or glow, as any woman of human flesh does in the light of a fire. Her dark ringlets too, where they escaped the shawls of brocade and velvet in which she sat at a plain deal table, glinted too glossily to convince. She had a certain personality, a measure of human presence, and yet…

"Holmes," I said, "this is only a dummy. A figure in wax."

"One can not say 'only' of the Marvel of Montmartre," Holmes replied, with some theatrical relish. He pulled up a seat opposite the wax woman, and gazed at her expectantly. I was unprepared for what would come next. When the woman's arm rose, with the jerk of a marionette's, I nearly spilled my Lapsang.

In her upraised hand, the dummy clutched a fan of cards. Her head twitched, as though her blind gaze were shifting across the faces. Then her other hand gave a sudden leap, a grab, and an almost graceful swoop.

Holmes considered her action with a knitted brow, before selecting a card from a hand of his own.

For twenty minutes, by candlelight, I watched the pair of them play a strange form of Euchre. I watched Holmes beaten by the Marvel of Montmartre, and then turn to me with a look of triumph on his face.

"I liberated her from Meadowbank School whilst you were entertaining the Headmaster and his colleagues," he told me, "playing cards and all."

I took one of these and inspected it, having had an interest in card games during my own schooldays. "Fascinating," I exclaimed. "They are a French deck, known as the Tarot. They appear to be exceedingly old, as does –"

At that moment, the woman startled me by springing into action once more. She spread her own pack with a painter's grace, halted a long moment, and selected a particular card, which she proffered in my direction.

"A mind reading act as well!" I spluttered with nervous laughter. "*Je regrette, madame*, you are incorrect this time. One shouldn't ask for miracles, I suppose."

"Can you see how she is worked?"

"A puppeteer?" I suggested. "Or is she run on clockwork?"

"Very good," he said. "They were my first guesses too – but it seems not."

"Then how…?"

"I haven't the faintest idea, my old friend. The best I can say is that she was not under-sold in her billing at the Langham Hotel."

"But what of the Meadowbank schoolmasters? How did she come to pass into their keeping?" I asked.

"That is a misassumption on your part, Watson," he replied. "The wax card player has a longer career than I first realised. In summer she entertained the great men of British society, four of whom, incidentally, have been sought in vain these past months. Then she herself was gone without a trace, like the gentleman exhibiting her. There is no record of the Marvel before June, but I have uncovered details of a 'Madame Fantastique' who toured the seaside towns of the south coast in spring. And a correspondent of mine in Paris recalled a certain Magicienne des Cartes playing nightly last winter, at a nameless café in the queer part of town."

"I still don't follow, my dear chap."

"All you need remember is Mr Crawthew's weakness for exotic young men," Holmes replied, "and then we may ask the greater question of why Madame and her friend should conclude their tour in the ignominious seclusion of a London public school."

"It is one of our very best schools, Holmes," I volunteered, defensively.

"Certainly," he said, looking at me suddenly. "The staff may be reprehensible, but the boys are likely to become great men. Did our friends from Paris accept a few of them in lieu of payment?"

I shuddered at the thought. "Do you think it wise to keep the, uh, good woman, here at Baker Street?" I asked.

"I am happier knowing she is not at the school," Holmes replied. "I think the boys are safe now to enjoy their Christmas holiday. We, however, must be prepared for a visit of some kind."

But Holmes was wrong. Days went by, shortening like a candle. We sat up at night, expecting at any time a foot on the stair, a ring at the bell. We wrote to Tiger and his comrades, and by return heard only good news, even invitations to their carol service. Holmes rolled his eyes at the very thought, though to me it seemed a jolly prospect for two childless bachelors at the darkest time of the year. No trouble came to Baker Street.

Having, in my time, played many a skilful hand at whist, I came to enjoy – with a certain frisson – the presence of our companion. She was a formidable opponent, despite the placid look on her modelled features, and after a day of treating the winter ailments of my patients I would relish an evening pitting my wits against her. Holmes grew competitive, advancing from novice to adept in no time, researching the history and permutations of card play in the cause of understanding his adversary. She could compete ably in any game a player initiated, so long as it did not require her to speak or use cards other than her Tarot pack. The adventure seemed to have reached a happy, even festive conclusion, save that Mrs Hudson detested "that awful thing" and refused to enter the sitting-room unless it was draped in its bed-sheet.

And then there came a morning, not five days from Christmas morning, when the sun seemed barely interested in troubling the abysmal sky, and a haggard face greeted me at the breakfast table. Its eyes were cracked with red and underlined in grey.

"You've not slept," I said. "I suppose you were occupied in understanding Monsieur Tournier's broken Hunter pocket-watch."

"Sadly, the significance of that detail still eludes me," he said. "But Watson, I have made the strangest discovery. Last night, the Paris auto-icon read my future."

"You mean," I corrected him, pouring us coffee, "that she performed her singularly unimpressive mind reading act."

"Watson, it is we who have misread the cards." He had one with him, its face downward, its black-and-red pattern blazing against the green linen tablecloth. "The Tarot are more than an exotic deck of playing cards. They are customarily used by practitioners of divination."

"Fortune telling? Why yes, I have heard of that."

"You and I, the schoolboys of Meadowbank, the gentlemen of Westminster and holidaymakers of Hastings, all assumed the wax woman was entertaining us. In fact, she sat in judgement."

"Judgement? For what purpose? You are exhausted, Holmes."

"Last night, while you slept, we played the Jeu de Tarot, the antique game for which the deck was first used. I thought, perhaps, it might bring some aspect of her strange mechanism to the surface. At its conclusion, I laid down my cards, exhausted – but she proceeded with her act, irrespective of my action, laying down her deck and choosing a card. The card she chose, she has picked before, from the Major Arcana: *Justice*. Without thinking, I accepted it from her.

"I passed an unpleasant night. I am not sure that I dreamt or woke, but I seemed to be constantly preoccupied with the design on the card's reverse. It resembles a city, you see? Silhouetted against a sky, a field of towers and windows. And it seemed that there were faces at the windows – in fact, I almost seemed to hear a voice inviting me to join them."

"Holmes," I said, my mind whirling, "What can it mean?"

"It seems too obvious now," he replied. "Whoever operated the Marvel has been watching her actions closely, observing what readings she gives. The machinery must surely, of course, be random, but for the owner of the machine, her readings appear to have some meaning: presumably he is a member of some hermetic society to whom the Tarot have significance. And the ones favoured by Madame, they spirit away to France, for induction into their order."

"Taking only the most promising members of British society," I said, "like yourself."

"And prior to that, the *crème des Français*."

"It sounds most unlikely," I said. "The cost, the travel, and the sacrifice of a year…"

"A most unpleasant choice of words," scowled Holmes. "It is typical behaviour of the fervid, secret society. You mention the year, and here we stand on the brink of a new century. Precisely the time when such a cult would be most active."

I hesitated. "Holmes," I ventured, "mightn't there be more to this?

Countless men – perhaps even women – have been transported by persons unknown. That much seems clear. Mightn't they, however, have been removed by less earthly forces…?"

Holmes narrowed his red eyes at me. "You think that a more convincing theory than mine?"

"How else do you account for your experience last night?" I glanced up at the ceiling, thinking of the wax figure seated immobile in the room above. For a moment, I envisioned the ghastly spectacle of her wandering about the room in our absence, poring through our papers whilst listening for our return. "How, in fact, do you account for the Marvel herself? You have perused her for weeks and uncovered no single clue to her autonomy, her facility with cards, and now her particular understanding of cartomancy."

"I refuse, absolutely, to admit the possibility of some infernal force within the four walls of 221B Baker Street," the wretched detective muttered.

"Might that not be the very reason she was unsuccessful in luring you from this mortal plane?" I said.

By way of answer, Holmes picked up his boiled egg and hurled it in my direction. Fortunately, his tired mind caused him some disadvantage, and Mrs Hudson was not there to witness it.

"In any case," I said, once I had removed the offending stain, "you did well to remove that foul object from Meadowbank. I am still curious about the relations between Monsieurs Lemaitre and Tournier, and the violent death of the latter."

"Probably the petty jealousy of cult members," Holmes replied, desultorily sipping his coffee. "One or the other may have received a favourable reading from their mistress, or perhaps even a crisis of conscience. In either case, I must say it is good riddance."

"Your disregard for men of another stripe does you no credit, Holmes," I replied. "Lemaitre, whom I have met, and Tournier, whose reputation we have both heard, seem wholly charming individuals. Their device – if it is indeed theirs – as you will admit, is remarkable in the extreme, and by your own reckoning, they have committed no injury to anyone but themselves. Gentlemen of an unusual philosophy, maybe, but far from the evils we have elsewhere encountered."

"I doubt that Arnold Bragg, wheresoever he now finds himself, would agree with you," Holmes replied. "Tournier's worth as a schoolmaster is much improved by his exiting this mortal realm. Since it is so much on your mind, might I suggest that a stopped clock, like the master's, will at least tell the right time twice a day? The sooner we take Lestrade there, and expose their sorry escapade, the better."

"It might do well, at least, to wait a day or so until you are more composed," I replied. "The case you have put before me will not be so easy to lay before a plain-minded policeman."

Holmes looked again at the mysterious card of the wax clairvoyant. "You are right about that, if little else this morning, Watson," he said, holding his head in his hands. "Why, it might do us well to wait until the first of January and hope the last men of the outfit take their own glass of arsenic."

With that morbid thought expressed, he rose from the breakfast table and went to ascend the stair. As he lifted his right foot to climb, he froze, his fingers curled around the wooden handrail. I watched him stand there, apparently deep in thought. I began to think once more of the peculiar effigy lodged in our rooms, and imagined her there at the top of the stair, gazing down at him with glass eyes, her arms outstretched to abduct him.

I rose to go to his aid, but in an instant he had returned to me. "Watson," he said, "I think we would do well to return to Meadowbank College."

"Of course, Holmes," I said, thinking pleasantly of the choir service.

"Today, that is," he added. "This very hour. We cannot afford to lose any time at all. I will ask Mrs Hudson to wire the police in our absence. Put on your hat and gloves – yes, and your thickest boots. It will be quicker for us to go through the park than call a cab and circumnavigate it, and the snow will be deep."

"I doubt the park will yet be open," I said, in protest, but it did no good. Within five minutes, we were scaling the high, spiked fence, dropping down into depths of virginal snow, which glowed with an unearthly quality in the deep gloom of the morning.

I have considered the strangeness of that journey more than once in the intervening years, attempting to estimate whether Holmes's calculation was correct, and whether we should have sacrificed a little time in finding a cab, instead of this direct but oddly encumbered route, the snow slipping and sucking at every tread like wet sand and sea mist. Distantly, the multitudes composing the metropolis rumbled and clattered on their way; closer to, I heard the denizens of London Zoo squawking and lowing in the frozen air, like something from an exotically sourced Nativity scene.

At last we crossed the brow of Primrose Hill, and the school lay before us against an evil yellow sky. Holmes picked up his heels and tore up the gravelled drive in several long-legged springs. The door, this time, was locked. No answer came to his knocking on its stout beams.

Joining him, I could hear another sound, faintly. It was the voices of schoolboys and the old song of King Wenceslas. Holmes set off at an impatient stride around Meadowbank's grey, gothic walls. I followed, still uncomprehending, and at last we gained the tradesman's entrance, also barred but more susceptible to two men's stout winter footwear.

Holmes skidded through the hallways on his frost-laden footwear, at last gaining the school assembly hall, where the remains of Meadowbank were gathered innocently together in rehearsal for their choir concert. Both boys and masters looked surprised at our invasion of the proceedings, but the boys gamely continued with their song as Holmes approached Lemaitre, the French master, and spoke quietly with him. Afterwards, I learned that he was warning the man of his imminent arrest. Seconds later, two schoolmasters had restrained the detective. His head rolled wildly, but not in escape – he was briskly studying the room.

"Watson," he called. "By the piano. A tureen. Get it out of here."

The Headmaster moved to stop me, but I was fortunately too quick for him, and scooped up the dish, making for the door as quickly as I could without dropping it. A boiled mixture within made the silverware hot to the touch, but since I still had on my gloves I held it with ease. The liquid within rocked and bubbled, and I could already smell the suspicious aroma of almonds amidst fumey notes of cloves and mulled wine.

Other schoolmasters stampeded to prevent me leaving the room, but at that moment, the boys abandoned their singing, and raced as one to assault their elders and defend me from their brute strength and immoral conviction.

Nevertheless, had the London constabulary not, at that minute, answered Mrs Hudson's urgent message and arrived to aid us, it is difficult to say how that winter solstice day might have concluded. We had not reckoned, Holmes or myself, on so many of the school staff (only, in fact, excepting their Headmaster) being members of that weird apocalyptic cult. Nor, though they did not appear to be armed with anything but their infernal beverage, could it be imagined what lengths the members would have gone to, to ensure their *fin-de-siècle* ritual.

"I have read of other cults in their ilk," Holmes explained afterward, to myself and the boys, as we all took a restoring cup of chocolate in the restaurant of the Langham Hotel. "They believe in a coming apocalypse, the snuffing out of the world on the last day of this century."

At this point, I began to argue that the twentieth century would surely not begin until 1901, but Tiger and co. overwhelmed me, begging their true master to explain his deductive process.

"A stopped clock, we know, is right twice a day," he replied, sipping his chocolate. "Specifically, it tells us the hour it stopped. In breaking his own watch as he passed into eternal oblivion, Tournier was able to demonstrate to his brethren, entirely covertly, the potency of their poison in their chosen disguise. The suicide note, of course, would describe the exact time he took the mixture.

"Watson argued eloquently this morning for the benevolence of your schoolmasters, and I must admit that their plans for today were meant as a kindness, to spare you from the earthquakes and rivers of fire they no doubt anticipated shortly."

"Zounds," cried Tiger, "but we've had a close shave. One can't but wonder, however, what the dooce happened to Arnold Bragg? Did he stumble across their ungodly scheme? Does his body lie somewhere in the grounds of the school, beneath these banks of snow?"

"Opinion is divided on the matter," I said, but received such a look from my friend that I retreated behind a café menu.

"It certainly strikes me as highly unlikely," replied Holmes. "I believe Bragg – and, probably, certain other boys who did not have the fortune to be missed – were the object of Lemaitre and his brethren, together with men of London, Sussex and Paris itself. Whether they have been smuggled out of London or off this earthly plane altogether will be established following the questioning of our friends."

Unhappily, in what proved to be Holmes's third error of this tale, the brethren never spoke of Arnold Bragg's final whereabouts. Through fair means or foul, they were each of them finally successful in the modest taking of their own lives whilst still in police custody, and took the secret of the wax card player with them to their graves. I must admit to feeling a strange excitement on the night of December 31st, as the chimes of Big Ben resounded through the capital and a new year swept away the old, the peculiar unspoken secrets of Meadowbank College along with them.

As for that weird effigy herself, though Mrs Hudson strenuously denied it, I believe she made arrangements for the sale of that Marvel of Montmartre to a passing rag-and-bone man whilst Holmes and I were both walking to the school. Holmes made some fruitless attempts to regain the effigy, visiting all manner of curiosity shops and esoteric bookshops, from Coptic Street to Whitechapel, before admitting the loss of her – into what hands, we could not guess.

Mr Crawthew, that lynchpin of the tale, returned to his role at Meadowbank and remained Headmaster into the earlier twentieth century without comment from any quarter. Whether he enjoyed any further adventures beyond the bounds of respectability, one can only imagine…

The pencil is still at last. The silence of the room appears to seethe. I come to, and realise I have been standing at the woman's elbow as her hand worked, feverishly, and apparently outside of her own control.

I don't know what to say about the story she has laid before me. I've never heard such an unlikely tale. Did she really dredge it from the river-muck of time, or merely her own, strange memory?

"Thank you," I murmur, my lips paper dry. "That is, Merci beaucoup."

My escort has been reading alongside me. Now he lays a fine-boned hand on my shoulder, the weight of a leaf. "One moment," he says, goes to the door and closes it. "I am not at all certain you can be allowed to leave with that story."

A cold dread fills my stomach, but I try to remain calm, and suppressing the thoughts that are already making themselves clear in my mind, I ask, "Why ever not?"

The young man lights a candle. "It is without precedent, I am afraid. As Dr Watson says, there are some names that must be protected." He places the candle on the woman's desk. "What say you, Madame?"

I do not want to look down, as she turns her eyes toward me. I know already the face I will see, the placid, carefully shaped features, unmarked by the flow of time. I look away as she lays down her pencil, rises stiffly from the table, and turns her sightless eyes upon me.

ABOUT THE AUTHOR

Nick Campbell is a writer and research student living in South London. Short stories of his are published by Obverse Books, including adventures with Iris Wildthyme and uncanny entries in *Shenanigans* and *Storyteller* (edited by Paul Magrs and Stuart Douglas respectively). He keeps a blog about books at leaf-pile.blogspot.co.uk and can't play cards to save his life.

THE CASE OF THE DEVIL'S DOOR

BY JAMES GOSS

I have met many different kinds of murderer during my adventures with my friend Sherlock Holmes, but I had never before encountered a house that killed people.

This singular case first came to my attention while I was on my rounds, when a running boy accosted me in some excitement. He bore a note summoning me to Baker Street. I hastily finished my last call and hurried there.

"What kept you, Watson?" my friend snapped as I was about to knock on the door, having taken the stairs two at a time.

"My last patient," I huffed. "The poor fellow's case was a mortal one." I stepped into the room.

"And so might this fellow be, Watson, thanks to your delay." Holmes was stood at the mantelpiece, gesturing towards the occupant of a chair by the fire. Barely had I noticed him when I sprang to his side, taking his temperature and pulse.

The man was in some distress. His skin, naturally olive in complexion, was drained of blood, his eyes were unfocused, and his hands clenched as spasms shook along his arms.

"What's happened to him?" I exclaimed.

"If you had got here sooner," retorted Holmes, "then I would know."

I was just beginning to protest, when he held up his hands, mollifying me. "Just do your best, Watson. He burst in upon me this morning, and such words as he has spoken are Spanish in origin and supernatural in nature."

I administered a sedative, and the patient sank into a brief doze. I took the opportunity to observe him. Aware of Holmes's eyes upon me, I started to describe the man.

"I should say he is in his early thirties. Extremely dirty and dishevelled –"

"Indeed?"

"But the clothes that he wears are good. Or were. Perhaps he has fallen on hard times?"

A gentle cluck of reproof. "The grime, Watson, is on the outside of the garments, not the body. A cursory examination of the back of his neck would reveal the shirt to be freshly laundered and worn against clean skin."

"So this is the result of some kind of attack?"

"Perhaps. Notice the marks on the knees and the scuffing of the palms. He has fallen over several times and righted himself. There are no bruises on his face, nor are the marks on his hands consistent with trying to protect himself from a beating. I would reckon…"

My friend fell silent. The giant brain behind his eyes was moving words as judiciously as a Chinese emperor constructing a *Mah Jong* wall. "Our patient here has been running for his life for a prolonged period. But from whom?"

I looked at him questioningly, and he rammed his hands into the pockets of his dressing-gown. "No, Watson, you would like me to describe the demons of his rantings – but I shall not. Those may remain the sincere conviction of our client. Ah, he awakes. The brandy, I think!"

Our patient stirred. He flinched, as though surprised to find himself in his surroundings and looked at us both for an explanation. My friend stepped forward, genuinely keen to learn facts to feed the racing engine of his mind.

"My name is Sherlock Holmes, and this is my friend Dr Watson. You may remember calling on me in considerable agitation?"

The man nodded. "My apologies," he muttered. "The devils have not found me?"

"No," Holmes shook his head, his tone soothing, "You are safe here. Now please, tell me your story."

The man frowned. His accent was thick, but his English was cultured. He shook himself like a dog, and then began. But his opening words were surprising. "The house – it tried to devour me!"

At some urging from my friend, our client began his story from the beginning. His name was Mendoza, and he hailed from that troubled Central American state of San Pedro. Recently, a counter revolutionary party called the Sons of the Tiger had swept to power, crushing the people under a new wave of brutality and darkness.

Fearing for the safety of his family, Mendoza had wished to return home. For an exile to do so openly was death, but word had spread among the *expatriate* community of an underground railroad that conveyed San Pedrans into their homeland in utter secrecy.

Mendoza had vowed to undertake this perilous journey. The voyage was said to be exceedingly dangerous, and many spoke out against it, preferring to risk an open sailing, or agitating for change from the safety of Europe.

"But I am a man of courage," Mendoza struck himself proudly on the breast, before collapsing his own bravado, "or at least, I believed myself to be, until the events of last night." He recounted how he had made contact with someone who had delivered him instructions of where to be, and at what hour. He was to embark without saying a proper farewell to friends, relations, or loved ones. As he described this, I had a sudden sharp memory.

It was of a woman, very prettily attired, sat in that same chair, sobbing hopelessly into a handkerchief. She was an heiress, and had called on Holmes just over a month ago, begging him to undertake an investigation into the sudden disappearance of her fiancé. Something struck a chord in my mind – had he not also been from San Pedro? I glanced across at my friend, and caught his slight nod. He was, as always, ahead of me.

Mendoza's narrative continued. "I will not elaborate the full details of the chain, as I fear it would bore you." Holmes gave him a sharp glance, and assured him that he had never been bored by details.

Mendoza became hesitant. "What I am about to tell you... you must remember, señors, that my country, my people, spans both the modern and ancient worlds. Some of our largest cities are built around ancient temples, cathedrals adjacent to altars where human sacrifices were once made. Some of the remoter tribes practise voodoo, and our late tyrant Don Murillo was said to have many demons on the payroll." His smile was grim. "I tell you this... because you are both rational men of the modern world. I wear your clothes, but you may easily dismiss me as a credulous fool. True, I was raised to believe in devils, ghosts and curses, but still, as an adult, I have no doubt of what happened to me last night..."

Holmes could, on occasion, be brusque, but he could also show surprising tact. "Rest assured, you will find a sympathetic reception here. Please, tell us where this supernatural attack took place."

"In Bayswater," said Mendoza.

If Holmes was surprised, it showed in little more than a twitch under one eyebrow. Mendoza explained that the start of his perilous journey was to be in London's embassy district, at the doors of the Consulate of Atoria, the neighbouring state to San Pedro. "There are," said Mendoza, "Many Atorians who remember the military aggression of our hated Tiger, and are in no hurry to see San Pedro return to a warlike footing."

He was told to report to the embassy in Leinster Gardens half an hour before midnight. He was warned not to visit the street earlier, for fear of being seen by the many spies of the new regime. "It was feared that they knew of the existence of the underground railroad," Mendoza permitted himself a bitter laugh, "but how... how it can have been taken over by demons... I do not know how they could..." He took a sip of brandy and shook his head again, as though trying to throw the nightmare free.

"It was a warm night, and the street itself was empty. The gates to Hyde Park had been shut, and any tourists had wandered home. I felt nervous as I approached the embassy, the flags of Atoria floating outside, seeming to offer me welcome. I knew that, once inside, I could look forward to a long and arduous journey, but I was excited – I would be going home, to make the land I loved well again." Mendoza paused, pride mingling with a reluctance to continue.

"I stepped closer to the embassy, and felt a momentary worry – its windows were dark. Perhaps it was closed for the night? And yet, I knocked at the door. There was no answer. I stood and waited, feeling all the time that I was about to be seized by padfooted assassins. But the only eyes watching me were the dark eyes of the embassy windows. And so, my heart in my mouth, I knocked again.

"I had been warned that, if I received no answer, I was to turn the door handle myself. I did so. I could make out few details of the hallway beyond, save a light at the end of it, and the impression of some picture frames ranged along the walls. I called out, softly, using the code word…"

Mendoza paused, and gasped. A sweat had broken out on his forehead, and I swiftly refilled his glass. He gulped at it, and continued, his accent thicker than before.

"As I spoke, it was as though I had summoned all the demons from hell. I stepped over the threshold, and plunged into the jaws of the underworld. It was truly, truly as though I was inside the mouth of a monster. A sulphurous roar erupted around me, and the most foul breath engulfed me. There was no floor, only the maw of that terrible beast. As I fell, I grabbed at the door handle. For a few seconds, I hung over the abyss, my senses assaulted by the hungry cries and screams around me, and then I flung myself back out, clawing and terrified onto the pavement. I was outside the embassy again, but the sounds, those terrible hell creatures I had unleashed, beat around me still, and I ran, heedless… running for hours, falling and screaming, until at last I tumbled senseless into an alleyway. When I came to, dawn was breaking, and I was amazed to find both body and soul intact. And yet, wherever I looked, I could sense those creatures. So I ran to your house, Mr Holmes. I had heard much of you – I did not dare trouble my countrymen (for it is clear that we are betrayed) and I worried that the police would laugh at me… and I feared that I was not in my right wits. I wonder… I wonder if I am now?" Mendoza looked up, startled. "Did you hear that, señors? They are come again!"

As his lunacy broke upon him afresh, I stepped in with another dose of sedative, and he lapsed into a fitful slumber.

Holmes regarded our patient. "Well, Watson, what do you make of it?"

"Perhaps he really has been chased by demons... but there are other theories, I'm afraid. As much as he says he wishes to go home, he may secretly be terrified of the consequences, and have summoned these fantasies into vivid life around him."

Half-expecting a rebuke, I instead received a friendly clap across the shoulders. "You are a commendable rationalist, Watson." Holmes seized his hat from the rack. "For myself, I rather fancy heading out to capture a demon house."

A short journey in the foetid air of the Metropolitan Railway brought us to the leafy streets of Bayswater, identical avenues of white-stuccoed buildings stretching between Hyde Park and the fairytale pavilion of Whiteley's department store.

We reached Leinster Gardens, and Holmes stopped. He swung his walking stick up and down the street and then turned to me.

"What do you see, Watson? Or rather," a small smile, "what do you not see?"

I wrinkled my eyes against the morning glare. The sun reflecting from the endless white plasterwork was a trifle blinding.

"Well, Holmes," I hesitated. I was always nervous. Like a man crossing a river on stepping stones, I knew I would, at some point, miss my footing. Every time I approached the stream more cautiously, my footsteps more ginger than the time before. This time, however, I felt sure of my ground. "The one thing I cannot see on this street is the Atorian Embassy."

Holmes nodded. "It's a long street, Watson. It may still surprise us."

We made our way up the serried white ranks. I found myself counting off the numbers as we passed grand residences and businesses, a public house breaking up the monotony like a stained tooth in an otherwise immaculate row of dentures.

Finally, hopelessly, we reached number 24 Leinster Gardens. Or rather, we reached its absence. A hiccup in the postal service. Number 23 was a promising-smelling Greek restaurant. And next door, Numbers 25 and 26 were a handsome-fronted hotel. The Clarion spread out along the street, from its grandiose entrance to a tea garden, its tables covered by gaily fluttering sun parasols. It was an oasis of tranquil gentility on a street already suffused with tranquil gentility. It was impossible to believe Leinster Gardens could be the home of supernatural horror.

The one hope was a narrow alleyway between the restaurant and the hotel, scarcely large enough to fit a carriage. I caught Holmes's glance at it.

"Could they…?" and I stopped. I felt my feet yet again placing their balance on a mossy stone. "Could someone have perhaps constructed something in the alleyway at night… and…"

The sheer preposterousness of the notion forced me to stop before I plunged into the burn.

To my surprise, Holmes fixed me with a smile. "It is a capital notion, Watson. Extravagant, but sound. The one flaw…" His walking stick rang out against the cobbles of the alleyway. "As you can hear, solid road. No gaping satanic maw." His lips thinned.

"Then perhaps this alleyway was once the site of a house," I persisted. "One which…" Again, the slippery stone.

Holmes continued my perilous train. "The ghost of that house returns to haunt the street at night, pretending to be an embassy and devouring exiled revolutionaries?"

We stood in silence, contemplating the alleyway.

"It is, I grant you Watson, a possibility that has some merits." I could not tell how dry my companion was being.

"I have another suggestion," I said, surer of my footing.

"Of course you do," said Holmes, looking up at the windows of the hotel.

"These streets all look very much alike, and have very similar names. Could not poor Mendoza in his confusion have mistaken one for another? The Atorian Embassy could still be somewhere hereabouts, or he could have mistaken another house for it. One which —" Something caught in my throat and I coughed.

Yet Holmes smiled. "A suggestion that warrants some investigation. Let us have a stroll around the area before returning to the hotel for tea."

I could not help but wonder if he was humouring me.

Our exploration of Bayswater yielded several promising hints, but nothing solid. We found several embassies with flags outside them. Using his name and reputation, Holmes gained entry, leaving me idling on the pavement until he returned, each time with a brief shake of the head. "We can, of course, discount Bulgaria, Sicily and Indonesia as being nowhere near, or having any real links to, Central America. But it was worth enquiring at their embassies."

"And what did you ask them, Holmes?"

"Why, if they had tried to eat any interesting people lately, of course!" Holmes clapped me on the shoulder. "Come Watson, let's go and have tea. I feel we deserve it."

The Clarion Hotel seeped respectability. The carpets of the lobby were plush and mossy. The brasswork was as brightly polished as the buttons on the bellboy's jacket. A smiling receptionist greeted us like old friends, and dealt with our enquiries as though he were often being asked the location of the Atorian Embassy. He answered in the negative with genuine regret, and then asked if there was anything further he could do for us, and professed himself delighted when Holmes asked if we could take refreshments outside.

We sat in the tea garden and watched the world go by. Precious little world goes by in Bayswater. The streets are sleepy by day and comatose at night. A perfume of calm hangs over the area. The only times it approached bustle were the endlessly revolving doors of Whiteley's, and the occasional whistle of a passing train. The horrors that Mendoza had described seemed far away from the languid afternoon around us.

The tea provided by the Clarion was excellent, but Holmes took little interest in it, his hands feeling their way indifferently among the sandwiches while he stole birdlike glances at the roofs around us, occasionally drawing my attention to how well-tended the hotel's window boxes were, and what a good showing of geraniums they had put on. If it struck me as trivia, I did not remark on it. I knew full well that many of my friend's best triumphs had been found among such minutiae as geraniums.

Eventually, Holmes pushed aside his plate and smiled at me.

"You have it, don't you, Holmes?" I asked.

He permitted himself a nod. "We have overlooked one detail, Watson. Our helpful receptionist would, of course, know nothing of what transpired, because the horrors of Mendoza took place near the witching hour. The receptionist's place would be taken by the night porter."

He swept back into the hotel while I settled the bill. When he returned, he looked satisfied.

"Are we coming back to question the night porter, Holmes?"

"No. His surname told me all I needed to know." Holmes began striding back towards Whiteley's.

"Indeed?" I found myself asking his back.

"Armentia."

"What does it mean?"

Holmes did not stop. "I don't know the exact derivation. But it is a clue to the terrors inflicted on our client. And, if I am right, on many other people. The tiger's roar may be heard long after his death, Watson." He strode through Bayswater, his chin set grimly. "To think that this has all been a lethal —" He tried to locate the exact phrase. "I think it is best called an impractical joke." He paused outside Whiteley's, grimness banished like a summer cloud. "Come, let us see if we cannot buy some soap as a gift for Mrs Hudson. I fear she has an arduous few days ahead thanks to her terrible lodgers."

Holmes spoke the truth. From that point on his hours became even more erratic, and his appearances and disappearances saw him coming and going in a variety of costumes and disguises. I devoted myself to my patients, and to supervising the recovery of Mendoza. Placed in a spare room of Mrs Hudson's, his health improved remarkably, although his night terrors required constant sedation, otherwise his cries would stir the entire household.

Holmes himself spent many hours closeted with him, and I would often hear the two of them talking and laughing animatedly, only for them to fall silent when I entered. I made no bones about feeling mildly disgruntled, but Holmes, in a rare attempt at mollification, explained that my arrival broke his concentration.

"Don't apologise, John," he told me, airily, "it is simply that you interrupt my flow of thought. Mendoza and I are, after all, conversing in Spanish."

"I did not know you spoke Spanish!" I exclaimed.

"I do now," replied Holmes.

One evening I returned from my rounds to find an elaborately moustachioed prospector taking up the best chair.

"Hullo, Holmes," I sighed.

"Watson," nodded the stranger. "As you perceive, I am every tea-stained inch the San Pedran exile. It would be so much easier if Mendoza were to take me into his society, but he must, for the moment, remain in seclusion. If it were known that he had survived his ordeal, then my appearance among the exiles would raise suspicions. For there are traitors among them, those still faithful to the memory of Don Murillo, the vile Tiger of San Pedro whose rule was distinguished by superstition and cruelty. I have become quite the expert on the politics of the region. The counter revolutionaries call themselves the Sons of the Tiger, and their reign has seen an increase in unholy and unnatural practice. It is this background of voodoo and sacrifice that has nurtured the notion of a devil house –" Holmes paused, "– in Mendoza's mind."

I was startled. "You mean that Mendoza himself is in on it?"

Holmes shook his head. "Merely that our friend was all too eager to place a supernatural inference on events which, gruesome as they are, are all too natural." Holmes cracked his knuckles. "I have done good work these last few days. I have spun a tale, Watson, that would pluck at the heartstrings of any valiant San Pedran. It is a tale of my homestead despoiled by the Sons of the Tiger; my heartbreak at the separation from my childhood sweetheart, who has written to me in terrible adversity, just one word: 'Come'. And so, like the firebrand I am, I shall return to liberate my country from the cruel oppression it has fallen into once more!"

He had struck a heroic pose. "Watson, there are some suitable clothes, moustachioes and a mountaineering rope in the next door room. Prepare yourself, for tonight we ride the underground railroad to San Pedro, to liberty and to freedom."

Had Holmes been wrong… had Holmes been wrong, there is every chance that we would have ended up in San Pedro. Knowing my friend, he would have then liberated the place single-handed. And that would perhaps have been no bad thing. But Holmes was not wrong. He was never wrong.

Our evening was arduous. We went from seedy bar to dingy club. We gathered around scrubbed deal tables, we stood on sawdust-strewn floors. All the time, my friend was transformed, speaking the rough and ready dialect of the streets of San Pedro. I hung back, my false whiskers drooping to the floor while Holmes hectored, lectured, pleaded and crusaded. He was clearly known to these people and treasured by them. At one stop, it was only the low ceiling that stopped them from raising him on their shoulders and cheering him around the room.

And the drinking! I knew the directions in which Holmes's vices took him, and they were never towards alcohol. He would take an occasional, appreciative glass, but I had never seen him drunk. But tonight he drank like a shipful of sailors. He sank glass after glass of the amber fire of San Pedro, and then he danced, whirling the women around with boisterous, passionate dexterity. I marvelled – not merely at the disguise, but at the sheer exuberance this swarthy revolutionary was displaying. I had seen Sherlock Holmes do many things, but I had never before seen him have fun.

It was clear that each watering hole, each basement was another step towards embarkation. Much was made of the brave journey the two of us were to undertake.

No one questioned why I did not speak, although, after Holmes reeled off a stream of words in my favour, the result was applause and a solid bear of a man wiped away a tear (Holmes later explained he had told them solemnly that I had vowed not to speak another word until I was on the soil of the motherland). I simply stood back, and watched his bravura performance, and tried not to drink too much of the amber fire.

I worried – what if my friend had forgot himself, and walked, reeling drunk, into the very jaws of death?

Finally, at a little after ten, we found ourselves standing in a rank-smelling cellar. In front of us a small, severe man stood under the green and the white, the colours of San Pedro. The man stepped up to Holmes, and pressed a single card into my friend's hand. Holmes pocketed it, then shook him by the hand. I did likewise. The grim little man saluted. We left.

Holmes stood outside, swaying slightly, and clasped me like a brother-in-combat. Arms locked as comrades, we staggered down the street, whistling the anthem of San Pedro. I might almost have missed my friend's whisper in my ear, "Say nothing. We are observed."

We walked on. A hansom for hire passed, but my friend's grip tightened before I could hail it. "We do not want to arouse suspicion." I wondered at that – was it so unlikely that two revolutionaries would hire a cab? But Holmes had his answer prepared. "Try as we might to conceal it, we would hail a cab as Englishmen, and our disguise would be for naught. The last thing I want is to be clubbed to death by the very people I am trying to save."

I saw the wisdom of his words, but I also saw a long walk ahead of us.

"Nonsense, Watson. This is Kennington. It is a little after half past ten, it is a warm evening, and we can be in Bayswater in time for our appointment. Besides, you could do with a little fresh air to clear your head."

There was no streetlamp to tell me whether or not my friend was smiling.

* * *

Although Kennington is by the river, its complicated intersecting roads baffled even Holmes, and we lost some time before we made the Strand. However, we cut through Hyde Park and, with only a little hurrying, arrived at Leinster Gardens just in time for our appointment.

The street was empty, the public house and restaurant closed, even the hotel's windows were darkened, the gay parasols of the tea garden drawn up for the night, surrounded by a neat array of bay trees in their tubs and boxed geraniums. I paid them little notice.

Instead, my attention was riveted by the remarkable apparition which confronted us.

I stood, I gaped, I shook my head.

Holmes himself held up the card he had been handed:

CONSULATE OF ATORIA
24, LEINSTER GARDENS
LONDON W1

There, ahead of us, was the Atorian Embassy. A light swung from the porch illuminating the bronze plaque on the door. Two Atorian flags fluttered in welcome.

I was astounded, and this time it was my hand that gripped Holmes's arm tightly. We had summoned it, and somehow the embassy had appeared out of nowhere. A grim foreboding seized me – what if Mendoza's fears were supernatural in origin after all?

On impulse I made to snatch the card from my friend's hand and throw it away, but he pocketed it, laughing.

"Oh, Watson! Our good intentions have led us to this spot – and here is the road to hell, freshly paved."

We walked forward towards the impossible building. As we trod on, my friend dropped to the ground, seemingly to tie a shoelace. He bobbed back up again, holding something to the porch light. "Sawdust," he said. "A little, but significant. Remember my instructions and be prepared."

I realised this was merely an attempt to distract me from the door in front of us. Black, like so many on that street, and yet somehow sinister. The door knocker itself looked demonic. Holmes seized it and rapped smartly once, twice, three times.

There was no reply.

Holmes gripped the sizeable bronze doorknob and twisted it. The door sprung open, the hinges well oiled.

Beyond was every appearance of an ordinary hallway. I could see a light at the end of it. I could even glimpse the darkened picture frames ranged along the wall.

"All seems well," I whispered.

"Indeed," said Holmes. It was a question. He stepped over the threshold, and all hell broke loose.

Holmes vanished, snatched away from me. As he went, I heard the terrible stentorian roar of some great, ravenous beast, and the hot, charnel stench of its breath consumed me. I felt myself toppling, tumbling into the endless hunger…

Then I remembered my instructions from Holmes. More by instinct than conscious thought, I had braced myself against the doorframe. I felt a tremendous pull, seizing me and hauling me inward and downwards, but I resisted the terrible strength as best I could.

The demonic howling and the piercing screams of lost souls subsided and I found myself, still struggling to grip on to the doorframe, my head giddy at the cloying stench.

For a second I was able to savour the silence.

And then a voice called out to me from the darkness.

"Watson, dear fellow, are you all right?"

I came to. "Holmes? Are you well?"

"Perfectly," echoed the answer. "Is the rope pinching?"

"It is, I have to admit, tight around my chest, and pulling me somewhat."

"My apologies. I'll try and find a foothold… ah, there we are. Better?"

"Much, thank you."

"I'll climb back up. I'm very grateful. I suspected this, but… ah, we needed to endure the ordeal to prove it."

Holmes's head appeared above the doorstep and he clambered back out from the abyss into which he'd vanished.

"What is this place?" I asked him once he was upright and had freed himself from the mountaineering rope that joined us.

In answer to my question, Holmes produced a lantern and lit it, waving it around the embassy hallway. The hallway had no floor. Just a vast darkness. The picture frames, under Holmes's lantern, showed themselves to be distant windows in the wall. And the lantern at the end of the hall was simply a light placed on a hook in a bare brick wall. At my friend's suggestion, I looked up and to the sides.

The Atorian Embassy was not a real house at all. Simply a wall.

I took a step back and looked up at the housefront. The windows were simply painted squares. The building was a facade disguised to look like a house.

"Who, who could have put this here?" I demanded.

Holmes laughed. "The Metropolitan Railway."

And so Holmes explained the workings of the deadly, impractical joke. The underground railroad was a literal underground railway. When the line was extended to Bayswater station, a house was demolished in order to build it, and in its place a facade was erected to avoid disrupting the aesthetic beauty of the street. Behind it a vent was needed to exhaust the noxious fumes from the steam engines. The fearsome noise and the hot air were made by passing late night trains.

"And the stench?" I asked.

"I am afraid," Holmes was grim, "that is the only authentic bit of the enterprise. The vent is blocked by quite a few honest San Pedrans. You yourself remarked on the smell when we alighted at Bayswater the other day."

"So, who is behind this?"

Holmes nodded. "Someone installed the door in the facade. And, when the trap was to be sprung, fixed the number on the door, unlocked it and lit the fake light in the hallway."

"But how did we not notice it?"

Holmes gestured up and down the street. "You remarked earlier how all these buildings look alike. By day, the hotel extends itself to take up the space of three housefronts with its tea garden. It even places geraniums on the window sills to make the facade look part of the hotel – after all, it makes the hotel look impressively larger. And then, at night, it is the job of the night porter to dismantle the tea garden. Of course, on evenings when the trap is to be set, the night porter – surnamed Armentia, a Son of the Tiger, no doubt – pulls the garden furniture in a little, takes down some of the geraniums, and turns a couple of parasol posts into flagpoles."

"Ah," I said. There seemed little else to say.

"And now," said Holmes, "we can warn our revolutionary friends about the traitors in their midst, and, once this false trail is closed, they can genuinely go about reclaiming their homeland. I wish them luck. But first, Watson, I think we should invite our friend Armentia to tea. At Scotland Yard."

ABOUT THE AUTHOR

James Goss lived on Leinster Gardens for nearly three years, and it was two years before he noticed the ghost houses. He's been unable to stop telling people about them ever since. He's written several *Doctor Who* and *Torchwood* books, two radio dramas, and stage plays.

The Adventure of the Coin of the Realm

⌒୨୧⌒

BY WILLIAM PATRICK MAYNARD & ALEXANDRA MARTUKOVICH

"**M**an overboard!"

Sherlock Holmes and I were strolling along the deck on our way back to our cabins following dinner when the call rang out. A Chinese porter was pulling on the bell as he repeated the terrible cry.

"Man overboard!"

By the time we reached his side, the deck was crowded with crew and passenger alike. Anxious eyes scanned the dark, roaring waves for some sign of life, but there was nothing to see.

"Who was it, Charlie?" Mr Blither, the first mate, growled.

"Charlie no see. Man fall."

The mate grabbed the Chinaman by the collar and twisted it until the porter's neck turned a bright crimson from the pressure.

"If Charlie no see, how come he say man fall, eh?"

The porter gently peeled the first mate's fingers loose from his collar as if they were banana skins.

"Charlie hear splash. See body go underwater. Charlie sure, you betchum."

The big man scanned the waters for a full minute, searching for proof of what the little Chinaman had claimed, but the waters gave no answer in response save the crashing waves that continued to rock the side of the ship.

"Bah!" Mr Blither roughly pushed the porter aside. "Be on your business. He doesn't know what he's talking about."

As the small crowd of interested faces began to disperse, Holmes stepped forward, clearing his throat.

"Would it be too much to ask a count of all passengers and crew members be taken?"

The mate glared at him until he noted the murmurs of consent from the other passengers whose interest had been rekindled by my friend's boldness.

"Certainly sounds reasonable," I added, nodding my head to the others in agreement.

"Bloody land-lubbers," Mr Blither grumbled, "alright then, let's have a head count."

As I stood upon deck watching the dark waves smashing against the side of the ship, my mind turned back to how different my expectations of our return voyage had been when Sherlock Holmes and I had first boarded the *Presumption* in New York five days before. At the time, I was eager to return home having exhausted both my finances and my patience indulging my friend's theatrical whims to their fullest. I was irritable and homesick and my thoughts were directed entirely inward. I now felt a pang of remorse as a sense of dread descended upon the ship as if the very spectre of Death itself had settled over us like a passing storm.

"It's Tyler, Captain. Milton Tyler has gone missing."

Mr Blither's voice cracked as he spoke. The big man's face was strained and showed a sense of helplessness as he looked from the porter he had unjustly bullied to the stern countenance of Captain Jamison, who had appeared by his side while my mind was lost in thought.

Instantly, I regretted my lack of charity in ignoring my fellow passengers. I hadn't a clue which of our small group had been the unfortunate Mr Tyler. Holmes quickly turned to me as if he had heard my unspoken thoughts.

"Tyler was one of the coin dealers. Roughly fifty-five years of age. Thinning grey hair streaked with white. Youngish face with a mouth turned downwards in a perpetual frown. Trim. He walked with a pronounced limp."

I nodded absently, recalling the man precisely as Holmes had described him. I recollected seeing him in conversation with one of the other passengers only yesterday morning over breakfast.

"Well, what are you going to do about this, Captain?" a stout, unpleasant fellow piped up from among our small crowd.

Captain Jamison turned his attention to the man who had spoken.

"I'll tell you what I am going to do about it. I'm confining the lot of you to quarters. I don't need a lot of blundering fools underfoot when I already have one *accident* to manage."

The fellow stood there, red-faced, and then turned to leave with the rest of them when Holmes stepped forward once more.

"Kindly spare me a moment of your time, Captain. I am Mr Sherlock Holmes of Baker Street. I am a consulting detective by trade with a private practice in London. It may be that you have heard of me. I have proven rather successful in assisting the official police on a number of interesting cases that my friend, Dr Watson here has committed to print."

Captain Jamison glowered at the two of us.

"No, I've not heard of you, Mr Sherlock Holmes and I don't have the time or the inclination to spend my days reading any *interesting* stories. While we are at sea, this is not a matter for the official police and as such I have no use for any unofficial consulting detective. Now… if you and your doctor friend would be so good as to return to your cabins as I have asked, I may be able to determine exactly what has happened to our missing passenger."

"What a rude man!" I said as Holmes and I turned back toward our cabins leaving the rather unpleasant captain to his equally sullen mate.

Holmes chuckled quietly, but spoke not a word in response.

I had just settled down at the writing table and begun recording my notes of what had transpired that evening when my peace was disturbed by a knock at the door of my cabin. I crossed the room and opened the door and was surprised to find Charlie, the Chinese porter who had sounded the alarm. He staggered towards me as the door opened.

"Good Heavens!" I cried as he stumbled into my cabin and collapsed upon the floor.

He sputtered and choked, gasping for breath as I hurriedly took his pulse.

"I saw… no man," he wheezed and then his head lolled back against my bent legs.

The light faded from his eyes and was replaced with the terrible glassy stare of death. I could do nothing to revive him. He had given up the ghost.

I rose to my feet and crossed the corridor and pounded furiously on the door of the cabin opposite mine.

"Holmes! I need you. You must rouse yourself at once!"

The cabin door opposite mine was thrown open a few seconds later. My friend stood there in his bathrobe, hair askew, pipe clenched firmly between his teeth. Without a word, he followed me across to my cabin, quickly shutting and locking my cabin door behind him. He knelt down by the dead man and immediately assessed the situation. I dashed for my medical bag next to my bed and had returned to Holmes's side in mere seconds.

"Did he say anything, Watson?"

My mind reeled for a moment as I struggled to recall the exact sequence of those unexpected events.

"Yes… he said that he saw no one. That was it, I'm afraid."

Holmes looked at me intently and puffed at his pipe.

"The question, Watson, becomes whether he was speaking of his own murder or of Milton Tyler's. There is little doubt the two incidents are linked."

I shook my head. "Not this time I think, Holmes. Look at his pupils. They're dilated. He was an opium-user. Let us see here." I unbuttoned the dead man's left sleeve and rolled it up past the elbow. "Needle marks! The man had a number of dirty habits, it seems. One of them cost him his life."

Holmes gave a thin smile in response to my harsh words against one with whom he shared the same despicable vice.

"Did it, Watson? I wouldn't care to wager on that conclusion just yet if I were you. Come along. We'd best inform Captain Jamison immediately."

As expected, the captain was furious that his porter had died in a passenger's cabin. However, I felt somewhat vindicated that he accepted my medical opinion that the man had died the victim of his own foul habit. After hearing my conclusion, Captain Jamison's attitude seemed to soften and he appeared grateful to have me aboard ship. There are times, I reflected, that Holmes, for all of his brilliance, is prone to the melodramatic and too easily convinced that every unfortunate circumstance must be the result of foul play.

It was quite late when I had finished with the attendant formalities and returned at last to my cabin for the night. I was awash in a feeling of exhilaration that made sleep a difficult state to attain. I lay awake and restless for nearly an hour before exhaustion finally overtook me.

I awoke to the sound of a beating drum. Gradually, I shrugged off my stupor and realised it was a fist pounding on my cabin door.

"Watson! Wake up, man!" Sherlock Holmes's voice hissed from the corridor between our cabins.

Rising and throwing on my dressing-gown, I crossed to the door and hurriedly unlocked it.

"Whatever is the matter, Holmes?"

My impetuous friend pushed his way past me into the cabin and responded in hushed tones.

"Milton Tyler is the matter, Watson."

"Tyler? Oh, you mean the fellow who fell overboard."

I stifled a yawn as I spoke.

"Keep your voice down. Captain Jamison has only just informed me of the latest developments in this matter. A telegraph wire was received a few minutes ago. It seems that Milton Tyler's body was discovered by the crew of the *Venture*. He was caught in their fishing net. It seems he had become entangled in seaweed and was floating just beneath the surface of the waves when they found him. You may recall that we passed the *Venture* only yesterday. You may also recollect your irritation that the *Presumption* had weighed anchor to allow the men to engage in conversation for a few minutes and conduct trade between ships."

I nodded my head absently.

"Well that settles it then, Holmes. The first death was either suicide or an accident and the second was unquestionably misadventure."

Holmes resumed speaking to me as if he had not heard my casual dismissal of the matter a moment before.

"Milton Tyler had been stabbed six times in the chest. His mouth was found stuffed with a blood-soaked handkerchief. Doubtless the handkerchief was initially placed in the mouth to prevent his rousing help when he was attacked. The handkerchief subsequently became soiled after he was violently stabbed multiple times by his assailant and vomited blood in his death throes."

I felt my face turn crimson as he continued.

"Strangely enough, Milton Tyler was still in possession of his wallet and various personal effects confirming his identity. This looks to be a most interesting case, Watson. Get dressed. I'm afraid you shan't have time for breakfast this morning."

Twenty minutes later, Holmes and I were squeezed in Captain Jamison's cabin alongside Mr Blither, the first mate. I was seated at the captain's desk while my friend busily paced the cramped room, smoke pouring furiously from his tightly clenched briar.

"Since we now know for certain that we are dealing with a murderer, it is reasonable to conclude that neither did the porter die from his own hand... intentionally or otherwise." Holmes paused to shoot me a glance before continuing, "The possibility that the Chinaman witnessed Milton Tyler's body being thrown into the sea cost him his life. Regrettably, his dying words were to persist in his claim that he had observed no one on deck that might be a suspect in the crime. Isn't that correct, Watson?"

"Yes, that's right, Holmes."

"The fact remains that he may have been lying. The murderer certainly thought so or, at the very least, determined that he could not afford to gamble on such a possibility. It is quite likely that the porter died pleading his ignorance since these were his only words to Watson at his moment of death. In any event, Captain Jamison, we cannot afford to delay a moment longer. The other passengers must be informed of the developments in the Tyler case and they must be interviewed as soon as possible. It is essential to a hasty and successful resolution of our investigation."

Jamison folded his arms across his big belly, leaning back in his chair. He took a deep breath and let the air escape through his lips in a melodramatic sigh.

"I suppose you are quite correct, Mr Holmes. You have my permission to proceed as you think best. Mr Blither, see that Mr Holmes has a list of all the passengers at once and follow his instructions to the letter about when and where they should gather."

"Aye-aye, Captain," the mate replied, rising from his chair and quickly exiting the cabin.

"Our first order of business shall be to determine whether or not the crime stemmed from an incident at the gathering of coin dealers in New York last weekend. Naturally, we shall not limit ourselves to this avenue of inquiry should any other lead come to light in the course of our conversations with the other passengers."

"*Gathering of coin dealers?* What are you talking about, Holmes?"

My friend stopped in his tread and turned to regard me in a new light, his eyes dancing with mischief.

"My dear Watson… can it be that you have been so obtuse as to remain blissfully unaware that we are among the very few passengers aboard the *Presumption* who did not attend the well-advertised gathering of antique coin dealers in New York over the weekend?"

I felt my cheeks redden with embarrassment as Captain Jamison chuckled at my obliviousness.

In due course, the passengers were informed that Mr Tyler had met with foul play and that Holmes was acting under instructions from

Captain Jamison to gather information to turn over to the authorities in advance of an official investigation. To this end, my friend was to meet with and question each of the passengers and I would take note of their responses as I had many times before with callers to the rooms we once shared in Baker Street.

The first passenger we interviewed was Miss Jane Portnoy, a very attractive young nurse. She entered the captain's quarters and seated herself for her interview opposite Holmes at the captain's desk. The time was exactly one o'clock in the afternoon.

"Miss Portnoy," Holmes began, "I am afraid I must first inquire as to the nature of your visit to the United States."

The young woman bristled at the indignity of being questioned in this manner, but only momentarily, for she quickly regained her composure and cleared her throat before addressing her response.

"I was visiting my sister and her husband. She married an *American…*" she pronounced the word as if we were likely to share her distaste, "…and, consequently, we do not see one another very often as you can well imagine."

Holmes smiled in quiet amusement.

"Did you have any other appointments while in the States apart from your visit to your sister and her husband?"

"No, Mr Holmes. I did not."

"And what was the duration of your stay in America, Miss Portnoy?"

"Three weeks, Mr Holmes."

Her voice rose in pitch as if the indignation of having her personal affairs discussed were nigh impossible to bear.

Holmes appeared not to notice her change in demeanour and continued to question her in the same quiet, relaxed tone.

"Were you at all acquainted with the deceased Mr Milton Tyler?"

Again, Miss Portnoy bristled at the question.

"No, I had never seen him before boarding this ship nor did we speak on any occasion while on board."

Holmes raised an eyebrow, quizzically.

"Not even a curt nod of acknowledgement while passing one another in the corridor?"

"Not… even."

My friend seemed oddly amused by her injured dignity.

"Do you know anything about coins, Miss Portnoy? Rare ones, perhaps?"

"Coins, did you say? No. Nothing at all. Why?"

Holmes shrugged, offhandedly. "Mr Tyler and several of the other passengers on the ship had a passion for rare coins. I thought perhaps that you might have heard something of interest from one of them. It seems highly improbable that an attractive woman such as yourself could pass five days in the close quarters of a ship of such a relatively small size without having made some contact with her fellow passengers."

The woman's nerves were frayed and I realised my friend was deliberately testing her reaction to his insinuating remarks.

"Perhaps I do remember something of interest after all, Mr Holmes."

I noted Miss Portnoy blushing as she spoke.

"Yes, I thought you might at that. What is it that you recall, Miss Portnoy?"

She held her hands together tightly in her lap and cleared her throat primly before she spoke. Her eyes were wide but she kept them cast on the floor in front of her and never looked directly at Holmes as she replied.

"I believe that I may have overheard something that one of the passengers had said… about collecting coins… only yesterday, in fact."

"Imagine! Go on, go on. We are all ears, aren't we, Watson?"

In spite of myself, I felt a pang of remorse for the poor woman. Holmes could easily make the most innocent action appear as a grave offence once he established his authority over the individual he was questioning. It was a useful tactic when dealing with those who were genuinely concealing information, but it could be devastating for the average person who found themselves questioning their every action for fear they would be interpreted as sinister in nature.

"I was with Catherine… Mrs Mendelssohn, that sweet old dear… when I heard a couple of the men speaking of a certain type of coin or… or maybe it was a collection of coins that Mr Tyler had. I… I'm not sure who it was that made the remark as I do not know most of the other passengers by name… or… or even by face. I'm afraid I'm not a very observant person, Mr Holmes."

"So few of us are, Miss Portnoy, so few of us are… there is little need to apologise."

Holmes sat back in his chair and crossed his legs, drumming his fingers on the top of the oak desk. There was a pregnant pause before Miss Portnoy found the courage to resume speaking.

"I'm afraid that is all that I can recall at this time, Mr Holmes." She waited for him to reply, but he continued drumming his fingers on the desk, absently. "May I go then, sir?"

"Hmm?" Holmes jumped as if startled by her question. "Yes, yes… of course. Good day to you, ma'am and thank you for your time."

Miss Portnoy smiled in relief and stood up to leave.

"One moment, ma'am," Holmes said as she turned toward the cabin door.

I noted her face was crestfallen as she stopped, but by the time she turned to favour Holmes, she had successfully regained her composure.

"If, by chance, you do recall anything else…" Holmes hesitated a moment, "…please don't fail to contact me immediately."

She smiled stiffly and nodded her head.

"Of course, Mr Holmes. Good day to you, sir."

Holmes watched her depart. I observed my friend keenly, waiting to see if he would impart any comment regarding our first interview. He chose instead to keep his thoughts to himself and left me to draw my own conclusions.

No sooner had Miss Portnoy made her departure, than the cabin door opened and Mr James Tetherspoon entered. Mr Tetherspoon, an elderly coin collector from Purley, came straight to the point as soon as he was seated.

"Poor old Milton," he shook his head sadly, "he deserved a better fate than what he found, Mr Holmes. He was the best friend I had in this miserable old world. I wasn't surprised to learn what happened was no accident. In fact, I was certain of it immediately. Milton Tyler was murdered in cold blood, I thought to myself, and I was right, too, as the both of you well know."

The old man wiped a grubby hand under his nose and then pulled absently at the grey and white whiskers that collected in a mottled bunch around his mouth. Holmes leant forward and rested his elbows on the desk, clutching his hands as if in prayer.

"What made you so certain that Mr Tyler had met with foul play, Mr Tetherspoon?"

The old man sighed and shrugged his shoulders.

"His behaviour, I suppose."

"What precisely about his behaviour suggested this fact?" Holmes asked.

"He… he seemed to change after we came aboard ship. He became very quiet and withdrawn. He was never like that before; he was gregarious… boisterous, even. I tried to talk to him, but every time he would give only terse responses or none at all."

"Do you know anything about a rare coin or collection of coins that Mr Tyler had either recently acquired or especially treasured?"

The old man smiled humourlessly at Holmes's question.

"Motive, eh? Very good, sir. Unfortunately, Milton's collection never really amounted to anything much over the years. He was quite the talker when we were younger, if you follow my meaning. I was grateful when he cut out the shenanigans, what with interested parties who don't know what from whom where coins are concerned. That's just the sort of dicey behaviour that does much to give coin dealers a bad name. Makes it hard for the rest of us honest sort to make a living at it, eh?"

"Of course," Holmes leant back in his chair, "if Tyler was keeping to himself, perhaps he had come across something of value over the weekend and wished to keep the knowledge from others… even old friends such as you, Mr Tetherspoon."

The old man stroked his beard once more as he considered the possibility. "That certainly may be, Mr Holmes. I hadn't considered that at all."

"Do you recall him speaking alone with anyone over the weekend… perhaps more quietly than normal? It may have been one of the passengers on board the ship or someone else entirely."

For a fleeting second, I thought I detected a glint of recognition in the old man's eyes, but then he smiled and shook his head. "No. I'm sorry, sir. You're a clever man, Mr Holmes, but I cannot help you."

Holmes smiled and reached across the desk to shake the old man's hand as he climbed to his feet. "On the contrary, my dear Mr Tetherspoon, you already have."

The old man smiled quizzically in response, but gave no outward sign of finding Holmes's remark unsettling. He bid us both a good afternoon and made his departure.

I frantically finished my notes of Mr Tetherspoon's meeting when the door opened once more to admit a diminutive old woman. I distinctly recalled seeing her rose-coloured, dimpled cheeks and cheery smile each time I had passed her on board ship these past six days.

"Ah, you must be Mrs Mendelssohn. Come in and take a seat." Holmes gestured toward the empty chair in front of the desk.

"Oh, thank you. Thank you, Mr Holmes. Good day to the both of you. It is such a lovely day, is it not? I was just remarking to that nice Miss Portnoy that it looks like we may not see much rain on this trip. Wouldn't that be wonderful, Dr Watson? Such a nice change from being at home."

"Yes, it would be wonderful indeed."

I shot a bemused glance in Holmes's direction.

Holmes cleared his throat, "Mrs Mendelssohn, I have a few questions that I need to ask you. It should not take much of your time. Now then, what brought you to America?"

Mrs Mendelssohn clung to her purse with excitement. "Oh, my. I'm sorry, Mr Holmes, but this is all so thrilling."

"Your reason for coming to the States, Mrs Mendelssohn?"

"Oh, yes. Just a visit, Mr Holmes. I was bored with the same routine. At my age, every week begins to look like the one before it and what with the awful weather we have… well, it makes it easy to forget the month, let alone the day."

"Yes, quite…"

"I have no family, you see. I'm a widow and my son, Robert – May God rest his soul – passed away nearly twenty-five years ago. It's a terrible thing for a mother to outlive her only child. I was talking with Mrs Richards whose husband runs the bakery and she said that what I needed was a change of scenery. I've been in England for over forty years now, can you imagine? I've been here ever since I met my late husband. So I took her advice and came to America. Though I must say, it's not a very friendly country from what I've seen of it so I'm glad to be going home. I do love England so."

She paused for a moment as if momentarily confused and trying to find her place again. "Do you know… it's been my home for over forty years? Quite an accomplishment, I should think."

"Tell me about the evening that Mr Tyler was murdered, Mrs Mendelssohn. Who were you with? Whom did you see? Was there anything of interest that you might have observed?"

Mrs Mendelssohn sighed. "There was such a lovely sunset that evening. I love to sit on the deck and watch all the beautiful colours disappearing into the ocean. I find the horizon is so much more soothing at sea, don't you? Did either of you see it? Wasn't it just marvellous?"

Holmes cleared his throat.

"I cannot say that I noticed it. Were you at all acquainted with Mr Tyler?"

"Oh, poor Mr Tyler. He was one of those coin aficionados. I find it very boring listening to them talk about their silly coins all day and all of the night. Have you ever tried to say anything to them? They always change the subject to talk about their tiresome coins. Oh well, they are nice people, though, I suppose."

"Miss Portnoy mentioned that she had overheard some of the coin dealers discussing Mr Tyler's collection while she was in your company yesterday. Do you remember anything specific that was said or which of the gentlemen were discussing Mr Tyler's collection?"

Mrs Mendelssohn frowned for a second, before chuckling.

"Now there you go talking about coins, Mr Holmes. Good heavens! I don't see what is so interesting about them. Everyone on this ship makes such a fuss over them except for Miss Portnoy and me. Well, everyone must have their own hobbies, I suppose. Mine is gardening. I love flowers; they are so pretty and they really do brighten up a yard. The ones in America are not as pretty as the ones we're used to back home. Do you enjoy gardening, Mr Holmes?"

"Not especially, Mrs Mendelssohn. Now, do you recall anything specific about the gentlemen who were discussing Mr Tyler's collection of coins yesterday?"

Mrs Mendelssohn bit her lip like a sulking child.

"Oh, dear. I do become so easily distracted, Mr Holmes. I'm sorry, but I'm afraid that I don't recall hearing their conversation at all. I do try to mind my own business, particularly when the subject doesn't interest me."

Holmes slapped his hands down upon the desk.

"Well, that is all that we need to discuss for the moment. Good day, Mrs Mendelssohn. It has been a pleasure."

The old woman smiled as she rose. "Good day, Mr Holmes and good day to you, Dr Watson. I didn't forget you over there in the corner. Goodbye, gentlemen. Cheerio."

She repeated her farewell several times before she made it out of the room. Each time she spoke her voice was a bit fainter and less assured than before.

I could barely restrain my laughter until she was out of the door.

"She was absolutely hopeless, wasn't she?"

Holmes glanced at me and smirked, but made no response.

After a wait of several minutes, the door opened to admit the stout form and sour face of Mr Thomas Whittingham. Instantly, I recognised him as the gentleman that the captain had chastised up on deck yesterday. I took an immediate dislike to him, even before he sat down, glanced irritably at his pocket-watch, and growled at us.

"My time is valuable, gentlemen. I am unaccustomed to having it wasted."

Holmes lifted an eyebrow.

"A sentiment we share then, sir. Kindly answer the questions put to you as best you can manage and you shall not have wasted any more of ours."

The businessman's jaw opened as if he were about to reply and then closed abruptly as he thought better of it.

"You are a factory owner, is that not correct, Mr Whittingham?" Holmes resumed speaking without giving him a chance to respond.

"Were you acquainted with the late Mr Milton Tyler?"

"Of course I was!" Whittingham snapped. "A loathsome little man Tyler was, but a man who took good care of his best customers."

"Of whom you were doubtless one."

"The finest, Mr Holmes. The finest beyond the shadow of a doubt."

"If he treated you well, what makes you judge him as loathsome?"

Whittingham spread his palms before him as if the answer were evident.

"He was holding out on me."

"Just on this occasion or was such behaviour habitual?"

"Of course it wasn't habitual! He was holding out on me concerning something big for an entire fortnight before our trip to the colonies. It seems that he took his secret to the grave now, damn his soul."

"What makes you so sure of that?" Holmes snapped.

"Why, I had his room searched, of course."

"When did you have his room searched?"

"What sort of damn fool do you take me for? A thorough search was conducted the first night that we began our return voyage. I knew something was amiss, but not a trace was found of anything valuable. Whatever item he brought to New York changed hands there, I am certain of it."

"Any pieces he was keen to get his hands on? Something rare, perhaps?"

"Don't be daft, Mr Holmes. He was a coin dealer. He was in the business of making money from money any way possible."

"If that is so, then why not include you on the bidding for this treasure of his? Surely, he would stand to make more from two or more interested parties competing for the same item rather than selling it to a single interested collector."

The businessman bit his lip for a moment.

"That's just it, sir. He didn't stand to make more from competition in this instance. He had a buyer willing to pay more than anyone else would even consider. There are such men who would sell their very soul for something they alone treasure. That's the only logical explanation."

"Someone who did not know the coin's true worth, perhaps, and paid a small fortune for what you would consider worthless?"

The gruff man considered this for a moment as if the possibility of his not losing out on a treasure had never occurred to him before. He smiled a hard, cruel smile.

"Possibly, sir, possibly. We're all rubes, Mr Holmes, every man Jack of us."

"There is one other possibility that you have overlooked."

"Oh? And what is that?"

"That Milton Tyler himself was being blackmailed."

Mr Whittingham laughed.

"No, Mr Holmes. If Milton had run into that sort of trouble, he would have come to me straight away as he had done in the past. We were both old hands at that game and he knew that I could be counted on for assistance in such matters should the need arise. Muscle can be bought as easily as anything else in this world and there is precious little it cannot put to rights."

"As you say, as you say." Holmes nodded sagely, but I knew him well enough to know that he thought Thomas Whittingham to be a fool.

"Kindly answer one further question, Mr Whittingham."

"Go on."

"You mentioned that you had Mr Tyler's cabin searched before his death. Whom did you employ to do so?"

The old man smiled and shook his head.

"There's no secret about that, Mr Holmes. It was the first mate, Blither. The second I set eyes upon him I said to myself, 'now there's a man who would do anything for the right price'."

"Who's to say you were the only one to make that observation? Perhaps you were bested, Mr Whittingham, by someone sharper who acted sooner. Someone willing to pay any price for an item would reasonably offer a substantial amount to protect it… perhaps even paying Mr Blither to deceive anyone else who expressed an interest in the contents of Mr Tyler's cabin."

Whittingham's eyes narrowed as he smiled grimly.

"You're very good at your game, Mr Holmes, but you'll not get my goat today. The item in question was sold to an interested party in the States and not one of the other coin collectors on board this ship. Who among this lot fits the sort that you described? Not a one of us. You said so yourself, we're all rubes."

"On the contrary, Mr Whittingham, those were your words."

The businessman frowned.

"What difference does it make who said what so long as it's the truth? That's the important thing, isn't it? Eh?"

"Is it now, Mr Whittingham? Is it indeed?"

Holmes held the man's gaze for a moment.

"Good day to you," he said dismissively and turned his attention to the notes that I had passed to him regarding the previous interviews.

The man's face soured. He rose with a sharp intake of breath and turned to exit the room, seething that he had met his match.

Holmes continued reading even after the door had clicked shut.

"Only two more interviews left, Holmes," I said, breaking the silence.

Our penultimate interview was with the Right Honourable Edward Smythe-Pedgwick, a thin man whose face was dominated by thick, round glasses. He hunched forward as he seated himself across from Holmes. His posture gave the appearance of a much shorter man than the gentleman who had entered the room.

"How do you do, Mr Holmes? Edward Smythe-Pedgwick."

He reached across the table to grasp Holmes's outstretched hand. I detected a Midlands accent partially disguised in an attempt to sound well-bred.

"A pleasure to meet you, sir. I understand that you are a coin dealer."

Mr Smythe-Pedgwick smiled confidently and nodded his head.

"That's right, Mr Holmes, quite right. You'll also be aware that the late Mr Milton Tyler was a man I considered my rival... business rival only, I might add... though I'm sure others have killed for less. I won't lie to you and say that I'm beside myself with grief, but I'd not be much of a man if I said I wasn't sorry to learn that old Milton met with such a miserable end. Why, I wouldn't have wished that fate on my worst enemy and that wasn't Milton, to be sure."

"Yes, I believe you've made that point several times already," Holmes drawled.

"I simply wish to be sure that we understand one another. I'm a businessman, Mr Holmes and as such I cannot afford to let any unsavoury dealings such as this reflect poorly on me. I have a reputation to uphold."

"Yes, I gathered from speaking with Mr Tetherspoon earlier that Mr Tyler was a bit… well, how should one put it? A bit unscrupulous in his business practices when he first began dealing in coins."

Smythe-Pedgwick's eyes narrowed and his thin face seemed to grow even more emaciated as if he were wasting away before our eyes.

"He was a cad, Mr Holmes. There's no two ways about it. Milton was once a scoundrel… a veritable blackguard who deserved a right thrashing for his antics. That was all many years ago, Mr Holmes. I was only one of Lord knows how many who had reason to resent Milton in those days. He cost me more than a bit of grief, but it was over and done with long ago. I'm not a man to wait decades to settle his debts."

"Of that I have no doubt, sir. There is perhaps one more item you could help shed some light upon." Holmes folded the tips of his fingers together and leaned forward in his chair, conspiratorially. Mr Smythe-Pedgwick raised his eyebrows with cautious interest, but spoke not a word in response as he waited for my friend to pose his question. "Did Mr Tyler come across any rare pieces recently that you are aware of? Perhaps his behaviour while you were gathered in New York indicated a change in fortune?"

Smythe-Pedgwick sat in silence for a moment and then shook his head slowly.

"The Mark of Cain was upon him as sure as it was anyone who wanted something so badly he'd sell his very soul to possess it. That's the true coin of the realm for a collector, Mr Holmes. Make no mistake about it. We're a breed apart and regular folk couldn't understand us if they tried. Do you follow my meaning?"

There was little more to the conversation and the hunched form of the thin man straightened as he rose from his chair and seemed to grow miraculously before my eyes. He was a peculiar sort, but I found him an oddly compelling figure.

Our final passenger to interview was Miss Hildegard Knopf. Miss Knopf was comfortably settled into the routine of a spinster. She was possessed of a matronly nature that was accentuated by her size and the severe bun her greying hair pulled back to form. Despite her appearance, Miss Knopf was also a very serious coin collector.

"Coin collecting is my passion, Mr Holmes," she began, "my only passion I might add. Collections afford one many hours of pleasure and unlike a husband, they can be easily set aside when they are no longer wanted."

She laughed with a deep throaty laugh. Peculiarly, I detected traces of her Dutch ancestry in her mirth although not in her speech, which was impeccable.

"I would like to ask you a question, Miss Knopf." The big Dutch woman smiled faintly and nodded her head. "What can you tell me of the history of this particular coin?"

I must admit that I was taken completely off guard as Holmes handed the woman what looked to be a stained and faded piece of gold. She took the coin and examined it closely. Her eyes squinted as she held it tightly between her thumb and forefinger, her mouth set in a painful grimace.

"Well now, that is something I haven't seen in many a year."

She let loose a low whistle of appreciation and smiled faintly, never taking her eyes from the coin.

"This is the Mark of Cain. Some would claim it dates back to the dawn of civilisation… to the time of the very first people in Mesopotamia. You recall the Old Testament story, of course? Cain killed his own brother so God placed a mark upon him that made him a pariah among his fellow men."

"Do you believe that this coin is actually that old?"

The woman shook her head in dismissal without ever raising her eyes to Holmes's face.

"The Mark of Cain was one of Giuseppe Balsamo's many swindles."

"Count Cagliostro? This coin was his work?"

She shook her head once more.

"No, Mr Holmes, merely the legend. This coin is a clever forgery, but it is not yet one hundred years old."

Holmes's eyes narrowed.

"How can you be certain?"

Miss Knopf sighed and stretched languorously.

"Milton Tyler was responsible for this particular forgery… when he was younger, I might add. Young, but far from innocent, he was."

She looked at the coin thoughtfully and then handed it back to Holmes.

"Where did you find it?" The words tripped off her tongue casually as if her interest in the answer was not great.

"It was found on deck shortly after Milton Tyler's body was thrown overboard."

My mind reeled that Holmes had somehow kept this knowledge from me. I realised that he must also have surreptitiously shown the same piece to Mr Smythe-Pedgwick earlier, as this accounted for the man's conspiratorial confidence regarding the Mark of Cain being the coin of the realm that set collectors apart from other folk.

The big Dutch woman clicked her tongue.

"What a pity. Poor old Milton was an unfortunate soul, to be sure."

Holmes leaned back in his chair.

"I am perplexed, Miss Knopf. If Milton Tyler's time as a confidence trickster was in the past, then what value would he place upon this coin?"

She considered his words, but again failed to look up at him.

"A man's sins always catch up with him, Mr Holmes. Whether it takes an hour or a lifetime, they are like a letter addressed to yourself that you dropped in the post one morning. They always come back to you sooner or later."

"Your philosophy is sound, but I'm afraid that someone else posted this to Milton Tyler. The question is who?"

"If I knew the answer to your question, Mr Holmes, I could save you a great deal of bother. Find out who had that coin and you have found Milton Tyler's murderer."

Holmes held the coin up to the light and smiled ruefully.

"It seems that the Mark of Cain was more than just a fable, after all." He stared at the coin for a few more seconds and then curtly dismissed her while still pondering the coin between his fingers. "I believe that will be all for now. Good day to you, Miss Knopf."

I watched Holmes closely as the door shut behind her retreating figure.

"Holmes! Where? How did you come into possession of that coin?"

He looked at me for a moment and then smiled faintly.

"Charlie the porter's inside breast pocket. Simple really. I checked his coat and trousers while you were retrieving your medical bag."

"But you just said…"

"I just said it was found on deck… and so it likely was."

"You don't think for a minute…"

"On the contrary, my dear Watson, I never cease to do so. Now be a good fellow and type up your notes for me and bring them to my cabin before dinner. I need a nap. We did not enjoy a very restful night last night and I suspect tonight will be even more unpleasant."

Now what the devil did he mean by that? I thought to myself.

I knew better than to ask such a question. Sherlock Holmes was not given to answering questions before his time. I did as I was asked and retired to my cabin to prepare my notes.

"Ah, Dr Watson, I'm glad that you could join us."

Captain Jamison indicated a place at the table opposite him next to where Holmes was already sitting. Dinner had been laid out. I took my seat and rather awkwardly set a large envelope containing my notes from the afternoon's interviews down on the table next to my plate.

"Splendid, Watson," Holmes reached for the envelope and hurriedly undid the seal to get at the contents. "This is just what I have been waiting for. Erm… some wine, Watson?"

I lifted my glass as Blither, the first mate, poured from the bottle. He did not make eye contact with me, but there was no missing the barely suppressed anger the man felt in having to wait upon us.

"Mmm. This is excellent sausage," Holmes made a bit of a

spectacle of himself as he chewed. "Watson, would you kindly read the notes that you typed up this afternoon? There's a good chap."

Holmes handed the contents of the envelope back to me. I glanced uncomfortably around the table, feeling ill at ease speaking so openly in front of Captain Jamison and his first mate.

"Come, come, Watson. We're among friends."

Holmes made a show of all but slurping his soup. I was uncomfortably reminded of his disastrous turn on the New York stage.

"Yes, well… let's see here. Miss Jane Portnoy…"

"Ah yes, the nurse who detests Americans… do go on, Watson."

I cleared my throat irritably.

"Miss Portnoy believes that she may have overheard part of a conversation between two men about Mr Tyler's coin collection…"

"Was she alone at the time?"

"What?"

"You heard me, dear fellow. I asked if she was alone when she overheard the conversation."

"Erm, no… no she wasn't. She was with Mrs Mendelssohn at the time. She appears to be the only passenger that she gets on with. A rather cold fish, our Miss Portnoy."

"Next?"

I shuffled through my notes. I loathed it when Holmes treated me like a cloth-eared schoolboy in the presence of others.

"Mr James Tetherspoon. Elderly coin dealer from Purley and a close friend of the deceased. Pleasant enough fellow, I suppose, but of limited value to the investigation."

"Ah, there I must disagree, Watson. Mr Tetherspoon told us a great deal."

I felt my face flush. I glanced round the table and noticed both Captain Jamison and Mr Blither were eagerly listening to Holmes.

"For instance?" I asked.

"Mr Tetherspoon noted the change in the late Mr Tyler's demeanour upon boarding the ship. He became withdrawn and sullen, in contrast to his usual personality, suggesting that something or someone had recently disturbed his peace of mind."

Holmes looked around the table, eager to feast upon the attention of his audience. "Good Mr Tetherspoon was also kind enough to reveal that he disapproved of Mr Tyler's behaviour when they first set out to deal in rare coins. It seems that Mr Tyler was a bit too sharp for his own good. He profited from those who knew less than him and generally behaved in a disreputable manner… although he later mended his ways."

"I don't recall hearing any of this, Holmes!"

"I assure you that it was said all the same." Holmes emphasised this in a way that left me eager to question him, but I checked myself and continued to the next page of my notes.

"Next was Mrs Catherine Mendelssohn. I daresay we learned naught from this dear lady, but I fear you would counter that the entire case depends upon her testimony, Holmes."

"You may proceed, Watson."

"Ah, yes… the unpleasant Mr Thomas Whittingham. Factory owner. A longstanding customer of the late Mr Tyler. Took a rather dim view of the deceased as he believed that Mr Tyler had acquired a rare coin and would not allow him to bid on it."

I glanced at Holmes for fear of a reproving look. Seeing none, I continued.

"Employed Mr Blither…" I paused for a moment, "…to search the deceased's cabin shortly after boarding the ship."

"Is this so, Mr Blither?" Captain Jamison appeared outraged.

The mate stammered for a moment before replying.

"Y – yes, sir. I did not mention it earlier only because it seemed of little consequence as nothing of value was found, sir."

"Eh… how much were you paid for rendering this service?" Holmes bent to light his briar and did not make eye contact with any of us while his question hung uncomfortably in the air. Mr Blither shifted from one foot to the other and appeared at a loss on how best to respond. "Doesn't matter, doesn't matter," Holmes replied. "It can't have been much or Whittingham would surely have complained bitterly about the sum."

"I don't like this one bit, Mr Blither," Captain Jamison stormed. "We shall discuss this again. I will not tolerate such behaviour on my ship. Forgive me, Dr Watson. Please continue, sir."

I cleared my throat and carried on.

"The Right Honourable Edward Smythe-Pedgwick and Miss Hildegarde Knopf were the final two passengers. Mr Smythe-Pedgwick corroborated Mr Whittingham's assertion that the late Mr Tyler was a bit of a scoundrel in the past. Apparently, Mr Smythe-Pedgwick was one of the victims of Mr Tyler's deceptions when they were both younger."

I looked to Holmes for approval. He nodded slightly for me to continue.

"Mr Smythe-Pedgwick alluded to an antique coin that Mr Tyler had recently acquired, known as the Mark of Cain. It has been suggested that this particular coin, the rare object whose existence Mr Whittingham so strongly suspected, cost Mr Tyler his life."

I looked around the room for a moment. Holmes and Captain Jamison were stone-faced. Mr Blither looked decidedly ill. I was startled when Holmes picked up the narrative in my place.

"Our final interview was with Miss Hildegarde Knopf. The lady in question proved very knowledgeable about antique coins and even more knowledgeable about coin forgeries of the past as well as of a more recent vintage."

Holmes reached into his jacket pocket and withdrew the same faded coin that he had examined earlier. "This is the Mark of Cain. This coin is a forgery and will convict someone on board this ship of two murders. I would ask you, Mr Blither, if you would be so kind as to assemble the passengers immediately after dinner. I believe it will not take long to draw this affair to a conclusion."

The first mate nodded sternly and left the captain's quarters.

A short time later, passengers and crew alike were gathered together on deck just as we had after Charlie the porter had sounded the dread cry of "Man overboard!"

Holmes was a bundle of barely restrained energy as he nervously paced around the cold and miserable group, hands clasped firmly behind his back and mouth clenched tight around his unlit pipe.

"This case is really quite a simple one, although cleverly disguised by the murderer to divert suspicion elsewhere."

I watched as the eyes of all the passengers followed Holmes closely as he circled them. All except for dear old Mrs Mendelssohn, who appeared to be contentedly lost in the gardens of yesteryear.

"It was of course presumed that possession of an exceedingly rare coin of considerable value was behind Milton Tyler's murder and, in a sense, it was, but under very different circumstances than all but one of us would have imagined. The truth behind the murder of Milton Tyler was made evident by Charlie the porter's dying words. What were they again, Watson?"

I paused for a moment, aware that I was suddenly the centre of attention. I was unsure how the Chinaman's words implicated Whittingham and Mr Blither for there was little doubt in my mind they were the guilty party.

"The porter stated that he saw no one. The man was murdered for a crime that he did not even witness."

Holmes shook his head.

"No, Watson. I made the mistake initially of accepting your paraphrasing Charlie's pidgin English. The truth became evident once I realised that what Charlie said to you and what you heard were two very different things."

I was flabbergasted. My mouth hung open as I recalled answering the door of my cabin and watching the poor Chinaman collapse in my arms.

"He said, 'I saw no one.' That is it, Holmes. Nothing more. I could not have been mistaken."

"Ah, but Charlie was not likely to use the phrase, "'I saw no one'" in his limited command of the King's English."

My mind raced feverishly. Again I recalled the knock upon my door and the shock of seeing the Chinaman there. I heard his words in my head once more.

"He said… 'I saw no man.'"

Holmes smiled. "That, of course, was what you heard. Charlie's dying words were in fact anything but a denial, he was making an accusation. 'I saw woman' was the phrase you misheard."

"'I saw woman.'"

I repeated the words aloud.

"Yes! Yes! By Jove, Holmes, you are correct. He said he saw a woman, but how? How could a woman have stabbed a man to death and thrown his body overboard? It scarcely seems plausible."

"No, Watson. Charlie was no liar. He heard the splash of the water and saw a body disappear under the waves. He did not see the murderer struggle to throw the body over the rail, but what he did see earlier stayed in his mind. It was the sight of a woman where she did not belong. A woman alone in Milton Tyler's cabin frantically searching among his belongings.

"Charlie's own reason for having been in the cabin was less than honourable. As a porter, he had the opportunity to pocket the very object that brought the woman in question to Tyler's cabin. The same object that Mr Whittingham would later hire Mr Blither to search for as well. The Mark of Cain. Charlie scared the woman away and would have thought no more of the matter had Milton Tyler not been murdered. Tyler's murderer likewise recalled Charlie and knew that she must also dispose of the porter who was the only person with reason to suspect her."

"So she was the killer!" I cried, pointing an accusing finger at Miss Knopf.

For her part, the matronly Dutchwoman looked aghast and held a trembling hand to her heart as the crowd parted and moved about to hold her should she attempt anything rash.

"No, Watson, Miss Knopf is innocent of murder as she well knows. No, our murderer is someone we would never suspect because she professed to have no knowledge of or interest in coin collecting in the first place."

"I didn't do it. I… I swear I didn't."

All heads turned toward the prim and attractive figure of Miss Portnoy.

"I don't blame you for not trusting me. I… I know I made a fool of myself when I sat down with you, but I swear I am innocent."

Holmes took a step forward and took the woman's right hand in his and patted it reassuringly.

"I did not suspect you then and I do not accuse you now, Miss

Portnoy. Forgive me for the unnecessary grief that I have caused you."

My mind reeled.

"Holmes, if it was not Miss Knopf and if it was not Miss Portnoy, then that only leaves…"

I stopped speaking at the sound of a solitary figure slowly clapping their hands in mock appreciation.

My eyes sought and found the face of Mrs Mendelssohn. It was a face strangely transformed. Gone was the expression of disarming feebleness and gentility. In its place I found hard black eyes that seemed to bore into my very soul. The old woman was smiling, but it was the face of a devil. Darkness seemed to shroud her features in shadows. There was a palpable malevolence about her that I would never have suspected lurked beneath her gentle features.

"Milton Tyler's death was not a crime of greed," Holmes spoke as he stepped forward, "but rather one of vengeance. Vengeance for your son, was it not, Mrs Mendelssohn?"

The old woman nodded, but those black orbs remained locked on Holmes's sad face.

"Milton Tyler killed my Robert as much as I killed him, but he killed for greed. Yet you judge me the greater offender."

"Milton Tyler ruined your son with his duplicity involving the Mark of Cain, did he not?" Holmes's voice was barely audible as he addressed the old woman. "Your son committed suicide because he was taken in by Tyler's fraudulent scheme and you waited twenty-five years to take your revenge. Never caring that Milton Tyler had reformed in all that time, letting your hate eat away at your soul until there was nothing left but your single-minded desire for meting out your own brand of justice."

The old woman laughed.

"How very theatrical, Mr Holmes. Perhaps you should give your useless doctor friend a respite and turn your own hand to chronicling your amazing adventures. How little you know of the larger world outside of this one. My son was young and impetuous. Eager to please, Robert sought advancement beyond his years and gambled heavily in purchasing the Mark of Cain from your precious Mr Tyler."

Holmes's face clouded with confusion. The old woman paused a moment, registering his failure to understand.

"My son was the treasurer for a very old organisation, Mr Holmes. An organisation you are likely unaware exists or, at best, consider the work of harmless cranks wasting their time in the riddles of antiquity. It is a powerful organisation that shapes your very world, Mr Holmes. Our precious Empire and the New World we have just left equally kneel before its might and majesty. We are kingmakers, Mr Holmes. We understand the true value of human life. Whoever controls a nation's currency controls the world. You wouldn't like us, Mr Holmes, for we would not fit your narrow view of human behaviour or your childish understanding of the workings of governments and monarchies."

"It was this organisation that my son failed. He squandered funds that he had no right to spend in the belief that he would win praise and prestige by presenting our High Council with a lost treasure of the half-forgotten past."

"The Mark of Cain," Holmes said simply.

The old woman nodded.

"Can you imagine the reaction of the High Council when he presented them with Tyler's useless forgery? Can you imagine how my Robert suffered in the hours before he took his own life?"

"Mrs Mendelssohn, I am sorry, but your son's death was his own choice…"

"No, Mr Holmes, you still do not understand. His fate would have been far worse had he not taken his own life first. Milton Tyler murdered my son with his greed. He took advantage of his inexperience and then slowly chipped away at the fortune he had stolen over the next twenty-five years. The justice that I brought when I paralysed him with the prick of a needle, stifled his screams for help, and stabbed him with the ritual dagger in the manner dictated of old was not a mother's revenge, Mr Holmes. Milton Tyler wronged a body that he never even dreamed existed. He sentenced himself to death many years ago. It was an honour to be allowed to carry out that sentence on behalf of the organisation. The Chinaman's life was an unfortunate necessity. I am not without mercy. His was a painless death."

"Tell me the name of this organisation that considers itself above the laws of every civilised land, Mrs Mendelssohn. Tell me and I swear that my brother shall…"

Holmes stopped speaking abruptly as the old woman began to tremble. Saliva frothed about her lips and a terrible gurgle escaped her throat.

"We are legion, Mr Holmes," she said as she collapsed in his arms.

Before I reached my friend's side, I knew that the old woman was dead.

Many hours later, a post-mortem would determine that she had injected poison into her veins as soon as she had learned that Holmes was gathering the passengers and crew to make his accusation. It was the same method that she had used to remove the poor Chinaman. The man I was ready to believe had died of his own addiction like so many of the denizens of Limehouse before him. Her actions in ending her own life seemed a terrible gamble, but I realised that she placed little value on her own life or the lives of others.

I knew that the knowledge of such an organisation with tentacles manipulating the events of the Western world would cause my friend no end of worry. I asked Holmes what he proposed to do about it. He stood staring out to sea for a moment, puffing at his pipe, hands clasped firmly on the rail of the *Presumption*.

"It seems one must broaden one's definition of evil, Watson," was his only reply.

After a moment, I turned and shared his view of the approaching island that we called home. I felt a chill snake down my back and wondered whether I would ever sleep safe in my bed again.

ABOUT THE AUTHORS

William Patrick Maynard was born and raised in Cleveland, Ohio. His passion for writing began in childhood and was fuelled by an early love of detective and thriller fiction. He was licensed by the Sax Rohmer Literary Estate to continue the Fu Manchu thrillers for Black Coat Press. *The Terror of Fu Manchu* was published in 2009 and was followed by *The Destiny of Fu Manchu* in 2012 and *The Triumph of Fu Manchu* in 2014. His first Sherlock Holmes story appeared in *Gaslight Grotesque*, published in 2009 by EDGE Publishing. He currently resides in Northeast Ohio with his wife and family.

Alexandra Martukovich spent her childhood in Garfield Heights, Ohio and currently makes her home in Parma, Ohio. "The Adventure of the Coin of the Realm" is her first published story.

THE STRANGE CASE OF THE DISPLACED DETECTIVE

⁊෴

BY ROY GILL

It was a most peculiar morning. The irregularity began as I wearily consulted the looking glass for the purpose of my ablutions. I was accustomed to this experience being a little dispiriting – for what established bachelor-about-town does not picture himself in the first flush of youth, despite all evidence to the contrary? – but I had not expected it to be alarming. And yet, for the slightest moment, as I peered into the glass I had the uncanny sensation of another's face staring back, regarding me with an expression of sorrow. I shook my head to clear it of the delusion, and all at once the phantom was gone.

"A rum do, old son," I said to myself, imagining a lack of sleep to be the most likely malaise, and an extra cup of Mrs Hudson's coffee the most suitable prescription. I might have thought no more about it, had a further visitation not presented itself...

It was a cold and overcast winter's day, and a murky light filtered in through the parted curtains of the sitting-room at Baker Street. Holmes sat wrapped in his dressing-gown, his meerschaum pipe clasped between his lips and his eyes closed, lost in moody contemplation. Upon the breakfast salver a scattering of letters lay beside a flask of coffee and a dish of eggs and bacon. I was about to fall upon this gratefully when I perceived I was being observed. A shadowy figure sat in the wingchair that Holmes usually favoured for clients.

"I do beg your pardon," I said. "I didn't see you. The light in here is so dim. I must adjust the gas." I crossed to the bayonet, turned up the flame, and banished a portion of the gloom.

"You said something, Watson?"

"I was simply remarking I hadn't realised you were consulting…" I turned back to the wingchair, expecting Holmes to effect some form of introduction, but the seat was quite empty.

"Good heavens!"

"I shouldn't have thought the matter that noteworthy." Holmes's eyes opened languidly.

"No?"

"Not at all. I haven't even decided if I will take the case. Why Mycroft should imagine a mechanism found embedded in a wall cavity in Richmond would intrigue me, I do not know."

"Of course, yes…"

Clearly Holmes had no notion of the "presence" I had noticed in the chair, and was discoursing on quite a different matter, drawn from his morning's correspondence. I told myself sternly it was a trick of the light, a shadow cast upon patterned fabric, that was all.

I followed my own prescription, and gulped down some scalding coffee.

"The method of the mechanism's concealment within the masonry might offer a diversion, but it's not beyond Mycroft's own faculties to resolve, if he would but stir himself from the comforts of the Diogenes."

I thought it a little rich for Holmes to remark upon his brother's indolence, given his own moments of torpor, but I kept the observation to myself.

"But where's the crime, eh? The entire affair's a curiosity, nothing more." The detective's eyes closed and he clamped his pipe back between his teeth, his manner reminding me of a crocodile I had once seen in Hyde Park Zoo. After eating its fill, it had sunk once more into lethargy, leaving only the knuckle end of its dinner projecting from its maw.

"Mr Holmes, Dr Watson – a caller for you!" announced Mrs Hudson from the doorway.

"Ah!" said Holmes, sitting up straight in his chair, "let us see what fresh intrigue awaits us. Mrs Hudson, you may show the gentleman in."

Time was, I might have wondered how Holmes had already determined the sex of our as yet unseen guest, but I had become wise to his methods. The tread upon the stair betrayed a distinct masculine presence, not the lighter feminine foot. As the visitor hove into view – a workingman shod in heavy boots – I permitted myself an inward smile at my accomplishment.

Our visitor was a tall bearded chap clad in oil-stained overalls. By his side he carried a carpetbag with an oriental design of serpents chasing their own tails. Such features as I could make out between his red neckerchief and flat cap were a somewhat protuberant nose and a lively pair of eyes, sparkling behind rounded spectacles.

"Mr 'olmes," he said, "you must 'elp, for I believe you are the only man in all London that can solve the mystery that vexes me –"

"Only man in London, indeed? Is that the limit to my expertise? Why then you must go further afield."

"Mr 'olmes!"

"Come now," I said, shooting my colleague a hard stare. "Holmes's sense of humour is a little caustic, but I've never known him refuse a case worthy of his talents…"

Holmes snorted. "I shall be the judge of that. But first, take a seat in the wingchair and tell us what it is like to be the mechanic responsible for maintaining a moving stairway. Are the crowds at Harrods appreciative of this new method of locomotion?"

The visitor's mouth dropped open in surprise. "By 'eck. 'ow could you 'ave known that?"

I too was astounded. "Is that indeed your profession?"

"It is, sir, and I 'ave left that very department store not 'alf an hour ago. How ever could you 'ave known?"

"Come, come," said Holmes. "It is writ so large upon your person, it needs no explanation, surely? Watson, what do you say?"

Cursing my earlier smugness, I studied the visitor for clues. "Well, the mechanical nature of his work is clear enough from the oil stains and smuts upon his face and hands, and I suppose his bag may conceal some tools peculiar to the task… but as to why a *moving* walkway, I cannot imagine! Are there some skills specially required for such a task?"

"No, no." The man rubbed his blackened forehead. "Any good engineer could fix her up and keep her runnin' steady. But it's the only moving staircase in England – what could let you know I work upon that?"

"It is the very singular nature of your employment that gives you away," declared Holmes. "Watson, you must learn to employ all of your senses in detection! Your eyes inform you this fellow is a mechanic; let your nose reveal a more detailed truth."

Feeling a little self-conscious, I scented the air. Alongside the expected notes of oil and engine fumes, the visitor carried with him distinct odours of ammonia and brandy.

"I understand," continued Holmes, "that travellers on the *escalator* are offered both cognac and smelling salts to revive them after their trip, further supplies of which are stowed in an alcove beneath the stairway, near where our visitor no doubt spends his day monitoring the running of the mechanism."

"And I've 'ad just cause to draw on both, after what I've seen!" The engineer brushed himself down, giving every appearance of embarrassment. "Who'd have thought the whiff off a geezer's clothes could be so revealing?"

"A small matter," said Holmes. "They reveal exactly as much as they are intended to."

A strange look passed between the visitor and Holmes, the meaning of which I could not discern. The visitor re-settled the carpetbag upon his lap, and said, "Maybe I should tell you of the mystery?"

"Pray continue," said Holmes. "It will be most illuminating."

"As you know, sir, the moving walkway is a new invention, and it's yet to be decided if it's to be kept on, or if it's all a bit too disturbing. Well, to that end, the store 'as been keeping logbooks, detailing the gents' and ladies' disposition as they get on, and their nervous state as they get off. A trial, as it were."

"Makes sense," I said. "A sound clinical investigation, before installing more of these infernal contraptions."

"Well, you see, I got to looking at one of these log books, sir." The man shifted in his seat. "What if I was to tell you, Mr 'olmes, that the number of people that gets off at the top of the stairway *is not the same as the number of folks that climbed on*?"

"Stop!" cried Holmes. "I've had enough of this foolishness. This story has not one iota of truth!"

The engineer was indignant. "Foolish it may be, but I've taken my life in my hands bringing it to you. Quality folks vanishing clean off a moving walkway! It's more than my job's worth –"

"Your job is worth nothing!" Holmes declared. "Just like the clothes you've carefully chosen, it's all a contrivance. And it is as false as the nose on your face!"

With a burst of energy, Holmes leapt from his seat. He approached the visitor, seized his blobby nose, tore it clean away and dashed it to the ground.

The visitor sighed and rubbed his face. An aquiline profile was revealed, now that the waxy disguise had been removed.

"As ever, it was a vain hope to deceive the 'Great Detective'," he said, in cultured, ironic tones. "It would seem I must try another tack." Opening his carpetbag, he drew out a curious contraption, rather like an over-sized carriage clock. Its sides were open, revealing an intricate latticework of cogs, brass valves and ivory bars. He depressed a tiny lever and set the gears spinning busily.

"What is the meaning of this charade?" I challenged. "Explain yourself, sir!"

"There is no time, Mr Watson – and too much time altogether."

The mechanism vibrated, the air shimmered, and before our very eyes, the visitor faded clean away…

"By Jove!" I said. "First a disguise and then a vanishing trick. I've never seen such a display of smoke and mirrors!"

"And all most carefully constructed." Holmes paced the room. "I had been planning a modest monograph on ascending chambers and moving stairways. New technologies always intrigue me, for men so swiftly find a way to subvert them for devilish purposes… This entire matter has been devised to intrigue and ensnare me."

"But how was the effect achieved? Some kind of image displaced from the street below?" I recalled the Adventure of the Haunted Townhouse, in which Holmes had uncovered a spectre created by means of a theatrical illusion known as "Pepper's Ghost". I hoped this might provide an explanation for the shadowy figure I had observed before the false engineer's arrival. Perhaps this had been a test of the method?

I opened my mouth to elucidate, but Holmes held up a hand. "No, Watson, the angles are not favourable. Besides, how would the illusion have knocked at the front door, and travelled up the stairs with Mrs Hudson? That would be a very substantial ghost."

"Well, damn it, what is the alternative? You can't believe a man just vanished clean away, like some penny dreadful phantom!"

Holmes smiled thinly. "Only the weakest minds believe in spirits. There was a method and a means behind this… Yes, and a singular intelligence too. I must consider the matter further." Seizing the tobacco-filled Persian slipper from the mantle, Holmes retreated to his room.

I moved over and examined the chair, cautiously testing the substance of its fabric and frame. It neither disappeared nor transformed into a bowl of goldfish, but was just as solid and as familiar as expected. If a substitution had occurred, I was none the wiser.

I ran my hands down the sides of the cushion, and frowned as my finger caught the teeth of an irregularly shaped cogwheel.

I drew it out, and examined it. In tiny etched letters, it revealed its maker to be *Wells & Co.*

I spent my afternoon in pursuit of the mystery of the cogwheel, Holmes proving impossible to dislodge from his smoke-ridden chambers, even when told of my discovery.

"Leave me alone, Watson," he said. "Once I've determined the method of our visitor's departure, all else will fall into place…"

Well, I've never been much of a man for contemplation! I prefer action to reflection, and truth be told, the affair had unsettled me. The usually homely environs of Baker Street felt haunted by the morning's manifestations, and I could find no peace there.

I began my enquiry at the premises of Pugh & Sons, a jeweller who had once made a fine job of restoring my late father's watch. I presented the wheel to young Roderick Pugh, and asked what he could tell me.

"This is a cam of some sort. Do you know what that is?" I professed I did not. "Its eccentric surface would suggest it is part of a machine of some complexity. The more cams employed in conjunction, the greater the sophistication of action."

"Might it be from a machine that could produce a vanishing effect?"

The young man adjusted his eyeglass. "Clockwork can do all sorts of things... It can make mechanical swans that swim on glassy lakes, marionettes that pirouette, and scribes that write complex sentences... In Austria they have an automatic Turk who can challenge the greatest grandmaster at chess! All manner of trickery is possible. But I cannot discern the purpose of the whole from so small a part."

"But do you know anything about its manufacture?"

"It's machine-made, that much I can tell, and it's been subjected to some considerable heat stress in the past, perhaps through excess operation? As to who created it... This company, 'Wells & Co.'; I'm afraid I'm not familiar with them at all."

I thanked him for his assistance, and went on my way. My progress onward was haphazard, calling in at such jewellers, clockmakers and engineering works as I could find, but none had any new information to share. As the day darkened, I realised I had wandered from the main thoroughfare. The businesses that lined the streets had changed from respectable traders to pawnbrokers and hawkers of shoddy second hand goods.

I was about to return to Baker Street, when a faded sign caught my eye, propped in the window of the dingiest shop of all:

Wells & Co.
Retailers of Antiquity
&
Chronologists of Futurity

I pushed the door open, causing a bell to dance and ring. The interior of the shop was cluttered, every surface littered with objects, although what philosophy had been employed in their collection, I could not tell. Costumes from ages gone by were draped on pegs, and books of all kinds lined the shelves, from crumbling scrolls to small green volumes with seabirds on the spines. I took them to be a range of mysteries. A complex array of pipes, retorts and tubes covered an oak table, and a foul dark liquid bubbled over a Bunsen. In a corner, a bell-shaped terrarium housed a curious lizard that stood upon its rear legs and tore at the branches within with its foreshortened front limbs. I bent over and tapped the glass, and it gnashed its teeth with such ferocity that I took a step back.

"Do not tantalise the tyrannosaurus, you will only give it indigestion."

I looked up. Hunched over a writing desk at the rear of the store sat an old man with flowing white locks, dressed in an embroidered smoking cap and jacket. Despite his great age, his watery eyes betrayed alertness and a keen intelligence. He was almost entirely obscured by an enormous stack of papers, and I had at first mistaken his hunched frame and rumpled clothes for another pile of clutter.

"I meant to make a study of the beast to pass the time," he continued, "but it was a foolish idea. It needs to be fed constantly, and grows at a most alarming rate. And besides, who would publish it, hmm?"

"It's certainly an unusual specimen," I said. "Presumably from some lost plateau in darkest South America?"

"A little further afield." The old man beckoned me closer. "Would you care for a coffee, Watson? There's some on the flame, and there are cigars made from a rare leaf in the humidor, if you would like one…"

"Never mind this talk of coffee and cigars," I said, in some irritation. "You have me at a disadvantage, sir. You know my name, and I do not know yours. I assume you are the Mr Wells whose card is displayed outside?"

"Pshaw!" The old man waved his hand. "That would be a borrowing, no more. A label so you'd know where to come. And I have been waiting quite a long time for you, Watson. You found the cam, of course."

I drew the wheel out of my pocket and the old man snatched it from me.

"It works as a regulator, you understand. Since it fell free of its mooring at Baker Street, my arrivals have become rather scattershot. If I want to target a precise date, I am forced to take the longest path of all, and simply wait it out." He smiled. "Hence my sad state of decrepitude."

"I'm sorry," I said. "I don't follow this. Am I to understand you're claiming some direct connexion to the Case of the Vanishing Moving-Walkway Engineer?"

"Oh Watson… You always had a penchant for melodrama. I can see you've already assigned a lurid title for your write-up in *The Strand*." The old man sighed. "Do you really not know me? Make a proper study of my features."

I stared closer.

Disregarding the shopkeeper's hunched bearing and withered skin, his high forehead and hawk-like aspect did hold a certain familiarity…

"You remind me, I must confess, of my colleague Holmes," I said slowly. "He is a private man, though, and has said little of his family. If you are some relation, then –"

"No relation." The old man stood up with a cacophony of creaks and groans, and thrust his profile into the light. "I am Sherlock Holmes himself."

"Good Lord!"

During our adventures together, Holmes had shown an aptitude for disguise that would put Drury Lane's finest to shame, throwing himself into roles from the rowdiest street tough to the most distinguished dowager duchess. Often I was quite taken in, and cursed myself afterward for not seeing through the greasepaint and whiskers to the familiar face beneath.

"Holmes, this is remarkable! This is surely your greatest disguise yet. But why the performance? Whom are you trying to baffle?"

"It's no disguise."

"What, then?"

"Merely the passage of years, my friend," the old man said. "*Tempus edax rerum*. Time devours all."

I stared at Holmes – for I was certain now that it was he – and said, "Old boy, if you've taken some kind of medication or accelerant to alter your appearance, you must tell me, I beg of you. There may be a counter-serum to return you to yourself."

"I have taken no drug."

Holmes regarded me with a weary patience. I took a deep breath and continued. "Well then, if you are asking me to believe that between this morning and this afternoon you've aged fifty years in five hours, I fear the reason for which you are so justly famed is now in doubt."

"A fair assumption. But if you will allow me, I will prove the truth of it." Holmes reached down the side of his desk and lifted up a carpetbag covered in serpents chasing their own tails; in design so similar to the carrier I had seen this morning I might have sworn it to be the same, had it not been much more worn.

"What if I was to tell you, Watson, there was a machine that could transgress the boundaries of time, allowing the operator to step from today to tomorrow, and tomorrow to yesterday?"

Opening the bag, he lifted out a carriage-clock-type contraption, and taking some tools from a workbox, he began to insert the cog I had brought into the mechanism's heart.

I laughed, a little uneasily. "Then I should wonder how even you had managed to uncover this marvel, while I spent all day in pursuit of a single cog…"

"But I haven't." The old man smiled. "I, or rather he, has yet to leave his room. If you were to take a taxi back to Baker Street right now and knock upon Holmes's door, there you would find my younger self, occupied in smoky contemplation."

"You mean to suggest *two* of you exist contemporaneously?"

"Of course."

"Two Holmes." I sat down rather heavily on a chair. "Good heavens. I hadn't realised when I had good fortune…"

"This morning's dematerialisation has stultified him." The old man sniffed. "It's not his fault. He is attempting to reason how a man may vanish into thin air, but the canvas of ideas he works on only allows for a limited number of dimensions... Soon though, he will discover another matter, apparently unconnected, is the key. And that we must not allow to happen."

I rubbed my head, wondering if the miasma of the shop, with its bubbling potions, strange artefacts and disagreeable lizard, had somehow addled me. Had I lost my wits, or had Holmes lost his?

"This is the knottiest conundrum you've ever asked me to understand, Holmes. You must take it a little slower."

"Shall we go for a stroll, and I will do my best to explain?" Holmes took my arm and lifting the carpetbag in the other, led me to the door. "Indulge the whim of an old man."

"The affair began," said the aged Holmes as we walked along the Embankment, "with the discovery of the first time machine. We do not know what became of its inventor... perhaps he found a future utopia and decided to remain there, or an encounter with a less civilised cousin forcibly prevented his return to the present; this is supposition, however, there is no evidence either way. What remains of his work is a scale model – a proof-of-concept, most likely – sent ahead to demonstrate the possibility of voyaging through time. A power failure or some automatic mechanism arrested its journey two hundred years in the past, and there – for reasons of superstition or covetousness or blind chance – it remained, bricked up within a wall."

"But this is the matter that Holmes – my Holmes, that is – spoke of this morning," I said. "He'd had a request from Mycroft to investigate such a device, and rather dismissed it."

The older Holmes snorted. "I've never enjoyed being at Mycroft's beck and call. My resolution will not last. The lure of the mystery is too strong. You and I will travel to a house in Richmond, currently undergoing demolition by its new owners, and we will examine the device *in situ* within the opened cavity in the wall. We will discover that the masonry is old, and aside from the blow of the builder's hammer that cracked it, shows no signs of previous tampering. We will see the blocks of stone below and above the nook are solid, ruling out the possibility of the device being somehow dropped in. We will note that the mechanism is rusted and corrupted by time, but that its parts are complex and of modern manufacture…"

"By 'we' you mean 'you', of course."

"Of course," said the old man. "But you know my precept, Watson, and how to apply it."

I nodded. "When you've eliminated the impossible whatever remains, however improbable, must be the truth."

"Quite so. Only a leap in time could create a modern day object sealed so completely within an ancient wall. And with the matter closed, I turned the device over to Mycroft."

"But why would that be a problem?"

"Mycroft's entanglement with the powers of state was greater than I ever realised," said the old man. "I had viewed the time machine entirely as a mystery to be solved and then put aside. Once unravelled, I dismissed it from my mind –"

"Yes," I remarked drolly, "that would be typical."

"– something destined to remain unpublished, like the Giant Rat of Sumatra or the Tragedy of the Weeping Candelabra; cases for which the world is not yet ready. Mycroft instead asked how the machine could be *used*. It might've been beyond the minds of our most brilliant scientists to devise it, but it was not beyond them to *copy* an existing template. A manufacturing company under the moniker of Wells & Co. spent many years analysing the decayed parts and painstakingly constructing a replica. And that is where it all went wrong."

The old man stopped and leant upon the balustrade. Beneath us, the sluggish waters of the Thames rolled by, carrying with them a scattering of tiny rowboats and goods ferries. Across the banks, yellow light glowed in the windows of Parliament, and above that august chamber, the chimes of Big Ben began to toll the hour.

"A blade may be used to harvest crops, or cut flesh. A telegraph might arrest a criminal's flight or provide the warning that prompts their escape," said Holmes. "It is in the unforeseen ends to which mankind puts his inventions that the devilment lies."

"But Mycroft would have no criminal intent, surely?" I said. I had met Holmes's brother before, and although he displayed a tendency towards the pompous, I never doubted he shared Holmes's passion for justice.

"No, that would've been easier to prevent... It was the maintenance of order that was his goal." Holmes spoke bitterly. "Imagine a world where no murderer goes unpunished! For whenever a body is discovered, a Chronological Detective traverses back through time – by means of his state-sanctioned machine – and apprehends the would-be culprit before the crime ever takes place. What would you make of such a world, Watson? Do you think it would be paradise, or rather a sort of hell?"

The old man's eyes studied me. I had the sensation my answer held some great importance to him. I leant against the damp stone wall, and considered my response.

"A world where all murderers see justice... It would mean no more need for consulting detectives, and a far easier ride for Inspector Lestrade and his cronies, but how could it be bad? Solving crime is what you strive for, surely?"

Holmes shook his head, and looked away. "Even good men on occasion hesitate on the precipice of crime. You and I know this to be true. Kindly souls, when pushed beyond endurance, lash out – a devoted man or woman can be driven to extremes to protect someone they love. Until the fatal blow is struck, is that person truly guilty?"

"These are dark questions you ask, Holmes," I said. "And I'm a doctor, not a philosopher. But I can only conclude, if your 'Time Machine' showed the person to be a murderer, then as a murderer they should be judged."

"And if these time-arrested perpetrators suffered the same sentence we now deal to murderers, what then? Would you allow that fate to happen to anyone, anyone at all? I tell you, Watson, when a man is condemned for a crime he has not yet committed, it is not a utopia. It is the very worst of tyrannies."

A chill ran through my bones that had little to do with the damp river air.

"This is the reason, then," I whispered. "The reason you came back. To prevent... an execution, of someone close to you."

"I had to try!" The old man's eyes danced wildly. "But each time I fail. And I have tried so many times to prevent the sequence of events. I have attempted to waylay my younger self, to mislead him, to distract him with other matters –"

"The engineer!" I cried. "You mean to say –"

"Not my greatest disguise, perhaps, but oh! I had set *such* a mystery to beguile him. Games within games! Months of planning, but he saw through it in an instant, and once more I had to give way…"

I smiled grimly. "Only Sherlock Holmes could ever outwit Sherlock Holmes."

The old man lifted his head. Even in his dotage, he was not immune to flattery.

"It all seems so long ago… And I fear I have reached my limits." He opened the handles of the carrier and removed the mechanism within, handing the carpetbag to me. "Time is like a parchment, scribbled over by a careless child… There are only so many occasions rough work can be scratched out before its substance tears irreparably. Fragments of the overwritten past have already started to linger, and manifest as ghosts…"

I recalled the sorrowful face in the mirror and the shadow presence in the chair. "Yes. I've seen them."

"Then you know I dare not go back again." The old man clasped my arm, his grip surprisingly strong. "It is up to you to prevent the younger Holmes from discovering the first time machine, and deducing its purpose."

"I will do my best," I vowed.

"Perhaps my mistake has been to rely on myself, and not confide in you before. You were always my greatest resource, Watson. Perhaps now you can be your own salvation as well."

He touched the control levers on the mechanism, and the air about him began to blur. "Goodbye my friend, and good luck!"

The older Holmes faded clean away.

I shall not set down a lengthy description of my visit to the house in Richmond that same night, for it would take the pen of a Dickens to depict the phantasmagoria that awaited me. I scarcely wondered that the new owners had sought to tear the place down, for the unearthly presence within was disturbing, even to one who had been forewarned of it.

I located the cavity and broke it open with a crowbar, allowing the mechanism to be fully drawn out. I dashed it to pieces on the ground, and the air cleared, as if an exorcism had taken place. I collected the fragments and bundled them into a sack that I cast into the Thames. As it sank below the roiling surface, I heaved a sigh of relief.

Returning to Baker Street, I was thankful to find Holmes – my Holmes – still closeted in his chamber. Taking the letter from Mycroft – the last evidence of the day's events – I threw it into the fireplace, and then at last sank into an exhausted sleep.

I rose late the next morning. Holmes – who kept whatever hours he pleased, especially when occupied by affairs of the mind – was still at the breakfast table.

"A fine day," I remarked, as I tended to the coffee pot. "Let us hope it sees no more conjuring tricks, eh?"

"Oh, that affair… I had quite forgotten it." Holmes's long fingers gestured towards the corner. "I was rather more occupied wondering where that object had come from."

The carpetbag!

I cursed myself. The older Holmes had presented it to me, and I had brought it back to Baker Street, casting it down as I sought Mycroft's letter. It was quite empty, so I prayed there was a limit to the damage it could cause…

"I happened across it in my wanderings," I said, "and rather took a fancy to it."

"Indeed?" Holmes raised an eyebrow. "A singular design, and not your style at all. It does seem familiar…"

"Ah yes," I bluffed. "As carried by that engineer chap. That's probably what put me in a mind to pick it up. In case it was a clue, or similar."

"Not similar. The very same, I should say."

"Now really, old man…"

"I am an excellent observer, and this carpetbag carries the exact markers of manufacture, and patterns of scratching about the clasp as its predecessor. And yet... it has clearly been distressed and moth-eaten... and not by any crude fakery. Which would mean..."

Holmes paused, and his brow furrowed. Then he steepled his fingers and remarked, "Yes, I see it all now. Well, well, well."

"Don't give the matter any more consideration. I beg of you." I snatched up the bag. "Unpleasant gaudy object. I'll have Mrs Hudson burn it."

"Your agitation surprises me, Watson," Holmes said. "But if you really think it best..."

"I do. I'll see to it at once." I pulled on the bell rope. "And then what shall we do with the rest of the day?"

"Oh, I don't know, Watson." Holmes smiled. "London is a busy metropolis. I'm sure some mystery will present itself..."

How much did he understand? How much did his future self know? I cannot be sure. I write these words in my diaries in the knowledge that he never consults them. I cannot let the episode go unrecorded. But it would not be the first or the last time I would be grateful for the wisdom of my friend, the detective Sherlock Holmes.

ABOUT THE AUTHOR

Roy Gill's first novel, *Daemon Parallel*, was published in 2012. A contemporary fantasy set in a transformed Edinburgh, it follows a teenage boy on a quest to bring back his father from the dead. A sequel, *Werewolf Parallel*, takes the story into a new dimension… Roy also works as a scriptwriter, and has contributed a feature length special, *The Prime of Deacon Brodie*, to Big Finish's audio drama series *The Confessions of Dorian Gray.* He was a Scottish Book Trust New Writers' Award Winner in 2010, and has been shortlisted for both the Kelpies and Sceptre Prize. Other publications include fiction and essays for *Algebra* (Tramway Theatre), *Kin*, *Critical Quarterly*, *Fractured West*, *Creeping Flesh* and the Iris Wildthyme anniversary anthology *Fifteen*. Find out more at roygill.com or follow @roy_gill on Twitter.

THE GIRL WHO PAID
FOR SILENCE

⊚⃝⚬

BY SCOTT HANDCOCK

s last year drew to a close, I found myself subject to one of the most peculiar encounters I have ever been privy to. Indeed, the meeting in question continues to defy explanation, even after having been presented to my long-standing colleague and friend, Sherlock Holmes – a detail that, in itself, is able to unsettle me a great deal more than many of those associated with the case – and it is for that reason that I have chosen to document it here.

The incident in question occurred on the last day of October, when the city of London had been subjected to the most terrible of crimes. A young girl had been found dead in the streets at the start of the month, her body having been defiled in the most appalling manner imaginable, and her killer still walked the streets freely. To this day, one cannot comprehend what would drive another human to behave in such a manner, and so one could only conclude that the culprit was some inhuman monster or somesuch, though a monster who had been adept at covering his tracks and eluding the attentions of Scotland Yard.

With the Ripper murders still fresh in all our minds, the city of London had shuddered. Women and children repaired to their homes before dusk, and even their husbands and fathers were scarcely to be seen on the streets once night had fallen. Fear gripped the city once again. Nightmarish thoughts filled our collective mind at every waking hour.

Could it be, people wondered, tacitly? Perhaps it truly was the Ripper, returned to us to seek revenge and complete his ungodly work? People routinely talk of devils and daemons walking among us – a sentiment I would usually have no time for – but in instances such as this, I could not help but question whether it truly was the only rational explanation? Or, at the very least, an explanation considerably less discomfiting than the notion that the culprit was a man such as you or I, a man who had developed a taste for such atrocities...

Though my associate, Sherlock Holmes, would never confess to such a thing, I knew that even he had been disturbed upon hearing the news of the young girl's death. Something about the details of the story punctured his typical arrogance, and instead he had become subdued and slightly withdrawn. Indeed, it was on account of the sudden change in his demeanour that I had taken to arranging luncheon one afternoon in our rooms at Baker Street, in the hope of raising his spirits or, at the very least, providing some manner of distraction from the matter in hand.

It was, as I have previously stated, the final day of October, and not a particularly pleasant day at that. The streets were strewn with drifts of muddy leaves and, at approximately two o'clock in the afternoon – the time, incidentally, at which I had originally anticipated the arrival of my friend – a heavy rainstorm broke in the skies above the city. Streams of water flowed along the cobbles, and insistent raindrops lashed against the windowpanes. I subsequently elected to light a modest fire in the sitting-room for, although I had taken the unseasonable weather into account previously, there was still a peculiar chill in the air.

A knock at the door drew me back from this diversion and, believing it to be my friend, who had mistakenly left his house keys behind that day, I went downstairs to greet him, Mrs Hudson having gone out. It was only upon opening the door, however, that I found myself presented with the most unexpected visitor, the memory of whom still haunts me.

It was a child, a girl, not much older than the one whose details had been reported in the press, and at first, she did not speak. Rather, she simply stood there, patiently, waiting to be addressed.

I could tell from the quality of her clothing that she hailed from a privileged family, which made her appearance on the doorstep all the more incongruous.

Her expression was not one that I was accustomed to seeing upon the faces of children. In the presence of nieces and nephews, one soon finds oneself infected by their joy and youthful abandon, all too easily transported back to the childhood mentality we all undoubtedly once enjoyed. But that was not the case with this young girl. Instead of joy, there was a peculiar sadness to her features, one that I had not witnessed in a great many years. Guilt, perhaps? Or the fear of a secret long-since broken?

She looked up at me, imploringly.

"Can I help you?" I asked, immediately imagining that she had come to the wrong address, or might be otherwise lost.

Her sense of sadness faltered for an instant, and the edges of her lips curled up into what resembled a hopeful smile.

"Would you be Dr Watson?" she asked, her soft voice betraying an innocence at odds with her air of confidence. Something about her suggested that she was unafraid of adults, such as myself. Though, given recent events, this struck me as a somewhat foolhardy attitude on her part. As such, concerned for the welfare of this young girl, I promptly answered.

"I am he," I confirmed, still a little perplexed by her arrival. It would, after all, be fair to say that most visitors come in order to speak with Mr Holmes himself. And yet, this child had been sure to ask only for me.

Our conversation was interrupted by a sudden crack of thunder and so, aware that this young girl had already been subjected to the elements, I invited her inside and out of the rain, leading her upstairs to the sitting-room.

I sat her next to the fire and asked if she would like me to remove her coat, an offer she politely, yet firmly, declined. I took my place in the armchair opposite.

"Have you a name?" I asked, aware that I was unsure what to call her.

"Emily," said she with a smile.

"A very nice name," I told her, attempting to put her at her ease. "And your parents, what are their names?"

Emily shook her head, as though that was an answer.

"What I meant to ask," I persisted, determined to learn more about my visitor, "is have you a surname?" I believed that if I was able to glean that detail from her, I might venture closer to discovering who she was and where she had come from.

"I have no surname," she answered, "only Emily."

As you can no doubt appreciate, I found this difficult to accept, but took it to be the response of a young girl not yet comfortable in her surroundings. And yet, this was at odds with the openness she had proffered to me earlier.

"Why have you come here, Emily?" asked I, not one for playing games.

Her response was swift.

"To find you, Dr Watson."

"But why?"

"Surely you've seen the stories in the press?"

I was momentarily thrown by this. Not only on account of the question itself, but also the manner in which it was delivered. It hung in the air for a matter of seconds until – sensing either my lapse in concentration or, more likely, my genuine sense of confusion at the question she had asked – Emily continued.

"The stories about a young girl, the girl who was" – she hesitated momentarily, before choosing the word – "murdered?"

"You shouldn't be reading about such things," I snapped instinctively, appalled. "The reports in the press are often sensationalist fearmongering, and I can personally vouch for the fact that Scotland Yard are on the case and have the matter in hand. It is being investigated by the very best men available. It is of no concern to a girl such as yourself."

"She was my friend," she responded, prompting a silence I hadn't anticipated. "Christine, the girl who died. She was my friend."

My heart sank in my chest at the very thought of it. Although it was obvious in hindsight, the fact that the crime might have some bearing upon anyone other than the victim's family had not occurred to me, less so the impact it might have on those too young to comprehend the motives behind such dreadful, inexplicable brutality.

Emily looked at me apologetically.

"Have I said the wrong thing?"

I shook my head and offered my condolences. "The whole affair makes me feel quite uneasy," I explained. "That it should extend to children as young as yourself simply does not bear thinking about." I paused. "Nevertheless, you should not have come to this place alone, whatever your reasoning. The streets of London are not a safe place to be at the present time. You are surely aware of that?"

"I am," she concurred, "and yet I am also aware that I have important information."

In spite of the dubious circumstances, I must confess that my curiosity had been piqued.

"What information?" I asked, unsure that I truly wanted to learn the answer, and it was at that point that Emily truly surprised me.

"I was there," she told me simply, casting her eyes toward the floor. "I was there when Christine died, I saw what happened."

As she uttered these words, I felt a suddenly gnawing sensation in the pit of my stomach, and my heart began to quicken in my chest. Either this was some macabre jape played by the most wicked of children, or Emily truly had been witness to the dreadful murder and debasement of an innocent girl.

I wished, with all my heart, that neither scenario was true, that there was, instead, another alternative that had not yet presented itself.

"You realise just how serious this claim you're making is?" Emily nodded. "Why then have you not spoken out before?"

"No one else would listen," she answered meekly, before raising her gaze to meet mine. A solitary tear rolled along her cheek. "That's why I came to you, Dr Watson. I knew that you would listen."

I responded in the only way I was then able: by thanking her for her kind appraisal of my character, and offering to listen to her account as she had requested.

Any doubts I may have had as to the validity of Emily's story were soon quashed by the level of detail she then shared with me. Her description of events went far beyond that of a girl's imagination and, as such, made for uncomfortable listening. To have such inhuman acts related by such an innocent tongue – that in itself was a crime.

She told me how she and the victim, Christine Saunders, had been playing in a local park one afternoon. They had been under the supervision of Christine's nanny when, apparently from nowhere, an unknown man came and snatched both girls away from their supposed guardian. She was unable to put up a fight. Instead, she could only report their abduction to the authorities.

That much of the story I was already well-acquainted with, thanks to the tawdry appetites of the London press. The atrocities Emily then went on to describe – actions I dare not repeat in my own hand, even now – were truly despicable, and crimes no girl should have ever been privy to.

Suffice to say that Emily escaped the killer's attentions; or, more accurately, he fled the scene and abandoned her. Whether this was because his ghoulish appetite had already been sated, or he feared the possibility of his actions being uncovered, I cannot say. But Emily remained with her friend, by her side, long after the poor girl's death.

She screamed and screamed until the authorities came and took the body away. And then, having come to terms with what had happened that fateful day, she said she came to find me.

"It was horrible," Emily sobbed, turning her attention back toward the floor, leaving me little choice but to agree.

Unsure what to say, or how to comfort her, I was unexpectedly relieved by the sudden – and somewhat alarming – noise of someone knocking loudly at the street door. I shall confess to being more than a little startled by the interruption and was then equally perturbed to discover, upon glancing over at the clock, that it was now almost four o'clock in the afternoon.

I left my seat and made my way to the front door where, two hours later than I had originally anticipated, Sherlock Holmes was standing, waiting to be allowed entry.

"Do forgive my tardiness, Watson," he muttered, by way of an apology. "As I am sure you have no doubt deduced, I misplaced my keys this morning; I am most grateful to you for granting me access."

He then barged straight up to the sitting-room, leaving me to close the door behind him.

I had expected him to pass some remark upon my visitor when he entered the room, but instead he refrained from making comment, or even acknowledging her presence. Instead, he stationed himself in the armchair nearest the window, waiting for me to address him.

Seconds passed. I stood there, more than a trifle flabbergasted by his behaviour. Even for Sherlock Holmes, a man not renowned for his adherence to social niceties, his snub of Emily seemed unnecessarily discourteous.

"Are you quite well?" he asked, once more overlooking the guest sat opposite us, and at that point, I must confess to almost having lost my temper with the man.

"Can't you see we have company?" I asked, struggling to maintain my composure in the young girl's presence.

Holmes turned to the chair where Emily was sat as though it had never once occurred to him that someone else might be with us.

"Ah," said he, with an air of vague curiosity, quite unlike him, before prompting, "please, do not halt on my account. Continue."

I took to my seat and turned to Emily once more, ignoring Holmes and his peculiar manner. His eyes followed me as I spoke with her.

"Are you happy to continue?" I asked, aware that our discussion had been abruptly interrupted by my colleague's arrival. She shook her head, not saying a word, and I immediately sensed her discomfort. I reminded myself that she had sought me out, not he, and in spite of the great man's reputation, she was clearly more than a little overwhelmed in his company and ill at ease.

"Would you like me to show you out?" I offered instead, and with a slight nod she rose from her seat and accompanied me down to the street door. I was keenly aware of the fact that the skies above the city were darkening and dusk was beginning to fall. With this in mind, together with my newly acquired knowledge of recent events, I elected to summon a hansom that she might be safely conveyed to her home.

"There really is no need," she assured me, not wishing to be any trouble, but it was not a chance I was willing to take. Understandably,

Emily was reluctant to share her address with me and so, when finally a cab pulled up, I determined to take care of the matter discreetly.

I handed over a not immodest sum of money to the driver in question and instructed him to take the young lady home, wherever that might be – and I handed over to him sufficient funds to transport her across half of Greater London, not forgetting a generous tip for his troubles.

Oddly, the driver seemed less than keen on this arrangement. Indeed, he made several attempts to protest.

"But sir," he cried.

"But nothing," I told him firmly. The instructions were clear, and the young girl's safe passage across the city was paramount. Not wishing to allow him any further opportunity to argue the terms, I opened the door to the cab and ushered Emily inside. "Get her home as quickly as you are able," I said, closing the door behind her, "that's all I ask," and dutifully, the driver nodded.

I watched as the hansom rattled away into the swirls of rain and fog. Then, as I returned indoors, I noticed Holmes watching me curiously from the window. His gaze met mine and, making my way indoors once more, I determined to get to the bottom of his behaviour.

Holmes had already made himself quite comfortable in my absence. Upon entering the sitting-room once more, I was confronted by spirals of thick tobacco smoke, emanating from his favourite pipe, and noticed an empty glass upon the table next to him.

He eyed me warily as I returned to my chair, though for precisely what reason I could not fathom. Then, as though to unsettle me further, he smiled at me. (A smile from Holmes without provocation is almost never comforting.)

"Would you care to explain to me what that exchange was all about?" said he.

"How do you mean?" I asked.

"Your guest," Holmes continued.

"What about her?"

He slowly refilled his pipe. "Tell me about her," he smiled. "How did she come to be here, for example?"

Reluctantly, I allowed my temper to subside and, recognising the greater implications for the case at large, I determined to share the details of Emily's visit.

"She arrived a matter of hours ago," I started, "when you were supposed to be here."

"So she was looking for me?"

"Not at all," I replied, and I must confess to taking satisfaction in momentarily puncturing Holmes's usually impenetrable ego. "She came here looking for me, and me alone."

"You?" Holmes asked, affronted. "Whatever for?"

"I dare say she was hoping to speak with someone who would take her seriously, someone a little more responsive? You saw how she reacted to your presence, Holmes. Your reputation precedes you!"

"Indeed," he agreed half-heartedly. "So what matter was it that brought her here? It seems to have cast something of a mood over you, whatever it might be."

Holmes took another drag on his pipe.

"It regarded the Saunders case," I told him, and immediately he set his pipe upon the table.

"Do go on," he prompted.

And so, at length, I related to my associate all the details of the case that Emily herself had shared with me, including her description of the assailant and his crimes. Holmes looked at me with a grim expression of pity as I recounted Emily's story, but there was also a peculiar curiosity that I had not witnessed in his countenance for several years.

This was not a straightforward case, I realised, though what I immediately assumed to be Holmes's discomfort at the nature of the crime transpired to be something altogether more unsettling. He allowed me to complete my extraordinary tale before revealing to me the reasons for his unusual behaviour.

He began by asking how the news of the Saunders case had affected me, and I confessed to having been somewhat disturbed by some of the details that had appeared in the press, not least because the description of the victim was not wholly dissimilar to the children of friends and relatives, and was thereby all too easy to identify with.

"Understandable," he concurred, and then he uttered the most outlandish thing I had ever heard anyone say. "You do realise, of course, Watson, that there was nobody else in the room when I arrived."

As you might imagine, I raised an eyebrow, not entirely sure how to respond to such a statement. Then, before I had a chance to challenge him, Holmes followed up his thought, as though to clarify.

"When I entered this room, there was only you," he claimed, and the expression upon my face must have betrayed what I was thinking, for Holmes immediately addressed the obvious issue. "I could see from the manner in which you held yourself that you believed there was someone else here, but I can assure you, there was not. And yet, the intriguing thing is that you still believe there was: a young girl, in that chair, witness to the crimes that have so disgusted you. Could it be that your mind is playing tricks?"

I did my utmost to counter this most absurd of accusations, but it soon became evident that I had no evidence with which to prove the young girl's presence. No more proof than Holmes himself had to confirm my alleged delusion. And yet, in spite of what I had seen, I could not deny there was something strange about the visitation. Not only had she found me, but she had left no physical imprint on our surroundings. She had not taken tea, or written a statement. Nor had she accepted my offer to take her coat upon her entrance.

By this point, I was unclear what I was thinking, or even what had happened.

"Perhaps it was a ghost?" Holmes ventured, clearly amused by the notion. It was unlike him to suggest the irrational, even in jest. "So shaken are you by the recent atrocities, you believe you are actually able to converse with the victim, perhaps in a daydream or somesuch? In so doing, you strive to ascertain precisely what happened to the poor child, or somehow hypothesise how such a terrible fate came to pass?"

"It was not the Saunders girl," I told him, having previously read descriptions and seen images of the victim in the press. The girl who had been in my home had been decidedly different. "Her name was Emily," I continued, "and she was quite exact about the fact that she was a friend of the deceased."

"Emily," Holmes repeated, musing to himself. "And did this 'Emily' have a surname, perchance?"

"Not one she was willing to share," I was forced to admit. Holmes remained unconvinced.

"There are certain features we associate with the human face," he asserted, "ones that the human mind will actively seek out in shapes and colours. They are how we recognise one another. Conversely, however, it is not impossible for people to see faces where they otherwise don't exist, whether that be in the flames of a fire, or the clouds in the sky. I would suggest to you, Watson, that my knocking awoke you from a dream, and in your drowsiness, your mind subsequently pictured a face within the hearth. In a matter of moments, particularly when coupled with the recent reports that have so clearly troubled you, it is quite possible that you invented the whole exchange."

"I am not a man prone to delusion," I insisted angrily, pointedly reminding Holmes that I had been awake since daybreak and, indeed, had been awaiting his arrival throughout the afternoon. My outburst seemed to amuse him to some extent, for he broke into a smile. Then he had me run through my tale again, sparing none of the details that the young girl had entrusted to me, before sincerely promising that he would refer the information to his colleagues down at the Yard. As one might expect, I looked at my associate, bemused, but Holmes had already pre-empted my reaction.

"You are, no doubt, now wondering why I have asked you for such details when I have already made it sufficiently plain that I believe the girl from whom you obtained them to be little more than a figment of your imagination," he stated, quite correct in his presumption. "In truth, I cannot answer that just yet, but I am curious. However you came to be in possession of these details – whether they are themselves some delusion, or you have gleaned them through some medium as yet to be defined by rationalists – I cannot choose to dismiss them out of hand. The killer of that young girl still roams the streets, and it is our duty to do all we can to prevent him from striking again. If this information should assist us in this task, it is not my place to question from whence it came."

And with that, he drew our discussion to an impromptu close. We did not speak of the case again for several days, neither with regard to the murder of Christine Saunders, nor the identity of her mysterious friend, Emily.

During the course of those days, I found myself beginning to question my sense of reason, and the means by which I had come to acquire the young girl's statement. It was not like Holmes to construct a fiction in order to make me lose my nerve, and so I had no choice but to conclude that Emily had, indeed, not been present in the sitting-room upon his arrival: a scenario I was not remotely pleased to have to accept.

Just as Holmes was not one to openly deceive me, I did not believe myself to be susceptible to hallucinations or delusion. Whatever Holmes's take on the case might be, I remained adamant that I had encountered Emily. She existed and I had met her, even if Holmes had not – and I trusted, more than anything, that Holmes would deduce the truth of her during the course of his investigation.

Until such a time came to pass, however, I elected not to address the issue any further, through fear that my friend might otherwise question my sense of reason and thus lose faith in me altogether. Instead we discussed commonplace trivialities. We spoke of the dreadful onset of autumn and the approaching winter, and made light of our plans for Christmastide: a time of year that neither one of us particularly looked forward to.

Holmes never divulged how his enquiries were progressing, nor did I ask. Then, one evening, when he had been due to meet me for a dinner appointment in Mayfair, he failed to arrive. As I have already made clear, this was not an especially odd occurrence, though he sent no note to apologise or advise of his lateness.

Quickly, the hours passed. Seven o'clock, then eight o'clock, then nine. When finally the clock struck ten, my appetite having been sated, I returned to Baker Street, where I was surprised to find that Holmes was not there either. I remained awake for several hours, awaiting his return, but eventually, and reluctantly, had no option but to repair to my bed for the evening, hoping that the following day might yet provide some explanations.

As luck would have it, my hopes were not only met but exceeded quite considerably. At sunrise I was awoken by a knocking upon my door, then the sight of a grinning Holmes drawing back the curtains of my window.

Without so much as an apology for his absence the previous evening, he perched on the edge of my bed and handed me several copies of various morning newspapers.

There, plastered all over their respective front pages, was the news that Christine Saunders's killer – one James Matthews – had been caught by officers the previous day, and that the suspect had openly confessed to committing the crime. To my additional surprise, the facts of the case corresponded exactly with those that I had provided Holmes with the previous week.

"Excellent news, is it not?" Holmes beamed, allowing me less than sufficient time to digest the story. Then, as I scanned the printed words in front of me, I idly suggested that this had been the matter that had kept Holmes from returning home the night before and, to my surprise, he faltered.

"It was, in a manner of speaking," he replied, taking the papers from my hands and casting his own eyes over them once again. "As you will no doubt appreciate, I was keen to impress upon the Yard how vital it was to catch the suspect before he had chance to suspect we might already be on his trail. Though I cannot claim that this is what prevented me from making our dinner appointment yesterday, for which I apologise, incidentally. No, Mr Matthews was taken into custody during the early hours of the afternoon and delivered a statement to confirm his guilt a short time later. I, meanwhile, had taken to pursuing further lines of enquiry."

"The girl?" I asked. Holmes nodded.

"How you came to be in such a position as to impart this information still confounds me," he confessed, and it was clear to me that he was not satisfied.

"Following Matthews's arrest," Holmes continued, "I made my way across town to the home of Christine Saunders. First of all, to extend my condolences to her family, but also to share the news that her killer had been found. They very kindly invited me into their home and, as you might expect, had questions about the arrest. I answered to the best of my ability, and then countered with some questions of my own."

"About their daughter?"

"No. About the girl who came here: Emily."

"Oh," I replied, warily, "and what did they have to say about her?"

"They said a great many things," Holmes confirmed, "but they were most intrigued to learn how I knew the name at all."

"How so?" I asked, somewhat alarmed by Holmes's change of tone.

"It was a name that nobody outside the immediate family had ever been familiar with."

"Then who was she?" I persisted.

"Just a friend," Holmes started, however I detected there was another aspect he was keeping from me, "though a friend only Christine could see: a figment of her own imagination, as is often the case with small children." He halted for a moment, allowing me to process what he was saying. "According to her parents, Christine would always talk of Emily. They would go everywhere together or, at least, Christine believed that they did. They believed she had long-since outgrown this belief, though perhaps…"

"Perhaps?" I prompted, still unclear as to what precisely Holmes was saying.

"Perhaps that might explain how Emily was present to witness her friend's demise?" he offered.

I was dumbstruck.

"You cannot possibly believe what you are telling me," I contested. "The very idea is ludicrous. Beyond ludicrous, in fact!"

"No more ludicrous than you conversing with an empty room," my friend retorted. "And let me assure you, Watson, I have spent many an evening attempting to tie all the details together, to try to make some rational sense of it. On that basis, I can honestly tell you that the only consistent explanation for your visitor is the one that I have now presented."

"An imaginary friend?" I repeated.

"Indeed," Holmes confirmed, before pausing. "I am, as you know, a rationalist, Watson, and so I am sure you can appreciate just how much it pains me to even suggest it. But it could just be that this girl, this figment, has visited our home a great many times before. Confronted by myself, it could well be that she found a mind unwilling to acknowledge her, as you witnessed. And yet in you, my friend, she found someone willing to devote to her the time she needed, and the attention she was seeking."

Flattering though this suggestion was, the very notion remained incomprehensible.

"Whatever the reason for her presence," my colleague continued, "the killer of Christine Saunders is now in custody. He will pay the highest penalties for his depravities, and we have you to thank for that, Watson. You and this mysterious Emily."

With that, he rose from the bed and stepped out onto the landing, turning back to address me one last time.

"Nobody has the right to take the life of another," he mused. "Perhaps that was Christine's gift to her. Emily lives on in spite of the child that bore her having perished. Perhaps there really are such things…?"

Then the door closed, and I found myself left alone with the morning's papers.

To this day, I cannot honestly claim to know precisely what occurred that afternoon. I would not wish to question Holmes's judgement or, indeed, my own. But the whole affair – the visitor in our home, the manner in which James Matthews had been traced – was somewhat incredible, however one chooses to examine it.

I live in hope that, one day, we shall ascertain what truly happened. Until that day, I comfort myself with the thought that we are probably better off never finding out… and that Emily honoured the life of her good friend, Christine Saunders.

ABOUT THE AUTHOR

Scott Handcock is a writer, producer and director based in Cardiff, best known for his work on a range of horror and science-fiction series from Big Finish Productions and the BBC. He has regularly contributed to the *Doctor Who* and *Dark Shadows* franchises, and is the creator and showrunner of *The Confessions of Dorian Gray* starring Alexander Vlahos. In 2013, he left BBC Wales after seven years of working on some of their flagship dramas – including *Doctor Who*, *Torchwood* and *The Sarah Jane Adventures* – and is currently contributing scripts to an upcoming TV drama series. Should you wish to follow his stream of consciousness, you can find Scott on Twitter: @scott_handcock.

AN ADVENTURE IN
THREE COURSES

BY GUY ADAMS

"This Friday," Holmes announced, his attention, as so often the case, lost among assorted alkaloids, "isn't that the first anniversary of Mary's death? We should celebrate."

I was willing to give Holmes the benefit of the doubt that he didn't mean that quite in the conventional sense.

"It is," I replied, "but no we shouldn't."

"Nonsense, I've received an invite to a new private dining club, and this provides an excellent excuse to accept."

Naturally there was little mileage in attempting to argue with Holmes; he was as intransigent as the government's views on foreign policy. This chain of events brought me to a small room hidden away off the Strand, surrounded by old oak, dark leather and so motley a collection of fellow diners one might find more convivial company on a prison ship.

Holmes was late. This was to be expected. Normally, if I wished to attend any social function in his company I would insist on starting at the same geographical point as my companion, some hours before the scheduled rendezvous. This allowed me to push him in the vague direction of the door at the appointed time, something he seemed incapable of doing himself. I would then keep pushing my companion in the preferred direction (towards the theatre, music hall or restaurant being aimed for) all the way, diverting his natural propensity for finding himself in the less salubrious parts of our city, knee deep in villainy armed only with a cane and a terrifying smile.

On that day, the choice had not been available to me. Holmes had conducted a gas experiment which had rendered our rooms uninhabitable for several hours so I had made my regular pilgrimage to Mary's grave and he had ventured to the British Museum, ostensibly to meet our mutual friend Roger Carruthers but really just to sulk.

Whichever task had delayed him, it had done so by nearly an hour.

The headwaiter, indeed the only waiter so far as I could tell, could not have made his disdain clearer had he spat on the table. It is in an interesting and altogether unpleasant development in dining, that the more exclusive the restaurant, the more overt the hatred exhibited towards the diners by its staff. I have no doubt that waiters have often been given due cause to resent the behaviour of those on whom they're tasked to serve, but it is a distinctly modern trend that has encouraged them to show that resentment so plainly. I now find dining in high-class restaurants an act of endurance not dissimilar to being bullied by my seniors at medical school. Perhaps I should resort to similar lengths in order to dissuade them. I'm sure it is not only medical students that grow to mind their manners when presented with a severed leg in their bed.

By the time Holmes finally arrived I had attempted to dull my irritation with a reasonable quantity of the house wine, a Bordeaux only a shade less aggressive than the man who had served it.

"Well," he said, settling down into the chair opposite, "this all seems terribly charming."

He draped his napkin across his lap, exuding a cloud of dust from his jacket that settled on the table linen like the result of a nearby explosion.

"Excuse the state of my dress," he said, slapping at his lapels, "Carruthers and I got rather carried away in the Egyptology room."

"I dread to think."

"Oh, nothing too unforgivable, just trying to solve an ancient murder."

"I'm sure it was diverting."

"Most definitely. It can only have been poison administered through ass's milk."

"How lovely that we can finally put the matter to rest. Should we inform the family?"

"You're in a mood. Why are you in a mood? This is supposed to be a pleasant evening."

"I have spent the last hour with nothing to do but be insulted by waiters."

"And drink wine."

"Yes, and drink wine, is that acceptable?"

"It depends entirely on the quality of the wine." He poured himself a glass, no doubt to toast his having successfully diverted the subject away from his poor time keeping. He took a sip. "Inoffensive, I suppose," he pronounced, "though I'm far from convinced that's a compliment anyone should aspire to."

"It's certainly not one that's ever been aimed at you."

"Thank you," he replied, taking another sip of his wine and avoiding the intended barb entirely.

"So," I asked, willing to be the grown man and move the conversation along, "does this place have a specific theme?"

"Apparently they only serve cold food," he patted his pockets, hunting for the letter that came with his invitation, "something about digestion I have no doubt. Everyone seems terribly concerned about digestion these days."

"Cold food?"

"Yes."

I sighed and poured myself more wine, the redeeming qualities of a nice hearty pie or steak having dissipated, leaving me with little hope for a pleasant night ahead.

Holmes was unpacking his many pockets, making piles of bizarre objects on either side of his plate. An ageing prayer book, its leather cover as cracked and uneven as a dry river bed; a pair of white gloves, their fingers stained red; a set of skeleton keys; a leather folder of darts from a blowpipe.

"Please tell me they haven't been in your pocket since the business with Tonga?"

"Hm?" He glanced at the darts. "Oh, no… they're a gift from Carruthers." He unwrapped the folder, exposing five darts and a vial of liquid. "The venom from a puffer fish, one of the most lethal poisons known to man. He thought it might be of interest."

"Perhaps we could toast with it later should the evening not improve."

"My, but you are surly this evening."

"Just reminded once again of the extraordinary company I keep." He was now trying to untangle a garrotte wire that was caught in the lining of his waistcoat. "To think you always ask me to bring my service revolver if we're heading into murky waters; on current evidence any given day will see you weighed down with a veritable arsenal."

"A revolver is less ostentatious."

"And far more likely to get me locked up. I'm not supposed to go waving it around in public you know."

"What member of the police force would dare? There isn't a court in the land that would convict you."

I settled into silence. Being reminded of Tonga and that business of the Sign of the Four had worsened my mood yet further. It had been during that case that I had first met Mary. She had come to us as a client, hoping we could solve the mystery of her missing father and also that of a mysterious benefactor who had sent her a single pearl annually in the mail. Naturally we did so; while Holmes might be a terrible dinner companion he's awfully good at mysteries. He received another justly earned feather in his cap and I fell in love. Twelve happy years. I suppose I should celebrate the time we did have rather than the future we now do not.

"It's no use," Holmes announced. "I've lost the letter. How can I possibly have lost it? I never lose anything."

"Perhaps it's stuffed into the dusty cavity of an ancient pharaoh," I suggested, "where it will cause future scholars no end of confusion. Anyway, it hardly matters," I reassured him, "we're here now. Your name was on the guest list, that's why they let me in."

"Yes, well, you only have to look around to see they're not too discerning about whom they give a table."

"Thank you very much."

"Oh hush, I don't mean you. Look though, observe!" He nodded his head towards our fellow diners, what few of them there were. Aside from ourselves, only four other tables were occupied.

"That old chestnut is it? Fine, I'm game. Let's at least attempt to enjoy our first course at the same time though, eh?"

The waiter appeared and ladled out two bowls of cold tomato soup. "Gazpacho," he explained, "very popular in Spain."

"So is fighting bulls with swords," Holmes noted, "I trust that won't be the evening's cabaret?"

"There will be something to divert you later, sir," the waiter promised, offering the first sincere smile I'd seen since entering the building, "but it won't be bull fighting."

"I dread to think," I said once he had gone, "I've never enjoyed entertainment with my food, I always end up having to clap halfway through a mouthful, making myself look like a circus animal."

"We make our own entertainment," he replied, "let the game begin!"

I sighed. "Very well." I took a mouthful of the cold soup. It was like drinking a Bloody Mary but with no discernible benefit.

I turned my attention to the patrons at a table in the far corner.

"The table by the sickly-looking aspidistra," I said, "man and wife I imagine…"

Holmes raised an eyebrow.

"Oh alright, it's a mistake to theorise without the facts, yes, yes…" I looked closer. "Fine, they're not married. While he wears a wedding band she does not."

"He looks to have spent a good deal of time inside," Holmes commented.

"I was getting to that, who's doing this, you or me? His skin is terribly pale and, given the summer we've just roasted in…"

"Intolerable," he added, "ovens are for poultry not people."

"…He must have missed a good deal of it to have retained such a complexion," I continued, ignoring the interruption. "I would place his age as being late forties. His hair is receding early, a hereditary condition I suspect, rather than a medical one. Though he is certainly not in the peak of condition. As well as his pale skin his gums are receding and the skin around his eyes betrays a man who has trouble sleeping. He has lost a lot of weight recently. Either that or the jacket he's wearing is not his own, though I suspect it is because the cuffs are tailored to a perfect length." I scowled at another mouthful of the cold soup. "More likely he's been coming here too much. I doubt one can sustain much of a girth on cold tomato soup."

"Are you going to complain through the entire meal?"

"That rather depends on whether the second course improves on the first. I make no promises either way."

"Had you finished your analysis?"

"My enthusiasm for it has dwindled, which amounts to much the same thing."

"You didn't notice the slight contusions on his wrist?"

"The cuffs were covering them."

"Not when he reached for the salt. I would suggest he has spent some time in manacles."

"Poor chap. His situation seems to go from bad to worse. Do you want to deal with the woman? I'm sure you're impatient to show me how it should be done."

"She's his sister of course, the nose betrays close familial connection and their similar ages don't really allow for any other connection. She rarely dines out. Her hair is combed unfashionably and her clothes are several seasons out of date. There's no sign of repair work or repeated wear so I would hesitate to suggest she was once a socialite who has fallen on hard times, rather a woman who once had cause to buy an expensive outfit and has rarely needed to wear it since. She briefly held a clerical job, possibly transcription, possibly secretarial."

"Calluses on the thumb and forefinger? You can see that from here?"

"I looked on the way in, it's not my fault you didn't plan ahead."

"How do you come to the conclusion she no longer has the job?"

"It would be difficult for her to maintain it without her buying a pair of spectacles, she had to ask her partner to read a letter to her, after several abortive attempts of her own. I don't believe she's so vain as to choose not to wear spectacles, not when you take into account the rest of her appearance…"

"She could have simply lost them?"

"Yes, she could, and I'll admit I'm stretching here, but her general demeanour is so fastidious, so precise, that I don't believe she's the sort of woman who ever lost a thing in her life. Perhaps they were broken so recently that she has not had time to replace them, but I'm inclined towards Occam's Razor in this case: she is clearly a woman of extremely limited funds, she needs spectacles and yet doesn't possess any. The most likely answer is that she cannot afford to buy any."

"And yet she can afford to be eating in a private dining club?"

"Yes, that is the point of most interest, I think. Neither of them shows signs of possessing the sort of money that one would expect in such circumstances. I mark that down as a point of singular interest, to be recalled once we have gathered more data."

"Joy. We're going to play this game all night then, are we?"

"I think you'll soon agree with me that it is in our very best interests to do so. Next table?"

I shrugged and moved my gaze to the gentleman almost directly behind Holmes, an elderly fellow with a professorial bent. "Late sixties, unmindful of his clothes, his waistcoat is incorrectly buttoned…"

"Look at his fingers. The way he holds his spoon."

"Ah… arthritic. Possibly not so much unmindful of how he buttons his waistcoat as incapable. Blind in one eye."

"Really?"

"He closed his left eye when reading the wine label."

"Very good! Of course I would have noticed myself, but his reflection in the glass of that horrid watercolour behind you offers a distinctly limited vision."

"Do try to be more graceful in your defeat, Holmes. I saw something you didn't, it's not the end of the world." The look on his face made it quite clear he didn't agree.

"The fact that he is a scholar of some kind is painfully obvious, but what do you think his subject might be?"

"Chemistry of course, you don't get acid stains on your fingers from studying astronomy."

Holmes smiled and held up his own hands. "It is possible that, like me, he is something of a jack of all trades but your supposition is logical enough. We polymaths are few. Perhaps that's how he blinded himself in one eye?"

"There's no sign of scarring on his eyelid, so if it was from a chemical accident it was some time ago."

"And so... we enter the uncomfortable arena of guesswork. Anything else?"

"He is doing his singular best not to make it obvious that he's terribly interested in our table."

"He's not alone there. I would say that's a common theme across the entirety of the room."

I did my best to appear casual as I took a final bland mouthful of cold tomato and glanced at the other tables. There was a young couple to my right and a woman sat on her own in the far corner. I couldn't help but note that all of them made considerable business of looking away as I glanced in their direction. "Interesting."

"Of course, given your continued efforts to make me the talk of the town, it's more than possible that it's simply due to my celebrity."

I chose to let the egotism pass; I knew Holmes well enough to appreciate he was being purely factual rather than showing off. "Or...?"

"Let's continue our game. The young couple next."

"No," I said, pushing my bowl away, "more food next, and one can only hope it will be solids."

The waiter was quick to clear away our soup bowls and just as eager to replace them with a pair of small salads.

"I believe fat rabbits have been known to exist," mused Holmes as he turned over a large lettuce leaf.

"I would have relished the chance to prove as much by having one baked and sliced all over my salad," I suggested. "It was your turn, the young couple..."

"Just so. Unlike our other pairing, they clearly *are* a couple: she is wearing a somewhat gaudy engagement ring – a clear example of excess winning out over good taste – and the gentleman's body language, while somewhat defensive in general, suggesting he is not altogether comfortable to be sat here, makes his affection for her clear. She is trying to restrain a considerable anger; her knuckles are quite white as she grips her knife and her hands shake when she lifts her wine glass. The anger isn't directed at her beau, though he is making a concerted effort to placate it, so one can only assume there is some other reason she would choose to sit and eat a substandard meal when so consumed with hatred."

"There we certainly agree."

"We do?"

"Yes, the food is very substandard." I had given up on my salad after having found the hard-boiled egg hidden in it to be the only edifying thing on the plate.

"She is clearly the dominant one of the two. They would not be sat here unless she expressly wished it. So, we must ask ourselves, what could make a young woman, so clearly not in the mood for a genteel evening, pretend so hard to be enjoying one? Our final test-subject?"

"That's it?" I asked. "No comment on the time the young man has obviously spent abroad? The fact that he has recently received a haircut and that he's a teetotaller?"

"I didn't think it relevant."

"Never stopped you in the past." I looked towards our waiter whose attention, like the rest of the diners', was squarely placed on us. I raised a querying eyebrow in an attempt to bring him to the table. He was quick, if sullen, in his response.

"Is everything acceptable sir?" he asked.

"I'm not an admirer of salads," I admitted, "the next course cannot come quickly enough. Plus another bottle of wine if you would be so kind." He nodded and retreated from the room.

"He is not entirely lacking in interest," I remarked. "Not many reputable waiters have skinned knuckles."

"Or badly hidden tattoos," Holmes agreed, tapping at his throat. "He is wearing his collar too loosely to entirely cover evidence of a gang marking around his neck. I believe it to be that of the Golden Noose."

"Golden Noose?"

"A gang whose members all proudly escaped the hangman."

"I suppose everyone needs a hobby."

"Theirs is particularly bloody."

"Dear Lord, Holmes, I was angry enough with you when I sampled the food, but if the staff are escaped murderers… where in God's name have you brought me?"

He smiled. "Wonderful, isn't it? Now… our last diner."

I shook my head, exasperated as I so often was with the misdirected enthusiasm of my friend. "She is elderly, the lighting makes it hard to offer an accurate guess but I would suggest she is somewhere in her late sixties. Her skin is dark; that combined with the styling of the ruby brooch she wears would suggest a background in India. She appears to have little interest in eating – though I can't blame her for that – and her interest in us is even more brazen than the rest, so much so in fact that I really can't look at her too closely for fear of giving the game away."

"And we wouldn't want that," Holmes smiled.

The waiter returned with two plates of cold meats.

"At last," I said, "something that might fill my stomach."

Holmes reached across and held my hand as I prepared to stab at a piece of cold beef with my fork. "One moment," he said, casually leaning forward and reaching down as if to fidget with his left trouser leg. In actuality I noted he was sniffing at his plate. After a moment he sat back up with a shrug and waved at me to continue eating.

"Worried the beef might be off?" I asked.

"Worse than that," he admitted, "but it's fine. Eat your fill."

"Anything to add to my summation of the lady?"

"Ah… certainly. You were quite correct in most of your assumptions. She has indeed spent a good deal of time abroad, though it was Persia rather than India. She grew up there and remained in the country until two months ago. She is actually only sixty-three years of age; the sun has not been kind. Your assumption was a perfectly logical one, however, as the stone is indeed of Indian origin. It's known as the Tiger's Heart and was rather famously won in a hand of cards by the lady's brother."

"Something tells me that you're playing this game with an unfair advantage."

"I know the lady, if that's what you mean. But then… after some consideration I know everyone in the room. As would you if you spent more time reading my files and less chuckling along to Robert Louis Stevenson."

I decided to channel my irritation in the direction of some cold pork. After a couple of mouthfuls, Holmes had still not elaborated. Finally I was forced to prompt him. "Well? Go on then! You must be dying to tell me."

"Oh, I'm sorry, you seemed so enthused by your cold meat I didn't have the heart to interrupt. The brother and sister are Ronald and Imogen Lacey. Until two years ago, Ronald was employed – if that is really the right word – alongside Imogen's husband, Harry. They were common housebreakers, though their reputation in that field is falsely inflated due to the fact that they cared not one jot if the house was empty when they broke into it. After their capture, they admitted to nineteen acts of murder, battering the sleeping tenants to death in their beds, before going on to remove anything of worth from the place. Naturally, Harry's reward was found at the end of a rope."

"But not Ronald's?"

"Ronald had the good fortune to escape custody. Until tonight I believed that he had vanished to distant climes. Noting his pallor and the fact that he has clearly served some time in gaol, I would suggest that his liberty was short lived. I imagine he was caught and imprisoned for some other crime abroad and has only recently returned. His sister is a woman of interest in that she was long suspected – though never proven – to be part of the gang. Certainly she made it quite clear at her husband's trial that she cared little for the lives he had taken. In fact, she served thirty days for contempt of court, having been dragged out of the building laughing. Clearly, as a single woman she has made some efforts to sustain herself with the aforementioned clerical job. Those efforts have recently floundered."

"She sounds charming."

"She's a terrible creature, they both are. The elderly chemist is Cyril Foster, surely you're familiar with that name?"

"The Lytchett Poisoner?"

"Not as far as the Dorset Police are concerned. They remain quite assured of his innocence. If you remember the details, Mr

Foster is a chemistry teacher at a preparatory school outside Lytchett Matravers. He stands accused of poisoning his entire class after they repeatedly made fun of his stammer. His trial is not to be heard for another month but the defence's argument that the boys were in fact poisoned when they tried to concoct a potion of their own – a stink bomb, no less – has gained great traction, mainly due to the fact that nobody can believe that anybody could be so devoid of humanity as to slaughter fifteen children over slurs regarding a speech impediment. He is, however, quite guilty. A fact I will prove at the aforementioned trial when I am called as the prosecution's expert witness."

"And the young couple?"

"She is Lucy Brentford, widow of Thomas Millan."

"The Aylesbury Strangler."

"The very same. If you remember she was implicated quite strongly in her first husband's crimes. Indeed, there were those who claimed she was the murderer and not him."

"'Those'?"

"Very well… *me*. *I* claimed that. But I was unable to provide sufficient evidence for her conviction. I received a charming note after Millan hanged, assuring me that I would one day pay dearly for my accusations."

"She sounds delightful, no wonder her new gentleman seems so timid in her presence. And finally…?"

Holmes held up his hand. "First things first, let's not forget why we are here." He turned to the waiter. "Excuse me, but do you have any champagne?"

"Of course sir," the waiter replied. "I'll bring you a bottle." He marched off.

"No discussion as to vintage?" I asked, smiling.

"I can't say that I'm surprised," Holmes admitted. "As you may have already guessed this place is not quite what it seems. We should be grateful they at least have a bottle to hand."

The waiter returned, with a bottle and two extra glasses. He popped the cork and poured us a small measure each.

"A celebration, sir?" he asked. For some reason he seemed to find the question amusing.

"Indeed," Holmes agreed, holding his hand out for the bottle, "may I?"

The waiter handed it over and Holmes perused the label.

"In fact," he got to his feet and cleared his throat to make an announcement, "if I may interrupt your meals for a moment. I am dining here with my good friend Dr John Watson, to mark the sad passing of his wife, Mary. Would you all think it terribly vulgar of me if I asked you to join me in a toast to her memory?" He handed the bottle back to the waiter. "If you would be so kind as to pour some for everyone?"

"I'm not sure there's enough to go around, sir," the waiter replied.

"Enough for a toast, I think," Holmes insisted.

"I don't drink," said the young man dining with Lucy Brentford, "but I'll happily join the toast as long as my water doesn't offend." He gestured towards his glass.

"Of course not," said Holmes, giving a small bow. "It's the thought that counts."

The waiter fetched a further five glasses and shared what remained of the bottle between them.

"Most kind," said Holmes, gesturing that I should get to my feet. I did so, in some embarrassment.

"To Mary," said Holmes, "a wonderful woman who made my best friend…" he looked to me and shrugged slightly, "my only friend… terribly happy. For that I can never praise her highly enough." He raised his glass and the rest of us followed suit. There was a mumbled refrain of "to Mary" and I found myself, quite absurdly, on the verge of tears. I know Holmes will always mock me for being an emotional man. He claims I let my heart dominate my brain. In that he is quite, quite right and I wouldn't have it any other way. And of course, as I have pointed out to him, that does at least compensate for the fact that he does exactly the opposite.

We sat back down, though Holmes turned his chair so that he was facing out into the room. "The final member of our dining party, Watson," he said, his voice raised, "is Lady Siobhan Moran, sister to our well-known acquaintance Colonel Sebastian Moran, and, I presume, the instigator of our delightful evening."

She stared at him from her dark corner of the room.

"Nothing to say on the subject?" he asked, before turning his chair back around to face me and tucking into his cold meats.

"The cold food was something of a theatrical step too far," he said, "evoking as it does the suggestion of revenge. I'm afraid we were not invited here to enjoy an evening of fine food."

"Just as well," I said, "as none was served."

"Indeed. Rather, this entire, grotesque little play was enacted with no other reason than to commit murder." He looked at me, a piece of ham paused between his mouth and the plate. "Ours."

"Dear God…" I made to stand up.

"Please, Watson, no sudden moves," Holmes said, gesturing for me to remain still. "We are surrounded by people who wish nothing more than to see us dead. It would take something far more grotesque and underhand to secure our freedom than a mad dash towards the door."

The waiter removed a revolver from his trouser pocket and levelled it at us.

"Though, of course," continued Holmes, "appreciating the terrible situation we are in, I have already taken such steps as necessary. Regretfully, yes… but I believe it was the only option open to us so, while I may find it distasteful, it was a desperate act of survival."

"Holmes?" I was, as is so often the case, confused.

The waiter was staring at the rest of the diners.

"Lucy?" the young man asked, panic creeping into his voice, "my God, Lucy… what's wrong?"

I looked around. All of the diners bar the young man had fallen back in their seats, their faces fixed in a paralysed mask. "The champagne," I said.

"And Carruthers' gift," Holmes replied, "yes. I poured some into the bottle while pretending to read the label. My apologies for forcing you to witness such a thing. I hope you will understand it was the only course open to us if we ever wished to leave the room alive."

"You killed them all!" shouted the waiter, staring at the results of Holmes's grim toast, the revolver quivering in his hand. I reached for the half-full bottle of wine on our table and hurled it with all my strength at the back of his head. There was an explosion of glass and cheap Bordeaux and the man sank to the floor.

I gripped the tablecloth, trying to restrain my anger, the sounds of Lucy Brentford's teetotal fiancé filling my ears as he tried to resuscitate her.

"You used a toast to Mary as a murder weapon," I said, "you killed them in her name."

"I did. And if she were here she would have understood. I did what it took to ensure you didn't die this evening."

As the young man's panic turned into tears I found my own eyes begin to follow suit.

"Dying is not the difficult thing," Holmes said, "no, in my experience dying is easy. Living, however, can be terribly difficult indeed."

ABOUT THE AUTHOR

G uy Adams is the author of over twenty books, from *The World House* and its sequel *Restoration*, to the weird western series *The Heaven's Gate Chronicles* from Solaris. He has written original novels featuring Sherlock Holmes for Titan Books – *The Breath of God* and *The Army of Dr Moreau* – as well as *Deadbeat* and the forthcoming *Deadbeat: Dogs of Waugh*. He has adapted classic horror titles for Hammer Books and his new horror/espionage series, *The Clown Service*, has just been published by Del Ray UK. He has also worked with comic artist Jimmy Broxton on *The Engine* for Madefire, as well as their creator-owned series *Goldtiger*.

THE SLEEP OF REASON

BY LOU ANDERS

Of all the tales I have related to you which concern the adventures of my good friend, S. Quentin Carmichael, the one that follows is the most singularly strange. I have held off publishing it until now, and even today I am not sure what to make of it. Although I have never known New York's most famous consulting detective to utter an intentional falsehood, the temptation to dismiss this tale as the fevered product of his more insalubrious vice is strong. But truth or falsehood, it is nonetheless an adventure as exciting as any of those that I have ever published in the pages of *Argosy* magazine, and so, on this, the anniversary of his final disappearance, I choose to tell the world of S. Quentin Carmichael's unusual adventure. If you, dear reader, chose to receive this account as fiction, neither I, nor I believe my absent friend, could fault you.

This remarkable story began some eleven years ago, on 23rd January 1900. I had an unusually trying day at my practice, and so was late in returning to the apartments that we shared atop two flights of stairs at 177B Bleecker Street. Entering our sitting-room, I saw the great detective stretched out upon the floor. As he was lying face up, arms crossed upon his chest, I did not at first suspect any health-related accident or other misfortune. Rather, I am sorry to admit, I assumed that he was merely in the grip of the opiates that were his preferred pastime on those rare occasions when New York's criminal underworld denied him more challenging diversions. Thus I set about to divest myself of cloak and hat, and pour myself a spot of brandy, before reluctantly returning to our sitting-room to see if I could assist in any way towards his comfort. As you, my readers, know, I disapprove of these episodes and their absence of late had rather lulled me into a wishful fancy that perhaps he had finally overcome the habit. So it was some ten minutes later that I returned and knelt down beside him. Only then did the extreme stillness with which he lay press itself upon me. My own heart quickening, I checked his pulse, and found to my horror that he had none. I do not wish to describe in detail the gamut of emotions my soul ran as I unlaced his tie, unbuttoned his shirt, and placed my ear to his bare chest to listen for a heartbeat. His absence today is painful to me, but has become easier to bear with the passing of years, whereas in that instance, the possibility of his sudden and unexpected death was a cut to my heart that I could scarcely bear.

For of a trace of a heartbeat, there was none.

I lay for some time, my head resting on his naked chest, and fought back tears that were unseemly for a man of my age and position, and then I slowly rose and settled with my back against our worn sofa, a shadow over my world like the blackest cloud imaginable. Many were the recriminations that I levelled against myself for not having fought harder to wean him off his addiction before this obvious and inevitable overdose.

How many minutes or even hours passed, I had no idea, but it was sufficient time that I had been able to work past my own considerable sense of loss to the beginnings of an understanding of how the city – nay, the world at large – would soon suffer from his absence. Who but the great S. Quentin Carmichael could have possibly solved "The Mystery of the Melodious Mummy", or saved the reputation of Mayor Van Wyck in a case the details of which I was ordered to keep confidential? But slowly I became aware of a knocking, a persistent gentle rapping in the room. I looked first to the door, but the sound did not come from there. Then, turning my eyes to the corpse of S. Quentin, I saw a sight that brought chills to my spine even as it rekindled hope in my heart. Devoid of pulse or heartbeat, the detective was nonetheless chattering his teeth. The sound was so faint, the movement so slight, that had I been other than completely still, I daresay I would not have registered it. As it was, I leapt again to his side, felt again for pulse and heartbeat, and drew back in some horror when I found neither. It was then that I noticed that he was still pleasantly warm, something one does not expect from a dead man.

I tried to revive him then, and I swear I saw his eyebrows twitch in characteristic irritation when the application of my mouth to his lips caused a momentary cessation of his chattering. But when my efforts produced no effects, I sat back, and was surprised when again his teeth began to rattle against each other. At first I thought this to be some bizarre nerve action, like the twitching of a dismembered limb, a residual impulse in an otherwise inanimate shell. But then something further about the sound caught my attention. It was evidencing a pattern.

It was, of course, a form of Morse code, that bastardisation known as American Morse or "railway code". Carmichael, or whatever now moved through him, was varying the interval of his bites to simulate the long and short elements of telegraph transmissions. The entirety being too faint for my ears to consistently distinguish, I gingerly pried his lips apart and slid one of my digits into his mouth, an action which I believe brought the slightest twitch of a grin to his sharp and otherwise lifeless features, even as it brought a wince of pain as his incisors bit down. But, thus situated, I could now distinguish the subtle differences in strength of bite. With my free hand, I grabbed the leg of our writing desk and pulled it closer, scrabbling to grab pen and paper so that I could transcribe the code.

Imagine my emotion when the first words that came out were:

Avery, is that you?

This followed by:

I can't hear you, man. My mind is quite literally elsewhere. But press firmly down upon my tongue when I release my grip if it is indeed you, dear friend.

And when I did this:

Good. Make yourself comfortable and then return to this exact position. I'm going to relate to you a most sensational tale, one that I imagine will puzzle your readers no end.

As you will have deduced, the story that follows is recounted just as it was told to me that evening, as we lay awkwardly together upon the floor of our Bleecker Street apartments. I have added only those literary flourishes and colourations of detail necessary for the purposes of drama, as Carmichael's original account was in the flat and unemotional manner that was his normal, business-like, professional self when he was in the service of a case. Which indeed this was: the queerest of his career to date. And so, without further introduction, for you to make of it what you will, I give you:

THE ADVENTURE OF THE PERILOUS PLANET
As Told by S. Quentin Carmichael to Dr Avery F. Wilson

It was a crisp January evening when S. Quentin Carmichael, Manhattan's famous Dandy Detective, returned to his rooms at 177B Bleecker Street to retire for the night. His longtime companion and chronicler of his adventures, Dr Avery Wilson, was not at home, doubtless engaged in the practice of his profession – the tireless ministrations to New York's ill, as vigilante an adversary to illness as his friend was to crime. Upon entering his flat, however, the keen mind of S. Quentin sensed that he was not alone.

"If you would be so good as to put the light on, my good fellow, it would make it much easier for me to address the matters of your case. As discretion is obviously your desire, if you like I can close the curtains as you light the lamp on the table next to you."

There was a moment of silence in which S. Quentin sensed an almost palpable bafflement.

"How did you…" a man's voice began.

"A Chicagoan by birth then, with a touch of Arizona doubtless acquired later. But to your first question before you ask another, I did not see the silhouette of my apartment mate's most treasured trophy, though it always rests upon the windowsill. A Readers Choice award from *Argosy* magazine – I certainly wouldn't want to see it damaged. That you took the trouble to move it, rather than knock it over as you entered through the window, indicates you came here seeking my advice not my bodily harm, and since you arrived in so unusual a fashion, and remain in the dark, that discretion is a serious concern."

This was met by a sigh, and a chuckle. "I'm glad to see first hand that you are as good as they say, Mr Carmichael. And I do apologise for my entrance. I hope when you hear my story you'll agree that my clandestine ingress was indeed necessary."

S. Quentin pulled the blinds closed, and after a moment, the lamp on his reading table swelled in illumination. A man sat beside the table, in his early thirties, with a bearing that suggested a period of military service, and a paunch that suggested a more sedentary occupation now. He rose, a grateful look on his face, and extended his hand, which S. Quentin took. But before the man could introduce himself, the great detective cut him off.

"Tell me, Mr Alderbert, how do you find your Oliver typewriter? I much prefer the new Underwood myself, but then, as I am not a novelist, I do not require the security of being able to instantaneously produce duplicate copies of precious work."

Despite having already witnessed this performance once, the man identified as Mr Alderbert was astonished.

"A simple enough deduction, my good fellow," the Dandy Detective continued. "Your hand, when I shook it, was calloused only on the tips of your fingers – due to years of punching typewriter keys, no doubt, yet there was also a permanent groove in the middle finger of your right hand where a pen has pressed against it – indicating that you first compose your thoughts by hand, then type up the manuscript, a trait common to many authors. Meanwhile, the carbon black stains on those hands can only have come from carbonic paper, and currently, the 'strike down' typebars of the Oliver hit the platen with relatively greater force than the side striking and upward striking keys of other typewriters, making it the machine of choice for those who need a solid strike to impress upon a carbonic sheet. And again, the calluses on your fingertips further indicate you are typing with some force in aid of a clean duplicate copy. This coupled with your combination of accents, as well as your recognition of and respect for an award from a pulp magazine, means that you could only be William Alderbert, whose stories have graced the pages of the same pulp magazines in which Wilson publishes my own exploits, the famous pulp fiction writer and author of the noted biography of the adventures of Joanna Carson, the War Mistress of Mars."

"Fictional biography," Alderbert said, stressing the first word. The detective, however, shook his head and gave a wry grin.

"I do not think so, William. Your other stories, while admirable, are written in altogether a different style, coming as they do from your own imagination and not the dictations of another mind. As you are obviously a man of intellect, and not a madman, it is simpler to believe that what you publish as fiction is actually fact. Before you protest, you must understand that I myself am engaged in a similar relationship with narrative, and more than once have I wished that Wilson would mask our identities with fictional names. Not having the good fortune to be on another planet, I am something of a reluctant celebrity."

Alderbert nodded, and slowly his face gave way to a grin. "Good, good. I thought that I would have to ease you in; it's not an easy thing to tell people, that our universe is teeming with life."

"Given the age and scale of it, I would have found the opposite a harder truth to swallow. But as to your own situation… your fiction first took off nine years ago in 1891, with the publication of *The Principia of Mars*."

"Yes, I was honourably discharged from Fort Grant the year before. That's when Joanna first contacted me via telepathic communication. A Yavapai chief invited me to share a sweat lodge, opening me to mental transmigration. She found me while I was in a visionary state. I didn't believe her voice was real for the longest time, but writing it down made it bearable."

"And then profitable," S. Quentin ventured, good-naturedly.

"Certainly. And I'm grateful for it."

"Indeed, so much so that you come seeking my aid now the Mistress of Mars needs my help."

"How did you…?"

"Because any purely terrestrial problem would have seen you enter by the front door. Not wishing to explain your visit to my consulting rooms, I imagine that the problem must lie outside our sphere."

William Alderbert then explained that yes, the Queen of Moosrab, as the Martians called their world, was indeed in trouble, though she refused to impart the details of the case. Her communication with Alderbert was mostly one-way, though she could sense when he was listening and when he was attentive enough to take dictation. On occasion, she could manage to get messages back from him, though how this was accomplished Alderbert would not say, hinting that it involved certain technological patents pending that had not yet been granted.

"And how am I to lend Queen Joanna the aid she requests?" the detective asked when he had heard enough. "I am fairly certain that the unique circumstances that lead to her Majesty's own crossing could not be duplicated in time and for a reasonable expense."

Alderbert shook his head. He had, of course, relayed in his pulp adventure stories the tale of how Joanna Carson, former captain of the only all-woman confederate battalion, the Roses of Alabama, had been unwittingly catapulted to the Red Planet by diverting an experimental rocket meant for the destruction of Atlanta by the means of her own person. "But the Moosrabians have another method of communication between worlds, a linking of minds more powerful than the telepathy that Joanna and I manage between us. A sort of shadow body is projected across the vacuum, which they manage to enhance until it is able to undertake independent action. Humans as a rule aren't capable of making the transfer – or I would have gone myself – but your superior intellect might put you in range of the possibility. I could teach you the meditative techniques…"

"That won't be necessary," the Dandy Detective replied, dismissively. "I studied under the eminent Chol Joon-Ho when he came here three years ago." At this point, dear readers, you will forgive me if I interject to point out that those of you who recall "The Case of the Vanishing Vapour" will of course know that far from simply studying under Chol, Carmichael received the secret Shadowsoul teaching in return for services rendered during the Tong-hak rising. "I require only the mantra that Queen Joanna doubtless furnished you with to allow the Moosrabians to lock on to my psyche and pull it across the void."

When the mantra requested was promptly provided, the Dandy Detective bid Alderbert goodnight, assuring him that he had the matter well in hand. Then, pausing only to refresh the flower that was his boutonnière, he set about to meditate, shutting down his higher functions, his soul cast adrift, a fishing line flung out into the ocean of night. For a time he floated in the dark waters of the soul, and then, surprisingly if not unexpectedly, he felt a tug. He experienced an instant of blazing cold and near-eternal darkness.

And when next S. Quentin Carmichael opened his eyes, he looked out upon the Red Planet.

Though he had been reclined upon his sitting-room rug moments before, S. Quentin found himself standing. He was in a recessed alcove off a rounded chamber. The walls were made of glass, crystal clear and multifaceted. Through their transparent panes, he saw that they were atop a vast plateau, the stone of which dropped away in near vertical descent until it reached a plain of rock and dust the red of iron oxide. He knew that he looked upon a different world from that of his birth. But as magnificent as the view outside the chamber was, there was more to see inside. The alcove he occupied was one of several set at intervals around the circumference of the chamber. Many were empty, but others contained inert figures, like crude wax mannequins standing at attention, awaiting an unclear purpose.

Furthermore, the chamber was inhabited by more than mannequins. Before him stood a man of the most strikingly bronze-toned skin he had ever seen. He was human, or human-seeming, with discerning eyes and firm lips. Tall, muscled, his physical perfection most obvious due to the circumstances that, as it transpired, the man was also completely nude but for a gleaming sword and a scarlet cape. The detective was running his eyes over the sword and other such protuberances when the silence was broken by an irritated cough. S. Quentin turned his attention to the figure beside the bronze man.

Her oval face he supposed many would declare beautiful in the extreme. Her finely chiselled features were doubtless no less exquisite than a masterpiece of art. Her eyes large and some would say lustrous, surely equal parts alluring and commanding beneath her wavy coiffure of blond hair. What must have been her once-pale skin now burned a light copper colour, perhaps glorious to behold, though not so dark as to overshadow the crimson of her lips. She wore only the same red cloak and weapon as her companion and in her nakedness could be deemed his equal in physical perfection. Before such stark indefectibility, few men on either Earth or Mars could manage to stand in a state of anything less than total and abject awe. Such a vision, however, was wasted on S. Quentin.

"Joanna Carson," he said, blushing at the display of unclothed femininity, "the Rose of Alabama and Battle Maid of Moosrab. I see you have succeeded in plucking my intellect from the stars. Now, how might I be of service?"

The Warrior Queen's mouth crimped in a momentary pout of irritation, doubtless not used to having so little effect on males in her audience. But she soon recovered.

"Sir, why it is indeed a pleasure to meet the renowned S. Quentin Carmichael," she said in a genteel Southern accent. "I don't always know how much dear William understands of my telepathic transmissions, so I am glad ya'll two were able to work it out."

She came forward and offered the detective her hand. Though flustered at the nearness of her unclothed form, he distracted himself by observing that her digits, though delicate in shape, were calloused precisely as one would expect from a lifetime spent wielding sabre and pistol.

"An honour to meet someone equally renowned," he said, careful where to direct his eyes. Seeing his discomfort, Joanna frowned, then dismissed her irritation with a good humoured smile.

"This is Salbatanu," Joanna said, indicating the bronze-tinged man beside her. "My trade minister, and an expert in mental transmigration technique. He can explain the method we employed to bring you here before we move on to weightier matters."

"You will doubtless find this fascinating," said the Martian known as Salbatanu. "Now, if you will permit me…"

"No need," replied the dandy, releasing the woman's hand with perhaps too much relief and gesturing around the chamber. "Our location, atop a plateau, combined with the absence of any other structures, is doubtless intended to raise us up above the level of Martian life, so that this room is open to telepathic transmissions from other spheres unhampered by the mental energies of the population below. That such a chamber exists at all bespeaks a certain frequency of its use. That I am apparently here in body, as well as spirit, is of further interest. This is no hallucination, and yet I am convinced that I still lie upon the floor of my apartment…" At this S. Quentin closed his eyes for a moment, looking into his inner self.

"Yes," he continued, "I can even feel a connection to that body far away across the aether." He opened his eyes again. "And so I conclude that the body I currently possess is not actually mine, but a simulacrum, an artificial vessel constructed for the purpose of housing transmigratory intellects."

"Oh my," Joanna breathed behind him.

He walked into another alcove and approached one of the inert, wax-like statues within. It was devoid of features, humanoid in shape but without detail. He prodded it with a finger and did not seem surprised when he found that its surface was pliant.

"The receptacle, then?" he pronounced. "When a mind is gathered to the chamber, it is impressed upon one of these simulacra, which then conforms in appearance to the mental image of the mind it hosts. Several such simulacra are missing from their alcoves, hence I conclude that this is a receiving chamber for migratory souls, an undertaking in at least fairly common practice. Thus this receiving chamber is a sort of Grand Central Depot for travellers between the worlds."

"Bravo, detective," smiled Joanna, clapping her hands. "You really are every bit the intellect your exploits make you out to be." The Battle Maid smiled, though S. Quentin noted that Salbatanu looked troubled. Perhaps the man resented being interrupted, or enjoyed hearing himself speak. A shame that such perfect forms were not always gifted with temperaments to match. He was dragged from such speculations when the Queen said, "Come, we will adjourn to more comfortable surroundings."

As S. Quentin stepped forward, he glanced down at his own attire, conscious of his clothing beside these two nude forms. His simulacrum was clothed just as he was always attired, with impeccably cut garments. The detail was accurate right to the customary green carnation of his boutonnière.

"It is how you see yourself," Joanna explained, noticing the direction of his gaze. "Your intellect is particularly strong to have rendered it so well. Though here on Moosrab, social decorum is quite different from how it was back home in Dixieland. You may dispense with your attire if you wish."

"Unthinkable," S. Quentin spat, and then realised his error. "For me, that is. A dandy is nothing if not properly dressed. I meant not to judge others or to cause offence."

"Nor did you, sir. I know nudity makes you uncomfortable, and your aversion to the female form, in art as well as in life, is well-documented."

"I assure you, madam, that did my inclinations run in such directions, I assume I would find you irresistible. As it is…"

"As it is you know not what you miss," said Salbatanu, with a look at Joanna that bespoke a silent longing. A shame that. "But perhaps to the matter at hand?"

"Yes," said the Battle Maid. "While it would be lovely to while away the time with an intellect such as yours, sir, we need to resolve this matter hastily and return you to your proper planet before placing too much stress on your real body. If you'll just come with me."

Joanna led them to another alcove off the chamber. When they all stood within, she passed her hand across a small, glowing gemstone set into its wall. An opaque crystal door slid up from the floor closing them in, and then S. Quentin felt the barest vibration as the entire alcove began to descend. Pulsing lights indicated, he presumed, the speed of their descent. And then the crystal door receded and he found himself in Joanna's palace proper.

In a spacious reception room in the palace, where rich tapestries and abundant plush cushions were artfully arranged across and upon walls and floors of gleaming Martian marble, the Battle Maid and her trade minister explained the situation to the Dandy

Detective. It seemed that Mars was the hub of an interplanetary diplomatic organisation known as the League of Planets, of which all the inhabited worlds of the solar system, bar the Earth, were members. The organisation existed to broker disputes, foster peace, and negotiate trade (largely trade in information given the distances involved) between the member worlds. Up until recently, Mars and Jupiter had been in a dispute, and only recently had the two worlds agreed to explore peaceful negotiations. Then, on the eve of talks, the Jovian ambassador had attacked and murdered his Martian counterpart. Afterwards, he appeared disoriented and claimed to have no memory of the crime. He was presumed to be lying and the conflict between Mars and Jupiter was poised to erupt again. However, the remaining League ambassadors demanded an impartial and impeccable third party be brought in to confirm the Jovian's guilt before they would sanction the resumption of hostilities.

"Which is where you come in," Salbatanu said.

"Your exemplary reputation, honey," smiled Joanna, "together with my former homeworld's lack of participation in, or even knowledge of, the League, makes you an ideal candidate."

"We have no doubt that you will ascertain the ambassador's guilt in no time," continued Salbatanu.

"For which we will be much obliged," said the Battle Maid. "And then we can get on with our conflict proper."

"I see," said the Dandy Detective, refraining from passing any other judgements on the display of naked bloodlust in Joanna's eyes. While he did not condone war, truth alone was his calling and the situation had him intrigued. "Very well, I should like to speak with the ambassador straight away."

S. Quentin next found himself seated in a comfortable chair, separated by a mostly invisible barrier evident only as an occasional shimmering in the air, from the strangest creature he had ever seen. The Jovian ambassador, whose name was Kralomoc, was a multi-limbed alien who resembled no terrestrial being but could perhaps be said to be least dissimilar to earth octopi. The ambassador had two small forelimbs, and a varied number of additional larger limbs, all descending directly from a bulbous head. He had a beaklike mouth, large eyes and a mottled purple complexion.

"You are the one sent here to condemn me?" Kralomoc said.

"I am here to observe you," S. Quentin replied. "To converse with you if you are willing. The outcome of that observation is unwritten despite what my hosts may think or perhaps desire."

"Then you are a singular being, as all others are convinced of my guilt."

"They do have the benefit, as I understand it, of having witnessed your assault on the Martian."

"That is what they tell me," replied Kralomoc, clicking his beak in a way that S. Quentin surmised was his equivalent of a dry laugh.

"You don't know yourself?"

"I do not. I cannot confirm or deny my participation in the murder of my Martian counterpart in any way. The time is a blank for me." He paused, his large eyes roving over the human before him before wandering up to the ceiling. "There is little, I'm afraid, for us to talk about."

"And yet I am here," said the detective, "and we will have to pass some time in each other's company to satisfy our hosts."

Again the beak clicking at the use of the word "hosts".

"Tell me," S. Quentin continued. "Do they have games of strategy here? Board games? We have one on Earth known as chess."

"There is something of the sort here," replied the Jovian, his large eyes now puzzled. "They call it Tejan. I do not know the rules nor understand much about how it is played."

"Marvellous. Neither do I. We will have to learn together and thus will be equally matched."

"You wish to play me in Tejan?" said Kralomoc, incredulous.

"We have nothing relevant to talk about, and time to spend. Surely you would welcome the diversion?"

"I am across a barrier from you," said the Jovian, waving one of his two short appendages in an obviously dismissive gesture. "I could not reach the playing pieces."

"Then I will come inside with you."

"With an alleged killer?" This time both of his short appendages spread wide, a gesture S. Quentin took for disbelief.

"An alleged killer with no intelligent motive to harm the one individual not convinced of his guilt."

Kralomoc nodded. "Singular, singular," he pronounced. His beak clicked. "Very well. The game is afoot."

"You have seen the ambassador?" said Joanna, when the dandy returned to her.

"I have."

"And you've come to your conclusion?" she asked with barely concealed eagerness.

"That I have as well."

"Marvellous," Joanna said, clapping her hands together. "That means that we can resume our hostilities."

"Your pardon, madam," he said, steeling himself to lay a restraining hand upon the flesh of her bare arm. "I said that I had come to a conclusion, but not what conclusion that was."

"But surely? In a matter so obvious…" Her eyes narrowed. "Mister, quit beating around the bush and tell me whatever it is that you are saying."

"You call the matter 'obvious'. Obvious indeed, madam, and yet I am the only one that reached the conclusion."

"The conclusion?" Her voice took on a wary edge.

"That Kralomoc the Jovian ambassador is innocent."

"Nonsense," said Salbatanu sharply, turning from the window where he had been contemplating the Martian landscape. "How can that be?"

"I played him in Tejan."

"You played board games with him?" the trade minister continued. "I don't understand."

"He proved to be a skilful opponent, both intelligent and adaptable to new situations."

"He is a shrewd one," said Joanna.

"And yet, a mind like his could not come up with a better alibi for his alleged crime than 'I don't remember.' Furthermore, an hour spent with him clearly shows that he has no love for Martians nor an aversion to the war. I doubt he would feel much remorse had he actually committed this crime, so it is unlikely that mental trauma can account for his memory loss. Ergo, he is not lying."

"And that is the basis for your claim?" Salbatanu's lips would have been gorgeous if they weren't lifting in disdain.

"Not claim. Observation. Based upon evidence."

"Just this evidence?" asked the Battle Maid.

"And other observations, which I prefer to keep to myself until I am further into this investigation." Joanna nodded, then stopped short.

"Investigation? What investigation?" Salbatanu looked displeased. S. Quentin ignored him.

"Tell me, Joanna, does your famed Southerner's hospitality extend to the maltreatment of prisoners?"

"Whatever are you implying, S. Quentin?"

"Kralomoc's forelimbs are badly bruised."

"We have not touched him. I will personally run a rapier through his eye at the moment he is pronounced guilty, but until that time he is inviolate. He suffered those bruises when he attacked our ambassador. He strangled him with those appendages. If they became bruised in the process, well, I hardly think he's due my sympathy."

"Curious," said S. Quentin.

"I fail to see the possible relevance –" Joanna silenced her minister with a wave of her hand.

"It is enough that I do, madam. Now, I should like for you to arrange meetings with the other ambassadors of the League of Worlds."

"On what pretext? Are they under suspicion now?"

S. Quentin smiled.

"Surely a pretext can be arranged for each of them to meet with Earth's greatest consulting detective on his first visit to the Red Planet. But it needs to be one on one. Let us tell them that I would like to play them at Tejan."

* * *

S. Quentin reclined on a curiously buoyant block of what looked like Martian marble that floated without bobbing upon the surface of a pool of crystal clear water. Cetus, the Neptunian ambassador, cavorted below, occasionally rising out of the waters to breathe through one or another of his multiple blow holes. An entirely unnecessary procedure, as he was, like the Dandy, present only by way of a simulacrum, and thus had no need of air.

"But old habits, like old ambassadors, die hard," Cetus laughed. And it sounded exactly like a laugh. No beak clicking or dolphin-like whistle, though there might actually have been one of the latter swimming underwater. No, this time S. Quentin heard the ambassador's voice piped out of speakers that floated in the air above the pool, obviously translating Cetus's shrill, underwater communication into something suitable for land dwellers.

"I'm sorry, I'm sorry," continued the Neptunian, "that may have been in poor taste. But they won't kill him easily now. You don't think old Kralomoc is guilty or else you wouldn't be talking to me."

"Perceptive," nodded the Dandy.

"We do have the largest craniums in the system," Cetus replied. "Though I suspect our cerebral patterns are organised differently from yours. Size probably doesn't make a difference."

"In this respect at least," replied S. Quentin, wrinkling his nose.

"At any rate, if you don't think it was the Jovian, I don't think you have to look far for another with motive."

Cetus rose out of the water then, opening his enormous mouth. The detective gazed into an imposing maw, for all that it was toothless, watching as Cetus's versatile tongue unwound, to grasp and move a Tejan piece across the board.

"You have an opinion?" asked S. Quentin, studying the board a moment before selecting one of his pawns and moving it forward a step.

"I have facts. Which lead towards a conclusion, as I'm sure you appreciate. Saturn's orbit lies nearest to Jupiter. In the past, there was conflict between them, but for some time now, hostility with the Red Planet has kept Jupiter occupied."

"And you think that if hostilities between Mars and Jupiter were to cease that Jupiter might again turn its aggression closer to home?"

"A conclusion as inevitable as the last move in Tejan," said Cetus. "Speaking of which: check," he said, his tongue placing a piece down on the board with a resounding plunk of triumph. The detective marvelled at his ability to talk while his tongue was otherwise engaged. A useful skill to be sure. "Whereas, as the third largest power, and being in a war with neither Mars nor Jupiter, Neptune has no need of this outcome. No, you would do well to look at Saturn with suspicion. They are the ones with obvious motive."

"What is obvious to one," said the detective, "is not always obvious to another." And with that, he slid one of his pawns forward to a new position. He sat back, allowing himself an indulgent smile. "Checkmate, I think you'll find."

The plant-like Venusian ambassador was strangely feminine. She, if indeed S. Quentin had the gender correct, watched the Dandy Detective shyly from out of mounds of rubbery, blue foliage. It was somewhat disconcerting, luminous azure eyes winking at him from the plants. The ambassador never came forward to move pieces on the board. Rather, various vines and creepers would curl up from underground to pluck a piece from the board and deposit it in a new position.

"But it is precisely because Neptune is the third largest power in the solar system that you must distrust Cetus," purred Inanna.

"Doubtless, you are about to tell me that I miss the forest for the trees," replied S. Quentin, noticing that although the green carnation affixed to his lapel was forged from the substance of the wax simulacrum, its petals had started to wilt. As had been explained, death here and death of the actual body were linked. He felt a vine questing at his ankle and brought his heel down on it sharply. It quickly withdrew.

"Any alliance between Jupiter and Mars would shift the balance of power," explained Inanna, "and grant them too much say in the League of Planets voting, diminishing Neptune's importance."

S. Quentin swatted at a creeping vine that had become too

familiar with the lapel of his jacket. Perhaps it was also puzzled by the cut flower of his boutonnière. As it was only a simulacrum, the flower would have no scent. So perhaps the vines were more a part of Inanna than he realised, the ambassador and the jungle she occupied two halves of a larger organism.

"Whereas you feel no such threat?"

"As a purveyor of trade, who seeks profit over influence, we are happy to deal with whoever has something to sell and something to buy."

"Naturally. And quite magnanimous of you. Still, knowledge is knowing a tomato is a fruit; wisdom is not putting it in a fruit salad."

"What does that mean?" said Inanna, the foliage parting temporarily to reveal consternation upon an inhuman face.

"It means," said the detective, as he executed the winning Tejan move, "that the petals may tell a different story than the roots."

"Surely a mind such as yours must understand that all matters revolve and resolve on issues of economics."

S. Quentin leapt nimbly aside as a column of rock, nearly his equal in height, burst from the earth of the Tejan square upon which he had been standing. The chuckle from Shabbathai, the Saturnian ambassador, sounded unnervingly like boulders clashing.

"Surely," said the Dandy Detective, lifting one of his own Tejan pieces and carrying it three squares across the board. Rather than utilising the small set that S. Quentin had played with up until this point, the colossal Saturnian ambassador had manifested a gargantuan Tejan game from the rocks of his cavernous quarters beneath the palace. Moving the life-sized carvings would have been impossible for S. Quentin back on Earth, but here the low Martian gravity permitted faux muscles – exact duplicates of his true muscles – to indulge in superhuman feats of strength. "Surely you understand that a mind such as mine is trained to look for weaknesses in others' arguments. Weaknesses are often clustered around rhetorical questions, themselves often framed with words like 'surely'. Rhetorical questions, as you must know, represent one's desire to take a logical shortcut, to embarrass or flatter the recipient into agreement without adequate proof."

A Tejan piece on the corner of the board crumbled into sand. When it re-emerged from the ground in a burst, the detective thought it was a little close for comfort.

"Venus provides a trade bridge between Mars and Jupiter and is worried the cessation of hostilities removes the need for a middle man. Whatever you think about rhetorical questions, facts are rock solid."

"In that, at least, we can agree. But tell me, does Saturn not seek trade advantages as well?"

"To what end?" replied Shabbathai. "As the most unusual of the life forms in the League of Planets, Saturn has no need of trade advantages. We do not eat. We do not amass wealth. We do not build from any substance other than rock, and even there, we do not distinguish our creations from ourselves."

"Indeed." S. Quentin looked around. There was no physical form or body that represented the Saturnian. His people were seismic vibrations able to move through and animate minerals and mineraloids. "An impressive array of facts. But then again, I've always felt that the only difference between stumbling blocks and stepping stones is the way you use them."

And with that, S. Quentin nimbly slid his Queen into the winning position.

"Sir," said the Battle Maid of Moosrab, her breasts rising and falling disconcertingly as her breath quickened in agitation. "Do I have my war or don't I? You have met three ambassadors now, and all ya'll have done that I can tell is play games."

"Games lubricate the body and the mind. Benjamin Franklin said that, and I always trust a man in a powdered wig."

"But do you have a suspect?" said Joanna, her eyes flashing like irritated diamonds. "Do any of them have a motive?"

"Motive?" said the detective in surprise. "Why, all of them do. We are not lacking in motive."

"All of them," replied the woman. Her hand fell to the hilt of her sabre. "I had not thought to take on the whole system. Still, if it's a whoppin' they're looking for, I shall be obliged to deliver it."

"Your pardon, ma'am, but let's not multiply entities beyond necessity, as it were. Whoever did perpetrate this attack was keen that Jupiter take the blame for it. But each of the three ambassadors I spoke with endeavoured to shift responsibility among themselves. Hence, I discount them as having participated in the initial attack."

"Who then?"

"I suspect we shall soon see."

The attack, when it came, was not unexpected. S. Quentin had walked alone to an observation tower in the palace. Indeed, he had placed himself alone on purpose, hoping to invite just such an action. He had counted on his own superb physical abilities, his mastery of martial arts, to provide him protection enough, and so was unconcerned when the tentacles first brushed his neck. But then he felt a tug at the back of his mind.

Again, he experienced a burst of blazing cold and a moment of near-eternal darkness.

There was a voice calling his name. No, not his name…

"Holmes? Holmes? Can you hear me?"

The detective fought his way through darkness thick as molasses. No, treacle. No, molasses. It was thick, anyway, no matter if he couldn't ascertain which continent his metaphors should come from.

He opened heavy lids to find he was lying on a floor, with someone bending over him.

"Wilson?" he asked.

"What? No, it's Watson." The man sat back from where he had apparently been attempting to revive him. "Holmes, it's me, John. Try and snap out of it, man. For a moment, I thought I'd lost you."

"Lost me?" the detective murmured.

"I think you may have overdosed, old chap. I found you on the floor. You may have been out for hours."

"Hours?" His thoughts wouldn't come easily, not a familiar sensation for a mind such as his. Breathing was difficult too. His neck felt constricted.

His neck.

"No," said the detective, knocking this "Watson's" hands off of him. "Leave me be. Must get back to, back –"

"Back, where?" the man who called himself Watson demanded.

"To Mars, of course," the detective replied, then he cast his mind adrift into meditative trance.

Darkness again. He was adrift in the ethereal realm, a transmigratory soul. When he first made the journey, the Martians had used their arcane sciences to snare his mind and reel him to the Red Planet. There would be no help from them this time. If he was to find his way back to the simulacra, he would have to do so on his own. The effort of will was colossal.

S. Quentin thrust with the fingers of both hands over each of his shoulders, finding a satisfying squelch as they lodged in the eyes of the Jovian. There was a yelp, and the tentacles constricting his windpipe relaxed and withdrew.

He turned around to behold the octopus-like alien hovering in the air behind him, blinking furiously through red and irritated eyes. "Kralomoc?" he asked. "No, not Kralomoc."

Joanna rushed into the room, with an escort of Martian soldiers. "S. Quentin, are you hurt?"

"I am quite all right, ma'am," replied the detective, making a show of straightening a lapel before winking at one of the soldiers, armour being as notably absent as other clothing. "Though I hope I haven't caused too much harm to this Jovian." S. Quentin let the end of his sentence lift up in a question.

"Tzedek," Joanna said, naming the alien. "The new ambassador, assigned to Kralomoc's post. And just as murderous, I see." She turned to her guards. "Take him away."

"What? What am I doing here?" stammered ambassador Tzedek. "I was in my quarters… I blacked out."

"That excuse won't work any more," snapped the Battle Maid of Moosrab, glaring at the ambassador as he was hauled off. But she hesitated when she saw the look with which S. Quentin studied the departing ambassador.

"Whatever are you thinking, sir?" she ventured. "Surely you see the Jovian's guilt now that two of them have attacked your person."

"Do I?" he replied, turning to face her. "There's that word 'surely' again. But as to what I was thinking, I was just noticing that Tzedek's two small limbs are badly bruised. Tell me, why do they keep attacking with those appendages if they damage so easily?"

Joanna sat now upon her throne, itself set upon a terrace that was carved from the rock of the plateau. The view of the Martian city below was breath-taking, though no less so than the court in attendance upon their queen. Salbatanu was again standing beside her, as were a great many Martians and other races. All the ambassadors were in attendance, Cetus in a tank, Inanna amid some sort of leafy portable canopy, Shabbathai at last partially present in the form of several large boulders, while both Kralomoc and Tzedek, surrounded by guards, stood before Joanna awaiting judgement. Tzedek seemed pityingly confused, still stammering that he did not understand the circumstances that brought him here, but Kralomoc embraced his fate with dry acceptance.

"Thank you for your attempts on my behalf, dandy," the Jovian said, "but they will have their execution as they wish."

"Silence," said Salbatanu. "Speak when Joanna gives you leave to do so."

"Well, I do hope she'll grant me leave," said S. Quentin, "as I believe I just might have one or two things to add before anybody runs off… half cocked."

He strode out into the middle of the throne room.

"Before I say anything on the matters at hand," he began, "I'd like to thank all of you for your hospitality and some invigorating games of Tejan. It's amazing what you can learn by indulging in simple pastimes. But then, I've never been one to shy from indulgences." He winked at one of the guards, who, surprisingly, winked back.

"Now where were we? Oh right. You all have plenty of justifications for your warmongering, but I'm afraid that Shabbathai has it when he says most matters have an element of economics to them."

"So I was right," the pile of boulders thundered. "Those Venusian vegetables are behind it all!"

"I did not say that," said the Dandy Detective. "Don't be so eager to cast the first stone, as it were. Leave that to more experienced hands."

"What are you saying?" Joanna demanded, as Shabbathai rumbled.

"In both attacks, that upon your late ambassador and on my own person, the Jovians used the first two of their appendages. Yet in my observation of Kralomoc, he only used those for communication, to add emphasis to his words like I would use facial expression." He winked again to illustrate his point.

"We also use them for mastication," offered Kralomoc.

"For what?" the Battle Maid exclaimed.

"For eating, ma'am," explained S. Quentin, barely concealing his exasperation at her misassumption. "Now," the detective continued, "their larger limbs are much stronger. Far better suited for attacks and strangulation. Why not use them? And their memory loss. Each ambassador experienced disorientation, not dissimilar to what I experienced when making the journey from Earth to Mars. But that only lasted moments, in the jump from body to simulacrum. I do wonder what prolonged separation from a physical shell would do."

"I don't understand," said Joanna, coming off her throne to approach S. Quentin. "What are you suggesting?"

"If you would be so kind as to indulge me, madam."

She nodded.

He approached Kralomoc.

"I do hope you'll forgive me for this," he said, then aimed a punch at the Jovian's eye. The ambassador flung out an appendage to block the blow. One of his large appendages. His two small appendages were busy gesticulating angrily around his mouth.

"You see?" said S. Quentin. "They do not use them aggressively at all. But I wonder what another mind, one used to only two limbs, would do if it found itself in an unaccustomed body with an abundance of body parts."

"The two small limbs…" said Joanna, beginning to work it out.

"Are roughly the size of a human, or a Martian's arms. And positioned in front of the face where they could be seen, making their selection understandable. If a soul can exit its body in favour of one of your wax simulacra, could not a superior mind impress itself upon an inferior one?"

"Watch who you call inferior," objected Kralomoc, gesticulating furiously.

"I mean that only in terms of meditative psychic technique. Mars excels at this, above and beyond all the solar system, else your League of Planets would be located elsewhere."

There were nods and murmurs of agreement at this.

"And so our perpetrator, someone of extraordinary mental ability, forced his consciousness to overpower first that of Kralomoc and then later, when my investigation was leading us away from war with Jupiter, that of Tzedek. During the period of each assault, each Jovian passed out, while their bodies played host to the true assassin."

"Remarkable," exclaimed Joanna. "But who could do such a thing?"

"You told me yourself that your trade minister was an expert in mental transmigration technique. Salbatanu is hardly ever more than a few paces from your side, and yet he was not present when Tzedek attacked me. Nor, I would guess, when Kralomoc attacked your ambassador."

The Battle Maid of Mars' eyes were incredulous, then they grew astonished, then furious. She drew her sabre and turned on her minister.

"Salbatanu… How dare you turn against me?"

"If only you had ever turned to me," Salbatanu said bitterly.

"I think you'll find that he was benefiting heavily from trade agreements arranged through Venus. Arrangements that would be threatened if hostilities between Mars and Jupiter ceased. He may have feelings for you, Joanna, but his pocket-book mattered to him more."

"Arrest him," Joanna said to her guards, then added, "and free these two ambassadors at once. They are innocent."

"I do apologise, ma'am," said the detective. "But with a Martian as the culprit, it seems you cannot have your war."

The Battle Maid had the decency to blush.

"I thank you, sir. You have shown me that perhaps I was too quick to race to violence. I will think twice about it in future. Just as soon as I have removed this traitor from his head."

She turned to Salbatanu, raising her sword menacingly.

He shook the guards off and launched himself, not at Joanna, but at S. Quentin.

"If I go," Salbatanu roared, "I do not go alone."

The dandy fended off the physical attack easily, but that hadn't been the point. The move bought time for the trade minister to make a mental assault.

Suddenly, S. Quentin found himself tumbling in darkness again, only this time he wasn't alone.

Salbatanu came at him with savage determination. In the darkness of the aether between worlds, S. Quentin was hopelessly outmanoeuvred. He had only a little experience of transmigration, and all of it recent. The Martian, by contrast, was an expert at out of body experiences, with the confidence of having recently overpowered two Jovians. As expansive as the Dandy Detective's intellect was, here he was a sheep lost in the woods and Salbatanu was a hungry wolf.

Each assault, when it came, manifest as a piece of S. Quentin's mind – of his life – torn asunder. At one blow, there went a poignant childhood memory, at another the sweet remembrance of a rare, shy kiss stolen at a boys' boarding school before his inevitable expulsion. So much pleasure and pain bound up in each memory, making him the man he was. And the man he wasn't. To suffer in this fight was not to suffer physically, but to lose part of oneself.

S. Quentin battled bravely, lashing out with his own intellect at the force bearing down upon him, but it was no use. As unaccustomed to panic as he was, when Salbatanu began to rend his more recent memories the true fear set in. There were some recollections the loss of which were too painful to bear. The loss of love he scarcely himself acknowledged.

"Avery," the detective cried. "Oh Avery."

In the darkness of the void, he heard Salbatanu laugh.

"You are finished, you twisted old thing," came Salbatanu's voice from the darkness. "Surrender to the inevitable."

Yes, thought S. Quentin, defeat was inevitable. Always inevitable. As inevitable as man's nature. As schoolyard bullies. As societal rejection. Perhaps he should make an end. But then, the Dandy Detective was nothing if he didn't know how to bear up under scorn. Defeat might be inevitable, but...

"A man is not beaten when he is defeated. Only when he surrenders."

And with that the detective gave up the fight. He fell back as Salbatanu rushed in. Invisible teeth tore at him, but freed from the necessity of defending himself, he cast his consciousness wide. As sweet memories of his peculiar existence were ripped from him, he cast his line not towards his body back on Earth, nor towards the simulacrum on Mars, but towards a new destination. A beautiful shell now robbed of its rotten core.

"Wait," came Salbatanu's alarmed response as he sensed something of S. Quentin's trajectory. "What are you doing? Where are you going? You can't go there!"

But S. Quentin had no time for a response. He had places to see and people to be.

He opened eyes that were not his own. He stood again in Joanna's throne room before the high terrace. He glanced down at hands that were gorgeously bronzed. Strong. Fine. Well-manicured. And locked around the throat of a replica of the Dandy Detective.

Releasing the image of himself, S. Quentin stood up straight in the body of Salbatanu. Mere seconds had elapsed since he had been thrust from his own simulacrum.

"What do you know?" he said aloud. "I met so many people on Mars, I even encountered myself."

He blinked and looked around. Joanna's guards were rushing at him, rushing at Salbatanu, he corrected himself. There wasn't much time.

S. Quentin ran, not towards the approaching soldiers, not towards the well-guarded exit from the room, but towards the one place that no one had bothered to block, the open terrace.

Without a moment's hesitation, he leapt from the platform. As the members of the court gasped in shock, he sailed out like a glorious, great bird into the air. It was tremendously liberating. He hung in the air for a moment, the full spectacle of Mars' capital city spread out before him, almost as though it awaited him with eager anticipation. Then he plunged down, a spear whipping through the wind towards the ground hundreds of feet below.

He felt something battering at his skull. It was, of course, Salbatanu, desperate to return to his body. The Martian had no way of knowing the predicament he was in, only that his own flesh had been stolen by another. S. Quentin lacked the skill to hold him off for long. But the longer he could resist, the better. He didn't want the treacherous trade minister to have anything more than mere seconds to assess his situation.

S. Quentin clung to the stolen form until the final moment. Then, as the rust red of rock and the dust of iron oxide rose to meet him, he abandoned the body of Salbatanu to its rightful master.

He felt the Martian's soul slide past him as he quit the body, felt its triumph turn to horror as it claimed its just deserts. He felt a moment of grim satisfaction all his own. And then he felt nothing.

Sherlock Holmes opened his eyes to find himself reclined upon the sofa in his 221B Baker Street apartments. His breathing was irregular, his forehead stained with sweat, his mind full of strange, half-remembered images. His collar was loosened, and his shirt unbuttoned. He had the sensation that he had been in a fight, had been fighting, in fact, for his life. A man was bent over him.

"Wilson?" he said. No, not Wilson. That wasn't correct. Not here, not now. Here the man had another face, another name. "Watson."

"Yes, Holmes, I'm here," replied Dr John Watson, placing a restraining hand on the detective's shoulder when he tried to sit up. "Steady there, old boy. You've given me a fright. You've been, well, you've been *away* most of the night. I always think it best to leave you alone when you are –" Watson stumbled over his choice of words, though he had no qualms about expressing his disapproval of the detective's use of cocaine. "When you are so indisposed," he finished, "but I do admit you were beginning to worry me."

"There was a case," stammered Holmes. "'The Perilous Planet.' A murdered ambassador. A woman."

"A woman?" said Dr Watson, raising an eyebrow. "Holmes, are you sure you're quite recovered?"

With his friend's assistance, Holmes eased himself into a sitting position on the sofa. He closed his eyes, long fingers massaging his temple, and tried to organise his thoughts. He saw a vision of red sands, an exotic palace built into the rock of a plateau, strange beings of fantastical appearance, red hands locked around the throat of a most flamboyantly dressed American.

"I do wonder, Holmes." John was talking.

"What is that, Watson? I suppose you're wondering again what I see in my seven per cent solution?"

"No," said Watson, wrinkling his nose in distaste. "You've explained to me on enough occasions how you cannot abide idleness and stagnation. I won't argue with your rationalisations nor impose my sermonising upon you again. No, I was wondering something else. Not why you would subject yourself to such substances, but rather what a mind like yours dreams when it is loosed from its moorings? Ordinary men have fantastical enough visions when they partake of such substances. What must the mind of the great Sherlock Holmes experience when it is cast adrift on a sea of hallucination?"

The detective pondered this a moment in silence.

"'*El sueño de la razón produce monstruos*'."

"What's that, Holmes?"

"A quote, Watson. By the Spanish romantic Francisco José de Goya y Lucientes."

"I'm familiar with Goya. 'The Sleep of Reason', wasn't it? I don't suppose you'll enlighten me as to its relevance."

"You suppose correctly."

Watson grunted. He turned toward the stairway leading down.

"Shall I ring for Mrs Hudson? Have her bring you up some food?"

Holmes rose unsteadily to his feet.

"I think not. Not yet."

He was not hungry. In fact, he felt quite invigorated, triumphant even. His mind played back to scenes of a New York flat. Pulp magazines. A Rose of Alabama. A man of bronze. A warm planet, and an even warmer sensation when he thought of the name Avery. Not monstrous at all. Quite a dream. If dream it was. It had all been so real. Perhaps it was a sign, admonishing him to consider that which was important. Singular natures afforded so few opportunities for the expression of true affection. It was a most uncharacteristic thought. He entertained another one.

"Come, Watson," he said, heading towards the stairs.

"A case, Holmes? Is the game afoot?"

"No case, not today," he replied, to his dear friend's incredulous stare. "Come and take a stroll with me. In the sun. Just two friends for once. Enjoying each other's company."

Holmes paused at the bottom of the steps, where Mrs Hudson had placed some freshly cut flowers in a vase on a stand. He selected one for his lapel, a green carnation. "For my comfort," he replied to Watson's surprised look. He wasn't sure the flower suited him; it wasn't really his style, but he liked it there for the moment.

ABOUT THE AUTHOR

Lou Anders is the Hugo Award-winning editorial director of the SF&F imprint Pyr books, a Chesley Award-winning Art Director, and the editor of nine anthologies. He has also been nominated for six additional Hugo Awards and five additional Chesley Awards, as well as the PKD, Locus, Shirley Jackson, and three World Fantasy Awards. His first novel, *Frostborn*, book one in a three-book middle reader fantasy adventure series called Thrones and Bones, will be published in August 2014 by Random House's Crown Books for Young Readers. Visit him online at www.louanders.com, on Facebook, and on Twitter @LouAnders.

THE SNOWTORN TERROR

BY JUSTIN RICHARDS

Holmes, as was often his wont, seemed to ignore our potential client. He stood at the fireplace, his back to where the man was seated, fiddling with his pipe or leafing idly through the various items of correspondence pinned to the mantel with a clasp knife.

For my part, I made a point of paying full attention and nodded encouragingly for the gentleman to continue. "Perhaps if you introduce yourself and tell us what brings you here," I suggested.

The man's inchoate smile was stifled by Holmes's snort of amusement. "Really, Watson," he murmured, "Mr Cooper need not waste his time on such obvious triviality."

"For my benefit if not for Mr Holmes's," I said stiffly. "I for one did not overhear Mr Cooper introduce himself to Mrs Hudson on his arrival."

"Neither did I," Holmes said, turning abruptly and sitting down. He steepled his fingers together. "But for my friend and colleague Dr Watson's edification, pray – tell us about the death. A relative, I assume."

"My father," Mr Cooper said. "But how could you know that?"

"I did not. As I said, it was an assumption. But the death worries you, no? Why else would you have come so far straight from the funeral? Your attire gives you away," he explained. "Not least, the embroidered name visible in the collar of your coat when you handed it to Mrs Hudson just now. The work of Stimpsons of Argyll, if I am not mistaken. The stitching is quite distinctive."

Not for the first time, Holmes's deductions and observations seemed simple once explained. But Mr Alastair Cooper, as he now introduced himself, was evidently impressed.

Holmes shrugged off the man's praise and admiration with a thin smile. "So tell us of this mysterious death that brings you from Scotland? Quite apart from the provenance of your coat, the ticket stub was in your hand when you arrived," he added quickly.

The deceased was, as Mr Cooper had intimated, his father, and the death was indeed mysterious.

"My father, Sir Fergus Cooper, was not a young man, but I had not assumed I should inherit the estate for a good number of years yet. He was fit and healthy and making plans to redevelop parts of the estate on the slopes of Mount Snowtorn."

The name "Snowtorn" sounded familiar, though I could not immediately place it.

"In what way 'develop'?" Holmes demanded, stuffing tobacco into his pipe and bedding it down.

"Given the environment, the land is not arable, and the snows descend over a large part of the mountain for much of the winter, as they do now, so sheep farming is also problematic."

"Hunting then," Holmes said, lighting his pipe and puffing out a cloud of grey-blue smoke. "Go on."

"Indeed. Father had plans to clear the few tenants remaining from the upper slopes of the mountain and convert their dwellings into hunting lodges which could be leased out."

"And these tenants are happy to be evicted?" I asked.

Cooper nodded. "There are as I say only a few, and all on short-term leases. Most of the area is already used for hunting, so no one is actually being put out of their home. In fact, father was returning from one of the lodges that night, having visited a tenant whose twelve-month lease is about to expire. A young widow, she took the property while recovering from the loss of her husband. But I get ahead of myself."

"Indeed you do," Holmes agreed. "Tell us how your father died."

Cooper drew a deep breath. "He was found on the mountain. His throat had been severed."

"Good Lord!" I exclaimed. "And the police…?"

But Cooper was shaking his head. "They want nothing to do with it."

"Interesting. Why?"

"Because, Mr Holmes, my father's throat was not cut by any human hand."

Holmes closed his eyes. "A hasty and undoubtedly erroneous conclusion. But nevertheless that is the first thing you have said which is of any real interest. Explain."

"I wish I could, sir. It was I who found the body. Or, perhaps I should say, it was I who first reached it. As I explained, the mountain is snowbound at this time of year. Much of it is covered with woodland, but there is a wide, clear path that runs up to the summit. The Cooper Estate includes this path as well as much of the woodland – right as far as the railway."

Holmes's eyes snapped open. "I thought I knew the name – you refer to the Snowtorn Branch that links the main lines for Glasgow and Inverness, yes?"

"That is correct. But the railway is not connected to my father's demise, for he was on that path which I described. One of the servants saw him at first light as she was collecting wood from the shed to lay the fires."

"She saw his body lying on the mountain path?" I said.

Cooper nodded. "A long way up, but it was the only blemish on the white of the snow. We did not know who it was, of course. I had assumed father returned after I myself retired to bed. But when the servants woke me it was because my father was not in his room. His bed had not been slept in. So, of course, I knew…" His voice tailed off and I could see him fighting to control his emotions.

"My dear chap," I said gently.

"Go on," Holmes urged, oblivious to the man's feelings.

"Well, I walked up to the body, of course."

"Alone?"

"What? Oh no. Mr Greville, a friend of mine who lives locally, had also seen the body and called in at the house. So we made the journey together. It took some time to get to the body through the snow."

"You say your father's throat was cut?" I prompted.

He nodded.

"And why do you say it was not cut by a human?"

"There are…" Cooper hesitated, searching for the right word. "Legends. Stories. Tales of a creature that lives on the mountain. Of course," he said quickly, "I set no store by such nonsense. I am a rational man, and do not easily give in to beliefs in a supernatural being that haunts the mountain, apparently envious of those who still have their own lives. A creature that preys on the living, an entity made of smoke and mist, conjured from the ether, leaving no sign of its passing save the death of its victims."

"Yet I perceive that you have indeed given in to such beliefs," Holmes said.

Cooper nodded slowly. "I do not know what else to think, Mr Holmes. When we found my father's body, his throat was slit as I said. But he was utterly alone on the path."

"You do not consider his suicide a possibility?" Holmes asked, tactful as ever.

Cooper shook his head. "It is easy, I know, to say that it was not in his nature though I do truly believe that. But if you want proof, Mr Holmes, how could he have cut his own throat without a knife or similar instrument? For nothing of that kind was found on or near the body. The police had the same thought and searched extensively."

"Could he have thrown it away?" Holmes wondered. Immediately he shook his head, correcting himself. "But no, his throat was cut. He would not have had the strength or the time to dispose of the weapon properly. Unless he was close to the trees perhaps?"

"He was in the middle of the path between the areas of woodland. Perhaps twenty yards from the nearest tree."

"Too far," I said.

Holmes nodded his agreement. "And how can you be sure that no one else was present, or later disturbed the scene of the crime?"

It was a good point, as Holmes's always were. "Someone else

could have taken the knife away," I realised. "Or slit his throat, come to that."

"No," Cooper said. "He was lying on his back in the snow. The *undisturbed* snow. Not only was there no one nearby, but the only footprints in the snow were my father's own."

There was silence for several moments as we absorbed this information. Then Holmes nodded as if he had expected exactly this. "Watson?" he prompted.

"Were your father's footprints deep?" I asked, struggling to find a possible solution to this singular problem.

"Not especially."

"Ah, good thought, Watson." Holmes jabbed the end of his pipe at me. "You are suggesting that the killer was somewhat lighter in weight than the deceased Mr Cooper."

"My father was not a heavy man," Cooper told us. "But how is this pertinent?"

"In that case, perhaps it isn't," I admitted. "But I did wonder if the killer's footprints were more shallow than your father's and a fresh snowfall had obliterated them while leaving those of your father still in evidence."

Cooper shook his head. "There had been no fresh fall since the previous day. In fact it did snow while my father was with Mrs Bennett, the widow I mentioned. Hence he walked back through the virgin snow, but his were undoubtedly the only footprints."

"It could not have snowed during the night?" I ventured. "Without your noticing?"

Again Cooper shook his head. "Impossible. Because the blood from my father's wound – and as a medical man, Dr Watson, you will appreciate that there was a lot of blood – was sprayed across the top of the snow, staining it as it sank in. Any fresh fall would have obliterated the stain. We have considered everything."

"I doubt that," Holmes said. "I do have one question, if I may?"

"Of course."

"How far is it from the railway line that borders your estate to the point where your father's body was found?"

The question seemed to surprise Cooper as much as it did myself.

But my experiences with Holmes meant that I was able to conceal my surprise, and I assured myself that his question would turn out to have some relevance.

"About a mile, I suppose," Cooper said after consideration.

"And am I right in thinking that some part of this line as it borders the estate was the location of the Snowtorn Line Robbery, as the newspapers have described it?"

"Ah!" I exclaimed. "So that's how I know the name."

"Most probably," Holmes agreed.

The robbery had garnered headlines about nine months previously. A freight train bound from Inverness to Glasgow had been carrying a large shipment of gold bullion when it was deliberately derailed on the Snowtorn Branch, killing the driver and badly injuring his footplateman. The gold was never recovered, and Holmes had been amused by the various speculations about how the thieves managed to move such a weight and volume of the precious metal through the snowy wastes of the Scottish countryside.

"Are they any closer to solving that one?" I asked Cooper.

"Not to my knowledge," he told us. "They did arrest a man soon after the event, as you probably know. Arvin Gunnarsson, I believe his name is. But the police were unable to connect him to the actual robbery."

Holmes nodded. "He claimed he was paid to sabotage the track, but had no involvement in the robbery itself and was long gone when the thieves derailed the train. The authorities had to content themselves with a charge of damaging railway property. I believe Mr Gunnarsson is currently serving out an eighteen-month sentence in Glasgow."

"You are better informed than I," Cooper admitted. "So, Mr Holmes – will you take the case?"

Holmes sniffed and regarded his pipe with interest. "Oh yes," he decided at last. "But I shall want to see the scene of the crime."

"The spot where the body was found – of course."

Holmes frowned. "Don't be obtuse, man," he snapped. "I mean the point at which the train was derailed."

* * *

Owing to other commitments, it was several days before we could escape the smog of London for the fresher air of Scotland. Cooper was the perfect host, sending a carriage to collect us from the nearest station, which was in truth not near at all.

Holmes was not at all interested in taking time to settle into our rooms at Cooper's substantial house, and before long we were trudging up the slopes of Mount Snowtorn. The view, looking back into the valley bathed in the early afternoon sun, was superb. A light pattering of snow covered my coat. Holmes cut a distinctive figure, retaining as he did the Inverness cape he had worn for travelling. I knew that he had sent the garment to be altered and only collected it again the previous day. I imagined, the air being so chill, that he was grateful for its return.

Mr Cooper showed us the spot, so far as he could estimate, where he had discovered his father's body. Holmes spared it little more than a glance, jabbing his walking cane into the snow to estimate its depth before heading off to the nearest trees.

When he returned, he announced shortly: "I have seen enough."

"And what have you deduced?" Cooper asked eagerly.

"Little of interest. I shall perhaps know more when I have inspected the scene of the train robbery."

Cooper looked puzzled, and I shrugged sympathetically. "His methods are not always conventional," I confided quietly to our client. "But they invariably yield results."

As Cooper pointed out the route we must take to the spot Holmes wished to visit, I perceived a figure hurrying down the mountainside towards us. A female figure, no less.

"Mrs Bennett," Cooper explained. "The widowed lady whom my father visited before…" his voice tailed off and he waved his hand by way of completing the thought.

Mrs Elizabeth Bennett was not the sort of widow I had anticipated. She was indeed young, barely out of her twenties, and a rare beauty. Her eyes were a pale blue and the hair escaping from the confines of the hood of her coat was as fair as spun gold. Her features were thin and well defined as she introduced herself to us. I thought I detected a faint trace of accent, Scotch I assumed until Holmes also remarked on it.

"I perceive that Bennett is your married name," he said, "since judging by your accent you yourself are from Scandinavia."

She seemed surprised. "How clever of you to notice. I thought my English was good."

"It is very good," Cooper assured her. "I had not noticed your accent at all."

"Norway, I think," Holmes murmured.

Mrs Bennett seemed more anxious to speak with Cooper than with myself or Holmes, so we waited politely while the two of them conferred.

"She is concerned about renewing her lease," Cooper told us as we made our way towards the railway line. "It runs out imminently, and father was assuming she would move on so he could renovate the property ready for the next hunting season. She initially took the lodge for twelve months only."

"Will you renew?" I asked.

"It is difficult. The workmen and the materials are already organised. My father had arranged to have a new floor put in next month and I have already confirmed the instructions."

"You are continuing with your father's project then?" Holmes said. "That is excellent. I'm sure it will be a success."

"I said I would call in on Mrs Bennett later this afternoon, once I have shown you the way to the railway."

The afternoon was drawing in by the time we reached the spot Holmes wanted to see. He stood for what seemed an eternity, looking around in all directions and nodding as if it was all exactly as he expected.

"Thank you, Mr Cooper," he called finally. "We can find our own way back if you wish to keep your appointment with the attractive Mrs Bennett."

"Attractive?" Cooper shuffled his feet and the colour rose slightly in his cheeks. "I suppose she is... if you are sure?"

"Quite sure," Holmes assured him. "Oh, just one thing," he called after Cooper as the man turned to go. "Make sure you are home before it gets fully dark."

"You don't really believe in this beast of the mountains do you,

Holmes?" I asked as Cooper disappeared into the distance.

"A man *is* dead," he replied thoughtfully.

"But surely…" I frowned. "You think Cooper is in danger?"

"I hope not. Now, Watson – you see how the landscape here undulates, yes? Although we are at a height, the railway climbs and descends slowly so that the locomotives can handle the incline."

"There is no road," I pointed out. "And in the snow there would be no way to get a carriage to this location. It would soon be bogged down."

"Especially with the weight of so much gold bullion pressing on the wheels," Holmes added. "Yes, as I suspected, there is only one way that the robbery could have been achieved."

It came to me with sudden inspiration as I looked back across the landscape and saw our footprints pressed into the snow. "Of course, Holmes – they buried the gold and came back for it once the snow melted in the spring."

Holmes seemed to be fighting the urge to smile as he dashed my theory. "Perhaps I should have said only one way for the robbery to be carried out *successfully*. What you suggest is certainly possible, but I imagine the police would have investigated any mysterious lumps in the snow. There is no woodland here, nowhere to conceal a pile of gold. And the snow would melt from it long before the ground was suitable for transportation, leaving the hoard visible to all. Highly visible once the sun was on it. No," he went on, "the solution is far more ingenious and terribly simple."

"Then what is it?" I asked, exasperated.

Holmes looked up at the darkening sky. "It is late. Let us hope that Mr Cooper heeded my warning and is already back at his house."

We arrived back before it was fully dark, to find a man of about the same age as Cooper also waiting for his return. This was Mr Greville, the friend of whom Cooper had spoken. Taking drinks before dinner, he was happy to give his own account of the discovery of Sir Fergus Cooper's body – an account that matched with young Cooper's own version of events.

"It's a puzzle and no mistake," Greville said as he finished. He checked his watch. "As is the whereabouts of Alastair. I am sure he said to be here for five o'clock and it is almost half past."

"Perhaps he had tarried at Mrs Bennett's," I suggested.

"A temptation he might not have been able to resist," Greville agreed with a knowing smile.

"A temptation that might well be the death of him," Holmes said, galvanised suddenly into action. He drained his glass and set it down on a side table before striding to the door. "Come along, Watson – a man's life could be at stake."

Before he reached the door, it burst open to admit another figure. Alastair Cooper staggered in, his face a mask of terror and his features streaked with blood.

"My dear chap!" Greville hurried to assist his friend, helping him to a chair close to the fire.

The man's clothes were soaked through, snow clinging to the fabric. His teeth were chattering and he shivered violently, though with the cold or with fear it was impossible to tell. I called for the servants and organised hot water to bathe Cooper's face and a stiff brandy to settle his nerves. The blood emanated from a deep scratch across his cheek, which I cleaned as best I could.

After a while, he recovered enough to speak of his ordeal. Greville and I listened in rapt silence while Holmes nodded and sighed as if everything was entirely as he had anticipated.

"As you know," Cooper said, his voice quavering, "I called to see Mrs Bennett to discuss further the situation regarding her leasehold. I offered to allow Mrs Bennett to stay on in one of the other lodges that has already been renovated," Cooper went on. "And at a reduced rent, which seemed to me to be a generous and equitable arrangement. But she was somewhat less enthusiastic."

"There's no place like home," I said.

"We talked for a while. Mrs Bennett is an easy person with whom to converse."

"I can imagine," Holmes murmured.

"She was the most generous of hosts. But when it got dark, she became a little flustered. She wondered what people would think if they knew that I was there with her alone at this hour and so I made my farewell."

"Probably as well," Greville said.

"Then, as I made my way down…" Cooper paused to take a sip of brandy, though he could scarcely hold the glass he was now trembling so much. "It's true – the legend," he stammered. "All true. I've seen it."

"Seen it?" I said, glancing at Holmes. But his expression was impassive as granite. "Seen what?"

"The creature. The beast of the mountain. Don't you understand – that is what attacked me. Its claws did this." He gestured to the scratch across his face.

"Good Lord," Greville said, and refilled his own glass. "There's devilry in this."

"Of that there is no doubt," Holmes agreed. "But tell us of the devilish creature you saw. Or think you saw."

"A dark shape," Cooper said. "Wings like a huge bat. I heard it coming behind me, the beat of its wings against the air, like the whoosh of a giant bird of prey. I turned – and there it was. Dark against the snow. Flying just above it, fast as the wind. If I had remained transfixed, it would have killed me."

"You moved then?" Holmes asked. "As the 'creature' slashed at your neck, yes?"

"I was petrified," Cooper confessed. "My foot slipped in the snow. The creature's talons sliced at me at just the instant I fell."

Holmes rose to his feet. "You were lucky. Did I not warn you to be back here before dark?"

Cooper nodded.

"Stay with him, Mr Greville," Holmes said.

"Where are we going?" I demanded as I rose to follow.

"Bring a length of rope," was Holmes's unedifying reply. "And it is cold out, so you had best wear my cape."

About the cape he was most insistent, despite the fact I had a perfectly fine overcoat of my own. But Holmes declared that the cold of the night would keep him alert and that the cape was my best option.

"This collar is rather stiff," I told him as I struggled to do it up.

Holmes merely grunted, and coiled the rope we had obtained with the help of one of the servants over his shoulder. We were also provided with lanterns.

"I assume you have your service revolver about your person," Holmes said as we set out to inspect the location of this most recent incident. I assured him that I had.

The snow was churned up where Cooper had been attacked. But, just as before, his tracks were the only footprints. Holmes set down his lantern and lay full length in the snow, inspecting the surface.

"It is as I feared," he said at last, leaping back to his feet in a single easy movement.

For my part, I was inspecting the area close to where the attack had occurred.

"There is some blood here," I pointed out. "But more importantly, Holmes – what do you make of *this*?"

I was sure that my find would provoke an enthusiastic response from my friend and colleague. As is so often the case, I was disappointed by his reaction.

"It is a hole, Watson. A hole in the snow, quite small but extending I imagine to a reasonable depth."

"It might be important," I said.

"I'm certain that it is," he agreed. "You will find another, unless I am much mistaken, a few yards further up hill. And again, down hill."

He was right of course.

"But what made them? Do you know?"

Holmes did not answer. He was apparently examining the slope of the path between the trees, and the distance to the nearest part of the wood on either side.

"Was some apparatus strung up here, is that it?" I asked. A series of supports for wires, perhaps."

"So that a sharp-edged object could be propelled down them?" Holmes asked without turning.

"Exactly so."

"I think Mr Cooper might have noticed such an apparatus as you describe, don't you?"

"What then?" I glanced up the slope, following Holmes's gaze. "I assume that Mrs Elizabeth Bennett is quite safe?"

"Elizabeth Bennett," Holmes repeated. "Yes... Yes," he decided, "you are right, Watson, as ever. It is time to lay this matter to rest. I don't know about you, but I am rapidly approaching the point where dinner would be most welcome. I shall return to Mr Cooper and his friend and acquaint them with our progress."

"I notice you use the singular," I said. "What do you want me to do?"

"Exactly as you suggest, my friend." He smiled. "You should go and check that Mrs Elizabeth Bennett is safe and well."

The prospect of seeing the young lady again did indeed appeal. But I was more concerned for her safety. "Won't you accompany me?"

"I have another small matter to see to." He turned and set off down the snow-covered path, the length of rope still slung unused over his shoulder.

I raised my hand in a vague wave before setting off in the opposite direction. Even with the lantern, it was dark. The snow reflected the light, creating eerie shapes and shadows. I glanced back, but there was no sign of Holmes at all. He must already be out of sight.

After perhaps five minutes of walking up the mountain, I heard it. Just as Cooper had described – a susurration like the breeze that became louder, like a sword cutting through the air close to my ear. I tried to dispel this less than comforting thought. But I could not deny what my senses told me – the creature was coming.

A moment later, I could *see* it. The dark shape that Cooper had described – bat-like wings spread out behind it as it sped across the snow, leaving no tracks. A long claw glinted in the light of my lantern. Inside my cape, my hand tightened on the grip of my revolver and I struggled to wrestle it clear of the heavy cape Holmes had insisted I wear.

Too late. The sharp claw lanced across my throat as the creature sped past. In the same moment, I finally managed to draw the revolver and fired at the creature. It emitted an unholy, high-pitched scream, and veered away with a "whoosh" of sound.

I had winged it, no more. But my own escape was nothing less than miraculous. The claw had ripped across my throat, and yet – there was no blood. I fumbled with the collar of the cloak, and felt the cold, hard surface. So that was why Holmes had insisted I wear it – the collar was stiff because the material was stitched over a strip of metal that had protected my throat.

Even as I made this discovery, I heard a loud cry followed by a dull thump from somewhere close to the path, in the trees. A lantern appeared, waving back and forth and Holmes's unmistakeable voice reached me as he called:

"Watson, over here! Well done, my friend – we have the murderer."

I hurried down the slope and across to the trees where Holmes was waiting. Behind him, I saw the rope he had carried was strung between the trees. Lying a little further on, stretched out in the snow, lay a figure. Wearing a long dark cloak that had billowed out behind like wings, still holding a long-bladed knife that I had mistaken for a claw, Mrs Bennett was bleeding from a wound to her left shoulder where my bullet had caught her.

A long wooden pole was attached to her wrist by a leather strap. One of the skis she was wearing had snapped as she collided with a tree after falling foul of Holmes's rope.

Dinner had seldom been more welcome. The barely conscious Mrs Bennett was taken away by a somewhat surprised representative of the local constabulary, summoned by Mr Greville.

"I believe she came from the Telemark region of Norway," Holmes explained. "Skiing with the pole as you saw, Watson – the pole that made those holes in the snow – has become almost an art form there. The skis developed in that region are shaped so as to leave the least impression in the snow. Even to an expert such as myself lying down at eye-level their tracks were only just discernible."

"But what was her motive?" Cooper asked. "Why kill father? And why did she try to kill me, and Dr Watson?"

"She attempted to kill Watson because she mistook him for me," Holmes said. So that was why he had insisted I wear his cape; any concern for my safety was probably secondary. He had wanted Mrs

Bennett to believe it was Holmes himself ascending alone while he observed events from the woodland. "Once I revealed her Nordic origins, and my interest in the bullion robbery," Holmes was saying, "she was afraid I might discover the truth."

"And what, pray, is the truth?" Greville asked.

"That she is no more a widow than I am," Holmes said.

"Good Lord." A thought occurred to me. "Perhaps Elizabeth Bennett isn't even her real name."

Holmes shook his head sadly. "Elizabeth Bennett is the fictional name of a fictional character. You really should read more, my dear doctor."

"So who is she really?" Cooper asked.

"I imagine her surname is Gunnarsson."

"But – that was the chap who derailed the train," I realised.

"The same. He and his wife derailed the train and made off with the bullion."

"But how?" Cooper demanded. "The police deduced that a gang of twenty or more would have been needed to shift the gold."

"No, just the two of them. And a horse."

"A horse?" I echoed.

"Pulling a sledge."

There was silence for several moments while we all took this in. It suddenly seemed so simple – as solutions often are when one finally has them explained.

"They didn't need to travel far," Holmes went on finally. "They took the gold to a nearby hunting lodge that Mrs Gunnarsson had leased under a false name, intending to move it once the fuss had died down. I imagine that twelve months seemed far longer than they would ever need."

"Except that Gunnarsson was recognised and arrested," I said. "That must have scuppered their plans."

"It meant a postponement, certainly, until he is released next year. But in the meantime, I think you will find the gold bullion stored under the floor of the lodge. The floor which both you, Mr Cooper, and your father made it clear you wished to replace."

Cooper nodded. "And since she could not remove the gold without her husband's help, Mrs Bennett – or whoever she was – had to make sure she stayed in the lodge and the floor remained intact."

"When charm failed, she resorted to more desperate measures," Holmes agreed. "I doubt she even knew the legend of the vengeful mountain beast, but she used the skill and expertise she brought from her homeland to despatch your father as quickly as she could. An unfortunate and desperate action. I am sorry for your loss."

I shook my head and accepted the offer of more wine. "Once again, Holmes," I said, "you astound me."

My friend smiled and offered his own glass for recharging. "Once again, Watson," he said, "so do you."

ABOUT THE AUTHOR

Justin Richards has written for stage and screen as well as writing audio plays, novels, and graphic novels. Before writing full time, Justin has worked in the computer industry, and as an odd-job man at a hotel exclusively for postmen. He is registered as an Inventor in the European Union and has patents in his name in, amongst other places, the UK, USA and Japan. Justin currently acts as Creative Consultant to BBC Books' range of *Doctor Who* titles, as well as writing quite a few himself. The first novel in his Never War series, *The Suicide Exhibition*, was published by Del Rey in November 2013.

A Betrayal of Doubt

BY PHILIP MARSH

"He's here."

The young police constable who delivered this message paused just long enough to utter those two words before pulling the door quickly closed behind him, in the manner of someone who has just tossed a hand grenade into a room and is trying desperately to escape the resulting blast. Certainly there can have been few occasions when a junior officer had had the opportunity to so startle his superiors, and I'm sure part of him had wished he could have remained to see the effect his brief appearance had on the officers present. Looking around the room, I noticed that each had reacted to the message in much the same way – experienced, professional men used to holding positions of authority, all feeling cowed and uncertain, like school boys who can hear that the housemaster is on his way.

I cannot claim to have reacted any differently.

A legend had arrived.

The room had been silent for several minutes, but now the silence took on a meaning all of its own, speaking of the anticipation felt by everyone present more eloquently than words ever could. Few of us who had gathered in the cramped Scotland Yard office of Inspector Barrett had met the visitor, whose last appearance in these rooms had been a good ten years previous, but those who had still spoke of him with a clarity that belied the passage of time.

Eventually the door opened. At last I was to meet the man that my father dedicated so much of his life to, and whom he had made famous. Indeed, had my father himself walked through that door, as though through a portal from the great beyond, I could not have felt such stirring emotions.

A uniformed officer entered the room before stepping respectfully to one side. And then, in he walked. He moved slowly, leaning heavily on his cane with every step, a shawl wrapped around his thin, hunched shoulders.

Barrett, who had been sat at his desk, rose to his feet instantly. Everyone else was already stood. Sitting at such a moment would have felt sacrilegious.

"Mr Holmes," said Barrett, "please allow me to say what an honour it is to welcome you back to London, and back to the Yard. My name is Inspector Barrett and I have admired your work in the field of detection for many years. Won't you take a seat?"

"Thank you, Inspector," said the visitor. "My legs are not what they once were." He sat, and I studied him closely. He was almost painfully thin, and his face was lined with deep creases, his skin waxy, its whiteness competing with that of his hair. His eyes appeared dulled with age and he peered as though trying to see through a permanent fog.

He looked around the room and his gaze suddenly locked on me.

"You," he said, pointing at me with his stick. "Come closer."

I hesitated for a moment.

"Come, come," he said tetchily, "don't dawdle."

I stepped forward and leaned down, unsure of how good the old man's eyes were. Suddenly his severe frown flashed into a smile.

"Well, well. Dr John Watson, Jnr. How appropriate."

I was instantly taken aback. "How did you know…?"

He let out a worryingly rasping laugh. "My boy, you really are just like your father, aren't you?"

I tried to recover my composure, thinking back through my father's accounts of his time with this man, remembering what I could of his methods. I was determined not to appear foolish. "My hands still smell of soap from regular washing," I hazarded, "and my pocket is dented where I keep my stethoscope. From that you deduced I am a doctor. Also I am wearing the pocket-watch that my father left me, and with which you must have been familiar from your time living together in Baker Street."

He chuckled again. "Nothing so extraordinary, I am afraid. You are the very image of your father in his younger days, and you also owe him your posture. My eyes are not as sharp as once they were but I recognised the way you were standing from the moment I entered the room. And I knew you had followed in your father's footsteps professionally from the letters he sent me before his untimely demise." And then, unexpectedly, he reached out and placed his hand on my wrist. "It was a great shock to me to hear of his passing. He was a brave and resourceful man, and a good friend. I was particularly saddened that a bout of flu prevented me from attending his funeral to pay him the respect that he was due." Then, as suddenly as he focused on me, he fixed his attention on Inspector Barrett, who had also taken his seat. "I must say, Inspector, it is unusual for me to be made so welcome in the offices of Scotland Yard. On most of my visits in the past I have been regarded as something of an irritant. I do hope you have dragged me all the way from Sussex to do more than perform cheap parlour tricks."

"Oh believe me, I have, Mr Holmes. I shall reveal all, but first allow me to introduce…"

"Please, Inspector Barrett. No disrespect meant to your fine, upstanding fellow officers, but I grew tired of the metropolis some time ago and would like to leave it as soon as possible. Pray, get to the point and explain why you have called me here."

"Very well, Mr Holmes," said Barrett, taking the snub of his fellow officers remarkably in his stride. "We have called you here because, to put it bluntly, we're absolutely stumped. A murder has been committed for which we can find absolutely no explanation."

"Such things must, if you will forgive my saying so, happen rather frequently. What is it about this case that makes it so special?"

Again, Barrett showed little or no irritation at Holmes's rudeness and continued in the same amiable tone.

"What makes it special, is that the body of the deceased was found in his own parlour, with the door to the room locked and no sign of any visitor or disturbance. Well, except for the knife sticking out of his chest, that is."

"Then someone must have had a key," said Holmes with a heavy sigh.

"Oh, they did, Mr Holmes. The deceased was a bachelor, no family in the local area. Only his housekeeper had a key. No one else. And she was staying with family in Hertfordshire that evening, with several witnesses vouching for her. She found him the next morning. We have no reason to disbelieve her when she says there was no other key, and what's more, the only footprints belonged to the deceased himself."

Holmes said nothing. The Inspector continued.

"But the strangest thing about the case, the thing that has prompted our unusual action of contacting you, is that when he was found his body was covered in symbols and lettering in foreign script. It is quite clear that these are occult in origin."

"The occult?" Holmes asked scornfully. "Not so much parlour tricks as fairy stories. Inspector, you disappoint me. You want a priest, not a detective."

"Oh I agree with you completely, Mr Holmes, don't get me wrong. I have no time for this kind of mumbo-jumbo normally. But the truth of it is," the Inspector leaned forward and spoke softly as though afraid his words could be overheard, "that it's gotten the public proper scared, and the longer this goes on without a resolution, the more they're starting to believe that maybe there's something to this supernatural business, and the more scared they get. People are starting to report all kinds of things; why only this morning a woman was found strangled in her own home, with a feeble attempt at mystical symbols drawn badly on her arms. Personally, I found the strangle marks around her neck that matched her husband's fingers to be more convincing. But if we don't get this thing solved, and solved quickly… why, there could be anarchy. At the very least, this business undermines faith, not just in the police force, but in logical reasoning and detection of any kind. And you of all people must appreciate how dangerous such a thing would be." Barrett leaned forward even closer. "So, what do you say? Will you help us?"

There was a moment of awkward silence. Then Holmes exhaled, slowly and deliberately. "Very well, Inspector," he said. "We can not allow anything to undermine the public's faith in the abilities of the Constabulary, can we?" Then he smiled again, and I could not tell if it was in mockery of the police force or inspired by his pleasure at having a new mystery worthy of his intellect to solve. "Take me to the morgue – I have a cadaver to examine."

"Capital," said Inspector Barrett. "I hope you don't mind my saying so, but I anticipated that you would not be able to refuse a case like this, and have arranged to have the Yard's saw-bones waiting downstairs to show you the body."

"Thank you, Inspector, but if you don't mind I would like Dr Watson to accompany us and provide a second opinion. I am sure that his medical skills were tested to the utmost by his wartime service, and a fresh pair of eyes is always to be appreciated."

Inspector Barrett chuckled. "Don't take me for an insensitive brute, Mr Holmes, but Dr Watson was not invited to this event simply for symbolic value. I know that you doubt the Yard's surgeons as well as its inspectors, and guessed you might like a more distanced opinion. Had Dr Watson Snr been alive I would of course have invited him, but seeing as he is no longer with us – God rest his soul – I thought you'd rather Dr Watson Jnr than a complete stranger."

"Most thoughtful of you, Inspector," he said before turning once more to me. "John... may I call you John?"

This sudden switch back to gentlemanly civility caught me out after Holmes's barbed conversation with Barrett. "Why... yes, absolutely."

"Good. John, would you mind coming and helping me to my feet? This chair is rather low."

"Of course," I replied, and stepped forward, taking hold of Holmes's arm and supporting him as he stood. I could almost hear the creaks of his joints as he rose and must confess that a betrayal of doubt assailed my mind – this man may once have been the world's greatest detective, capable of supreme feats of concentration and deductive brilliance, but now he appeared frail and worn, just another old man in an old body. Did those famous wits still work sharply enough? Could this delicate frame take the strain of another investigation?

"You may remove your hand now, John, I am capable of walking a short distance, I assure you."

I removed my hand with a start and Holmes made his tentative way towards the door, which Barrett held open for him. Despite the slowness of his gait, I fell into step behind him so naturally that it did not seem an inconvenience to alter my natural stride. As we walked Barrett kept up a stream of comments about the corridors and offices, noting any changes that would have taken place since he last entered the building. Eventually we arrived at the morgue, which I doubt I need to describe in any detail, especially to those familiar with my father's stories – I'm sure I do not need to remind anyone that my father's first meeting with Holmes took place around a dissection table.

At Inspector Barrett's command, one of the cooling cabinets was opened and a body produced. The corpse was around five feet eight, of average build and with dark-brown hair. These details however only registered later. Before then I was distracted by two features. First was the stab wound in the unfortunate man's chest. This distracted me not from horror but rather because it triggered the attention that my medical training and experience had conditioned me to focus upon sight of a wound. And the second distracting feature was that the corpse was covered in strange, intricate symbols, drawn into the skin.

"The deceased is a Marcus Sanders," stated Barrett. "Age thirty-eight. Bachelor. Owner of a small tobacco shop which made a modest profit, and which enabled him to afford a small property with a housekeeper in one of the slightly poorer, but not too rough, parts of town. Neighbours reported nothing suspicious about him, no noise, few visitors, largely kept himself to himself. None has been able to provide any suggestion as to why anyone might wish to kill him."

"Your opinion?" said Holmes, and a moment passed before I

realised he was addressing me. But once more, my experience quickly took control.

"The wound is remarkably clean. A single blow straight to the heart. Do we have the murder weapon here?"

Inspector Barrett took a knife from a tray and held it up for me to see.

"Yes, that blade would match this wound exactly. The blow must have been struck from close up to be so precise – this was no wild stab and there are no other knife-marks on the body."

I looked at Holmes but his expression gave me no clue of what he was thinking. "Continue," was all he said.

"This suggests that the victim knew his assailant as he does not seem to have put up any kind of struggle."

"Could he not have been restrained?"

"There are no marks on the skin to suggest so."

"Drugged?"

"A possibility," I confessed. "But we will not know that until a full autopsy has been carried out."

"There is one factor you seem to have overlooked," Holmes said.

I thought hard but could not work out what he meant.

"The knife was still in his chest when he was found. Unless our killer removed it and replaced it to allow for the victim's clothing to be removed, the killing blow must have occurred after Mr Sanders was already undressed. I had to continually warn your father about coming to conclusions until all the evidence was in our possession and fully considered. Still," and at this point he smiled, "I did rather goad you into it, and your conclusions were rather intelligent given the information you had to work with. Your father would have been very proud."

Inspector Barrett harrumphed pointedly – the first sign of irritation I had seen from him. "There is another rather unusual feature on this particular cadaver, as I am sure neither of you good gentlemen could have failed to notice. The markings."

"Ah yes," said Holmes, who reached into his jacket and pulled out a magnifying glass, through which he peered at the strange symbols, moving around the table to view them all.

"It appears that they were drawn after death – the deceased's clothing was found in a pile next to the body. Our theory is that after the murderer gained entry – however he did *that* – he delivered the killing blow, then stripped the body and drew them, although what they signify no one can tell. Still, they don't appear random, so someone must know what they mean – the murderer at least."

"You are right about them not being random markings, Inspector," said Holmes. "They are too elaborate – whoever drew them must have practised them many times in order to be this precise, especially given that they would have wanted to complete them as quickly as possible to avoid detection. They have a very definite meaning."

"Which is?" asked Barrett keenly.

"I have no firm conclusion on that point just at this moment," Holmes replied. "But three possibilities occur to me. One, the patterns are there to identify the killer, a serial killer's marker. Second, that they are some kind of message. Thirdly, that they are as the Inspector suggested, occult in origin, and their very presence on the body was considered sufficient to have some kind of impact on the world."

"Like a magic spell, you mean?"

"Exactly, John. We may dwell in the light of rationality, but some of our brethren choose to live in the shadow of superstition. However we must guard against assumptions and consider each option thoroughly before favouring one over another."

"But who would write a message on a dead body?" I asked, feeling once again how my father must have felt on many occasions during his time with Holmes. "I mean, how could they know it would be received? Even if the newspapers get hold of the story they could not possibly describe the patterns in such detail as to be recognisable."

"Well, should that second possibility turn out to be the correct one – and it is far too early to assume anything of the sort – we are again left with two possibilities. First, that the patterning itself is the message, and a report of it would be enough to alert the intended recipient. Or second, that the intended target of the message is someone who would come into direct contact with the body."

"I think," interjected Inspector Barratt, "that we're becoming rather guilty of what Mr Holmes has just warned us against;

speculation without accumulation – of evidence, that is."

"Touché, Inspector," said Holmes. "Touché. Speaking of evidence, could you kindly furnish me with a series of photographs of the body so I can study the markings at my leisure? I do not think that the atmosphere in this room is particularly conducive to my joints working as they should. Also, for John here to attend the autopsy when it is carried out – I would like to hear his findings as well as those of the official surgeon. You would have no objection to that, would you, John?"

"Why, no. Not at all," I replied. "In fact, I would have no objection to carrying it out now, if that would be acceptable, Inspector?"

"Fine by me, Doctor. In truth the surgeon's been getting itchy about it."

"Excellent," said Holmes. "I shall leave you gentlemen to it. Inspector, if you could find me a comfortable chair and a medicinal cup of tea while this lifeless unfortunate is carved up, I would be in your debt."

The Inspector led Holmes back to the main part of the Yard and I could not help but reflect on how time changes us all. The Sherlock Holmes I knew from my father's stories was as fond of cocaine as of a wholesome cup of tea. My father had always feared that his use of the drug would impair Holmes's faculties, those unique powers of logic and deduction. So far in my acquaintance with him, I could not see any evidence of this – his body might be gradually slowing down but his intellect seemed to remain strong.

While I had given the impression of being eager to commence with the autopsy, in truth I did not like the idea very much. I am not squeamish – no man in my position or with my experience can afford to be – but I have never relished the cutting up of the human body, the revelation of the internal world of the human being. While many surgeons seemed to delight in this procedure I find it to be a necessary but unpleasant evil. I was happy therefore to allow the hospital surgeon to carry out the work while I merely observed. Despite Holmes's reservations, I found nothing to disagree with in the surgeon's techniques or observations. There seemed to be no evidence of any drug as Holmes had suggested there might be. As I went on to explain to Holmes, the knife appeared most strongly to be the cause of death, with no other suspicious injuries or unusual features.

"In short," I finished, "we have no further information than we had before the autopsy."

"Oh, do not sound so downhearted, John," said Holmes. "Your work was not in vain. We have eliminated some of the possibilities, meaning we now have less to distract us from the correct one. So, the next step is to examine the scene of the crime."

"Now?" I asked. I was concerned that after all the travelling Holmes had done he could do without more exertion.

"Yes, John, now. The longer we leave it, the less there will be to discover. Inspector, is the housekeeper back from…" He paused for a moment, searching for the right word, "…her family's home?" he finished, but I could tell he had been trying to remember exactly where the Inspector had told him that was. I could also tell from an unguarded expression that lasted for a second at most that Holmes was annoyed with himself for not remembering.

"I agree," said Inspector Barrett. "Sergeant – please help Mr Holmes to a car. I need to collect a couple of things and speak to Dr Watson, so we shall catch you up."

After Holmes had left the room, Barrett leant across his desk and fixed me with the kind of stare I imagined he normally reserved for suspects who were withholding evidence. Such was its intensity that I found myself nervous even though I knew that I had done nothing wrong.

"Well?" he asked.

"I assume, Inspector, that you are asking me about Mr Holmes, and whether I think he is still capable of dealing with this kind of case."

"I am."

"He is certainly quite frail, and perhaps his memory and vision are not what they were, but from the little I have observed, his intellect seems intact."

"Your tone suggests that you are refusing to say the word 'but',

Dr Watson. Please do not refrain from doing so."

I sighed. "*But* it is too early to say with any confidence."

"I need you to keep an eye on him, and feed back to me how capable you think he is as the investigation progresses. With all respect to his past record, if he is past his best I can't afford to be sent down blind alleys."

I felt an immediate flare of anger at the Inspector's rudeness towards Holmes and my temper momentarily got the better of me. "I understand, Inspector," I said, levelly but firmly, "although the fact that you have asked Holmes here at all suggests you have already investigated a fair few of those under your own initiative."

A flicker of surprise twitched across Barrett's face at my rudeness, and for a moment I thought it might be accompanied by an eruption of temper, but it lasted for a fraction of a moment and was gone.

"A jibe, Dr Watson," he replied, good-naturedly, "but a fair one. You seem to have inherited some of Mr Holmes's strength of character, as well as your father's qualities."

"Not at all, Inspector. You will be familiar with my father from his own written accounts of Mr Holmes's cases. It is my experience that he wrote his part in those cases down to emphasise the prowess of Holmes, at his own expense. The man I grew up around was more than capable of standing up for himself, I assure you."

"Well, keep in mind what I said, Doctor. We need to wrap this case up, and quickly. So we had better follow Mr Holmes to the car. I would hate to give him something else to complain about!"

Holmes remained mostly silent throughout the journey, and I did not consider it wise to disturb the thoughts that were clearly wheeling around in his mind. The noises he did make seemed to be prompted by the changes that had taken place in London since his last visit – redrawing his mental map of the capital street by street. Each change seemed to distress him, as though by changing in his absence, London had been somehow unfaithful to him. The only complete sentence he uttered was when he turned to me and, with a nod towards a side street as we passed, asked if that was the way to the Strand. It was heart-breaking to have to tell him that his bearings were totally off, and that the Strand was in the other direction, but I felt it would have patronised him to have done anything else. He responded with a simple "Hmm", before lapsing back into silence.

We arrived at the deceased's house and found a uniformed officer on the doorstep, ensuring the integrity of the crime scene.

"We have replicated the scene of the night of the murder for you to the smallest detail, Mr Holmes," said Barrett proudly.

"You mean, you re-locked the doors," said Holmes. "Nothing else should have been altered as a matter of simple procedure."

"Well, I can assure you, Mr Holmes, that procedure was followed very closely. All possible routes into the room were checked. Would you care to examine the door?"

Holmes retrieved a magnifying glass from his coat pocket and carefully studied the lock. "John, would you do me the great favour of seeing if there are any other ways of gaining entry that a reasonably young and able-bodied gentleman could make use of?"

I took a step back from the house to get some perspective, feeling slightly intimidated by the request to act for Holmes in such a manner and anxious not to miss anything. I tested the front ground-floor windows but all were fastened securely, and certainly could not be broken into without causing obvious damage, of which there was none. There were no footprints on the window-ledge, but I stood on it anyway to see if I could gain access to the upper-floor window. So narrow was the ledge that I had to stand side-on to provide enough of a surface to balance on. I could reach the upper window-ledge, but pulling myself up was a tricky task – it was hard to keep a grip whilst hoisting yourself up.

"Dr Watson," said Barrett, with a touch of smugness in his voice, "most modern criminals, when trying to gain access to a property through an upstairs window, use this most modern of inventions called a 'ladder'. Perhaps you have heard of them?" Barrett chuckled at his own joke, and I took this as revenge for my jibe earlier.

"Is there a way round to the back of the house?" I asked, ignoring the Inspector's comment completely. The constable who had been watching the front door took me to the rear of the property, but again I could find no evidence of forced entry. When I returned to the front of the house I found that Holmes had completed his own examination, and was awaiting my return.

"Nothing that I can see to suggest that this lock has been in any way tampered with," he said to my unasked question. "Shall we proceed inside, gentlemen?"

Barrett took a key from his pocket and turned it in the lock. "One moment, Inspector," said Holmes. "Where did *that* key come from?"

"This is the housekeeper's key, Mr Holmes. She has already given her statement and is staying with her family until this matter is settled. The deceased's key is, of course, evidence and so it would not be appropriate to use it."

"And there is no spare key?"

"No, Mr Holmes. The housekeeper swears there have only ever been two keys."

"And if the housekeeper were involved, and lying to your officers? Her being away from the house is a perfect alibi, and also something of a coincidence, is it not?"

"She has almost an entire village's worth of witnesses who swear she was nowhere near London on that night."

"But she might have had a copy of her key made and given it to her accomplices."

"To what end, Mr Holmes? No robbery has taken place so no material gain appears to have been sought. If anything, Mr Sanders' death gives her reason to be rather put out, as she now needs to find a new position. And it took an hour to stop her wailing before an officer could get a statement from her, and I'll wager she's not that good an actress."

"Is the lady available to be questioned by me?"

"I'm sure she could be, Mr Holmes."

"Good. Could she be brought here now?"

Barrett's expression made his surprise clear. "Well…"

"Splendid," said Holmes. "You send an officer to collect her and bring her here, and I shall begin my investigation. John, would you accompany me please?"

Barrett muttered something ungentlemanly-sounding under his

breath as I followed Holmes through the now unlocked door. The house was modest, both in its size and its decoration. For a moment I panicked as Holmes sank to the floor, but I realised that he was only examining the carpet intensely with his magnifying glass.

After I helped him back to his feet we went through every room in the house, examining it in the most minute detail, but Holmes never gave any impression of what he was actually looking for or whether he found it. We checked the kitchen, the hallway, the bedroom... everywhere in fact except the parlour where the murder took place.

"Mr Holmes!" called Barrett from downstairs.

"That will be our housekeeper," said my companion, and we went back downstairs, Holmes taking each step worryingly carefully as though he feared pitching over at any moment.

At the foot of the stairs stood a rather anxious-looking lady whom I estimated to be in her mid-thirties, who glanced around the hallway as though expecting a dangerous animal to burst out at her at any moment but not being sure exactly where the attack would come from. With Holmes on the prowl, I thought with a smile, she might not be too far wrong.

"Mr Holmes, Dr Watson – this is Mrs Gainsborough, the late Mr Sanders' housekeeper," said the Inspector. "Now, Mrs Gainsborough, Mr Holmes will have some questions for you, and I want you to answer them as fully and honestly as you can."

Mrs Gainsborough managed a nervous nod.

"Actually, Mrs Gainsborough," said Holmes, "I have no questions for you. At least, not yet. Rather, I have a request. I would like you to re-enact the events of two days ago when you returned to the house and found the body of Mr Sanders. Can you do that?"

"Oh, begging your pardon, Mr 'olmes, but I don't think I could," she replied, still clearly upset. "I mean, the thought of finding 'im there like that... I've not been able to get it out of me mind as it is, and going through it like that'll just make it worse."

"Mrs Gainsborough, I do appreciate your feelings," said Holmes in a tone that suggested that he in fact did not, "but it is very important that you do this if we are to work out what happened to him."

"Well, we know what happened to 'im, don't we?" she replied. "It was magic. That's what everyone's sayin', and I happen it must be true. I mean, I swear no one could've gotten in and out again without a key, and he had the other one still on 'im. And all them things drawn on 'im. I'm a good Christian woman, Mr 'olmes, and I'm not much of a one for superstition…" – at this Holmes cleared his throat loudly to hide the derisory snort that squeezed itself between his lips – "…but we know about the Devil and the people who do 'is works, don't we? An' that's what we got 'ere as far as I can see."

"If that is the case, Mrs Gainsborough, then surely it is even more important that the guilty parties be found before they receive any further orders from Lucifer, for the sake of society."

"If they can walk through walls and locked doors, Mr 'olmes, I doubt there's much the law can do wiv 'em."

"Mrs Gainsborough," I said, cutting in. "I understand your position completely. Indeed, it makes a lot of sense. But please consider the other possibility – that whoever is responsible for this act is as human as you or I. And that at present they are at large, free to commit another murder. Don't you think we should be doing everything in our power to prevent such a thing happening to someone else? If we are truly dealing with the demonic, then you are right, there is nothing we can do. But if they are not, then while it is too late for Mr Sanders, the next death is preventable, if we can only work out who is responsible and stop them. Can we afford to take that risk?"

"Well… if you put it that way, I suppose you're right," she replied.

"Well, now that we are all agreed, perhaps we can get on?" said Holmes tetchily. "Let's go outside, and re-enter the house. Mrs Gainsborough, it is essential that you carry out as closely as possible the movements you made when you found the bod…" Holmes caught himself, "when you found your employer."

Mrs Gainsborough nodded, and we went outside, re-locking the door. The Inspector gave Mrs Gainsborough her keys back. After a moment's hesitation she opened the door and went inside, this time with the three of us following.

She walked through the hallway and straight through to the kitchen at the back of the house, where she took off her coat and hung it behind the door. Then she proceeded to prepare a breakfast, or rather to mime making one at Holmes's insistence. When asked to actually make the same motions despite no actual breakfast being prepared, Mrs Gainsborough looked at me for support but I could not offer her any. She continued her absurd-seeming performance, until she eventually picked up a tray (loaded with cutlery, again at Holmes's insistence) and carried it through the hallway to the entrance to the parlour where the breakfast was to be served. She placed the tray on a table and tried to open the door. It was locked. She took out her keys and inserted the correct one in the lock. It turned with a solid click. She opened the door.

"And then?" asked Holmes, with perhaps an unnecessary level of relish, when Mrs Gainsborough paused.

"And then… he was there," she replied.

"Describe what you saw to me, in every detail. Omit nothing."

In truth, although I saw the point of it, I found Holmes's pressing of this lady slightly distressing, given that he was asking her to re-live a terrible moment in her very recent history. But again, I did not feel I could take her part, given what was at stake.

"He was lay there, God rest 'is soul, naked as the day he was born. Laid out on the floor, just there," – she indicated the floor directly in front of her – "covered in this strange writing or drawing; it was something between the two. And there was a knife sticking out of him, out of his chest…" And then she started sobbing. Her tears, however, did not give Holmes the slightest pause.

"And the knife. Had you seen it before?"

She shook her head as she pulled a handkerchief from her pocket and pressed it to her face. "No sir."

"And did you notice anything, anything at all, unusual about the rest of the room? Anything out of place, anything you had not seen before?"

"No sir. Only that Mr Sanders' clothes were piled up next to 'is body. Everything else was as it should have been."

"And was it unusual for that door to be locked?"

"Yes sir. I can't remember it ever being locked in all my years of service."

"Thank you, Mrs Gainsborough," said Holmes distractedly, not even looking in her direction. "You may go now."

Mrs Gainsborough glared at Holmes for such a casual (and some might say, callous) dismissal, and then left the room.

"Now, gentlemen," he said, "we must examine this room for any indication of intruders. So far we have two locks, either of which could have been picked by a skilled burglar. However, such a person would do well to hide all traces of themselves from me within this room."

I must admit that at this point I remembered my first meeting with Holmes earlier that morning, when he could not make out my features from a few feet away. Once, years ago, Holmes's confidence might have been justified, but now?

The next thirty minutes were among the most dispiriting I had experienced since the end of the war. Holmes shuffled painfully around the room on his hands and knees with his magnifying glass, looking for even the slightest clue. When he found nothing there he examined the furniture – the table Mr Sanders ate his meals at, the chairs, the lamps… everything in fact that could be examined came under his most intense scrutiny. Occasionally he asked me to look at something through the glass and asked me if I could see anything unusual. Unfortunately, on each occasion I had to report that I could not. At the end of the examination, Holmes turned to face us, his magnifying glass pressed to his chin. Inspector Barrett and I waited for him to speak, to reveal his findings, but he stayed silent, in contemplation. Barrett's impatience did not allow this state of affairs for long.

"Well?" he asked. "What have you found?"

The forcefulness of his question seemed to catch Holmes unaware, and he jerked out of his reverie.

"Nothing," he replied.

"Nothing?" echoed Barrett. "What do you mean by 'nothing'?"

"I mean I can find no evidence that anyone has been in this room for the last few days. For example, it rained quite frequently during the past week, yet unless an intruder was polite enough to remove their footwear before entering the house I can not see how they could failed to leave some kind of clue as to their presence. But there is none."

"Well, Mr Holmes," said Barrett with a sigh, "I suppose there is nothing left but to thank you for your time…"

"Oh, I am not beaten yet, Inspector. I shall remain in London a few days at least, and endeavour to unmask our culprit. If you might recommend me some lodgings…?"

"I wouldn't hear of you staying anywhere but with my wife and myself," I said. "I could not think of allowing such a dear friend of my father's to look for hospitality elsewhere. We have a spare room, and we live not far from here. On top of which, my wife would very much like to meet you."

"Well," he replied, "if you put it like that, I would be delighted."

The Inspector dropped us off at my house. Although he knew my address he was unfamiliar with the area and I directed him through the streets. When I glanced at Holmes he was again wrapped in his thoughts, hardly seeming aware of the journey at all.

I held the door open for Holmes and called "Millie! We have a guest!"

She emerged from the parlour, and I must confess that as always the sight of her made my spirits – which had taken something of a pummelling watching Holmes's failure to find any clues – rise, as it had not ceased to do since we first met.

"Mr Holmes, I want you to meet my wife Millicent."

She stepped forward and offered him her hand, which he accepted. "Please, call me Millie," she told him. "It's a pleasure to meet you, Mr Holmes. I would say that I had heard a lot about you, but as there can hardly be anyone who has not it would be a redundant comment. Please come through and sit yourself in front of the fire while I prepare something for us to eat. Not knowing when John would be returning today I have put a stew on to cook slowly, and it should not require much more attending to before it is ready."

She showed Holmes through into the parlour, where he warmed himself in front of the fire and glanced around. "You have a very cosy home here, John," he said.

"Millicent is rather house-proud," I said, "but you are in luck in that regard as she has not been at the hospital today and has clearly been using the time waiting for our arrival to get the house into order."

"The hospital? Is she unwell?"

I laughed. "Oh no, she is in the rudest of health. She is a nurse and tends to work longer hours than I do at the practice!"

"You have taken over your father's practice?"

"Yes. It is not large, as you are probably aware, but there is enough of a living from it to keep us. Millicent insists on working, says that she would feel useless otherwise."

"Children?"

"Not yet. But we are in no hurry. And what with taking over the practice, we both feel that it is not the best time for children."

"Indeed," said Millicent from the doorway, "but I'm sure we all agree that now would be an excellent time to eat. Dinner is ready!"

"So, how did the two of you meet?"

The three of us were sat around the dinner table, and while I was aware that Holmes had a rather unusual attitude to the kind of relationships that most people take for granted as one of their aims in life, the question seemed to be asked entirely in good faith.

"It was the war brought us together," Millie replied. "I was a nurse, and while I did not believe in the reasons for the war, I knew that my services would be needed to tend to the soldiers, so I volunteered. And after a while we were joined by a young, handsome doctor, who needed to be very quickly taken in hand and shown the ropes or else he would have most likely been sent home again."

"It's true," I confirmed. "It was such a shock to be thrown into that situation, so many injuries, such poor equipment and facilities."

"Anyway, I quickly decided that the hand should be mine. And I watched him find his feet, and grow and become the best field doctor we had."

I opened my mouth to contradict her.

"And *don't* you contradict me, John Watson." She turned to Holmes. "He's much too modest for his own good."

"An unusual situation to meet a future spouse in," said Holmes.

"But in many ways a good one," I replied. "As we've already been through so much together the stresses of civilian life seem less arduous."

"It also allowed us to begin our relationship on a more even footing than normal society allows," added Millie. "When you are in conflict together, certain… conventions become more elastic. Once the war ended, they quickly re-asserted themselves. That is the arduous part."

"Come now, Millie," I said, eager to head off this particular topic. "We're talking about our marriage, not society at large."

"It's society at large that sets the standards that we are expected to live by, and that includes marriage. You cannot disagree that you have enjoyed much greater opportunities than I have since we became man and wife."

"I took over my father's practice, that was my opportunity."

"While I spend my days doing little more than emptying bedpans despite all the experience I gained in the field. Why, I know more about the treatment of wounds than most of the doctors at the hospital, but of course I am merely a nurse and know nothing of anything except how to keep wards clean and curtsey to a lot of ignorant and patronising doctors." She took a deep breath. "I'm sorry, Mr Holmes. It is very rude of me to invite you into our home and then take out my frustrations on the limitations of the place of women in society on you. I do hope you will forgive me, and allow me to fulfil a stereotypically womanly role by collecting the plates, as we all seem to have finished."

After Millie had gone to the kitchen I turned to Holmes. "I'm sorry about that. She does get very excited over the issue. She's right of course, but there is a time and a place." I was aware from my father's stories that Holmes was a confirmed bachelor and rather old-fashioned in his views on the positions of the sexes. I was somewhat surprised therefore by his reply.

"Not at all, John. She is absolutely right. She is clearly an extremely capable young lady and it must be extremely frustrating for her to be put in a subservient position purely because of her sex while those less capable are valued more highly because of theirs."

"A very modern viewpoint, if I may say so."

"Not at all, simply a logical one. If a society has skills at its disposal it should make the most of them to function most effectively. And anyone who doubts the ability of women to make a contribution to society should look no further than Queen Victoria – a most formidable woman. Had our involvements with her not been considered too secret to be revealed, your father would have had the utmost pleasure in writing of his personal admiration for her."

"You took on a case for Queen Victoria?" I asked, stunned.

"Perhaps, 'service' would be a better term than 'case' in these instances. Certain matters of high state importance that required absolute discretion to bring them to both a satisfactory, and secret, conclusion. I rather suspect your father failed to resist the urge to write them up for his own archives, even if he could never publish them. If you have any of his notes you might even find them."

My mind immediately turned to the stack of old diaries and papers my father had left. I had never felt like looking through them before, considering them too personal, but I must confess the thought of unpublished cases, with such an illustrious client…

"Anyway, I think it is time for me to withdraw," said Holmes, rising slowly to his feet. "I find myself in greater need of sleep as the years advance, and feel now would be the moment to go to bed – if you would not mind showing me the way?"

That night I found myself wide awake into the small hours, the excitement of the day's events acting like an incessant buzz in the back of my mind, preventing me from relaxing into unconsciousness. Millie, in contrast, was asleep within minutes, no doubt due to the long shift of tiring work she had undertaken while I had been with Holmes.

I must admit that the more I thought through the details of the case, the more certain I was that Holmes had finally met his match – a mystery that even his powers could not unlock. This concerned me not for his reputation – no one outside of a carefully chosen few at Scotland Yard was aware of his involvement – but for his state of mind. Holmes had retired with an almost spotless record of success. He would have had scant opportunity to use his powers in the last few years in his cottage, and so would have had less opportunity to notice his waning abilities. His failure to solve this most impossible of cases would bring that diminution into stark and sudden relief – one that he might struggle to come to terms with.

These most depressing of thoughts were disturbed by the creak of a floorboard downstairs. I did not wait for further evidence of an intruder – I had seen too much of battle to distrust my senses. I slipped as silently from my bed as possible (taking care not to wake Millie) and crept to the sideboard, before sliding open a drawer and taking out my revolver. I quickly checked that it was loaded and ready – a reflex, as I knew it would be – and edged my way slowly out of the room and to the top of the stairs, looking down from the shadows.

I could see nothing, but was rewarded for my vigilance with the creak of another floorboard, this time coming from the parlour. I made my way as silently as I could down the stairs, one careful step at a time, until I reached the hallway. I crossed to the door, took a breath, and shouldered the door open, jumping into the room with my gun raised.

Holmes was wrapping his scarf around his neck when I appeared. Despite the time he was fully dressed, but did not respond to my sudden entrance or to the gun in my hand. Instead he looked at me, somewhat confused.

"John? Ah, what luck. I was just about to set out on a mission of the utmost… the utmost…" He paused, seemingly unsure of the word he was looking for. "Importance! Yes. I hope I did not wake you, Mrs Hudson has re-arranged everything and I couldn't find what I needed. But I am ready now. Would you care to join me?"

Part of me was devastated by the sight before me, but I banished my own personal feelings as my years of medical practice had taught me to do.

"Do you know what time it is?" I asked.

Holmes paused, considering the question for a moment, despite the fact that there was a clock barely a foot from where he stood. "Well, it must be nine o'clock by now. It's not like you to rise so late, John. Whatever will your practice do without you?"

"Holmes, it isn't nine o'clock yet. It's only a quarter to three in the morning. Now, let me help you back to bed and we can start the investigation again in the morning."

"Oh… are you sure?"

"Can you see that clock?" I asked, pointing it out.

Holmes turned to follow my gesture and looked at the clock for several moments, as though trying to remember how to decipher the meaning of the numerals and hands. Then he turned back to face me.

"Of course I can see the clock! What are you trying to imply?" he asked angrily.

"And can you see the time it says?" I replied, keeping my voice level.

"Well… it says a quarter to three doesn't it? You just told me. Why are you asking me all these questions? Whatever has gotten into you this evening, John? I haven't got time to stand here like this anyway, I have to go to sleep." He turned and took a step across the room, towards what I assume was where the door to his bedroom was in Baker Street.

"Your room is upstairs now, Holmes," I said. And took his arm to guide him.

"Take your hand off me," he snapped and pulled his arm free of my grasp. "I am perfectly capable of managing a flight of stairs you know."

I was worried that he would attempt to take the stairs at the pace he would have done as a younger man, but some element of memory or self-preservation flared into life and he made his way carefully, one hand on the bannister, the other pushing down on his stick. Once at the top, he made his way straight to the guest room.

I returned to my bedroom. Millie was awake, waiting for me.

"I heard raised voices," she said. "Is something wrong?"

"Oh Millie," I said, and I pressed my face into the nape of her neck as the tears arrived before the words.

The next morning I rose with some trepidation. Seeing Holmes in such a state had affected me deeply – the contrast between the heroic figure of my father's stories and the befuddled old man I had seen the night before was devastating, and on reflection I think I was mourning my strongest link to my father unravelling before my eyes. However, as Millie reminded me, I am a doctor, and if Holmes required medical help then it was lucky that I was in a position to provide it to him in a way that my father's sudden passing had not allowed.

I had just settled myself for breakfast when the door opened.

"Good morning, John!" said Holmes as he positively strode into the room.

For a moment I wondered if I had dreamt last night's events, as the Holmes before me now seemed sharp and alert, and showed no sign of disorientation or agitation. But then I remembered that in the initial stages, people often experience isolated episodes of confusion which gradually become more frequent and of longer duration, and which not infrequently occur at night. I also realised that there was every chance that Holmes would not even remember what had happened – either that or he was doing a very good impression of it.

"Excellent timing, Mr Holmes," said Millicent as she came and placed bowls of porridge down in front of us both. At that moment there was a firm knock at the front door. I began to stand but Millicent was already on her way to answer it. A moment later Inspector Barrett entered at a gallop, looking flustered and holding the morning's edition of the *Standard*.

"Good morning, Inspector," said Holmes. "Do we at least have time to consume our breakfast before you take us to the crime scene?"

Barrett was clearly surprised by Holmes's question, but recovered quickly. "Well, I dare say it won't matter to the deceased if we take an extra few minutes. But how…?"

"Inspector, yesterday you expected my involvement in the case to be over. Today you arrive at the crack of breakfast looking, if I may say so, somewhat flustered. It was not hard to deduce what might have caused such a visit and demeanour."

I must confess it took me a moment to catch up, so quickly had this new information been thrown at me. "You mean, there's been another murder…"

"…in exactly the same manner as the one you looked into yesterday, yes," completed Barrett. "Once again, the deceased was in a locked room and there is no evidence of intruders. Obviously we recognise that Mr Holmes failed… I mean, was unable to find any clues at the first crime scene, but seeing as the body is still at the premises and the scene is still fresh, I thought maybe he might like to take a look at this one."

"A capital idea, Inspector," replied Holmes. "I would be greatly interested in doing so."

"Good. There is, however, another matter which has come to light unexpectedly. Take a look at this."

He handed me the copy of the newspaper. My heart sank when I saw the front page.

"What is it, John?" asked Holmes.

I read the headline and the beginning of the article aloud:

LEGENDARY SLEUTH SHERLOCK STUMPED BY IMPOSSIBLE DEATH CASE!

Famous Consulting Detective Sherlock Holmes has been called in by Scotland Yard to look into the seemingly impossible death of Mr Marcus Sanders, who was found murdered in a locked room inside his own home. Scotland Yard detectives were so baffled that they called Mr Holmes out of retirement and united him with the son of his former investigative partner Dr John Watson. However even Mr Holmes confessed himself at a loss to explain how the murder took place.

"How on Earth did they get that amount of information so quickly?" I asked, incredulous.

"That's what I want to know," said Barrett, "and I intend to find out, have no fear."

I glanced at Holmes. Given his admittance of initial defeat yesterday I expected to find him at least a little concerned. Instead a smile played its way across his face.

"Well then, gentlemen," he said, after swallowing the last spoonful of porridge. "We had better re-double our efforts and give the press something more positive to write about, hadn't we?"

As we were driven to the scene of the crime, my frame of mind was not at its brightest. I had had to postpone a second day's appointments at the practice, and Millie had wanted to join us in what she clearly saw as something of an adventure, but she had recognised that she did not have the luxury of being self-employed. But what was really concerning me – even more than the magical-seeming murderers that appeared able to strike anyone at will regardless of the levels of security they had to bypass – was the newspaper article. I had already been worried about the effect it would have on Holmes to have to admit defeat, but that was when the matter was a private one, a personal realisation. Now that the whole of London knew of Holmes's involvement, any failure on his part would stain his reputation forever, something that I was sure would be even more painful to him and could speed the rate of his mental deterioration. Despite my immense personal pleasure at meeting him, I was beginning to wish that Holmes had never been invited back to London.

We pulled up outside one of the nondescript houses that pack parts of London like pens in a farmyard. Not that it was a particularly poor area; rather there were many small houses crammed together in a space so small it was hard to imagine that there was not some magic involved.

I do not consider it necessary to describe most of the next hour as it replicated so closely the visit to the previous crime scene. Again, the house was left locked so Holmes could look for ways in and out. Again he failed to find any, or to find any evidence of intruders inside. Again, he examined everything in minute detail before finally viewing the room that the killing took place in. The major difference on this evening was that, as the crime had only been discovered a few hours previously, the corpse was still exactly where he had been found – stripped of all clothing, killed by a knife to the heart, covered in the same strange markings.

"Such precision," commented Holmes as he examined the body.

"The angle of the blow?" I asked.

"No, the markings. They are exactly identical to those on the first body."

I had my doubts that Holmes's sight and memory were up to the job of recognising such precision, but I kept my own counsel.

"Speaking of which," he said, turning to Inspector Barrett, "do you happen to have the photographs of said markings?"

"Why yes," said Barrett. "Apologies, Mr Holmes. What with all the kerfuffle earlier about the body and the newspapers I quite forgot." He turned and shouted out through the door, "Constable Wilson! Fetch the photographs from the car."

Moments later a fresh-faced young officer came running in with the pictures and Barrett indicated that they should be handed to Holmes.

"Thank you, Constable," he said. "Right, John, I don't think we need stay here any longer."

"So, no ideas? No clues you've spotted?" asked Barrett.

I expected Holmes to give the same answer as he had when Barrett had last asked the question, but he surprised me by chuckling.

"Oh, I have ideas, Inspector. No clues, but definitely ideas." He turned to me. "John, would you kindly accompany me further? Seeing as I am back in London I feel as though I should take the opportunity of visiting one or two people and places from my past while I am here. Your company would be most appreciated."

We were driven back towards the centre of London in the police car but Holmes refused the driver's offer to take us directly to where he wanted to go – indeed, he told neither the driver nor myself where this was. Once we had been dropped off we hailed a cab and

Holmes gave the driver an address in Marylebone.

"It would have been much quicker to let the driver take us all the way."

"I have cultivated the useful habit of only letting Scotland Yard know what it needs to know, and no more. I have a feeling that such a policy is the correct one in this instance also."

We pulled up a little distance from the main high street, outside what appeared to be some kind of shop. The windows were dark – whether through tinting or dirt I could not immediately tell – and there was no sign above them. In fact, I would have assumed that whoever had owned this place had long since left it to ruin. Holmes, however, made confidently for the door, which opened easily. I followed him inside.

The interior of the shop belied its unpromising exterior. Rather than an abandoned shell, I found myself in a well-maintained bookseller's, with bookshelves from floor to ceiling, stuffed so full of volumes that it appeared that several could be squeezed out by the sheer pressure at any moment. And these were no ragged-edged penny-dreadfuls – most of the books in question were quality volumes with fine leather covers. Rather than some shabby thrift store, I realised that I was in a collector's emporium.

Behind the counter was an elderly man with a shock of white hair, who appeared to be around Holmes's age. He looked up and smiled in recognition.

"Why, if it isn't Mr Sherlock Holmes," he exclaimed. "It must be at least… oh, a good twenty years since you last crossed the threshold. That business with the Cult of the Scorpion. I do hope you have been keeping well. I had heard you retired."

"You heard correctly, Simmonds. Indeed, I was summoned back to the metropolis by Scotland Yard only yesterday."

"Ah. So it is business that brings you back to my humble establishment?"

"Indeed. I am in need of your expert, but discreet, services."

"You know full well you only have to ask, Mr Holmes. I can never pass up the opportunity of allowing myself to think that I helped the greatest mind in the field of detection in some small way."

Holmes laughed. "Not so little, Simmonds. Why, I would have never been able to pin down the Cult of the Scorpion without you, and more besides."

Simmonds looked over Holmes's shoulder at me. Holmes noticed immediately.

"Oh, forgive me my lack of manners. Simmonds, this is the son of my dear departed friend Dr Watson – Dr John Watson Jnr. John, this is Isaiah Simmonds, owner of the finest and most secret collection of occult books and knowledge in the whole of the country. Isaiah has been of incalculable help to me down the years whenever I have crossed swords with the world of the supposedly unnatural."

"A delight to meet you, Doctor," said Isaiah, holding out his hand across the counter to me. I took it and I was surprised at the firmness of the older man's grip. "Alas, I did not have the pleasure of knowing your father well, but I know he was a fine gentleman."

"Thank you," I replied. "Tell me, why is your shop such a secret? Surely you could make a small fortune with the books you have here?"

"Not so small, Doctor, not so small. The truth is that these books are some of the most powerful in the world – although Mr Holmes of course remains a sceptic in such matters – and few of them are actually for sale. I choose not to advertise as there are many who would desire to gain possession of my books, and would find few depths too deep to stoop to if it meant satisfying that desire. In some ways this is more of a library than a shop, but one that only allows admittance on the strictest of criteria. In your case, Dr Watson, being brought here by Mr Holmes is all the criteria you are required to meet. Now," he said, turning back to Holmes, "I assume that this is not simply a social call? Do you require my humble services for one more occasion?"

"I do indeed," he replied. "I would be most obliged if you could take a look at these for me." Holmes handed over the file containing the photographs of the markings left on the body of Marcus Sanders.

I watched Simmonds carefully for his reaction to the pictures, but he exhibited little more than an academic curiosity, a solitary "Hmm," escaping his lips as he studied them. Such a reaction suggested to me only two likely explanations – either the man was able to focus entirely on the markings as though viewing a puzzle on paper, or he had seen corpses before.

After several moments, in which Simmonds looked through each photograph and peered at them through a pince-nez, he looked up.

"Well?" asked Holmes. "Do you recognise them?"

"They do seem familiar," said Simmonds. "I feel as though I have seen them quite recently. A new cult, I think, or at least one that has only recently given any indication of its existence. You would think, Mr Holmes, that as science provides more answers to the mysteries of life that people would feel the need of the occult less."

"An odd sentiment from a life-long believer," noted Holmes.

"Oh, I did not say that such a decrease in belief would be the *correct* response," he replied with a chuckle, "merely an understandable one. In fact it appears that we have more cults springing up than ever before. I personally hypothesise that it is in fact a reaction *against* the scientific world, and the idea that all aspects of life and death can be broken down into the realm of the mechanical. Science has lain down the gauntlet and challenged the traditional beliefs, and those beliefs have taken it up and are fighting back."

"Running scared from reality more like," said Holmes. "Frightened by the idea of their long-cherished certainties being exposed as the foolish myths they are, and hiding in any dark corner they can fester in."

"No offence taken, Mr Holmes," said Simmonds, who had obviously heard similar from him in the past. "Anyway, my point was that with so many new cults springing up it's hard to keep track. New reports are coming in all the time and I am afraid that these days I find it harder to keep up with it all. I am sure though that I saw an illustration very similar to these photographs in one of my more recent acquisitions. If you will excuse me, gentlemen, I shall endeavour to find the volume in question." And with that, he turned and disappeared behind the curtain that separated the public area from what I assumed was the storage area. Despite Holmes's confidence in Simmonds I could not help but question his ability to help us, and found myself unable to prevent myself from expressing my doubts.

"If this cult is so secret, how is it that a shopkeeper in Marylebone knows of it?"

Holmes laughed uproariously, and suddenly the room did feel like a library as his mirth filled the space. "A *shopkeeper?*" he repeated. "My dear John, do not let Simmonds hear you refer to him as that. He is so much more. And the information he receives is not available in even the most well-stocked library. Simmonds is the end of a chain of information, each link of which is a man – and sometimes, a woman – prepared to risk their lives to ensure that these secret groups are discovered and that the information is accessible to those who find themselves in opposition to them. That is why Simmonds does not advertise his services."

"But if this information is so vital surely it would be better that the chain leads to Scotland Yard so they can act upon it?"

"*Scotland Yard?* John, if you ever require a piece of information to be publicly known, tell it to the police. It shall be known to the criminal underworld within twenty-four hours. No, it is imperative that Scotland Yard know as little of this place as the cults themselves, as the one will certainly lead to the other. Wouldn't it, Simmonds?"

"Indeed it would," said Simmonds, who had emerged from behind the curtain so silently that I had not noticed him – although he had obviously not managed to evade the attention of Holmes. "Have you found the information we require?"

"I believe I have, Mr Holmes," he replied. He placed a modest volume on the table – simply bound and lacking the expensive finish of so many of the books in the room. And then he opened the book, and I found myself more impressed by the content than I could ever have been by even the finest quality of leather and binding.

Each page of the book had originally been blank, and had been filled in by hand. The pages were covered not only in script but also elaborate drawings that showed the author to be a fine draughtsman. I saw what I took to be crests and profane images no doubt used in occult ceremonies. Simmonds turned the pages until at last he found what we were looking for – diagrams that matched those found on the bodies.

"A perfect match, I believe you will agree," said Simmonds. Holmes examined the page with his magnifying glass before confirming.

"Then, gentlemen, allow me to introduce you to the group these markings belong to: the Cult of the Magic Age. Allow me to read what my source has written about them:

> "The Cult of the Magic Age are a relatively new group, whose core belief is that there is a battle raging at all times between the forces of magic and chaos on the one side, and rationality and reason on the other. As their name suggests, they favour the former. Their primary objective is to attempt to tip the scales of this battle in chaos's favour in whatever way they can, including acts of murder and human sacrifice. If forced they will act as simple assassins, but their preference is to kill in ceremonial fashion, which involves covering the body of their victim in magical symbols which they believe will provide strength to the forces of chaos. Their stimulus does not have to be mystical in origin; they look for any event that disrupts people's faith in the rational structures of modern civilised society and will endeavour to capitalise on and, where possible, inflate those problems."

"But in what way does the killing of the two victims contribute to the cause of chaos?" I asked, baffled. "Neither were important men."

"I have been following the case myself," said Simmonds, "both through the information received via my own channels and in the newspapers. I have a theory."

"Please," said Holmes.

"Well, perhaps the identity of those killed is not the important factor. Rather it is the manner of their deaths that matters. News of the occurrence of two impossible murders would spread like wildfire in the press, and then pass into legend. That in itself would strengthen the cult's cause."

"Inspector Barrett said something similar when he asked Holmes to take the case on," I said.

There was a moment's silence, then Holmes tapped his stick on the floor. "Right, well, thank you, Simmonds, for your assistance, which as always has been most useful and illuminating. May I have the photographs back? I need to return them to Scotland Yard."

"Of course," he replied, handing the pictures over. "Do you feel that you have the case in hand now?"

"I am expecting developments in the immediate future," Holmes replied. "Come along, John. Goodbye, Simmonds."

"Goodbye, Mr Holmes. If you are ever passing..."

Once outside Holmes hailed a cab, then appeared to change his mind and waved it away. He did this again when the next cab came.

"Where are we going now?" I asked, thinking it might be better if I took responsibility for the taxi.

"As I said to Simmonds, I need to return these pictures to Scotland Yard, then we shall return to your home for the evening. I have done more than enough gallivanting around for one day."

He finally allowed us to enter a cab and we were driven to Scotland Yard. Once there, we were shown to Inspector Barrett's office but he was absent. Holmes suggested I wait in the office in case the policeman returned, while he went to see if he was in any of the nearby rooms. It seemed obvious that these roles should have been reversed but I knew that Holmes would accept no argument so kept my own counsel.

He was gone several minutes, and I was about to go and look for him when Inspector Barrett entered.

"Ah, Doctor. Just the man I wanted to see. Is Mr Holmes with you?"

"He just went looking for you, actually."

"But I am back now," said Holmes from the doorway as he shuffled into the room.

"Good. Now, as you know, news of your involvement in this case has gotten into the press somehow, and I can't help thinking that this makes you both – and your lady wife, Doctor – a target for the killers. So, I have instructed an officer to be in attendance at your address at all times for your protection. I was just about to dispatch him, so if your plan is to return home you can travel together."

"Most kind, Inspector, most kind," said Holmes. "Let us hope that a killer who can walk through locked doors can not do the same with policemen."

Despite the worrying truth behind Holmes's frivolous remark, I made doubly sure that all the doors were locked once we arrived home. The officer who had been sent to guard us waited outside the front door. I explained the precaution to Millie.

"Is an attack on this house really likely?" she asked.

I was about to attempt to reassure her that the officer was there purely to cover all possibilities, when Holmes startled me by announcing, "Oh, I fully expect an attempt to be made on our lives. And very likely quite soon."

"Right," said Millie, in that unanswerable tone I knew so well, and she strode from the room, returning moments later with two shotguns and my old service revolver. "I don't hold with this idea of mystic killers who can move like ghosts, and I would wager that if anyone attempts to break into this house they'll bleed like anyone else."

"Quite an arsenal you keep here," said Holmes, amused.

"I am a country girl at heart, Mr Holmes, and was brought up shooting rabbits. Every year John and I spend a week with my family and keep ourselves in practice. I assure you that anyone who breaks into *this* house will have reason to regret it."

"Well then," said Holmes, "I shall take this opportunity to rest for an hour or two, now that I realise how safe I am."

"Wait, Mr Holmes," said Millie. "What about the officer outside? Should I inform him of our preparations?"

"No, I think it better that we leave him to do his job as he would normally. At the moment we have the element of surprise – we must guard it at all costs. I shall return in a couple of hours. I feel that it will be a long night – possibly even a few, depending on when they choose to mount their assault."

* * *

Millie and I sat in the parlour in silence, each armed and alert to the slightest sound. Somehow there seemed nothing to say – we had our lives to defend, and we could do so better with silence than conversation, so silent we were.

Gradually the evening darkened, and we lit the lamps as we would have done of an evening, and then switched them off at the same time as we would have done had we been going to bed. And we waited.

After a few hours, Holmes re-joined us, and I was relieved to see no sign of his confusion of the previous night. Instead, Holmes seemed invigorated by his rest, and eager to see how events would play out.

And so we waited, in darkness with only the ticking of the clock to disturb the quiet.

There was a knocking at the front door.

I glanced at the clock. It was nearly one in the morning. For a moment, none of us moved. Surely no killer would attract their victim's attention by knocking?

I glanced at Millie, and we both stood, and made our way slowly to the door. I went to open it, and Millie stood just inside the parlour, invisible from the door but ready to level her shotgun. I opened the door.

"'Scuse me, sir, can I come in and use your lavvie? Only I've been out here for hours an' it's gettin' to be a serious matter, if you get my drift."

It was the police officer.

"Yes, of course," I said and allowed him to pass.

"I'll only be a moment, sir, then I'll be back out front. Through the back, is it?"

I nodded and he made his way to the WC. I went back into the parlour. Luckily, due to a mixture of caution and the gloom he had not noticed Millie's shotgun by her side, and I had slipped my revolver into my pocket. After a couple of minutes I heard the officer come back downstairs and let him back out, locking the door behind him.

We resumed our vigil.

After another hour of complete stillness, an hour in which I started to wonder if Holmes's prediction of attack had been nothing more than confused paranoia, it happened.

The back door slowly creaked open.

We stayed sat on the floor, not wanting to betray our position by moving, but we levelled our weapons at the parlour door in case of discovery. We heard footsteps, muffled and (I surmised) shoeless, creep past the parlour door and up the stairs. Once they reached the upper landing, we allowed ourselves movement, rising from the floor and preparing for combat. It was not hard to imagine what was going on upstairs – the would-be killers searching our bedroom, ready to dispatch us in the same manner in which two men had died previously. Millie suddenly stalked silently across the room and opened the door a fraction, peering into the hall before, to my horror, slipping through. I could not go after her for fear of drawing the attention of the intruders. And then, the footsteps made their way back down the stairs, towards us, and I had to focus on our immediate survival.

The parlour door gradually opened. Shadows entered the room, human shapes made of gloom.

Light filled the room, surprising the intruders who raised their hands to their faces as Holmes held out the lamp (minus shade), momentarily blinding them.

I made a show of cocking my revolver. "Drop your weapons," I commanded, taking aim at the nearest.

"All of you," said Millie, from behind them, her shotgun held steady and sure.

"Oh, and in case you're hoping your accomplice at the front door who unlocked the back door for you earlier will come to your aid, I am afraid he's just been rather surprised too," said Holmes. "As you have been, Inspector."

Now that their eyes had become accustomed to the light from the lamp, the intruders had lowered their hands from their eyes, and I was astounded to see that the leader of the group of three was Inspector Barrett.

"I don't know what you mean, Mr Holmes," he said quickly. "We heard there had been a disturbance at this address and of course, came over immediately to see what was happening."

Holmes reached forward and pulled Barrett's long coat open. "Stopping only to collect ceremonial daggers and, I assume, a copy of the markings that you expected to find on our bodies?"

"I wouldn't be so smug, Mr Holmes," Barrett replied, his tone becoming stony. "Your dead bodies will tell as few tales as those you have examined over the last two days. Our version of events here will be the one believed. We are officers of the law after all."

"So are we," said a new and unexpected voice from the hallway. "And I'd call that a confession."

"Ah, such perfect timing," said Holmes, as four further figures entered the room. "John, Millie, let me introduce Inspector Pemberton," he said, indicating the figure who had spoken. "I had the good fortune to find his office earlier on when we stopped in at Scotland Yard. I… *assisted* him in a case back at the beginning of his career, and there's not a more honest, upstanding officer in the whole of the force. So, I asked him to do me the favour of waiting circumspectly outside until I shone a light, and then to come in and make the arrests."

"Although you didn't tell me *who* I'd be arresting," said Pemberton. "Good job really, as I'd have struggled to believe it if I'd not heard with my own ears. Put the cuffs on them, lads."

"Hang on," I said, feeling as lost as my father had while dealing with Holmes in the past. "I'm afraid I'm not following this. You mean you knew this afternoon that a police officer was involved?"

"I would not go so far as to say that I knew, but I strongly suspected not only that there was police involvement, but that the good Inspector here was at the heart of it."

"But how?" I asked. "I have been with you nearly continuously since your arrival in London. What did you see that I did not?"

Holmes laughed. "Nothing, John. You saw as much as I. However, I followed the facts and arrived at the only logical conclusion. Allow me to explain. As you saw, I examined both of the so-called crime scenes, and found no evidence of an intruder in either. Therefore, once I was satisfied of this, there was only one possible solution – there was no intruder in the first place."

"No intruder?" asked Pemberton, obviously as bemused as I. "Then how did Barrett kill them?"

"That's the beauty of this whole little mystery, Inspector," said Holmes, clearly relishing the opportunity to show off his amazing deductive powers once more. "He didn't. No one did. Those men were killed by the only people to have access to those rooms – themselves."

"Why on Earth would they kill themselves?" I asked, trying desperately to see the logical thread that Holmes had so skilfully reeled in.

"Ah. Well, I am rather afraid that is where I come in, John. They died to give Inspector Barrett here an excuse to invite me back to London – the perfect murder. I realised this when my presence was publicised in the press this morning. I – and you, John, to complete the symmetry of the deaths of Holmes and Watson together – was to be sacrificed on the altar of chaos. My failure to solve the case – which the newspaper so clearly emphasised – would be compounded by our deaths at the hands of the same cult that was supposed to have murdered the other two victims. What better symbol for the death of rationality and logic than the murder of, if I may say so, their greatest proponent? The symbolism would be rather potent."

"So the dead men were cultists?" said Millie, who as usual was a step ahead of me.

"Exactly. Fanatics who thought they were laying down their lives for a worthy cause, rather than the insane promises of a deluded Order."

Barrett was glowering at Holmes as he said this, but Holmes met his gaze. "Even had your plan succeeded, Inspector, you would have found that the world is too complex a place for your simple-minded philosophy. Your little group would have been washed down the well of history anyway. I am however gratified that I, and my friends the Watsons, have prevented you doing any more damage and avoided being washed down with you."

"Well," said Pemberton, "I don't know about you, but I could certainly do with my bed some time soon, so we shall be taking these gentleman to the Yard. Could you attend tomorrow to make your statements?"

"Of course, Inspector," said Holmes.

"Well, then I shall wish you goodnight," he said, and led Barrett and his accomplices away. "We'll go out the back door, save you unlocking the front."

"The spare key?" I asked, already knowing the answer. Holmes nodded.

"Well, we won't be leaving that on a hook by the door any more!" said Millie. Once the officers had left and she locked the door behind them, she turned and embraced me, and we kissed deeply. "You were magnificent," I whispered to her, and meant it completely. "I love you."

"I love you too," she replied, and we held each other for a few perfect moments.

We found Holmes putting the lamp back in its original position in the parlour.

"Well, that's that then," I said.

"Hmm? Oh, this matter is far from over, I am afraid."

"What do you mean?" asked Millie.

"Well, for one thing I doubt that only four cultists infiltrated the police force. Pemberton – or whoever the job is given to – will have a hard time of it, ferreting them all out."

"But their leader is caught, that's got to be worth something?" I said.

"Barrett? Their leader? I don't think so. A senior lieutenant, possibly. The leader would not have come here tonight and risked capture. No, Barrett was trusted but reasonably expendable. There is another hand behind this particular game. Another mind."

"Then we are still all in danger. What is to stop them simply coming back for us?" I asked.

"Oh, I wouldn't worry, John. We have proven their supposed magic to be nothing but a particularly grim parlour trick. The plan won't work twice. And to make another attempt on our lives now would just increase their risk of being caught, for no real advantage. No, we are perfectly safe for the time being, I am sure of that. Unless we cross swords with them again, of course, in which case their hands might be forced."

He sounded almost pleased with this thought.

"Well, I must a-bed. It has been an extremely tiring night for a man as old as I. Goodnight." And he shuffled his way to bed.

After he had gone I marvelled at the intellect and drive still present in his aged frame, and felt a moment of shame for the betrayals of doubts that I had experienced over the last couple of days. Then I took Millie by the hand, and we ascended the stairs.

ABOUT THE AUTHOR

Philip Marsh is a Manchester-based writer and editor. He is a graduate of the Creative Writing MA course at the University of East Anglia. He has contributed two chapters to an academic study into the use of politics in British telefantasy in the 1970s and 1980s, to be published in early 2014 (Cambridge Scholars Publishing).

ABOUT THE EDITOR

George Mann is the author of the Newbury & Hobbes and The Ghosts series of novels, as well as the original novels *Sherlock Holmes: The Will of the Dead* and *Doctor Who: Paradox Lost*. He is also the author of numerous short stories, novellas and an original *Doctor Who* audiobook. He has edited a number of anthologies including *The Solaris Book of New Science Fiction*, *The Solaris Book of New Fantasy* and two retrospective collections of Sexton Blake stories. He lives near Grantham, UK, with his wife, son and daughter.

SHERLOCK HOLMES: THE WILL OF THE DEAD

GEORGE MANN

A rich elderly man has fallen to his death, and his will is nowhere to be found. A tragic accident or something more sinister? The dead man's nephew comes to Baker Street to beg for Sherlock Holmes's help. Without the will he fears he will be left penniless, the entire inheritance passing to his cousin. But just as Holmes and Watson start their investigation, a mysterious new claimant to the estate appears. Does this prove that the old man was murdered? Meanwhile Inspector Charles Bainbridge is trying to solve the case of the "iron men", mechanical steam-powered giants carrying out daring jewellery robberies. But how do you stop a machine that feels no pain and needs no rest? He too may need to call on the expertise of Sherlock Holmes.

SHERLOCK HOLMES: THE SPIRIT BOX

GEORGE MANN

Summer, 1915. As Zeppelins rain death upon the rooftops of London, eminent members of society begin to behave erratically: a Member of Parliament throws himself naked into the Thames after giving a pro-German speech to the House; a senior military advisor suggests surrender before feeding himself to a tiger at London Zoo; a famed suffragette suddenly renounces the women's liberation movement and throws herself under a train.

AVAILABLE JUNE 2014

THE EXECUTIONER'S HEART
A NEWBURY & HOBBES INVESTIGATION

GEORGE MANN

When Charles Bainbridge, Chief Inspector of Scotland Yard, is
called to the scene of the third murder in quick succession where
the victim's chest has been cracked open and their heart torn out,
he sends for supernatural specialist Sir Maurice Newbury and his
determined assistant, Miss Veronica Hobbes.

The two detectives discover that the killings may be the work of a
mercenary known as the Executioner. Her heart is damaged, leaving
her an emotionless shell, driven to collect her victims' hearts as
trophies. Newbury and Hobbes confront many strange and pressing
mysteries on the way to unearthing the secret of
the Executioner's Heart.